The Heart of the Graystone

M.K. Brown

This book is a work of fiction. Any resemblance to actual events or persons, living or dead, is entirely coincidental.

"The Heart of the Graystone," by M.K. Brown. ISBN 978-1-60264-555-4.

Published 2010 by Virtualbookworm.com Publishing Inc., P.O. Box 9949, College Station, TX 77842, US. ©2010, M.K. Brown. All rights reserved. No part of this publication may be reproduced, stored in a retrieval system, or transmitted in any form or by any means, electronic, mechanical, recording or otherwise, without the prior written permission of M.K. Brown.

Manufactured in the United States of America.

This book is dedicated to my nephews.

Table of Contents

The Omen	1
A Curious Day	3
Uncle Murro's Tale	15
An Unexpected Detour	23
On Wings	31
King Geraldi	39
Bethë Dien	49
The Great Prairie	59
In the House of Leyrea	73
Voices in the Night	85
The Marnalets	97
Bethë Khür	107
Revelations	119
A New Day	135
Delasur	139
Solia's Word	149
Into the East	159
The House of Pendi	169
The Token Crucible	177
The Days of Sanctuary	189
The Golem Strikes	195
Finding Heart	203
The Coming Storm	213
The Battle for Locnomina	229
Broken Circles	243
A Hard Rain	251
The Great Desert	261
Kara de Sten Yah	271
The Servant and the King	283

Acknowledgements

My most heartfelt thanks to those who supported me in the most tangible ways as I struggled along with Kazareen on his journey: Romona, Daniel, and Louis. Dearest thanks also to those wonderful characters in my life whose courage, grace and tenacity helped to inspire me. I also wish to express my gratitude to all of my steadfast friends for their unending words of encouragement. Finally, I must give thanks to the one whose name I do not know, The Creator, for the time, breath and experiences I've enjoyed among the wondrous circles of this creation, but most of all for allowing me to seek the light of infinite grace.

The Omen

Geraldi's days had become nightmares, his nights non-existent. The dull gray creep of death to his door was silent, unyielding, inevitable. He shuddered and pulled the scarlet robe tighter round his thin frame. An icy shiver stealing through him, even in summer, did not seem odd. It was a feeling to which he'd become all too accustomed, for the ancient walls of the tower were haunted by cold, dank memories. He stroked his wiry beard, buried his chin in his chest and seated himself in a poplar chair upon which no heraldry was carved. As he placed the golden scepter on the table, he heard a faint click from behind, followed by the sour creak of swollen wood.

King Geraldi's counselor stepped from the shadows of the doorway. He drifted in like a vapor, as quietly as the fog that rolled in from the sea and blanketed the capitol on a cool summer morn. The hulking shape of the counselor's brother loomed behind him in the shadows of the threshold. They paused to share a few hushed words, entered the high turret of the tower of Pente Kaleán, and approached the hunched figure that was King Geraldi. They did not bow.

The king sat quietly with his back to the door. He knew their footsteps well, so he sat and stared out the east window, as if watching for some advancing army or pillaging enemy hoard. None had come.

"My Lord." The counselor's coarse voice defied his spidery frame; it was thick and rough, like a rasp tearing through the hardest oak.

"What news?" asked Geraldi.

"It seems the day we have awaited for so long draws nigh. The Seer has beheld another vision, this one of a great sign in the sky. I believe the time has come to make our play, though the Seer advises we stay our hand until the sign appears."

"Tell me the fashion of this sign," said the king, more interested.

"He could not divine as much, saying only that it would not be missed by any who had eyes to see."

"And the old man?"

"No sign of him."

The king eyed his chief counselor carefully. "You are certain?"

"We passed undetected."

"Very well. But where is the boy? I need to know where." Geraldi's voice had raised a notch.

"Well within our reach it would seem, for the Seer has felt great tremors emanating from near the town of Feria."

Geraldi's eyes widened as he reached for quill and parchment. "Send for my messenger."

But the counselor did not move. It was his brother who stepped forward. "When shall I depart for Feria, my Lord? I've already mustered my best troops."

"You will remain here, for you draw far too much attention to yourself. I need the boy at ease, if he is to be taken without incident."

The king eyed the massive bulk of his general and found himself drawing back slightly, wishing he could retreat into the grain of the chair, but as usual, his gaze was drawn, slowly, inevitably, to the sword that hung from his general's belt. With a great effort, he shifted his eyes back to the parchment, hoping his lingering glance at the dark blade went unnoticed.

But the general saw. His greedy eyes flashed as his hand drifted to the hilt. The counselor placed his hand gently on his brother's shoulder. The general allowed his hand to be stilled once again, but Geraldi knew that the idleness of the blade at his general's hip gnawed ever at him.

"We shall let the local magistrate seize him. I need him alive," Geraldi said.

"For a while." the counselor added.

Another shudder ran through the king and he paused to collect himself, then continued to scratch out his decree on the parchment.

As he wrote, Geraldi imagined that just for a moment, a fleeting glimmer of sunlight passed through him.

Was it—?

He swallowed hard and buried his thoughts. The feeling passed quickly—if it had ever existed. And the perpetual gloom of the turret closed in around him once more.

A Curious Day

Kazareen de Pendi went to the wide door of the stable, pulled off his gloves and wiped the sweat from his forehead. He didn't mind grooming horses, or even polishing saddles and tack, but he loathed shoveling the stalls, especially in heat like this. He propped his arm on the shovel and took a moment to catch his breath. A fair breeze blew in from the west, helping to cool his brow and whisk away the thick odor of fermenting manure hanging over the stables. Kazareen watched as a small trade caravan went rattling by. With a smile, he nodded to the driver that looked his way, but the sun-beaten man only scowled in return. The recent surge of summer heat had evaporated most folk's willingness to engage in even the simplest of courtesies. It was high summer now, and the caravans making their way west to the capitol clogged the streets of Feria.

Kazareen paid no mind to the sour face the driver had shown him. As usual, he was looking forward to the afternoon. He tried to whistle a happy tune, but the staccato rhythm of his uncle's hammer on the anvil in the smithy next door scattered the melody into fragmented phrases. At least he was almost done; only two more stalls to shovel. And Kazareen wasn't too concerned about having to make a midday meal for his Uncle Murro; in heat like this, Murro rarely had much of an appetite, despite his tiring work. A few titanic draughts of water and a short nap was all he required—then back to work, for the money they earned at the height of the trade season would have to see them through the slow periods of winter.

Town life was bustling and loud and hurried. So Kazareen passed most of his free time lying around in the shade of the tall trees in the forest of Bethë Dien, where nothing and no one could bother him. There were always strange and unfamiliar faces passing through Feria, and while Kazareen was as friendly as any, for some reason he always longed for something quieter. Closer. More familiar. And the forest, despite its reputation of queer happenings, afforded him that much. It made living in Feria a little more bearable.

The forest was a fair walk, three miles or more up and over the big hill north of town, but the soft fragrances and gentle quiet of the forest always made it worth his effort, especially after enduring hours of drudgery in the steaming reek of the stalls with only the monotonous accompaniment of his uncle's hammering to distract him.

It never bothered Kazareen much that others thought him odd for his regular treks into the forest and he never believed any of the whispered rumors he'd heard about Bethë Dien, some so horrible they'd curdle the buttermilk if one were inclined to believe them. They were just stories—or so he'd been tutored.

Uncle Murro, he'd say "Horse pies!" and "Don't you believe everything you hear, Kazareen. Those are just tall tales and pigwash."

Still, it did seem a bit odd for Uncle Murro to say such things and yet never venture near the forest himself. Maybe there was more to the gossip than his uncle would admit. Even Kazareen could never bring himself to plumb the forest depths. It was enough to simply find some shade and quiet. After all, who really knew what dangers or mysteries might lie hidden within? For the forest stretched for long miles until it met the river that marked Pendoria's northern border, and few knew what lay beyond.

Now the Kingdom of Pendoria lay between the two great rivers: Laché Dien to the north and Laché Khür far to the south. And the rivers stretched for hundreds and hundreds of miles out of the East, their waters born of the melting snows of the towering, impassable mountains of Atán Beruth. And the wise hand of King Geraldi ruled over all this fair land, or at least so said the folks of Feria, for the king's ancestral lands laid all around the trading town and much of the western part of Pendoria, and his ascension to the throne had become a point of regional pride.

But Kazareen paid little heed to pride or politics. They seemed remote and unimportant to him—just more boring grown-up talk. His greatest source of joy came from the time he spent alone in the forest. As far as Kazareen knew, he was the only soul in Feria willing to venture into those infamous woods, which was probably another reason why he had so few friends.

The breeze died for a moment, and with it, Kazareen's improvised tune, but the clanging of Uncle Murro's hammer carried on. He wiped his forehead again and went back to work.

Streams of perspiration poured down Murro's face as he beat out the glowing iron of another in an endless line of horseshoes. He was nearly black from the soot of his labors, and the bulging muscles of his arms glistened under a sheen of sweat. Murro's arms had grown to gigantic proportions from swinging his hammer for so many years, but his middle saw less work, and as a consequence his belly bulged out and over the belt of his breeches. Through the long wavy locks that hung

The Heart of the Graystone

about his face, he caught a glimpse of a tall figure standing under the awning of the smithy. He stopped hammering and looked up.

"Well, Murro. I see the heat hasn't slowed you down much," said the soldier.

"Dargon." Murro wiped his brow, and it left another dirty, black streak. "What brings you here this time of day?"

Dargon Feluz, Murro's next door neighbor and newly appointed Captain of the Town Guard of Feria, held up his long sword. It was notched in several places.

Murro shook his head. "What have you been doing? Practicing against a stone wall? I'm more an armorer than a sword smith, you know that."

Dargon chuckled; he was a good-natured man who seemed to find humor in everything, despite his weighty responsibilities. "Just doing a lot of sparring. Something must be stirring on the borders. Word came down from the magistrate to step up the training regimen. He's a bit of a stickler about it I'm afraid." He held out the sword.

Murro frowned. "Borders, eh? Any word on where?"

"Just rumors so far—all started by the men. If I hear anything definite, I'll let you know. In the meantime, I think you'll be seeing more of my men than usual."

Murro's frown turned to a scowl. "I've an awful lot of work. Can it wait?"

"Sorry. You know Du Fe," Dargon said.

Murro sighed and took Dargon's sword. He hadn't quite gotten used to the idea of his neighbor as Captain of the Town Guard. Dargon's smiling face seemed to clash with the fierce eyes of The Dragon that stood as the centerpiece of the royal seal stained onto his thick leather armor. Murro's paying customers would just have to wait. The work required of him in the king's service always came first. It was his way of paying taxes, in lieu of gold or Graystone.

"I'll have it to you by the end of the day." He eyed a particularly deep notch in the sword. "If I can. Come back at sunset, and I just might have it finished."

"Thanks, Murro." Dargon turned and left.

Murro considered the rather large pile of unfinished horseshoes on the ground. "Kazareen! Come in here!"

Kazareen appeared at the door. "Uncle?"

"I've got to re-work this sword, but we can't afford to fall behind shoeing, not this time of year. I need you to drop what you're doing and get to work shaping and flanging these shoes, while I see to the king's work."

5

Kazareen's heart sank when he saw how many horseshoes still required work. The forest would just have to wait. "Yes, sir."

Now Kazareen wasn't much of blacksmith, and both he and his uncle knew it, but he knew better that arguing with Murro was fruitless. If there was anything he hated more than shoveling stalls, it was hammering shoes next to the diabolical heat of the forge. He put on a thick pair of leather gloves and a wide apron, grabbed a hammer from the wall and went to work on the anvil while Murro took the sword to the grinding wheel and began pumping the pedal at a firm and steady pace.

Kazareen worked slowly. The heat in the smithy was withering, and the sweat kept rolling into his eyes, blinding him. He'd only managed to finish shaping four shoes in the first hour, but in the same time, he'd rapped his fingers five times. Murro kept watching him from the corner of his eye, knowing how little aptitude Kazareen had for the work.

"Lords!" Kazareen shouted, as he smashed his fingers again. He threw off his glove and shook his hand to rid it of the pain. His fingers had already turned a deep and ugly purple.

"Kazareen, don't curse." Murro looked at Kazareen's discolored fingers. "That's enough. Go ahead and finish up in the stables."

Kazareen felt bad he couldn't help out his uncle more, but he was more than happy to escape the hellish heat of the forge. "I just finished the last stall when you called, so I'm done in there. Are you hungry?" His fingers continued to throb.

Murro surveyed the large pile of shoes on the ground and the sword in his hand, which was proving to be a tougher job than he'd first anticipated. "No," he replied.

"Is there anything else you need done today, Uncle Murro? Around the house, I mean?"

"I think you've done enough damage today," he said, looking at Kazareen's hand again. "But be home by suppertime."

Murro watched silently as the young man he called nephew peeled off his apron and sprinted out of the smithy. "Oh, Kazareen...Happy Birthday," he called out.

Kazareen stopped and smiled back at Murro, then he tore off for the house.

With a smirk, Murro shook his head in silent bemusement; the chances of Kazareen becoming a blacksmith were slim. He had no idea what the future held for Kazareen, but somewhere inside, in a place he'd kept hidden for many years, he knew it wouldn't be an easy one.

After washing up, Kazareen grabbed an apple to nosh on and began making his way through town. He paid little attention to the surge of

The Heart of the Graystone

traders as he slipped through the maze of the marketplace; his mind was already carried away to the forest, even if he wasn't. He felt a hand on his shoulder.

"Kazareen?"

He turned and saw the familiar face of Talisa du Fe. He couldn't help but smile. Talisa was the only other person besides Murro who really seemed to enjoy his company, and he thought of her as his only friend, though he didn't see her as often as he wished. Few of the boys his age would lower themselves to associate with Kazareen, due to his questionable family background. He'd grown accustomed to deflecting their taunts, but they still hurt.

Talisa, on the other hand, didn't seem to mind being seen with him, which Kazareen found odd; her father was Feria's magistrate and therefore the most powerful and feared man in town. He thought it was probably a good thing Garthon du Fe didn't know how close he and Talisa had grown over the last year, but he was a busy man and paid little notice to his wife, let alone his only child.

Talisa was a year younger than Kazareen, just thirteen, and despite her youth, she was at least an inch taller than Kazareen, probably two, which was the only thing about her that made him uncomfortable. Her curly red hair poured over her shoulders and hung in her face rather messily. She had the whitest skin Kazareen had ever seen, except where it was covered with freckles. Even in this heat, she kept her bright green shawl pulled over her head; it matched her eyes perfectly.

"Oh, hello Talisa."

"Going somewhere?"

"Oh, nowhere in particular, just out for a walk," he replied, still smiling.

"You don't think I believe that, do you? You're headed off to..." her voice shrank to a whisper, "...to the forest again, aren't you?"

Kazareen shrugged. He needn't answer, because they both knew the truth well enough. He just kept smiling his broad, toothy grin as he turned and walked away, his fine jet-black hair flaying in the breeze.

"I want to come too," she called out.

Kazareen turned and looked at her with his usual curious expression. This was, without a doubt, the last thing he expected to hear from her. Talisa was his only friend, and he knew her pretty well, but she had never shown such an adventurous streak before. More often than not, she only wanted to sit by the fountain and talk. Or laugh at the jiggling bellies of the traders as they bounced along the potholed avenue. Kazareen gave into her wishes from time to time, when he felt more like talking than being alone in the forest, but today he had no intention of sitting around idly in town. The sun was bright, the sky a clear blue, and the forest beckoned.

"Aren't you afraid of the horrible Bethë Dien?" he asked with a devilish grin. He used its proper name, knowing full well that it conjured up the more distasteful side of its reputation.

"No, not really. Anyway, I'm taller than you, and if you go to and fro unscathed, so shall I." She stood up straight to display fully her height advantage over Kazareen.

His smile faded a little. "What about your father?"

"What about him?" She shifted her weight to one leg and looked a little shorter now.

"If you're caught. Won't he—"

"Oh, don't worry about him."

His smile brightened again. "Alright, then. If you dare." For once, it would be nice to do something together that he really enjoyed, though he'd never expected her to want to come along. Not to the forest.

Talisa squealed with delight, and a few of the traders looked at her sideways.

"All right, all right. Enough already. Let's go. But without so much...commotion."

They made haste for the edge of town, and before long found themselves making strides up the large hill that stood on its northern flank. At the top of the hill, two tall poplars stood proudly together, swaying in the breeze. As they climbed the gentle slope, they passed through wide patches of wildflowers covering the hillside—delicate blooms of purple, yellow and red—all dancing together in syncopated waves. The sun was bright and warm, but more welcome now that Kazareen had finished his chores. The gentle breeze already carried with it the familiar aroma of the forest, and he relished it. But he understood well this was all new to Talisa. To his knowledge, she had never smelled or even seen the forest, for it lay well hidden behind the big hill. She certainly was not the only person in Feria who'd never seen it. There were folk of sixty or more summers who had never laid eyes on it, and would probably say so with pride.

As they crested the hill, they came to a halt in the shade of the twin poplars and gazed down on the forest. Slowly, Kazareen turned to Talisa. Was it what she expected? For Kazareen, it wasn't dark or treacherous looking and didn't loom in the least bit. In fact, it seemed to radiate a friendly light, a soft golden-green glow that stood in stark contrast to its rather sinister reputation. Still, her first sight of it was enough to give her pause. And she seemed suddenly unwilling to take another step.

The Heart of the Graystone

"Come now, there's nothing to fear. Especially not here, we've still another mile or more to go." Kazareen saw the flat expression of apprehension on her face. Teasing her in the marketplace was one thing, but to antagonize her now was quite another, for she was seeing Bethë Dien for the first time, and oft-repeated warnings died hard. He took her by the hand and she responded with a sheepish grin.

As the sweat of their hands mingled, his heart began to beat a little harder.

"I'm fine. I'm coming," Talisa said, glad for the reassurance. To his dismay, her hand slipped away from his own, and they began to make their way down the far side of the hill. The forest was farther away than it looked from the top of the hill, and they walked on for another twenty minutes or more, but with a little less talk.

At last, they approached the sparse eaves of Bethë Dien. To Kazareen's surprise, Talisa seemed as much at ease here as he did. A serene smile began to spread over her face as she took it all in. Small birds flew gleefully from tree to tree, chirping and singing. Wild berries grew in patches here and there, and not a single thorn bush was to be seen. The fresh scent of life abounding enveloped them fully and they surrendered themselves to its warm embrace. Sharing this moment with Talisa filled him with a quiet delight unlike any he'd felt before.

"Mmmm," she intoned.

Kazareen took a few steps deeper into the forest, found a ring of bluebells hugging the ground, and with arms outstretched, fell backwards into the thick carpet of grass. He gazed up through the limbs of a wide oak into the endless sky above and felt the peace of the forest wash over him. Unlike Talisa, he was quite accustomed to it.

But she warmed to it quickly. She spun around in circles with arms wide, tripped over a fallen branch and fell laughing at the feet of the mighty oak.

"My! It really is nice here." She pulled the shawl from her head. "Oh! I almost forgot. Happy birthday, Kazareen! Fourteen already. Hard to believe. Tell me, what did you get?"

Why did she have to bring that up? It was the one thing he didn't want to talk about, and now the mood was suddenly spoiled. Kazareen rolled onto his side, away from her.

"Does it matter?"

He knew deep in his heart that his uncle loved him. What did it matter that he never gave gifts? It was harder to see as a younger lad, but as he grew, he thought he was beginning to understand his uncle better. It wasn't the things that Uncle Murro said or didn't say, or his indifference to the outward gestures of custom, but his quiet strength that spoke loudest to him. Kazareen saw an indomitable force in his uncle, one that could not be turned or easily swayed from his chosen path. Would he ever grow that strong himself? He wasn't sure, but it gave Kazareen a vague sense of satisfaction and hope.

When Kazareen was orphaned, Uncle Murro was the only one willing to take him in. Some said it was because Murro was a lonely widower who needed a hand around the house. But Kazareen never went hungry and Uncle Murro never, ever beat him. He wouldn't even chide him about what he did in his spare time. Over time, Kazareen began to see that his relationship with Murro was far different from those that other children had with their parents. Even though Murro was not his father, it seemed to be built on something firmer. Something more akin to respect, the kind of esteem many parents never afforded their children until much later in life. Uncle Murro loved Kazareen deeply and he knew it, even if his uncle's rough exterior prevented him from expressing it in gentler ways. At least he'd remembered today was his birthday.

Kazareen was now fourteen years old. And in Pendoria, that meant he really was an adult, though he didn't feel any different than he had the day before. For most, the day a boy began his fifteenth year was a very special one indeed. Relatives and friends would gather round and offer rare gifts or nuggets of wisdom to guide them into manhood. Hopefully, the boy put these special blessings to good use as he crossed the threshold into the world of adult responsibility. But Murro was a man of few words and even fewer tender words, and since Kazareen had no other living relatives—that he knew of—the day would pass with little notice. Still, Kazareen realized it really didn't bother him that much. Murro's gift to him had been a home. And that was enough for content. If it weren't for his uncle, who knew where he might be at this moment?

"To tell you the truth, I was given something very special. Something precious," Kazareen said as he rolled onto his back.

"Really? What?"

In his heart of hearts, he saw his uncle shaking his head and smiling back at him through his bushy beard, in a way few others were ever privy to and only he could fully understand.

All he wanted to do was change the subject. "Do you ever wonder how far up the sky goes? What's behind it? Where do the stars go during the day? Why can the moon come out in the day as well as the night?"

He could see no moon today.

"Why! Don't you ever stop asking why? I've never met anyone as curious as you. Sometimes I think you're mad—quite mad, my dear friend." She giggled a bit, but kept after him. "Now tell me, what did you get?"

Kazareen shook his head and said nothing. It wasn't something he could express to her. Not yet.

She leaned in toward him, her eyes glowing with expectation, as she bit her lower lip. Kazareen waited her out patiently, until she saw she could not wheedle it out of him.

"Fine. Keep your secrets," she said, leaning back on the oak once more, but she didn't seem too put off by his silence. "Still. It really is beautiful here. I quite love it, and should have come with you before. I can't believe people say such dreadful things about it. Why do you suppose?"

"Why! Why? You must be mad, my dear Talisa. Quite mad."

They laughed together now.

Kazareen and Talisa sat in the shade and among the bluebells for what seemed like hours, talking, laughing and singing the afternoon away. Yet thankfully, the time passed slowly—the way summer days seem to last forever when you're young. At times they spoke softly, sharing their dreams and hopes for the future, and the beauty of this place they both now found so special. Later, they sang songs that folk had sung in Feria for years beyond count: merry songs and full of mirth. Even a few silly songs they still remembered from their cribs. And all the while Kazareen felt the urge to take her by the hand again, but the opportunity never came.

The forest itself seemed to grow more cheerful as they whiled away the day. When at last the sun's light began to dim, Kazareen knew they would have to be getting back. After all, there was real life to return to, supper to be made and dishes to be done. Still, Kazareen thought life with Uncle Murro was going to be better than ever before, having finally realized his uncle's great gift to him. A gift that no words could express or describe, and no material present could ever hope to truly represent or replace.

Then something struck Kazareen very odd. A great hush had fallen over the forest. The quiet grew menacing, and a strange feeling, like an ancient and powerful predator stalking its prey began to hem him in. Looking around, he saw the shadows of the trees had barely lengthened at all, and yet it seemed to be getting darker by the moment. The sky was not turning the soft amber color to which he was accustomed, but a sickly gray.

Kazareen stood.

Talisa picked a bluebell and twirled it between her fingers. "Getting dark already. I can't believe we've been here this long. My father will—"

"Look," he said, pointing toward the sun. It was still fairly high in the sky. "There is something very queer happening. Daylight fades, yet the sun, it's..."

Talisa looked and saw the untimely darkening of the sun. Instantly, she leapt to her feet. She let out a short, sharp scream and immediately began to run back toward town.

"Wait! Talisa! Wait!" he shouted after her, but she kept running, and no words of his would stop her.

Then suddenly, he heard a voice behind him. It reminded him of something out of a nearly forgotten dream.

Kazareen!

He turned, but there was no one.

Kazareen!

He was sure he heard it this time. Coming from deep in the forest? Or had someone followed them?

"Yes?" he replied to the voice in his head. "Who's there?"

Now any normal lad would have run, but his insatiable curiosity held him in check. He couldn't deny he felt a twinge of real fear, but he found it exhilarating. Darkness continued to descend, but he ignored it and began to creep forward. His eyes darted back and forth through the hardwoods, looking for the owner of the voice he'd heard, and without really thinking about what he was doing, he began making his way deeper and deeper into Bethë Dien.

He heard little but the soft rustling of leaves from his own footsteps for long minutes as he walked. Then crickets began to warble as if night had indeed fallen. Here and there, fireflies began rising from the ground, softly flashing. He caught glimpses of the sky through the trees and saw that a few of the brighter stars were now visible overhead.

Kazareen was beginning to feel very uncomfortable, for now he realized he'd never ventured this far into the forest before, and certainly not on such a queer day as this! He had nearly made up his mind to turn and leave when he saw a wide clearing in the trees just ahead. In the middle of the clearing stood a small knoll with a gnarled woody hedge, nearly leafless, hugging one side. The sight of it made him uncomfortable, and part of him insisted that he turn and run, but his curiosity demanded that he stay.

Gathering his courage, he stepped forward with a bold stride. With that, the last remaining rays of the sun receded. Looking up, he saw that the sun was gone, or worse yet, changed somehow. A white shimmering ring stood in its stead. Wispy strands of pale fire flowed out from an abysmal black hole in the sky. What great things were happening in the heavens?

Then suddenly, the strange voice came to him once again. But it was no whisper this time, but like the voice of many waters, pouring over a thunderous waterfall. It filled his head, saying:

"When the midday sun wilts,
When the heart that beats through me sings,
Come seeking! Come seeking!
Follow on wings, and you shall find
your lost one, your heart's desire,
and the grace to overcome
the silence of frozen fire."

"Who's there?"

I am Dien.

"Where are you?"

There was no reply.

He stood motionless for some time, listening to the rhythm of his pounding heart. But the moment passed. The ring in the sky disappeared, the sun's light began to grow again, and he thought—just for a moment—he heard music or singing.

Wait.

No, it was just the normal sounds of the forest.

He shook his head, for he felt disappointed. The voice was gone and though its words were strange indeed, it seemed that it had all come to naught. Surely, it had been an altogether confounding and curious day in the forest, but he felt it had ended all to quickly.

He waited in the clearing for a long while, hoping the voice would come to him again, but he would never hear it again in this world. Soon the sky was nearly as bright as it had been when he and Talisa sang merrily in the grass. He decided it was time to go.

At least he had a good tale to tell his uncle, he thought. But knowing Murro well, the idea was quickly banished. Who would believe this? Maybe Talisa was right and he really was going mad.

Kazareen turned to leave when a sharp flash of brilliant light caught his eye. It shone from a moss-covered and rotting stump at the foot of the knoll. His curiosity aroused once more, he went to see what held the light. Careful to give the twisted shrub a wide berth, he peered inside the shallow hollow of the stump. There he saw a beautiful Graystone, shimmering and twinkling in the growing sunlight. Why someone would leave it here, he had no idea. He looked around cautiously for a moment and then snatched it from its hiding place.

Now Graystones are much coveted by the traders of Pendoria as the most valuable of all jewels. And though the sight of them had become rare indeed, Kazareen still saw a few small ones changing hands in the marketplace from time to time, but never one as large or as expertly cut as this one. It was bigger than a walnut and had no sharp facets at all. It was as smooth as still water. Someone with great skill had fashioned it into the perfect likeness of a water droplet, like the ones that hung from the tip of the icicles on the eaves of his home as winter began its slow retreat.

What luck! He shoved it in his pocket. At least now he had something his uncle could see to believe.

Kazareen turned and ran for home.

When he reached the top of the hill, he stopped to catch his breath. Turning back, he peered at the forest once more. Though he couldn't be certain, he thought he heard a gentle sigh, like long suffering patience fulfilled, quiet and low. As Kazareen started down the hill—just for a moment—he thought he smelled smoke, but the scent was gone.

Uncle Murro's Tale

It was late afternoon by the time Kazareen hit town. Everyone was still wondering at the darkening of the sun, and a great buzz of excitement permeated the streets of Feria. Some of the old folk were saying they'd never seen anything like it before and that it was a bad omen. "Somethin' terrible's gonna come from it, mark my words," said one trader as Kazareen sprinted by. All business had come to a halt, and the market still hummed with talk, and very little of it cheerful.

A thousand things seemed to be running through Kazareen's head about what to do next, and for a moment he paused in the marketplace to catch his breath again. *Maybe I should see how Talisa is. Should I have one of the jewelers look at my Graystone to see what it's worth? I have to get home. What happened to the sun? Did I really hear that voice in the forest? Have I gone mad? I have to show this to Uncle Murro!*

Kazareen turned and made for home.

When he arrived at the workshop, Murro was nowhere in sight. The fire in the forge was dying, so he went to the house. When he burst through the back door, to his surprise Uncle Murro was sitting at the kitchen table, staring out the window, his brow furrowed. It was quite unlike him to sit idly while the day's work was yet undone.

"Uncle Murro, you won't believe what I found!"

"I believe I will," he said, not shifting his eyes from the window.

"I found the most wonderful—"

"Graystone?"

"Why yes...how did you know?" Kazareen asked.

"Come in here young man and sit down. The day I hoped would never come has arrived, and on your birthday no less. It's time for us to talk. More likely long past the proper time, but that can't be helped now."

Kazareen was still out of breath, and his shirt was plastered with sweat. Panting, he walked over and sat in the chair next to his uncle. Instantly he felt something inside him shift, like a wall of earth unleashed, and he got the feeling that his uncle was about to be furious with him.

"You know me. I'm not much for idle chatter. But right now, there is quite a lot that we need speak of," Murro said, but he remained quiet for a long while.

"Uncle Murro?"

"I suppose I should start at the beginning. This is going to be hard for you to hear, but you must. You may even find it hard to accept." Murro peered into his eyes and put his hand on Kazareen's shoulder. "First of all, I'm not your uncle."

Kazareen gasped. "What? I am—"

"Shh, just listen. Today is your birthday and that means you're a man now, and like it or not Kazareen, you should know the whole truth." Murro paused to take a deep breath, then leaned back in his chair, as if dreading to go on.

"When you were still but an infant, a man came to this house in the night and bade me take you in and raise you as my own. After much talk, which I will explain soon, I agreed. But I could never bring myself to call you son. It was only a year since my beloved wife and son perished in the siege of Beruthia. I took it hard, and vowed to move far away into the west to forget my pain. That is how I came to live in Feria," Murro said, shifting in his chair.

"After the siege was broken by Lord Geraldi and his host, he was made king over all the lands, the good King Smidon having perished in battle before the gates. Most of the surviving host began clamoring for Geraldi to be named the new king, having proven himself of true and noble character in the gauntlet of battle, myself included, may I be forgiven, because I believe he is not what he seems. At least, that is what the one who brought you to me said. At first, I doubted him...and those doubts have waxed and waned over the years. But now, there is no doubt left in me."

"But I stray off the path a bit. As for the man who brought you..." Murro paused for a few moments as if sifting through his memory.

"I had only lived here six months or so, when the man carrying you knocked at my door. It was late and I was tired, but being more soft-hearted then, and poorer in spirit, I bid the old man come in from the cool of the night and have somewhat to warm himself: tea and cakes. I thought it odd, an old man carrying a swaddling child in the night, but there are as many ways to live as there are people in the world, and those in need deserve our aid when we are able to provide it, I say."

The old man nodded politely as he came in and began warming himself by the fire. Standing in the flickering light, Murro now saw this was no ordinary man. He was shorter than Murro had first guessed, and though his long, tangled hair did well to hide much of his face, it could not disguise the extraordinarily odd shaped ears peeking through his silver locks. Leaves of green and gold clung to his hair, nearly forming a wreath about his head, and his robe smelled of damp earth.

The Heart of the Graystone

"Murro de Pendi, I have come far to charge you with the care of this child," he said, fully entranced by the glowing coals.

"How do you know me?"

"Ah, the world is full of mysteries."

"By what name are you called?" Murro asked.

"I am Dien."

Murro gave an uneasy chuckle, but the odd man took it poorly and frowned.

"You take your name from the great river to the north, or the forest named there for," said Murro.

"It is the river that is named for the forest. Nevertheless, I am Dien."

"Very well old man, then from whence have you come such a great distance?"

"The forest, of course," he said, finally turning his face from the fire.

Murro was becoming a bit annoyed now. "The forest is but a few miles north of here, and that is no great distance." Murro then muttered under his breath: "Old fool."

The old man smiled wryly at the remark.

Murro saw that his nose was very long and thin, and his eyebrows curled up in the most peculiar way.

"Can you travel but a few miles into the sky? It is no great distance," he said, raising a finger while still cradling the child. "I would wager the heaviest Graystone you could *not*. Still, I am Dien. You might say I am the forest. It is my home, just as this village is yours. Travel in the heavens is beyond your power. But being as I am now, I have endeavored to seek you out this night. If I were a vulture soaring, could you, even once, seek me out there?"

Murro could make no reply. While the old man spoke with an odd skill, Murro thought him nothing more than a doddering old fool who had wandered out into the night with his grandson.

"I have come for a purpose: to bear this child to you to raise as your own blood. Will you accept this charge?"

Murro had had enough. "Out you go, old man." He threw open the door. "Mind yourself and make your way home before your son misses his."

But the old man didn't move. He only stared at Murro. "Seek you a sign?"

"Leave my home! I've little patience for your ramblings."

"Very well...men always seek signs. You will be given signs you shall not soon forget!" In a flash, the old man lay the sleeping infant at his feet and threw off his cloak. His eyes blazed with a silvery incandescence, and he spoke in a commanding voice.

"I am the wind in the forest!"

A great gust of wind rushed through door, knocking over a lamp, which was thankfully unlit. Murro struggled to keep his feet.

"I am the sway of the trees!" the old man shouted. The house shook violently, as if a mighty hand toyed with it. Murro fell this time, as did most of the things from his shelves. The infant began to cry.

"I am—"

"ENOUGH! Enough! Stop, please."

The old man lowered his arms and the fire in his eyes died away. He took a deep breath, as if suddenly very tired and bowed his head. A mischievous grin spread across the deep lines of his face. "Now do you see?"

"Well enough," Murro said, struggling to his feet. He brushed himself off and surveyed the mess. Though he could hardly believe what was happening, he tried to make light of the situation, as was his custom. "I suppose I will need someone around the house to help me clean up from time to time."

He turned to where the old man stood, but he had vanished. Then a voice filled Murro's mind.

Now a word of warning. This child must never come before the king, who is not what he seems, and who should not be trusted, or all hope will be lost.

"Wait! Hope for what? Who is this child?" Murro turned and looked at the baby, and for a split second he thought he saw the infant's eyes twinkling with the same silvery glow he had seen only a moment ago in the old man. But he convinced himself he must have imagined it.

Then Murro heard the old man's voice in his head, saying:

"When the midday sun wilts,
And the child of the forest comes seeking,
Tell him his tale
And ne'er shall he fail,
For the heart of the Graystone is waking."

"I never saw the old man again." Murro stared out the window as he told his story. Finally, he looked at Kazareen again. "Neither did I hear his voice again...until today, just before the midday sun wilted. I heard the same words of prophecy I heard on the night I first saw your precious face, but I had not forgotten them. Long have they haunted me." He put his hand on Kazareen's.

The Heart of the Graystone

Kazareen expected his uncle to ask him many questions, but he kept silent.

"Uncle Murro, would you like to know what happened to me today?"

"If you wish it."

So Kazareen told his uncle all about the darkening of the sun as he saw it, and the strange verse he had heard in his head, by a voice calling itself Dien, and the finding of the Graystone.

"What was the verse?" Murro asked.

Kazareen repeated it for him.

Murro thought for a moment. "The prophecy I heard has been completely fulfilled. The sun has wilted in midday. You came seeking me. I have told you the tale of who you really are, as far as I know it, in any case. And apparently the heart of the Graystone has awoken. Look!"

Kazareen was so engrossed in Uncle Murro's tale he hadn't noticed that the stone he held in his hand was now burning with a brilliant silvery light. Kazareen held it up and for a moment, and it burned all the brighter. It did not grow warm, but touching it made Kazareen feel peculiar and a tiny bit afraid. He placed it on the table between them and its light faded quickly.

"I see now that the prophecy you heard is only beginning: 'Follow on wings, and you shall find your lost one, your heart's desire, and the grace to overcome the silence of frozen fire.'"

"This is your destiny, Kazareen—there can be no doubt. But I fear for you, for this is a strange business. Still, exactly what this prophecy portends, I don't know."

Kazareen was beside himself. "What should I do, Uncle Murro?"

"I am afraid it is a mystery much beyond my wits. Why the old man chose me to look after you. Where you came from. The meaning of the prophecy, or the significance of the Graystone. What you might do, now or later. You should seek wiser counsel than I."

"Who?"

"Perhaps a man I know of can help us, or should I say: help you, Kazareen. My part was to raise you as my own, and as of this day, that part is now over. If you ask for counsel, I will give it, for you will always be dearest to me, even as my own blood. But you are come of age now. If the words spoken are true, only you can find your heart's desire."

Kazareen was beginning to feel a gulf widening between Murro and himself. He didn't even know who he was anymore. The story Murro had told him of his parents was a lie. Who were his real parents? Surely, not Dien.

"You don't really know who my father was then, do you?" he asked.

19

"I'm afraid not. My brother and sister both died very young. I'm sorry, Kazareen. I had to tell you something until you were old enough to know the truth."

Kazareen's heart began to ache. "You named me then?"

"Aye. I had no idea what your real name was, or if you had one at all. I delayed in naming you for some weeks. But you grew on me. And since I had indeed taken on the task of raising you as my own, I gave you the name of my own blood. I gave you the name of my son who perished at Beruthia."

For the first time in his life, Kazareen saw tears streaming down his uncle's face. He went to his uncle and embraced him. "I do love you, Kazareen," said Murro.

"I love you, too. Uncle Murro. Don't cry."

They held onto each other for a long while and it helped to ease the uncertainty Kazareen felt. Suddenly, he wished he hadn't been so curious about the forest. He wished he had taken more interest in his uncle's work. But blacksmithing wasn't his destiny, this he felt.

"Tell me Uncle, who should we seek counsel from?" asked Kazareen.

Murro wiped his face with his dirty sleeve.

"Long ago, before the siege of Beruthia, I heard tell of a man of great learning and wisdom, though I have never met him and only one man who has. His name is called Arpento. They say he lives quietly among the wood-folk of Bethë Khür far to the east. He keeps to himself, and dislikes visitors. But it is also said that if there be real need, Arpento is willing to lend aid, but always at a price. Yet the price is not in gold, silver or Graystone; rather, he requires some deed in exchange for his help. Most have shrunk from performing the deed, for it is always fraught with the greatest peril."

"The man I knew who sought his counsel was called Juazeer, a merchant I knew somewhat in Beruthia. He never told me the reason he sought out Arpento, but he told me the task that Arpento demanded as payment. Juazeer was to pass through the great Northern Gates and retrieve a bundle of plants that grew beyond the mountains. No one has passed the Northern Gates nigh on two centuries. His fear of the barbarian hoards that dwell beyond was too great, and Juazeer refused the task. Alas for Juazeer, for he also perished at the siege."

"I notice you said 'whose counsel we should seek.' I am afraid that I cannot go with you. Like it or not, you are a man now and you are responsible for yourself and your actions. I must stay here, continue my work, and never cease to ask blessings upon you after you go. For go you must. There is some mystery here that I do not see, but I feel in my

The Heart of the Graystone

heart that your task is an important one. Perhaps more important than we could possibly guess."

Murro sat for a moment in quiet reflection. "Like Juazeer, I think it would be best not to say anything about your purpose. Your business is best kept your own, for it is an odd business, and the odd man is often out, I say. But for tonight at least, let us put this matter aside, and eat in peace. I grow weary," said Murro.

"But there is something else I am curious about..."

"There is always something else you are curious about. What is it?"

"Why not seek the king's counsel? I mean, if this is as important as you think it may be...shouldn't I go to him?"

"No, absolutely not. Don't forget the words of warning Dien spoke. Never let the king know what has happened to you, or what you are doing about it. Since his reign began, many things in Pendoria have turned for the worse."

"What things? Life is not so bad here."

"You don't know any better. You're young, and there are many things of which you know nothing, things that have come to pass over the years. But never mind that now; we shall speak of them later. For now, you would do well to avoid him. Flee his servants. Be wary. The king is not what he seems, and he has many spies. Again, keep your business to yourself! Otherwise, things may go ill. Now promise me and make your first solemn oath as a man that you will not seek the king's counsel."

Kazareen suddenly felt the heavy mantle of responsibility that came with manhood, and he wondered if he could bear it. But he trusted Murro without reservation, so he took a moment to search for the words he imagined a grown man might say. "Very well. I will put my faith in you, who took me in and raised me as your own. On my honor, I will not seek out the king."

An Unexpected Detour

Kazareen awoke the next day with Murro's tale still haunting him. He went about with his chores as usual, but something was gnawing at him. He couldn't get his mind around the fact that the king was not to be trusted, but there was something else. *Wait! What about Talisa?* She was there with him and knew at least some of what had happened. True, she had bolted before Kazareen heard the voice and found the Graystone, but there was no telling how much she really knew.

"Forget it, she left and knows nothing of what happened after," he said aloud. Still, he was uneasy about it and so went to the workshop to ask Murro's advice.

"Talisa du Fe was with you? Why didn't you tell me this before?" Murro dropped his hammer and wiped his brow.

"So much happened so quickly, I just forgot."

"She heard what you heard? She saw what you found?" An urgency filled Murro's voice.

"I don't think so. She ran away, towards town, when we realized the sun was growing dark. She was afraid," Kazareen said.

"Are you certain? Did you turn to see that you weren't followed?"

"Not after I heard the voice. I just assumed—"

Murro shook his head. "This won't do. You must find out for certain what she knows. Finish your chores and go find her this afternoon. But don't tell her any more than you must. I don't have to remind you who her father is. I doubt he'd be very happy to see you spending time alone with his daughter, no matter what the circumstance, least of all, the two of you alone in the forest."

"You know she is my only friend."

"Yes, I do. But I am not the Town Magistrate. I am a common blacksmith in my own employ. Garthon du Fe is in the Royal Service and selected by the king himself. He is also a snake, and a prat with a nose for other people's business. Do you remember what I said about dealing with the king's men?"

"Yes, sir."

"Good. Then mind it when you find her. Now go about your chores."

Kazareen hurried through his chores and it was not yet midday when he finished. He headed through the market and its loud jumbling masses, keeping his head down and wishing he had chosen a different route. One of the merchants recognized him with a nod, but Kazareen said nothing. Finally, he reached Talisa's street. The wide cobblestone avenue was lined with the neatest, largest houses in Feria.

He didn't recognize any of the few people walking in the street, so he began to make his way up to number seven. As luck would have it, when Kazareen neared the door, Talisa happened to be coming out.

Talisa blinked and took a step back when she saw him. "Kazareen, what are you doing here?"

"Do me a favor, will you? Come out of the street for a moment." He took her by the arm. They stepped quickly down the alley that ran two doors down from her house. "Tell me, what do you think happened yesterday while we were out in the forest? I mean, what did you see? What did you hear?"

"What's this all about?"

"Please, just tell me."

"Well, I saw the sun disappear in the middle of the day, as you did, and then reappear later."

"But did you hear anything?" Kazareen asked.

"Hear anything? I heard you calling me as I left—"

"Left from where?" said a voice. "Take your hands off my daughter! What have you two been doing?" Garthon du Fe rounded the corner. His tall, thin frame hovered over them, "Well? Answer me!" His face was already verging on a bright crimson.

Kazareen kept his eyes low. "Nothing really, sir. Yesterday...we were...in the forest... just enjoying the afternoon, when—"

"Enjoying my daughter you mean! That's it! You're coming with me. I will not have my family's name sullied by the likes of you!" Du Fe's fingers dug into his arm.

Kazareen thought about running.

"Father, no! We were just—" Talisa cried.

"Do not waste your breath defending this urchin my daughter, I've had my eye on him for some time."

This caught Kazareen's attention. *Why would he be watching me?*

"Up to no good...wandering around in Bethë Dien. Now come with me, you're going to the guard." Du Fe dragged Kazareen out into the avenue.

Kazareen's mouth went dry. His heart bumped and rattled in his chest. He was about to make a break for it, but to his surprise, two armed guards were standing at the ready as they rounded the corner. Seeing Du Fe emerge from the alley, they ran over quickly and took hold of Kazareen and began leading him away to the Royal Constabulary.

The Heart of the Graystone

"I have broken no law sir, nor have I dishonored your daughter," Kazareen said over his shoulder. "What is it that you intend to have me charged with?"

Du Fe trailed after, but said nothing.

Kazareen was in a fix and he knew it. Hadn't Uncle Murro told him to keep clear of the king's men?

Talisa ran up from behind. "Father, stop! I swear we did nothing wrong. You must—"

Du Fe stopped with a jerk and turned to his daughter. "I must what? Don't dare presume to order your father! Now go inside and stay there until I return. I'll deal with you when I return."

Talisa didn't move.

"Now!" he shouted. Talisa burst into tears and ran into the house.

Du Fe threw open the door of the constabulary and the guards followed with Kazareen in tow. "Lock him up." Du Fe ordered.

A tall soldier that Kazareen recognized immediately took hold of him. It was his neighbor, Dargon. There was wonder in his eyes to see Kazareen, for they knew each other well. He frowned, but did as he was told. He led Kazareen through a long corridor, down a flight of stone stairs, and then put him in a small, dank cell. It stank almost as badly as the stables. Kazareen heard the metallic clank of the lock as Dargon turned the key in the door.

"Don't worry, Kazareen. You'll be fine. I'll do what I can," he whispered through the door.

Kazareen was not at all reassured.

The only source of light in the cell was a narrow horizontal slit near the ceiling through which shone a thin ribbon of sunlight. When his eyes began to adjust to the darkness, he realized he wasn't alone. In the corner lay a dark figure in tattered clothes. He looked at the man, but did not say a word. Kazareen hoped he would not stir. His hands began to tremble uncontrollably as the realization of his situation set in. Then he heard Du Fe's voice coming from beyond the door, instructing Dargon. He put his ear to the door.

"Have a wagon readied. This criminal must be taken immediately to Pente Kaleán and brought before the king. Rouse the off-duty guards and instruct them to report to me. I'll stay here until they arrive. Hurry!" Kazareen recognized the urgency in Du Fe's voice.

"To the king? What is his crime?" Dargon asked.

"Do as you're told!"

Kazareen imagined Dargon cutting down Du Fe with his eyes. But after a moment of silence, he heard Dargon's heavy feet stomping away.

25

"Young man, I do not envy you. But today is the day. Your fate is now sealed. Long have—" Du Fe paused. "Never mind. I would not wish to spoil the king's surprise." Then he chuckled, but said no more.

"And what's that?" Kazareen asked.

No reply came.

Kazareen wrung his hands while he listened to Du Fe's footsteps grow faint as he left the door.

He slid to the floor of his dim cell and considered his plight. There was more to this affair than Du Fe had first hinted at. Surely, he had feigned offense at the appearance of any impropriety between Talisa and himself. It was only an excuse to lay hands on him. Was it possible that he knew about what happened in the forest? Did they know about the Graystone?

"The Graystone!" he said aloud. He reached into his pocket and wrapped his fingers round the smooth gem. Yes! Dargon had not searched him. Whether his failure to do so was because of their familiarity as neighbors or simple forgetfulness, he didn't know, but he was grateful nonetheless.

Suddenly a groan came from the dark corner of the cell. Had Kazareen spoken aloud? Oh no.

"Graystone?" the old man grumbled in the shadows. His voice was hoarse and weak, and he spoke with a strange accent. It reminded him somewhat of Murro's eastern accent, yet with a slightly different lilt. Kazareen realized his foolishness and felt certain the other prisoner would quickly be upon him to steal the Graystone. He hopped to his feet to defend himself.

The old man struggled to sit up. He considered Kazareen wearily, and saw that his hand was grasping something in his pocket. "Hmph. What good be riches in this place? No bribe shall buy your freedom now." The old man shook his head as he saw the aggressive stance Kazareen had taken.

"At your ease, young one. If you've a Graystone in your pocket, then yours it shall remain. I am no thief—despite what the king's men think. Ha!" The old man spat on the floor. "That's for the king and his den of snakes. Besides, I doubt if I could take anything from you by force. Look at me, if you're able to bear the sight."

Kazareen drew a bit closer, but remained on his guard. The man appeared older than he had first thought. His unkempt beard hung pitifully from his face, and a drawn and haggard mask it was, chiseled with deepening lines of wear. The wretch's filthy hair hung about him in a thousand tangles, like a thick bramble of thorns. His eyes were sunken into the large, dark sockets below his heavy brow. His arms and legs

The Heart of the Graystone

were frail and thin, like he had not eaten a substantial meal in years. Sores blotched his pale skin. The man seemed to be standing at the threshold of death's very door, needing only one step to pass within. Kazareen relaxed a bit, but the old man's appearance had made him wince.

The old man turned away. "I fear you too will appear as I do—before long," he said, with a hollow, self-effacing laugh.

Kazareen finally realized he was grimacing and took a step back. He suddenly felt pity for the old man. "Who are you? Why are you here?"

"Why should you care?"

"I don't, really," Kazareen said, taking another step back.

A withering sigh escaped from the huddled shape in the corner. He was silent for a long while. Nevertheless, he must have secretly wished for and welcomed Kazareen's company, for soon he began to speak.

"If you really wish to know, I am Florin from near Delasur. Long ago, though I've no longer a true sense of exactly how many years have since passed, I was a hunter, a trapper and a trader of fur in the great forest of Bethë Khür, far in the east. Do you know it?"

"I have never left Feria in my short life," Kazareen replied.

Florin paused for a moment, as if contemplating whether he had the energy to tell the boy his tale. Finally, he drew a deep breath and spoke slowly. "It wasn't long after the Siege of Beruthia when the newly crowned King Geraldi and his party began their long march back to Pente Kaleán to set up court. But being a lonely hunter and hearing little news, I knew not yet what had befallen in the East. By chance, or strange fate, the king's company overtook me on The Great Road as I was making my way to Delasur for some trading. Seeing my stores of meat, they bid me give to them half for the feeding of their company. Now I was wary of bandits crouching in the wilds, so despite how well armed they were, I refused." Florin sighed again, then added ruefully: "I didn't know he was the king."

"Needless to say, I was overwhelmed and they helped themselves to my harvest. Taxes, they said. But little of my own did they see fit to share with me. Long I marched behind them in heavy bonds, until we came to the city of Crosston. There I endured many months, or perhaps it was years, in the tower dungeon. From time to time, they see fit to move me between different dungeons throughout the kingdom. Don't ask me why. Yet, here I am—still. Tis a joyless tale, is it not? And I have grown weary of my lot. The only blessing I count now is that I do not think I will have to endure this life much longer."

Indeed, the tale was sad. Kazareen tried to hide his sympathy for the old man and turned his face to the door. "Do you think they'll move you to Pente Kaleán when they return for me?"

"May hap. Who can say? But I have told you my tale, and now I would return your questions, for I entertain so few guests."

Kazareen thought he heard the slightest hint of good humor in Florin's voice, though his jest was grim.

"Who are you? Why are you here?"

Kazareen thought for a moment about the words of warning Uncle Murro had given him. "I am called Kazareen de Pendi. Why I'm here...well, it's...a tale you would not believe, even if I told you. Let's just say the Magistrate of Feria has had me arrested for...dishonoring his daughter." Kazareen thought this a good answer, as it was true enough, yet revealed nothing of the Graystone.

A lecherous smile appeared on Florin's face. "Was she worth it?"

"It's a falsehood! I did not touch her. And that is the truth," said Kazareen, but the thought of touching her hand made him flush.

Florin's smile disappeared and he humphed in disappointment.

"Aye, I suppose tis more likely you speak the truth. The king's men trouble themselves little with real criminals these days. When I do have guests, too often have they been innocent men. Curse the king and those that do his foul bidding! Curse him!" He spat on the floor again. A fire had grown in Florin's voice. Perhaps he wasn't so near death as Kazareen first thought.

Kazareen was quiet for a while, but thought carefully about what Murro had told him. Should he ask this stranger? Finally, feeling bold, he said, "You say you are from Bethë Khür. Do you know of a man called Arpento?"

Florin raised an eyebrow at the mention of the name. "Aye." He paused for a moment. "But I am curious how a lad who says he has never left his own town would know of Arpento. Why do you ask, boy?"

"I turned fourteen yesterday. I am now a man," Kazareen stated.

"A thousand pardons, young master," Florin said, bowing his head, "but you haven't answered the question."

Kazareen was trying not to reveal too much to this stranger, though after hearing his story and his curses on the king's name, Kazareen felt he was someone he could trust—at least a little. "My uncle told me of him. He said he was a man of great wisdom and could offer counsel to those who sought him out."

Florin laughed. "Wise he may be. At least, that is what is said. Never have I heard of a soul who could pay the price for such counsel however, for tis always too high. He is a queer fellow and courts only solitude. Greater wisdom may be found in the hearts of those who steer clear of him. The hunters of Bethë Khür always gave a wide berth to the home of Arpento, and I was no different." Florin's eyes seemed to dismiss Kazareen.

"You know where he dwells? You have seen this place?" Kazareen asked, a glimmer of hope rising in his voice.

Florin nodded. "But if you seek the counsel of Arpento to untangle the web you find yourself in now, I'm afraid my knowledge of his whereabouts will avail you not at all. Look around, young master," his voice beginning to rise toward something like anger. "We are prisoners; and falsely accused or nay, prisoners we shall remain! If the counsel of Arpento is your only hope, then I'm afraid hope has deserted you—as it has deserted me." Florin's body eased slowly.

The haggard old man was certainly devoid of hope, and for that too, Kazareen felt sorry for him. But hope was not yet extinguished in Kazareen. "I must seek Arpento."

Florin raised his head slightly and stared back at him, his lips parted, but did not move to speak for some time. "There is no escape. I have watched and waited for many years, but never have I found opportunity to even attempt escape. Do you think that the king's men will lower their guard, even for a moment?"

Kazareen tried to keep a brave face, but soon found it was a lost cause. Florin was right. There would be no escape.

Murro set his hammer down for the third time in the last hour. He went to the stables, then the house. "Kazareen?" There was no reply. The worry began to show on his brow. He sighed and went back to work in the smithy. Kazareen had left nearly two hours earlier and he should have returned.

Murro raised his hammer to start work again when Talisa appeared before him. She was out of breath. Before she said a word, Murro felt the pit of his stomach run cold.

"Mister de Pendi?"

"What is it Talisa? Where is Kazareen?"

"He's been arrested. Father took him to the Constabulary. But it's not true. It's not true what father thinks happened," cried Talisa. "It's not true!"

"Say no more. I believe you. Is he still at the Constabulary?" Murro ripped off his gloves and apron and wiped his hands and face with a tattered cloth.

"I don't know," she said. "Father told me to stay in the house after he took Kazareen away, but I had to warn you. I had to tell you the truth. We did nothing...unseemly."

"Don't worry, dear. I believe you. I know Kazareen better than anyone. You run along back home before your father finds you missing. I'll take care of this," Murro said, though he didn't know how. Kazareen was under Royal guard and there was little he could do to change that. Murro looked at Talisa and tried to give her a reassuring smile. Talisa nodded slightly and slipped out of the workshop.

Without changing from his dirty clothes, Murro made his way across town in long, lumbering strides. Up the stairs of the Royal Constabulary and through the doors he burst like a whirlwind. "Where is Kazareen?" he said in a booming voice.

Dargon was standing guard alone now, and despite his friendly relations with Murro, he knew his duties came first. He drew his poniard, but kept it lowered. "Hold on a minute, Murro. Just calm down," he said.

"I've no reason to be calm! So I ask again, where is Kazareen?"

Dargon moved the long dagger to his left hand and held his right hand up in a gesture of peace. "The Magistrate ordered he be taken immediately to the king. He has seen no harm, I assure you. But there was nothing I could do."

"When did they leave?" Murro asked.

"There is nothing you can do about it either, now please, Murro—"

"When?"

"About a half hour ago, but—"

Murro ran out before he could finish. Dargon ran after him, shouting. "Murro wait! He's under heavy guard. Don't do anything foolish! If you interfere, you'll be arrested too, or worse!"

Murro paid no heed and ran out of sight. By the time he arrived home, he had calmed his mind somewhat. He leaned upon the dining table to collect his thoughts. If Kazareen was under heavy guard, as Dargon said, that meant at least three, possibly as many as six guards. Dargon was right; there was little hope of freeing him. Even if he did manage to slay the guards and free Kazareen, where could they possibly go to hide? They would be wanted men. Eventually, they would be captured again. But Dien's words of warning still echoed in his mind, and he knew he couldn't allow Kazareen to be brought before the king— under any circumstances.

Murro thought quietly for a while, musing on what had transpired. He peered down at his calloused hands and soon it became clear to him what must be done. He would free Kazareen, no matter the cost.

On Wings

Murro stood up from the table with his plan laid firmly in his mind. It was not a particularly good plan, but it would have to do. Haste was needed if he intended to overtake the caravan before it reached Pente Kaleán, for it was a little more than a day's ride from Feria. He went quickly to the storeroom in the back of the smithy, and unlocked an old wooden chest. From it, he drew a shining breastplate, where it had laid undisturbed for nigh on fifteen years. He struggled to squeeze his bulk into it, for its intended owner was a smaller man than Murro was now, but he soon had it secured. Somewhere deep inside him, Murro's pride began to stir, seeing the great royal seal embellishing the work of his own hands from long ago. At last it would see battle. Reaching back into the chest, he carefully uncovered the helmet that went with the plate mail. It was cool and smooth, and he pulled it down firmly over his brow. The cheek and nose guards hid his face well; he would not be recognized. On his way out, he took hold of Dargon's long sword, which he had only managed to finish that morning, and a stout swinging axe for good measure.

In the stables, he threw a saddle onto a sleek, muscular stallion. The horse belonged to Du Fe, and was named Wingfoot. It eyed Murro curiously at first, but knowing well the sight and smell of him, his presence caused the stallion no distress. Murro laughed to himself at the prospect of waylaying the king's caravan on the horse of one of his own appointees.

Murro mounted the great, gray steed. "Let us see now if you live up to your name. Ho! Away!" he cried, as he ground his heels into the horse's great flanks. The tall stallion burst into a gallop that nearly unsaddled Murro. The animal was indeed swift and Murro had to hold on tightly as Wingfoot tore through the dusty avenues of Feria.

At the edge of town, four guards stood upon the road with long spears. The road was barricaded with a large logging wagon, still laden. As Murro approached, the guards spied the royal seal upon his breast. After only a moment's hesitation, the sergeant of the detail ordered the wagon moved aside: "Clear the way for the king's man!" It seemed that fear of retribution for halting a royal messenger, especially one in such great haste, outweighed any order Du Fe's might have issued to halt traffic in and out of Feria. Murro barely slowed as he passed them. When he cleared the barricade, he steered Wingfoot northward.

Four months before the siege was laid at Beruthia, while the rumors of war with the wild Northmen were unsettling the kingdom, Murro had had another unusual visitor. Not as unusual as Dien, but unusual nonetheless. The great King Smidon himself had walked into his smithy in Beruthia.

All the best steel was forged in the foothills of Atan Beruth, for the iron mines were near at hand, and the blacksmiths there had practiced the crafting of metal longer than anywhere else in Pendoria, honing their technique to a high art. The king knew this well, and when word of the young Murro de Pendi and his innate and sublime skills of fashioning armor reached his ears, he sought out the young artisan.

Murro stood in awe of Smidon, and stammered when he tried to welcome the great king when he entered. But soon, the king's warm smile and familiar way of speaking quickly put Murro at ease. After looking over his wares and seeing the mastery of their crafting at Murro's hands, the king commissioned Murro to fashion for him the mightiest suit of armor he could devise; one suitable not only for what appeared to be impending war, but also to signify to all those who saw it that the man who wore it was sovereign of Pendoria.

The king ordered that the royal seal cover the entire front of the breastplate. The seal must not only be engraved there, but also inlaid with the finest gold, topaz and Graystone to be found in the kingdom. Now at that time, Murro took great pride in his handiwork and readily accepted the king's commission. It would be a daunting task, and much of his other work would have to suffer in order to complete it, but if did his job well, his renown could only grow.

However, war came to Pendoria much sooner than any had believed. The Northmen circumvented the great North Gates and managed to traverse the cruel heights of Atan Beruth, where no other path or pass was known to the men of Pendoria. It was a feat none had believed possible, at least not with a great war party. Appearing unexpectedly from the southeast, they laid siege to the stronghold at Beruthia with a force greater than ten thousand men. And it passed that King Smidon perished in the great battle, before his suit of armor was completed.

So great was Murro's grief for the loss of his family, and of the kindly king, that he spurned the pride he had once taken in the works of his hands. He could never bring himself to finish the suit of armor. Neither had the new king come calling for it, as King Smidon had commissioned it himself, and Geraldi knew naught of it. Murro had only finished the breastplate and helmet; and the breastplate, while engraved with the royal seal, had never been finished to the state of glory

The Heart of the Graystone

envisioned by Smidon. No stores of gold, topaz or Graystone ever came to Beruthia from the royal treasury, as Smidon had intended. Sudden war had overtaken his concern.

Kazareen and Florin lay quietly in the steaming reek of the prisoner wagon. The roof was low, barely high enough to sit up in, and its impenetrable black wood, hewn from the hard timbers of Bethë Dien, made the wagon feel more like an oven on wheels. The door at the rear was locked from without and held the only window, which was very small and barred over. The dark stench of the wagon had, before long, quelled Kazareen's enthusiasm for escape. How would he get out of this thing? There had been no chance at escape when they were taken from the cell and thrown into the wagon, as both their hands and feet had been bound, and remained so. The leather straps of his bonds cut into his wrists and ankles, which had long since gone numb. Kazareen was beginning to see that old Florin was right. There was no hope of escape.

Then Kazareen heard one of the guards cry out, "Ey, what's this? Sergeant?" The wagon rocked and slowed.

"I'll take care of this!" shouted the sergeant of the guard. The wagon set off again, but at a great pace now, making the old timbers of the wagon groan in protest. It tossed and shook the occupants around violently as it rambled down The Great Road.

Kazareen gained his knees and crawled to the back of the wagon to peer out the miniscule window.

"What is it?" Florin asked.

But Kazareen did not answer. He saw a great knight riding a tall ashen horse. He bore him down on the sergeant with terrible haste.

As the two riders were about to clash, the sergeant spied the royal seal borne upon the rider's armor and he hesitated. The knight did not hesitate. He lifted his swinging axe high and brought it down in a mighty blow. The sergeant crashed to the ground and did not move again.

Kazareen's eyes widened as the knight immediately began to make up the distance with the wagon. The remaining guards must have seen this as well, as the crack of whips on the horse's flanks rang out. But the wagon was too heavy to outrun the knight's swift mount. As the tall stallion drew nearer, Kazareen gazed at the knight, but his shining helmet hid his face, all save his eyes, and those glowed with the fiery rage of battle. The horseman passed out of his sight as it caught the wagon up. The wagon slowed once more.

The clash of metal on metal rang through the dell, followed by the cries of anguish and death. Finally, the wagon lurched to a halt. As he heard the slow footsteps of what could only be the victor of the battle,

33

Kazareen was suddenly afraid. Trying to hide, he squirmed into the far dark corner of the wagon. "Someone's coming."

A key went into the lock, turned, and the door opened. "Kazareen?" asked a familiar voice. Then Murro removed his helmet.

"Uncle? Is that you?" Kazareen asked from the darkness. He was amazed to see Murro's face.

"Uncle!" Kazareen squirmed toward the door as quickly as he could. To Kazareen's horror, he saw Murro's eyes roll back in his head as he collapsed in a heap. "Uncle!"

Kazareen threw himself from the open door unto the ground. Next to him lay Murro, his chest heaving under the shining armor, which was now stained with blood. There was a gaping wound on Murro's neck. Blood was flowing freely from the gash and Murro's face was already growing pale. "Kazareen?" he said weakly.

"I am here, Uncle," Kazareen said. "But my hands are bound. Help me, then I can help you."

Slowly, Murro opened his eyes. "Here," said Murro. He fumbled to remove the strap from Kazareen's wrists. Murro managed to loosen the strap enough for Kazareen to finish taking it off with his teeth before he fell limp again.

"Go now. Take the horse, Wingfoot. Promise me you'll find Arpento," Murro said, gasping and coughing weakly.

"I will, Uncle. I promise," said Kazareen. "But I won't leave you here. Don't give up!"

Murro placed his hand on Kazareen's head. "Blessings on you, young master," said Murro, and his hand fell to his side. Kazareen leaned in close and put his head on his uncle's breastplate. His tears mingled with Murro's blood.

"Go," Murro managed weakly. And then he was gone.

Kazareen would have wept long at Murro's chest had Florin not broken the bubble of his grief. "This was your uncle?" asked Florin, now at the small door of the wagon. Kazareen said nothing; his world was now turned inside out.

"You should listen to the dying words of your kin. We need be off. Free me. When the caravan is missed, they'll send out more soldiers to look for us. There's nothing you can do for your uncle now. Honor his memory by heeding his word!"

Kazareen realized the old man was right. He looked on Murro's face and gently closed his eyes. whispering an inaudible goodbye.

After freeing his legs, he removed Florin's straps as well. Wingfoot stood nearby, its head hung to the ground, but it was not grazing. It seemed to Kazareen that the stallion was mourning Murro's loss as well.

The Heart of the Graystone

Florin stood up slowly and rubbed his wrists, trying to revive them. To Kazareen, he looked even more frail and helpless in the bright of day. When the blood returned to his hands, he went to the horses that had been drawing the wagon and struggled to unyoke the one that looked the healthiest, though both seemed old and worn from their long, thankless labors.

Kazareen came over to help Florin with the draw horses. "We can't just leave him here. He was my...only kin," he said. Kazareen would always think of Murro as his uncle, though he now knew otherwise.

"We've no time to raise a mound to his noble sacrifice nor to bury him in pauper's grave. We must be off, and soon," Florin said. When the horse was free of the wagon, Florin saw that Kazareen would not leave Murro behind. "Very well. Help me ready the other horse and we shall bear your uncle's body away."

When they'd finished freeing the other horse, Kazareen searched the soldiers for any useful items while Florin hunkered down and tried to find his strength of breath. His labored pants sounded more animal than human. Kazareen hopped onto the wagon, but was disappointed to find only about two days rations stored in a compartment under the seat. He also found a good length of strong rope, a sharp dagger, a flint stone and two woolen blankets there. Kazareen stowed them all in Wingfoot's saddlebags. Florin rose slowly; his aged back still bent, and went over and picked up a sword and scabbard from one of the fallen soldiers. Why, Kazareen couldn't imagine really, he seemed barely able to walk, let alone fight. But seeing that Florin was at least thinking clearly, Kazareen took the axe from Murro's hand and slung it through his belt. It was still smeared with the sergeant's blood.

Soon they had put Murro's body on one of the drawing horses, and Kazareen helped Florin mount the other. He hoped Florin could manage the beast bareback. Kazareen climbed atop the tall Wingfoot, though his feet barely reached the stirrups. He sat atop the great horse and Dien's words came suddenly back to him.

> *Follow on wings, and you shall find*
> *your lost one, your heart's desire,*
> *and the grace to overcome*
> *the silence of frozen fire.*

"On Wings," Kazareen said to himself, as he stroked the horse's mane. "It seems our fates have been tied together." Wingfoot stomped the ground.

35

Florin pointed. "We should go south. There should be fewer patrols there for few dwell in the hills southwest. We'll head for Khürasé, then drive east—"

"No. We should make for Bethë Dien," Kazareen interrupted. He thought perhaps the spirit of the forest could aid them, though he didn't know how.

"The forest? Only a fugitive would go there. Which is why we must not. They will certainly search there first, and we won't be able to hide for long. We must do what they expect least."

Kazareen paid no heed to Florin's advice. "We'll be safe there...for a while. Come." These were mostly empty words. Kazareen did not know what would happen to them now, but in his heart, it seemed to him the best course—the only course.

Florin looked at Kazareen curiously, but decided not to argue when he saw the determination chiseled on his face. They made their way back to the fallen sergeant and Kazareen searched him as well. He had carried a small purse attached to a thick belt about his waist. Inside, Kazareen found a letter and a stash of twenty silver pieces; they would certainly find use for the coin. He opened the letter. It read:

Your Majesty,

It is my privilege to present you with the prisoner, Kazareen de Pendi. He is of the right age, and is the oddest sort of creature, and an orphan, venturing oft into Bethë Dien. In my judgment, he must be the one you seek. Your Majesty will find him uninjured, in accordance with your wishes.

Garthon du Fe
Magistrate of Feria

Dismissing it as useless, Kazareen foolishly let the note drop to the ground.

He remounted and they set off for the forest. They rode hard for about an hour until they found themselves approaching the eaves of the Bethë Dien. By then, the sun had sunk below the horizon.

Kazareen had never been in the forest at night, and the trees now seemed like menacing guardians, standing vigil over some forgotten hoard. The moonless night smothered them with darkness in the thick wood, doing its best to drain away what little hope still remained with Kazareen. It was the fragrance of abundant life flourishing there that brought him the familiar comfort, and that kept his fear in check. The fugitives dismounted as they reached the edge of the forest.

Florin surveyed the trees for a moment. "Come," he said. "We shall search for a hidden dell to shelter in for the night, where prying eyes cannot see. Though I am not sure I like the feel of this forest."

"I can barely see. How shall we find anything?"

"You forget, I lived and hunted long in the great forest of Bethë Khür. I may be old and weak now, but thanks to Geraldi, I'm accustomed to the darkness. I can see much, and hear nearly all. Come." There was a surprising amount of confidence in his voice for one that had been imprisoned for so long, and the sound of it managed to assuage Kazareen's fears, if only a little.

The thought that they might pass through the hidden meadow where Kazareen had found the Graystone leaped to his mind, but he said nothing of it. He wasn't sure if it would be proper or even safe to shelter there, as he thought of it as Dien's home. But they did not come across the clearing. The wood was thick and close as they pierced the darkness. Kazareen tripped and stumbled often, though Florin and the horses seemed to have less difficulty. After making their way along slowly for a long while, they came upon a small hillock, and Florin suggested they make camp at it's northern foot.

They found a dry spot in which to camp and after eating a bit of the rations they had taken from the soldiers, they laid Murro's body down to rest in the sparse grass. His burial would have to wait until morning. Later, Kazareen thought it would have been a harsh night in the forest but for the blankets they had plundered from the wagon. The summer's heat did not hold well at night in Pendoria.

King Geraldi

A lone rider sliced through the crowds surrounding the gates of the castle. Pente Kaleán, the great fortress of Pendoria, sat perched upon the high rocky point at the edge of the expansive sea. Between two squat towers of stone the heavy gate of oak and iron stood open, yawning like a sleepy giant. The drawbridge was down, as it had been for many years, spanning the chasm below. Tall, thin openings dotted the tower's outer face; squinting like aged eyes that gazed ever into the rising sun. A heaving throng of people milled about in the markets before the bridge. Many homes and shops had sprung up around the citadel over the years and Pente Kaleán was becoming a great city, though almost all of it now lay outside the protection of its high walls.

Looming over all was the high watchtower of the royal keep, from which the approaches to the city could be spied for more than ten miles in every direction. Four tall spires rose from the top of the great tower and on the pinnacle of each, the flags of the four Great Houses of old fluttered in the breeze. For it was from the four Great Houses that had joined forces so long ago that the kingdom of Pendoria was born, in a time of great peril for the people of those days, for they were beset from both the north and south with pillaging and war.

The wild men of the north and the ambitious and arrogant men of the kingdom of Farak to the south hemmed the people of Pendoria in, requiring them to join together to defend themselves. In time, the people became one and built great strongholds throughout the land. And to this day, here the seat of the kingdom still stood, and a truly unassailable target it was. On three sides, sheer craggy cliffs led down to the crashing waves of the sea. The only approach came across a wide crevasse spanned by the huge drawbridge. And the ramparts astride the ancient twin sentinels were manned ceaselessly with archers of deadliest skill.

"Make way! Make way for the king's messenger!" the soldier shouted. Startled people scrambled to get out of his way. After trampling through the gate and into the courtyard, he dismounted and hurried up the wide marble steps that led to the keep and main hall. Many barracks and storehouses lined the courtyard, and at their feet a fair number of soldiers were sitting idly by in the fading light, while others seemed intent on winning some game of chance. The messenger reached the top of the stair and approached the entrance to the grand keep.

"Halt! Name your business," demanded the captain of the door guard. He stood with drawn sword, backed by four more guards with long spears and shields. Their red cloaks signified them as the High Royal Guard. The captain scowled at the messenger. His weathered face spoke of the years of hardship that only a soldier could know.

"I bring urgent news from the king's post in Feria, I would speak with King Geraldi."

"The password?" asked the captain.

"Aruthe," the soldier replied in a hushed voice.

"Follow me."

He led the messenger through a broad, many-columned portico until they came to tall bronze doors, fashioned in an age long past, on which was carved an ornate relief depicting some ancient battle between Pendoria and Farak. Though the images stood as an artful testament to the strife of those days, all the tales of the great war between the neighboring kingdoms had long since faded from mortal memory.

Just inside the doors stood another guard detail; alert and at the ready. The captain walked past them without saying a word and the guards did not challenge him.

The messenger followed along, eyeing the inside of the great hall. It was not what he expected. Several broad stone columns still supported the high ceiling of this once-fair meeting place, but now, low and hastily built rooms filled the space that ran along either side of the narrow corridor. The corridor was open above, and the messenger could still see sunlight filtering through slender windows of colored glass in the original walls. He'd never seen the inside of the great keep before, so he wanted to burn the image of it into his memory. Though he was disappointed to see that great feasts would never again be held in this once-hallowed place, he was still in awe; the raw strength of its construction was something to behold. There was no fortress anywhere to rival it—or so the soldier believed. When they reached the far end of the corridor, the captain drew out a key and slid it into a much older looking door, handsomely framed in the stone wall.

"Leave your weapon here," he ordered.

The soldier drew his sword and set it in the empty rack standing next to the door. The captain turned the key. The door led not to a room, but a staircase: steep, narrow, and dark. Up, up they climbed, twisting through the small passage. So steep it was that the messenger found his head level with the captain's feet as they climbed the stairs. The spiral stairs ended at another door, illuminated by torches, at which the captain knocked firmly. "A messenger carrying urgent news from Feria has arrived, my lord."

The door opened and the brightness of the light blinded the soldier for a moment. He heard a voice. "Enter."

The Heart of the Graystone

The soldiers entered the chamber and bowed. King Geraldi sat in his plain chair at a small table, littered with scrolls and documents. A heavy golden scepter kept them from blowing away. The last rays of sunlight still filled the room, but the soldier felt a stale darkness enveloping him. The king did not turn to him, but stood and gazed out the window toward the sea. The room was much larger than he expected, with gaping windows facing the four cardinal directions, and four small anterooms behind closed doors. The throbbing crash of waves breaking on the rocks below was as little more than a whisper in the wind in this high place. The soldier saw two other men, one of which he recognized as General Gueren, standing near the king.

"Well? What is the message?" said the king.

He stood forward a bit, but was halted when the captain took him by the arm. "Kneel," he whispered.

The messenger dropped to one knee. "By your leave, my lord. I bring word from Garthon du Fe, Magistrate of Feria. He wishes to inform my lord simply that the boy is in custody. A wagon bearing the prisoners makes its way to the castle as we speak. It should arrive by morning. I was ordered to ride ahead with all haste to bring you word," said the soldier.

"Prisoners? More than one?" asked the king, still avoiding eye contact with the guard.

"Yes, sire. The boy and an old criminal, long in custody. A routine transfer, only."

"Routine? Hmph." King Geraldi turned and faced the messenger. "By what names are the prisoners known?"

"The boy is called Kazareen de Pendi, my lord. A lad of fourteen summers. Begging your pardon my lord, but the name of the old man I know not. A common criminal of little note, I am told."

"And how many guards did Du Fe assign to this prisoner caravan?"

"Three, my lord."

"Is that all? Captain, dispatch a sortie of ten more soldiers to intercept the caravan and escort them here. See to it."

"By your leave, my lord," said the captain. He bowed as he withdrew, taking the messenger with him.

When the soldiers had gone, the king turned to Alerien. "Kazareen? And of the Great House of Pendi, no less. We shall discover the truth of that," said Geraldi. "Very well. If this be the boy we have sought, it will not be long before we know all. I trust you are ready for his arrival?"

"As always," Alerien said.

41

"Very well. At least this boy is the right age. Du Fe had better be right about him," Geraldi said. "His last message said he had at least twelve boys of the proper age in the town."

"It seems the Seer's vision was true. The occulting of the sun was surely the omen of which he spoke. And very soon our enemy will be in our hands. I have no more doubts," said Alerien.

"We shall know surely soon enough. If he is the one we seek, I will know it when I see him," said Geraldi, turning to the east window. He gazed out upon his kingdom, searching the horizon in vain for the caravan. "Leave me, now. I wish to think."

The brothers exited without a word.

For hours, the king was left alone, pacing ceaselessly throughout the night, pondering the fate of both the boy and himself, so inexorably linked. Time stretched out into a rope that only seemed to grow in length the longer he waited, his gaze turning ever to the east. What would be their final doom? He could not see it.

As the first rays of morning peeked through the eastern window, a knock sounded at the chamber door. The King had not slept at all. "Urgent news, my lord!" said the familiar voice of the Captain of the Guard from the other side.

"Enter." The door opened and the captain stepped into the room and knelt. "Well? Have the prisoners arrived? I saw them not."

The captain seemed hesitant and fumbled at the words.

"What is it, Captain? Speak."

"The caravan, my lord, was...waylaid. The guards...all dead," said the captain.

A fire grew in Geraldi's eyes. "And the prisoner?" he asked.

"Gone, my lord."

Geraldi shouted. "Escaped, you mean!"

"Apparently so, my lord."

Alerien and Gueren burst into the room. "Are you all right, my lord?" asked Alerien. Gueren had drawn the dark blade from its sheath, and held it at the ready.

"No, I am not all right. The boy has escaped, and someone has slain three of my soldiers!" shouted Geraldi.

No one spoke as the king seethed.

Finally, Alerien broke the silence. "One thing at least seems certain, my lord. This Kazareen de Pendi must be the one we have sought."

The king threw him a dagger glance, but took a deep breath and thought for a moment. "We do not yet know this for certain, though it is likely. If true, then it is not the only fact here revealed. Someone else knew the boy's importance, and is helping him," said Geraldi.

He turned to the Captain of the guard. "Do we know whither they fled?"

"Yes my lord, they took the horses from the wagon and rode north toward Bethë Dien. They left a clear trail and had no more than a five or six hour head start. Men are already in pursuit. We should have them soon," said the captain.

"Send thirty more soldiers to aid the search. Gueren, the time has come for you to do what you best. Find him and do not fail. Send word also to the constabularies at Feria, Crosston and Dienaté to send every spare soldier to the area. I want every road, path and pig trail watched. He'll not slip through our net if we tie its knots closely together. But remember, we need him *alive.*"

"We'll need a description of the fugitive, so I'll go to Feria first and have a little talk with this Du Fe," said Gueren. The thirst for blood in his voice laid bare his intentions. Geraldi thought of protesting, but held back. Du Fe had failed them and deserved his punishment. Geraldi knew Gueren would do as he pleased no matter what he said now.

Gueren grinned as he exited with the Captain. Geraldi sent Alerien away. He needed to think. As he became lost in his thoughts, his mind returned to the time before the siege at Beruthia and the events long past that ever vexed him.

How had it all gone so wrong? The king bowed his head and the fine, pitch-black hair swung before his eyes.

Verdio du Phenoa saw his brother standing at the edge of the camp with two men. A large, bearded hulk of a man stood behind the tall thin one who spoke with Geraldi. He didn't recognize either of them. They slipped into the woods and out of sight before he made it to his brother's side. "Who were they?"

Geraldi turned, surprised to see Verdio. "Ah, just some locals. Craftsmen who managed to escape Beruthia before the siege. But they had little to tell we didn't already know, so I sent them away."

"Nothing, eh?" Verdio's voice rose. "So little brother, are you ready for your first battle? All the time spent at swordplay will certainly avail you, but tomorrow shall be far different from a friendly sparing session. The barbarians of the north are wicked, wily and strong—at least, so it is said. And you will receive no quarter."

"Don't worry about me. I've everything in hand."

"Perhaps. But you should spend more time practicing your skills from the mounted position. There is great advantage to be gained from remaining horsed, height and speed not the least." Verdio loathed his brother's arrogance, especially his pride in his skill as a swordsman, but he was glad his brother would be fighting with him rather than against him.

"I do practice mounted," Geraldi protested.

"Not enough. When we arrive at the approaches to Beruthia tomorrow, you will see why. One of the scouts reports there are at least ten thousand barbarians laying siege. If his estimate be true, then we are outnumbered nearly four to one. The only way to survive will be to remain atop your mount."

"That I can do. And I am willing to wager to prove it."

Verdio raised an eyebrow. He knew he was a far more accomplished rider than his brother. "Speak, brother."

"Twenty gold pieces. Do you see that grove of trees on that escarpment?" Geraldi said, pointing to the south. The trees stood at least four miles away. "First one there shall claim victory."

"A contest of speed. Ha! Your horse is outmatched, little brother. Deneb is no match for Bellatrix. You're on."

"That old hag? Not a chance. She'll buckle under your girth in three furlongs, brother. I'm surprised she can bear you at all," said Geraldi.

"We shall see. We shall see."

They each went to their squires, and had them ready their mounts. Before long, word began to spread through the camp of the brother's competition and a crowd began to gather to cheer them on. A great many side bets were laid, though none as rich as the brother's.

"I hope your purse is full, little brother. I expect my reward before we go into battle tomorrow. I wouldn't want you to die while still in debt to me." Many of the soldiers looking on broke into laughter. Verdio was popular among the men, and they relished in his jests.

But Geraldi only seethed. "You'll get what's coming to you, don't worry," Geraldi said with a sneer. "Now, go!"

Geraldi's horse burst into a gallop, leaving Verdio and Bellatrix standing unready.

"Yah!" cried Verdio, and he bolted after his brother. The onlookers laughed and shouted as the brothers tore out of camp.

Verdio urged Bellatrix on, but Geraldi's head start was difficult to make up. The ground was uneven and soft, and Bellatrix soon faltered. The smaller Deneb and lighter Geraldi moved through the trees and brush with great agility, making quick, sharp pivots, as if they knew the path they would take instinctually, though no trail was cut.

The Heart of the Graystone

Verdio knew there was no way his brother's horse could keep up with Bellatrix in the open, but he soon realized Geraldi held the advantage here upon the wooded hills.

They were little more than a mile from the war camp when Verdio finally lost sight of his brother. He slowed Bellatrix, realizing there was now no way to win the wager. His brother often proved cleverer than he thought, especially where gold was concerned, and he had pressed his advantage again.

"That's alright girl," he said, stroking Bellatrix's mane, "you can't help it if your so large and strong. We'll just take it easy, no sense in risking your legs for a race we can't win."

As they walked into a small meadow, Verdio saw his brother stopped on the far side, waiting for him.

"Given up already?" he shouted back.

"You laid your wager well, little brother. Bellatrix cannot get rolling in this land. I should have known better. Now, if we were on the open plain..."

"We aren't. Are you going to continue or nay?"

"What's the point? I'll just give you the ten gold—"

"Twenty!" Geraldi corrected.

"Very well, twenty," Verdio said, as he came even with his brother. He began digging in his purse.

"Wait, I don't want your gold—yet. Not unless I win it. How about a handicap? I'll give you a ten count head start from here, and we'll make it fifty gold."

"Fifty? Are you sure?"

Geraldi smiled. "I won't lose."

Verdio thought for a moment. "Ten count, now. And not a moment less. You promise?"

"On my honor."

"Your purse had better be deep, little brother, because Bellatrix runs ever harder when she finds herself in the lead. You're on!" Verdio dug his heels into the mare's great flanks and they thundered off.

Geraldi had to hold back Deneb, as he lurched forward to follow. Five seconds passed. Eight. Ten. Then twelve.

Twenty seconds passed, and still Geraldi did not move. Finally, they set off after Verdio, slowly following his trail.

Verdio lay in the mud, struggling to find his breath. Nearby, Bellatrix struggled to gain her feet, but her front legs were broken and bleeding. She would never stand again.

Bolts of pain shot through Verdio's chest with each attempt he made to inhale. Bellatrix must have landed on top of him, though the fall happened so fast, he could not remember. He tried to cry out, but couldn't bear the pain. As he looked around, he saw what caused her fall. A web of heavy hemp rope wound with metal barbs and camouflaged with vines stretched from tree to tree.

Then his vision began to fade. A wave of chill rolled over him and he felt himself slipping away. But he could still see: a figure hovering nearby, or was it two? The pitiful cries of his suffering horse grew vague and distant.

"Brother. Help me," he said, though he could manage little more than a whisper.

The shadowy figure drew close, and Verdio saw it was not his brother at all, but the tall, bearded stranger he'd seen talking with Geraldi earlier.

"Help," Verdio repeated.

"Very well," said the man. He reached down and put his rough hands on either side of Verdio's head. Verdio was helpless to stop him.

"Gueren! Not yet!" Geraldi cried, as he rode up to the scene of the crime. He dismounted and walked slowly, confidently to Verdio's side. "Time's up, big brother. I just wanted you to know who it was that got the better of you."

Verdio was still limp, but his eyes were filled with rage. "No."

"Yes. I tired long ago of enduring your jests and foolish pride. I will live in your shadow no more. And I shall be king. As for you...well, Gueren here has a job to do. Goodbye, brother."

"Rosari!" cried Verdio.

Geraldi turned his back on his brother and nodded to Gueren. The crack of Verdio's neck sounded through the wood.

Search parties were sent out after the brothers did not return when expected, and they found Geraldi cradling his brother's body, struck with grief and bemoaning his shame for laying such a senseless wager on the eve of battle. Verdio's body was slouched over a stump, his neck broken, the victim of a clumsy, overzealous mare, or so it seemed. All felt the loss of Verdio and morale in the camp plummeted. The heir apparent to the throne had died in a simple riding accident, the day before they were to assail the siege at Beruthia. How could they possibly prevail now?

But the next day, Geraldi, seemingly filled with a monstrous wrath, led the vastly outnumbered Pendorians into battle against the barbarian hoard. Most believed his rage burned all the brighter because of the loss of his brother. Oft he shouted Verdio's name as he hewed away enemy

The Heart of the Graystone

limbs. His skill in battle and his fearless charges into the midst of the barbarian lines were like nothing the men of Pendoria had ever seen. It seemed he had no fear of death, and he slew score upon score, while suffering not the slightest injury to himself.

When their enemies lay dead upon the marches, all were quick to ply for the crowning of Geraldi. The death of King Smidon, cut down early on in the battle, as he tried to match Geraldi's bold charges, came as a terrible blow, leaving the land without a king. They had won a great victory, but without a king, the land would surely wither and fall into disarray. And so The Counsel of Patris, the leaders of the Great Houses, met soon after the battle and appeased the clamoring masses by presenting Geraldi with the scepter and the crown.

In the weeks and months that followed, a scant few in the rival houses whispered their suspicions about the role Geraldi may have played in Verdio's death, for it was believed by most that the eldest brother of the House of Phenoa would be found most worthy of the crown when the aging Smidon finally passed. But the Counsel of Patris knew well that Pendoria would always have to come first, so no word of accusation was ever uttered against Geraldi publicly for fear of tearing asunder the alliance of the Great Houses. To the deceived masses, Geraldi had earned his throne.

Bethë Dien

The forest came alive as dawn gave way to the new day. Kazareen and Florin rose and took some of the rations to break their fast. Florin saw that they had little in the way of food, but said nothing of it. If he still had the wits to tap his old hunting and trapping skills, they would not go hungry. The horses were grazing just a few yards away, nipping idly at scattered grasses.

"We should have set a watch last night. I wasn't thinking clearly, I guess. Old fool. Our freedom is not free," said Florin.

"Our freedom..." Kazareen said, nodding slowly. "Where will you go now?"

"Go? Away, that's where—far from those who seek us," Florin said, then took another bite of dried salmon.

"Of course. But I mean after, if we should steer clear of the king's men."

"Hadn't given it much thought. Home, I guess."

"Bethë Khür?" Kazareen studied the old man carefully from beneath his dark eyebrows.

"Aye, they'll never find me there—not again," Florin said. Feeling Kazareen's stare, he stopped gnawing on the rubbery fish mid-chew. "What?"

Kazareen's mind was set on the promise he made to Murro, and on the Graystone in his pocket. "I would still seek out this Arpento, and you said you know where he lives. If you're going that way, could you...I mean would you, lead me there?"

Florin spit out the fish. "I don't know why you're so determined to find that old hermit...not that it's any of my business. What I do know is that you and I are now wanted men, so listen, and listen sharp. We'll each have a better chance at staying free if we go our separate ways, divide up their forces. Frankly, I don't know why I came here with you." He threw the fishtail over his shoulder and stood. "Should have headed south yesterday. Must be losing my wits." He turned and walked away.

Kazareen bristled. "Ungrateful old—"

"What's that?"

"You're only free because of Uncle Murro. You say freedom isn't free. In that at least, you were correct. And the cost was the blood of my kin—which he gave freely! For me, not for you," Kazareen said. The skin of his face burned with anger.

Florin stopped cold in his tracks.

49

"I could have just as easily left you bound there on the road. But I didn't, did I?" Kazareen added.

Florin turned to face Kazareen, his eyes wide. His face looked even paler than before. Slowly, he came back over and sat down across from Kazareen. For a while, his eyes searched the ground.

"You're right, of course," he said, finally looking Kazareen in the eye. "Forgive me, I've thought of nothing but my own problems for so long, I'd nearly forgotten who I was...who I am. I am many things: old, weak, and more than a little selfish now. But one thing I am not is ungrateful. You and your kin saw to my freedom." He sighed. "And so I shall repay that debt—if our fortunes hold."

There was a long uncomfortable silence neither seemed willing to break. Kazareen felt both like apologizing and not. How many times had Murro shamed him into doing the right thing? And that often with a heavy, dreadful silence. Finally, Florin nodded and offered Kazareen his hand.

"Deal?"

Kazareen took his hand and they helped one another to their feet. The old man's grip was not as weak as he imagined it might be. "Deal," Kazareen said.

"And I shall not forget my vow. I so swear."

The last of Kazareen's anger was washed away as Florin's words planted a bit of hope to take its place.

"Now I believe it's time we honored the one who freed us, and find him a place to rest." Florin said, placing a reassuring hand on Kazareen's shoulder.

A pall of dread fell over Kazareen. He did not relish the thought of burying Murro, or saying his last goodbye. Slowly, they shuffled over to where they'd laid his body in the night.

"Where? Where has he gone? We laid him right here!"

"Aye," Florin said, gasping. He kneeled to the ground and touched the grass, which was covered with a thin layer of dew. "The grass is laid low in this spot. His body certainly was here. Don't move," he said. He began to examine the area carefully.

Kazareen simply stood and watched, he was too aghast to do anything else.

"Here is a mystery, indeed," Florin said, after reading the ground for some time. "All round our camp the dew is undisturbed, save where we or the horses have tread. But how can this be? There is no sign of carrion fowl or wolves. No sign of any living creature except us—and no drag marks. If soldiers had come to the camp, they would not have taken

The Heart of the Graystone

your uncle's body and left us. If wolves or other creatures came at night there would be tracks. This mystery is beyond my woodcraft."

Kazareen fell to his knees and hung his head. Just what was going on? Kazareen had thought they might find protection here in the forest, but this he had misjudged, clearly. Then a strange thought occurred to him. And under his breath he muttered: "Dien?"

"Hmm?" Florin uttered.

Kazareen did not repeat it. But he pondered on the spirit of the wood. Could it be?

"Come on, Kazareen," Florin said, placing his hand on Kazareen's shoulder in an effort to console him. "I'm afraid we have no time to investigate this riddle further. We must be moving on. And the sooner, the better. We have to get as far away from Feria as we can."

Kazareen wiped the scant tears from his face and stood. "You're right. But this—all of this—is my fault. Uncle Murro would be alive if not for me."

"Perhaps," Florin said. "'Tis often difficult to see why men choose the paths they do, or how fate and chance play out their part. Murro did what he thought was best, and now, so must you. If you wish to honor his memory, you must carry on. Besides, there may come a time to avenge him. Come."

Vengeance. The word stabbed at him. Kazareen felt his heart begin to pound with the thought of repaying Garthon du Fe, or even King Geraldi himself, for what they'd done to Murro. He felt full and hot; a burning in his soul the like of which he'd never imagined.

The world fell silent.

Kazareen's hand slipped into his pocket and grasped the Graystone. Its heat grew and Kazareen felt the anger and frustration within him growing with it. Soon, a bleak darkness filled his mind; he could see nothing, and once again, he caught the faintest odor of smoke. Just as the thought of swearing vengeance for Murro crept into his mind, the light he saw in his mind's eye turned to blackness and Kazareen heard a familiar voice.

No.

"Kazareen, are you alright?"

Kazareen opened his eyes to see Florin hovering over him. His hand still clutched the Graystone, safely in his pocket. He looked up at Florin with a puzzled expression.

"What happened?" asked Kazareen.

"I think you fainted. You've been out for several minutes. Can you stand?" asked Florin.

Kazareen was a little dizzy still, but allowed Florin to help him to his feet. "Yes, I think I'm alright. But, I heard Uncle Murro's voice, I'm sure of it."

"You've been through a lot," Florin said. It was obvious Florin didn't believe him. But he put his arm around Kazareen's waist and steadied him as they walked. Kazareen said no more to Florin about the episode, but was quite sure what he had heard. He tried to put all that out of his mind now, for now haste was needed.

Within a few minutes, they were ready to set off again. They left the older looking horse from the wagon behind, as there was no use for him now. At least it would have plenty to eat here in the forest and a life markedly easier than the one he'd been living.

Making their way toward the rising sun, they found the going slow through the thick underbrush of the deepest stretches of the forest. In a small clearing, they came across a patch of wild raspberries, which they stopped briefly to collect. They were ripe and sweet and they ate them as they walked.

Florin scanned the trees and forest floor constantly, watching for any sign of pursuit. He would often stop them with a raise of his hand. They spoke little. But for a few squirrels, rabbits and the odd gopher, there was little movement. After a couple more hours of trekking slowly through the forest, Florin halted them again. Kazareen stood quietly behind.

"Running water. Nearby. We must be close to Laché Dien," Florin said in little more than a whisper. "Come, we shall look first. Tie the horses here."

Kazareen tied the horses to a sturdy branch and followed close behind. The sound of the running river grew as the pair made their way through the brush. Almost before they knew it, the riverbank was at their feet. They kept themselves hid as they looked up and down the wide river, but saw no one. On the far bank and beyond there were no trees to be seen in any direction. North of the river lay a land brown and barren, a wide sea of tall, golden grasses that stretched on over long rolling hills, seemingly forever.

After watching carefully for a while, Florin decided it was safe and they brought forth the horses and watered them in the river. They seemed thankful, especially the brown drawing horse they'd taken from the caravan.

"Do you think we should cross the river?" Kazareen asked.

"There is no crossing point for a great distance. The river is too wide this far west. The nearest ferry is at Dienaté, at least three days ride to the east. But we must avoid towns and settlements if you wish to meet this Arpento," said Florin. "I still think we should have gone south into the hills. Our path is more dangerous in the north."

Kazareen saw now that Florin was right. They should have gone south. But it was too late now. "I think you're right. I've led us into greater danger. From now on, you shall decide the safest road."

"A good choice. For I am crafty in the wilds and woods. This has been a strange day, but the best I have seen for years. Sunlight. The smell of the wood. I almost feel young again," said Florin.

Florin was standing straighter, taller than before. Something seemed to be giving life back to the old man. Was it the forest? Or was it hope restored that had put spring into his step and strength in his heart? After living so many years in the dark squalor of the king's dungeons, Kazareen supposed the sky and the fresh air were enough to work at least a bit of healing magic in Florin.

Florin watched the flowing river. For a moment he became lost in the shimmering rhythms of light that pranced like countless jewels upon the water. He looked to the horses. "Perhaps tis not such a bad idea. We *could* cross the river. But it will be perilous. Then again, peril has followed me everywhere in my days. Why should this be any different?" Florin gave a light chuckle.

Kazareen did not.

"Horses are strong swimmers, even when bearing a burden, though few folk are brave enough to cross such a wide expanse. Tis the currents that'll give the horses the greatest problems." Florin paused and thought for a moment. Laché Dien was at least two hundred yards wide at this point.

"We shall head east and see if the river grows narrower. If we seek to cross, we must do so no farther east than a day's ride from the edge of the forest. What do you say?"

"It's up to you. I follow where you lead," Kazareen said.

"Very well. We'll seek a narrower crossing come the morrow. In the meantime, we must find some more food. Our packs have already grown too light. Since we have no bows, I'll set snares. We shall spend one more night in the forest. This will give its creatures ample opportunity to fill my traps. Rabbits and squirrels beware!" Florin's voice echoed oddly through the trees. He covered his mouth for a moment and lowered his voice. "Draw the horses back from the river; they will be easily spotted if a patrol comes along. Give me that dagger, and I shall begin work on the snares. Look around and see if you can find more berries nearby," Florin said.

Florin busied himself cutting sapling branches and tearing away the thin strips of green bark to make twine for his snares.

Kazareen gathered the horses and led them back some way into the trees. He didn't tie them, but left them free to graze. Kazareen searched the area around their new camp for quite a while, but found no new cache of berries. On his way back to the camp, he found the horses huddled together beneath a tree. They'd discovered a lone apple tree not far from where they had set up camp, and were munching away happily. Kazareen gathered as many apples as he could carry in his arms and pockets. When he returned to the camp, he saw that Florin had nearly finished making his snares.

"Florin, look! I found apples. Actually, we can thank the horses for finding them. But we have at least two dozen here, and there are yet more to gather."

"My, my. Yes. Let me see. That's strange," Florin said.

"What?"

"A fruit tree? Deep in the forest? I would expect to find nut bearing trees here, but not apples." Florin stopped work on the snare he was fashioning. He picked up one of the apples from the blanket and smelled it. "And ripe fruit. In high summer, no less. This is odd. Have you eaten one?"

"Well, yes. Two of them, actually. Are they not sound?" asked Kazareen.

Florin sniffed again and took a bite. It was sweet as any he'd ever tasted. "They seem to be. You say the horses found this tree? Show me where."

Kazareen put down his load and led Florin back toward the apple tree. They found the horses huddled together, apparently waiting for Kazareen and Florin to arrive. "Here we are," said Kazareen.

Florin looked around and shrugged. "Where? I see no apple tree," said Florin.

"It must be a little further, I guess," said Kazareen, a bit surprised. Certainly, this was the spot where he had collected the apples just a few minutes earlier. The horses flicked their tales and watched carefully as the men searched for the tree. They wandered around aimlessly for a minute or two with no luck. Kazareen looked to the horses and they stared back at him. He thought if horses could laugh, they would be doing that very thing.

"I don't understand it," Kazareen said, giving up the hunt. He hung his head in frustration. "Everyone always spoke ill of this forest. Said it was queer and dangerous place. I never believed them. But after the last few days, I'm beginning to understand. First the Graystone, then Uncle Murro, and now—" Kazareen leaned his head against Wingfoot's neck

The Heart of the Graystone

and stroked his mane. He felt like everything he knew of the world was but a pittance. "All my ill fortune springs from these trees."

"You speak of ill fortune. Think again. The trees did not slay your uncle. Neither did the forest imprison you falsely. Your luck's been bad of late, but the forest is not to blame. We have found sanctuary in these trees for a day, and now we have sound fruit to eat. If anything, the forest has been your benefactor. I too have heard a few strange tales concerning these woods, but from what I have seen and heard, it is King Geraldi who brings you ill fortune, not the forest. The king is your enemy, as he is mine. Come."

It seemed Florin's preference for the company of trees wouldn't allow him to suffer Kazareen blaming his problems on them. Kazareen felt humbled by Florin's words, but he was right. Wherever his problems were rooted, they were sprouting from the king, not the forest. But he wasn't ready for what Florin asked next.

"But tell me, what does the forest have to do with your Graystone?"

Kazareen's mouth fell open for a second before he snapped it shut. He'd let it slip.

Kazareen tried to act as though he hadn't heard Florin's words. Every nerve in his body tingled as he ducked under Wingfoot's neck.

But there was no escape.

He threw his arms across Wingfoot's back and rested his chin in his wiry coat. Kazareen faced Florin now, but his thoughts were turned inward. Dare he? Uncle Murro's warning had been about the king and his men, no one else. Could he trust Florin with such a secret? Surely, here was a man who would not betray him—wronged as he was by the king.

"Kazareen?" Florin said.

But would Florin believe his story, even if he told him? *There's one way to make him believe.* The empty space in his heart left by Murro's death demanded filling. The desire to find a friend, an ally, someone he could trust, was too great.

Go ahead. Do it.

Kazareen pulled the Graystone from his pocket and held it out for Florin to see.

The old man's sparse eyebrows rose. "Whew. That is quite a stone, but—"

"Just watch..." immediately, the inner light of the Graystone sprung to life. It glimmered weakly at first, and then its light grew until it began to make Kazareen uncomfortable again. When he saw the glazed look of amazement on Florin's face, he slipped it back in his pocket, glad not to have to look upon something so far beyond his comprehension.

55

Now it was Florin who was speechless, but he could not manage to close his mouth.

When Florin finally seemed about to speak, Kazareen began telling him the full tale of the eclipse, the prophecy, the Graystone, Murro's story, Du Fe, everything. Florin listened carefully, and Kazareen left nothing out.

"I don't believe it," Florin said.

"No?" Kazareen pulled the Graystone from his pocket once more.

"May I see it?" Florin asked, as he came for a closer look.

Kazareen held it out. Having no more fear of Florin, he placed it in the old man's palm. The light began to grow once more. When Florin seemed to accept what his eyes were showing him, he handed it back to Kazareen and he pocketed it quickly.

"Very strange. It's just so—"

"Hard to believe, I know. It is for me too. But that's why I must seek Arpento. That's why I must find some answers to this...mystery. Besides, I promised. Still, there is one thing even more curious than all that. Why was I arrested? The note I found on the guard makes it certain it wasn't just Du Fe's idea. It is the king himself who seeks me. But now that Uncle Murro is..." he couldn't say the word, "no one but you and I know of this thing. Why does he want me?"

"I know not," Florin said. "But whatever the case, tis certain he means to have you."

"Not if I can help it."

"Nor I," Florin said. In Kazareen's eyes, Florin seemed suddenly taller. Or was it younger?

"I think the Graystone is— "

"Perhaps it is wiser to speak no more of it, until we find Arpento. But I don't know if he can help you, Kazareen, for the price for his help is terrible. If he is able—or willing—to explain the mystery of the Graystone, then perhaps he could divine also why the king seeks your capture. Perhaps this is the key, discovering the king's interest in you. If you know that, then I believe the rest of the riddle might be explained more easily. I pray he can help you," Florin said, "but I have my doubts."

Kazareen said no more, but they nodded to one another as if some unspoken agreement had been struck. And Kazareen's feet seemed to feel the reassurance of the earth beneath him once more.

They turned and led the horses back toward the camp. Whatever had happened to the apple tree they would never know. At least it had not unsettled the horses, for they are beasts quick to flee danger and the unknown. To the contrary, they seemed bound to stand there in peace

The Heart of the Graystone

until the end of time, if left to themselves. There was no doubt that the tree had indeed existed, for when the pair arrived back at the camp, the ground was still littered with fruit.

After Florin finished making and setting his last snares, it began to grow dark. The thought of another night in the forest and the strange events that might come to pass there weighed heavily on both their minds. Still, the power of Dien seemed to be working for them rather than against them, so Kazareen's worries were mostly of being discovered by the king's men. Kazareen volunteered to take the first watch. His eyes grew heavy in the darkness, for they could certainly not build a fire, lest they be discovered. But the darkness held no fear for him, only doubts. His whole past and future were unknown to him and the uncertainty that ignorance brought covered him like a shroud.

Florin woke Kazareen. "Dawn approaches, Kazareen. Break camp and prepare yourself for the day. I'm going to check the snares," Florin said.

Kazareen rose and went to the river to wash himself. The water was cool, but not cold, and helped to open his eyes. He returned to camp and after gathering the horses, he began to load their gear and scant provisions. Soon Florin came walking back, but he was empty handed.

"My snares have failed to catch a thing. Perhaps I have lost more of my woodcraft than I care to admit," Florin said, kicking at an old branch.

"Let's just go. At least we have a good store of apples, which seem now like a gift," said Kazareen.

Florin agreed and soon they were under way. Within a couple minutes they came upon the spot where Kazareen thought the apple tree had been. They passed through without saying a word. They moved cautiously through the forest for many hours, keeping the sound of running water to their left. The going was still slower than Kazareen's liking, for the dense growth forced them to go it on foot. It was midday when they finally arrived at the eastern edge of Bethë Dien.

"Cautiously now, Kazareen. We cannot be seen," Florin said.

They crept into the sparse eaves of the forest. There they laid for a long time, watching for signs of movement along the river and to the south and east. When Florin felt certain no one was around, they led the horses out into the sunlight.

"It is still at least two days ride to the town of Dienaté, perhaps three. We must trust to luck for a while as we follow the river east and search for a narrows to cross," Florin said.

Kazareen nodded and they mounted their horses and left the mysteries of the forest behind. He sighed in relief, for he had grown footsore from their long trek and was glad to finally ride. Feeling his own weariness, he wondered how long Florin would be able to continue on, how long before his neglected body was sapped of the strength given him by fresh air and sunlight. For now at least, they could ride and that would make the going easier, but the danger of being seen or caught would only grow.

As they rode, Kazareen saw that the land they found themselves in now was mostly open. There were sparse groves of trees and bushes here and there, so they rode through cover when they were able.

His long journey to find Arpento had begun at last.

The Great Prairie

The day passed slow and sticky-hot as they rode east. At Florin's direction, they strayed at times a mile or more south of the river, passing through small garths. He said that if they were being tracked, the signs they left behind would appear more random. Their trail might also become lost among the trees and shallow streams that fed Lachë Dien. Florin's craftiness in tracking game had also taught him how to avoid being tracked himself, for they did not simply ford the tributaries, but rode in them for long stretches, if he judged that their mounts could find safe footing.

Florin's care in choosing their path only made Kazareen's trust in him grow. Any doubt lingering in the back of his mind about the old man soon blew away with the warm summer breeze. To pass the time, Kazareen spoke of his home and Uncle Murro and Talisa and how poor a blacksmith he was. Florin too began to tell tales of his life before his incarceration, his home in the forest, long and successful hunts, but Kazareen always felt like he was holding back more than he was sharing.

As the sun steadily sank in the west, they began watching for a spot with good cover in which to make camp for the night. As they crested a low ridge, they spied ahead of them a thick grove of trees in a small dell through which another small stream ran.

"What about there? That looks like a fair place for two hardened criminals to make their lair for the night," Kazareen said, pointing ahead. Florin began to chuckle, but it quickly caught in his throat as he turned to look at Kazareen, who followed close behind.

"Look! We are found out! Fly now, to the river!" Florin cried.

Kazareen turned and saw about a dozen horsemen riding hard, making directly for them. They were at least a mile behind, but Kazareen and Florin had been spotted as their silhouettes stood out against the clear sky atop the ridge.

Fear gripped him and in the terror of the moment he froze. His heart felt as though it would burst through his chest, it pounded so. His ears filled with the roar of blood coursing through his veins. He couldn't even hear Florin's pleas for him to flee. Florin stopped, turned and rode back to Kazareen to loose him the stranglehold of terror.

"Come! Follow me!" Florin shouted as he circled Kazareen.

It was the sight of Florin that finally shook him back into the moment and they rode north to the river at a full gallop. Approaching the river basin, they saw it was already shrouded in a damp mist. When

59

they reached the river, they found it not much narrower than it had been at the eaves of Bethë Dien. It was difficult to judge in the growing darkness and veil of fog, but it was still at least a hundred yards across. They had no choice, so they urged the horses into the river.

"Stay high in the saddle and hang on tight. The current is strong. It will try to sweep you away!" Florin warned.

Kazareen feared for himself, but he knew Florin would have a much more difficult time, for he was riding bareback, and both he and his mount were old and weak. They had only gone a few yards from the shore before the horses lost their footing in the riverbed and began to swim. Florin wrapped his arms around his mount's neck and hugged its wide girth with his legs.

The strong current was sweeping them downstream, and he struggled to hang on. Wingfoot kept his head high and pumped his legs furiously. He tried to steer the great steed toward Florin, who was still slightly ahead of him and to his right, but it made no difference—Wingfoot's survival instinct had taken hold.

They were more than half way across when Florin turned to look back at their pursuers. They were still riding hard down the long sloping bank to the edge of the river and they would reach its edge in a matter of seconds. But in turning, Florin lost his grip, and he disappeared below the rippling eddies.

Florin felt the current sweeping him away, but just as he felt about ready to give in to the chill of the waters, he slammed against a great churning mass of muscle; he reached out, but could find nothing to grasp. Finally, he felt a hand pulling him up by the back of his tattered shirt, which began to tear, but did not give way. He burst to the surface gasping for air and coughing.

"Hold on! We are almost across! Just a bit further!" Kazareen cried.

Florin managed to keep his head above water as they approached the bank. Just as the soldiers reached the far side, Wingfoot caught his footing in the muddy bottom and he lurched forward. In three great strides, he climbed out of the river. They had made it across—barely. Florin fell coughing into the sloppy bank as his tattered rag of a shirt finally tore away. A bit farther downstream the older horse, now exhausted, trudged slowly out onto the bank as well.

On the far side, the soldiers hesitated. Either they had no orders to leave Pendoria in pursuit, or their fear of the treacherous currents held them back. Several of the soldiers drew bows and launched arrows that fell harmlessly into the water several yards short. They set themselves to launch a second salvo, but the captain stopped them. The fugitives were wanted alive, and the light was almost gone. The captain ordered his

The Heart of the Graystone

men to remount and follow as he spurred his horse into the river. But several refused the order, for they held a greater fear: that of the barbarian Northmen, and those fears were ancient and did not die easily. Who knew how many might dwell on the great prairie to the north? An argument broke out and soon the clash of swords came ringing over the water.

Kazareen helped Florin to his feet. "Look, they're fighting among themselves. Let's go," he said.

Florin wearily made his way over to collect the old horse, which stood shivering near the bank. He mounted the beast and urged it forward, away from their pursuers. But the old horse was shaken from the crossing and could manage little more than a hastened walk.

Kazareen climbed back atop Wingfoot, still dripping wet. Suddenly, Kazareen had a terrible thought. *The Graystone! Had it been swept away in the river?* Holding his breath, he checked his pocket and felt it there still. He sighed in relief. They rode north, still shivering from the cool waters of Laché Dien, leaving the soldiers behind to settle their quarrel.

Though Kazareen and Florin would never know it, the soldiers had slain their captain and dispersed. None wished to face the peril of the wide river or the Northmen they imagined might live beyond, nor the wrath of General Gueren for the slaying of their captain. The survivors stripped themselves of their rank and livery and melted back into the population, deserters. Most rode east to find new lives as hunters or farmers in the lands to the north and west of Bethë Khür. But no word of the mutiny at the river ever reached the anxious ears of General Gueren, only the report of entire patrol gone missing.

As the waxing moon rose in the east, it shone down upon the land and helped to guide their way. But it made little difference, for the land they rode in now was a bare and mostly featureless prairie of high grasses. The long, rolling hills stretched on seemingly forever.

Kazareen was a bit surprised when they came upon the ruins of a dwelling, long since abandoned. He didn't think anyone lived north of the river. But hoping they might find a scrap of food or some useful tool, they dismounted and began sifting through the fallen timbers of what had once been a simple longhouse. The logs that still held some shape were charred and rotting with age. Kazareen thought he detected an air of decay hovering about the ruins.

Kazareen kicked through the coals for a while but found there was little left to salvage. Evidently, it had been picked over many times. The sharp scent of burning stirred up by their search filled his nostrils and immediately he began to feel uncomfortable, like maybe they shouldn't have stopped here. But there was something else—something fainter—hidden in the memories of this place.

He kicked again in the black dirt and saw something round. He leaned down to see. Brushing away the surrounding coals, he quickly realized what he'd uncovered and he jumped back with half a shout. In the dim moonlight, the white of bone shone clearly among the coals. His skin began to crawl as he recognized the pall of death that lay over this place. Whoever had lived here had apparently died here as well.

"What is it? Did you find something?" Florin said.

Kazareen realized he'd broken one of Pendoria's oldest and strongest taboos: that of disturbing the dead. He kept retreating from the pale crown of the skull until he tripped and fell over a rock.

"Watch yourself."

"I'm alright. Let's just get out of here," Kazareen said as he stood and brushed the ashes from his bottom. His eyes were wide, but in the dim light Florin didn't notice.

"Yes. We should keep moving."

They mounted again and rode off, but Kazareen said nothing about the remains he'd accidentally disturbed.

They rode on for many hours in the darkness, unsure if they were still being followed. By midnight, they began to feel they had made a clean escape, at least for the time being. Despite slipping from his aged horse in the river, Florin felt grateful toward what was surely a noble beast.

"You may be old and slow, like me," he said, stroking its tangled mane, "but you refused to give up. You have earned my admiration. So I shall now give you a name. And I shall call you Vala, which means 'worthy' in the ancient tongue." It seemed they had a new friend among them now, for Vala shook his head in agreement.

Kazareen smiled a little, but he was still unsettled by what he'd touched in the ruins of the longhouse.

Soon their weariness overtook them, and with their fear of the pursuing soldiers abated, they stopped in a shallow dell to bed down for the night. They would have built no fire to give away their position, even if they had been able to find fuel in this barren land. So they took the last bit of dried meats and an apple each from their humble store and soon laid down to rest under the crescent moon. Their clothes were still damp from the crossing and the cool night air bit them easily. Kazareen rested his head in the grass and listened to the crickets as he drifted off into a dream of his lost home and his soft bed that lay empty there.

The Heart of the Graystone

Dawn broke and Kazareen woke Florin. They were both tired and sore, for neither of them was much accustomed to riding. Shaking off their pains, they broke their fast. The apples were now all that remained. They took one each and tightened their belts.

"These won't last long. And this land is so empty. What'll we do for food?" Kazareen asked.

"Don't worry Kazareen, our needs shall be met. This land is rich with sustenance—though it may not be much to your taste—at least, until you become hungry enough. Where there is life, there is food enough to survive. We shall not grow fat here, that much is certain, but the earth provides. For now, let us be content with what Bethë Dien has given us," said Florin.

But Kazareen's curiosity would not let the matter go. "And what, pray tell, is this food? Grass? I am no horse. I cannot eat that."

"Your food sings to you yet."

"What?"

Florin grinned and began searching the ground. Spotting his quarry, he leaned over and snatched a cricket from the grass. He popped it in his mouth, gave it a good crunch or two and swallowed it down, still grinning.

"Ew! I cannot eat that. I am—"

"When your belly growls from hunger you'll be glad for it. That is just one of many foodstuffs for the likes of us, though they are easiest to catch and most plentiful. There are wild grains here that can sustain us as well, though we cannot take the time to harvest them. Haste is still our ally. For now, be content with your apples." Florin seemed to savor the insect, for as he turned he spotted another and ate it as well.

"Eating grass does not seem so bad to me now," Kazareen said. The thought of living on crickets or locusts made his stomach twist. He found he was no longer very curious about what other things Florin might have them eat in this wide-open land. Instead, he took Florin's advice and grabbed another apple.

They collected the horses, which seemed quite content with such an abundance of grasses to graze upon. Kazareen guessed that for them it was a kind of heaven. Kazareen whispered into Wingfoot's ear. "You don't know how lucky you are, Wings," he said, giving a sideways glance to Florin. Florin heard this, but said nothing.

They mounted and Florin led them toward the rising sun.

This land had a stark beauty all its own, but there was little to please the eye or break the monotony of the endless prairie. Worse, there was no shelter or cover from prying eyes, and it began to weigh on Kazareen. He reckoned they were twenty or more miles north of the river now, but he had no knowledge of the fate of the soldiers who had nearly ridden them down. And while it seemed that they had not pursued them directly, he assumed that word of their whereabouts would reach the king and a greater number of soldiers would soon be seeking them.

The heat of the day began to wear on them and their thirst grew. They would have to find water again soon. Vala seemed to have recovered from his efforts from the crossing the day before and while his footfalls were heavy as always, his mood seemed brighter. Before long, they came upon a trickling brook that flowed south to the river and they stopped to refresh themselves in its cool waters.

"Where are we? I mean, what is this place? If you know," Kazareen asked.

While Florin had not traveled widely in his younger days, he had, on occasion, seen maps depicting the kingdom and the lands that surrounded it. "We are on the great prairie that borders the edge of the northlands. Tis considered a wasteland by most and it extends for more than a hundred miles until it meets the western slopes of the great mountain range of Atan Beruth. We are unlikely to find any settlements in these lands, except perhaps more ruins. Tis a harsh place with little shelter and few hiding places, so we must make our way east without delay."

"The stronghold of Dienaté guards the westernmost ford, but yet lies to the southeast. It was still at least a full day's ride east of where we crossed the river, so it shall soon be directly south of us. We may even happen upon the remnants of the old North Road. The good people of Pendoria had, for a time, tried to farm these lands. But they abandoned it for richer lands in the south long ago. It would be hard to carve out a life here. Tales tell that terrible winters with howling gales curse this land—winters that few could survive. Now, fear of the Northmen prevents even the hardiest and bravest souls from crossing the river."

"Then we are close to the barbarians? Do you think they destroyed the longhouse we found last night?" Kazareen asked, suddenly wary.

"I think not," said Florin. "Despite people's fears, I have never heard tell of Northmen venturing this far west."

"Where are we headed?"

"East. We should ride due east for three full days. Perhaps four. Then, we turn south. With a little luck, we can cross the river again, but in something like safety this time. The river is narrower and shallower east of Dienaté, so the crossing should not be as treacherous as before. From there..." Florin seemed to drift off for a moment, as if caught suddenly in a dream.

"From there?"

The Heart of the Graystone

Florin's eyes seemed to be seeing far beyond. "From there...we continue south. Only two more days ride and we'll come upon my old home that I have not seen in many years, the greatest forest in Pendoria: Bethë Khür, where, I believe," he turned to Kazareen now, "an old man named Arpento awaits the arrival of two weary outlaws."

Florin's words were meant to reassure Kazareen, but he took little comfort from them. They had been so busy in their flight that the thought of his business with Arpento had nearly escaped him. The dream of home he'd had the night before came back to him.

Why has all this happened to me? Why me? All I wanted was to go on living as before. Now, Uncle Murro is gone and I'm a fugitive, not only from the law, but from my life as well.

They spoke little for the rest of the day as they continued east. Florin kept turning to eye the dark clouds gathering behind them. "There is a storm rising in the west. We'd best be seeking some kind of shelter, and soon," said Florin.

They gazed at the emptiness of the land around them and resigned themselves to the fact that a wet night was coming. Their mood darkened with the sky. The sun had already slipped behind the clouds as it descended into the west, and summer's warmth seemed to be slipping away with it. A chill wind carried the storm clouds ever nearer.

Eventually they came upon the remnants of the old North road—or what was left of it—just as Florin had predicted. Through years of disuse, it had grown over with grass, leaving only two thin tracks of hardened ground upon which no seed would grow. They almost passed over it without notice, as it lay nearly hidden in the tall grass of the prairie, their stalks waving wildly in the cool wind. They stopped and considered the old road for a moment as it led north over a long ridge and south toward the river town of Dienaté. It gave Florin a bit of hope.

"If we are granted a bit of luck, we may actually find some shelter this night," said Florin. "As I mentioned before, there were hearty folk who tried to farm these lands, long ago. We may happen upon an old dwelling that still stands. Let's hope we find one soon. Our chances will be better if follow the road south, for a while. But we don't want to draw near the ford."

Kazareen strained his eyes in the fading light for any sign of civilization. They turned south along the old road, and went four or five miles, but saw no sign of a dwelling— whole or decrepit. Kazareen's hopes for the simple comfort of a roof over his head faded.

65

When Florin grew wary of riding further south, they turned to the east once more and rode along in silence. The darkness grew around them and the cricket's song began anew.

Finally, the rains came, first in a light mist, then a sprinkle, and finally in a torrent that soaked them to the skin. But they continued on, not wishing to lie in the cold and the wet. They dismounted and walked for some time in an effort to keep warm. Kazareen broke out the wool blankets from his saddlebags, and they draped them over their heads like cloaks. It seemed to help for a while, but the rain was relentless and the blankets were soon soaked as well. By then, the storm had kicked up a swift gale that bit them as ravenously as any wolf from the wilds.

Onward they stumbled into the gloom and rain, bearing the sting of the wind as well they might, until at last their strength began to wane. Kazareen was young and strong, so despite his miserable plight, he bore it well. But Florin, in spite of the near-miraculous change that seemed to have come over him since their escape, began to falter.

"What's that?" asked Kazareen, pointing to the southeast. A dim light twinkled through the tempest, but just how far away its source lay, neither could say. "A fire. Let's go," said Kazareen. Immediately he set off in the direction of the light, thinking of nothing but relief from his soggy torment.

"Not so fast!" Florin interrupted. "It could be a soldier's camp. We are still not far from the old road. The king may have dispatched patrols this way. We cannot stomp heedless into their camp." The thought of being thrown back into the king's dungeons struck him like lightning and he began to cough.

Kazareen stopped cold. "Not even the king's soldiers could keep a fire lit in this downpour. It can't be a camp. It must be a dwelling of some kind. Maybe someone still lives in these parts. Besides, we have to get out of the rain."

Florin's head was pounding. He had no energy left to dispute Kazareen further. "Perhaps you're right. So be it. We'll go and see the source of this light—be it friend or foe. But we should approach with caution. Be prepared for anything. Draw your weapon."

Kazareen did this, but did not relish the idea of going into battle. He knew nothing of warfare; besides, they were tired and cold. If they had to fight, their chances of victory were miniscule.

They walked slowly toward the light, clutching their weapons and shivering. They endured more than a mile of the drenching rain before they finally made out the source of the light. As they approached, they saw a small dwelling dug into the side of a hill. It looked old and in ill repair, but the light of a small fire shone from its lone window.

The Heart of the Graystone

"Wait here for a moment," said Florin, dismounting. "I shall take a closer look. Be at the ready."

"No, I'm coming with you. If we must fight, then we fight together," Kazareen said.

"Very well, but stay behind me. And be quiet. Come, and we shall see what we shall see."

They left the horses standing pitifully in the rain. Kazareen gripped the axe as best he could, measuring its weight in his hand, but his fingers were tingling from the chill of the stinging rain.

Stepping as lightly as they could, they approached the dugout. When they reached the front wall, Florin looked at Kazareen, placed his index finger to his lips, then ducked under the broken window and rose on the far side. He took a deep breath, held it and peered inside. He watched intently, but gave Kazareen no sign of what held him motionless. Curiosity got the better of Kazareen once again and he looked too. But it was not what he saw that first caught his attention, but the sweet aroma of fresh meat cooking. Immediately his mouth began to water. It seemed that he'd never smelled anything so savory.

Kazareen saw a lone figure huddled by the fire, back to the window and seated on a low stool, turning the meat slowly on a spit. No one else seemed to be inside. The sounds of a crackling fire and sizzling meat were now barely audible over the din of the blasting rain. Florin looked at Kazareen and they stood back from the window. There didn't seem to be much danger for them here, so Florin decided to risk making contact. They needed shelter badly, but it was the smell of the roasting meat that drove away any remaining hint of caution.

Florin sheathed his sword, much to Kazareen's surprise, for in doing so, its metal blade rang loud enough to be heard in the dugout. Before Kazareen knew what was happening, Florin rapped on the door.

"Put away your weapon," he said to Kazareen, "we are fugitives, not brigands." Kazareen stowed his weapon in his belt. But no one came to the door. Florin beat on the door again. Still no one came.

"We are lost and cold and hungry on this night!" Florin shouted. "We mean you no harm, will you not let us in?"

Still no one came. Finally, as Florin reached to try the latch, the door swung open. The point of an arrow, bent upon a great longbow of yew, greeted him. The hooded figure stood as motionless as a pointing hound, ready to loose the arrow if Florin moved.

Florin raised his empty, upturned hands above his waist in gesture of parlay. "We mean you no harm, we—"

"We?" said the figure. Florin looked over at Kazareen who still stood shivering next to the window. "Step back!"

67

Florin took two steps back and the stranger stepped out and pointed the dart at Kazareen for a moment, then aimed it back Florin.

"We seek shelter only until the rains pass. Will you not—"

"Who are you? What are you doing in these lands?"

"I am Florin of Bethë Khür, this is Kazareen of Feria. We are but travelers caught in the storm."

The figure stood silent, bow still drawn, as if searching the old man's eyes. "You lie."

Florin was becoming frustrated at the stranger, whose face remained hidden under the deep, hooded cloak. "It appears you will not trust us. Very well. But let me remind you that we had it in our power to slay you at unawares and take your home and dinner for ourselves—but we did not. For we are armed and approached by stealth. If our intent were other, you would have died while turning your spit, none the wiser," said Florin.

Still the figure made no move to lower the weapon.

Florin's frustration suddenly faded into despair. "Loose your arrow if you must. But do it now! It will be a more merciful death than the one that awaits us in these wastes."

"No!" Kazareen shouted.

The stranger's bow slowly went slack.

"In this at least, you speak the truth. Come in from the rain," said the dark figure, turning back into the dugout.

Kazareen and Florin both hesitated. The stranger halted just inside the threshold. Then the voice said more softly: "Please enter...and be my guests."

Kazareen and Florin traded a cautious glance but passed into the dugout and shook off the rain. It was warm and dry and that was a relief, but their mouths were watering from the aroma that filled the single room abode. The dwelling was larger on the inside than it appeared from without; being dug some depth into the side of the hill. On their right stood a table and two benches near a tall cabinet of wood in which were stored a small array of sundry items. A single cot was situated not far from the fire, covered with tanned animal hides. At the back of the dugout, the half-butchered carcass of what appeared to be a small antelope hung from a sharp hook.

The scene reminded Florin of his own lodge in the wilds of Bethë Khür, so many years ago. In a strange way, he almost felt at home.

They drew near the fire to warm themselves while the lonely hunter sat down again upon on the low stool and began turning the spit. "You'll find dry furs in the back. You'd best get out of those wet clothes. Neither man nor beast should be traveling on a night like this."

The Heart of the Graystone

"The horses." Kazareen looked to Florin who stood shaking. "I'll get them."

Florin coughed. "And what, pray tell, will you do with them? Bring them in here? Let them be," he said and coughed again.

"Go get them boy, you can stable them in the lean-to. They'll have some shelter and company there, and they will be glad for it."

Kazareen resented being called a boy, but thought better of arguing with their host, lest the offer of shelter be withdrawn. "Where?" he asked. "We saw none."

"Thirty paces to your left as you exit," said the hunter.

Kazareen was surprised that they hadn't noticed the lean-to, but the darkness of the night was complete, except for the small fire they'd seen. He went back out to gather the horses, and when he returned Florin had already shed his rags and was seated next to the fire, wrapped in animal furs. The hunter was removing the roast from the spit. Kazareen had gathered the remaining apples in his blanket and poured them onto the table. He shook the rain off again and went to the back of the dugout to remove his drenched clothes. When he'd wrapped himself in one of the animal skins, he gathered his clothes and hung them from the mantle to dry.

"Eat. It will help to warm you as much as the fire." The hunter saw the fruit lying on the table and looked at Kazareen, but he could not make out the stranger's face in the dim light. "I thank you for sharing. I've not tasted fresh fruit in some time."

Florin still sat shivering as he stared into the fire. Seeing his friend's weakness, Kazareen went to him and helped him to his feet. They seated themselves at the table, facing the fire. The hunter had placed the meat on a platter and was carving it with a large hunting knife. Kazareen and Florin thanked their host and ate what they were offered. The hunter sat facing them, still cloaked, and ate quietly with the guests. At times, the stranger paused as if studying their faces, but said nothing during the meal. They each took an apple and ate them for dessert. It was as fine a meal as Kazareen had had in what seemed to him like weeks—though it had only been a few days since he was seated at his own table with Murro.

When they finished eating, their host spoke again. "There are no travelers in these lands. Tell me truly now, why do you flee Pendoria?"

Kazareen looked at Florin, but he was intent now upon their host. "We thank you for your hospitality. Food and shelter on a night such as this are greatly welcome. But before we discuss our business, we would first know our host's name so we may thank him properly," said Florin. He was still wary, for as fugitives from the law, they could not share the whole truth of their escape and flight from the king's men with just anyone.

The hooded figure chuckled a bit under the cloak. "Very well. But mind you, I am quite skilled with this," said the stranger, holding up the hunting knife.

Kazareen was puzzled by this statement, but only for a moment. The hunter, still holding the knife in one hand, drew down the hood of the cloak and they saw their host's face for the first time.

Kazareen's mouth fell open. The hunter was a woman, neither very young, nor very old. Her face was shapely and tanned, and her short blond hair hung gently around it like a golden wreath encircling a face as fierce as the sun, yet with a stillness as gentle as the moon.

"I am Leyrea. Leyrea of Khürasé—until about three years ago, that is. Now I am Leyrea, huntress of the Northlands."

Kazareen was still taken aback, but it seemed to him that Florin was not. Perhaps Florin had caught a glimpse of her face by the fire.

"Leyrea of the Northlands, we thank you again for your hospitality. But please, lay down your knife, you have nothing to fear from us," said Florin.

"When the need arises to protect oneself, a woman on her own is put harder to the test than a man," she said, laying the knife on the table, but still at the ready. "You are not the first guests I have had in my home of late. Yesterday, a small band of Pendorian soldiers passed this way." She glanced furtively at Kazareen. "It seems they were seeking an old man and a boy they called Kazareen, who had escaped their prisons."

"I am not a boy, I am in my fifteenth year."

Leyrea stared him down for a moment, then turned back to Florin. "It also seems these fugitives killed four of their soldiers, including an officer, and another band of soldiers has gone missing. So you see, they were in rather a foul mood. They helped themselves to—" she paused for a moment, "whatever they desired. I could do nothing to stop them. Now I have lost most of the stores. I shall have to start anew, and I will be hard pressed to make it through another winter. So now that I have spoken, are you willing to tell me the truth?"

They were in a hard place. Florin had already told her their names, so there was no denying that they were the fugitives the soldiers sought. His only choice was to tell the truth. But what if the soldiers were simply using her as bait to trap them? The enemy could be closing in around the dugout as they spoke.

Florin rose slowly. As he did, Leyrea picked up the knife again and rose to match him. Florin walked slowly to the window and peered outside, but saw nothing but the dark and the rain.

The Heart of the Graystone

Leyrea understood Florin's suspicions immediately. "There is no one else here but us. Do you think me a spy? After what they did! I'll put an arrow in the gob of the next soldier I see—count on it! Don't think I couldn't."

Florin saw now that she had been wronged by the king's men as much as he and Kazareen had. "I believe you can and would," he said as he walked to the fire and sat down again. "Come, I am still chilled from the rain, let's sit by the fire and talk a little treason." These words, more than any others they shared that night, allayed Leyrea's fears.

As they warmed themselves by the fire, Florin spoke of their wrongful imprisonment and their flight from the king's men at the river. Kazareen spoke of Murro's sacrifice on the road to Pente Kaleán. He even spoke of their goal: to reach the house of Arpento in Bethë Khür. But neither spoke of the Graystone.

After listening to their story, Leyrea began to feel a kind of kinship with the fugitives. And so before long, she too began to speak of her plight and why she had fled the rule of King Geraldi.

"Five years ago, my father and brother were slain by a party of soldiers at the direction of one of the king's generals, who called himself Gueren. Our family farmed a plot of the richest lands in Pendoria, just east of Khürasé, along the banks of Laché Khür. But we came upon hard times when great rains in the East caused the river to flood its banks. That year, all our crops were lost in the deluge. So in an effort to make ends meet, my father and brother set out for the great desert to the south, seeking riches in the form of Graystones in the desolation of what was once the kingdom of Farak long ago. It was rumored that, in places, Graystones lay upon the ground like leaves in a forest. I never believed it, and I am not sure my father did either, but our situation was dire, so they set off in search of the precious stones, despite the hardships that awaited them in that accursed place," she said.

"They were gone for more than a month, so Mother and I had to make due in their absence. By the time they returned, the waters had receded and the soldiers stopped them at the crossing. Word had apparently spread to the constabulary of their trek into the forbidden lands. I never knew if they found what they had sought, but they may have, because they fled from the soldiers. Gueren cut them down. There were many who saw what happened, but thankfully, my mother and I were spared the sight of their deaths."

"We could no longer work the land by ourselves, nor afford to hire hands. Mother was so grief-stricken that she passed into a malaise that ultimately consumed her. She died that winter. And so I left Pendoria, vowing never to live under Geraldi's rule again." Leyrea's gaze never left the fire as she spoke.

They sat quietly, absorbing the warmth for a while, and it grew late. The rain was still falling, but they were warm and dry now. Soon the weary travelers, glad for their luck, lay down and drifted off to sleep.

Leyrea however, sat up by herself for a long while as her guests slept, remembering her lost family. She allowed herself no tears that night, but as she lost herself in the dwindling tongues of fire, thoughts she had long tried to suppress filled her mind and darkened her heart. Twice now, the king's men had wronged her, and so she set her will and made a new vow: never to allow them a chance at harming her a third time.

In the House of Leyrea

Kazareen awoke well after sunrise, refreshed, but still sore. Florin lay in a fitful sleep beside him. There was no sign of Leyrea in the dugout. An early riser, no doubt. To Kazareen's eyes, Florin looked pale and weak from their long and soggy trek through the rain. The fire had nearly gone out; only hot coals smoldered in the hearth. He stood and felt their clothes, which were still damp. Turning to the window, he saw that the rains had subsided, but still no sunshine graced the prairie. Gently, he put the back of his hand on Florin's forehead, as Murro had done for him so many times in the past, and felt there the burning fever of Florin's blood.

Leyrea entered the dugout bearing a small faggot of dry wood. She dropped it next to the hearth. "Your friend is fevered. Help me put him in the cot. Had I known, I would have lent him my humble bed, but my thoughts were elsewhere last night."

Kazareen rose and they lifted Florin into the small cot. He stirred, but did not awaken. Leyrea covered him with more skins.

"We cannot linger here. If the soldiers already know of this place, they may return," Kazareen said.

"Your friend is in no condition to travel. He needs rest until the fever passes," she said. Kazareen looked into Leyrea's eyes, which glowed blue, like sapphires in the light of a midday sun. "You should be prepared for...the worst. He looks old and weak to me. How long was he in prison?"

"A long time. Almost fifteen years I believe, maybe longer," said Kazareen.

"Well, it's taken its toll. His strength is sapped. And he will have to fight hard to survive," she said. Leyrea saw the concern and worry in Kazareen's eyes. "If you feel you must be off, don't worry. I will care for him as best I may."

"I can't leave without him. I don't know the way to...our destination. I must stay here until he is well again. And hope the soldiers don't return," said Kazareen. "Where did you get the wood?"

"There is a small grove, an acre or two, to the northwest, not far from here—about five miles. It supplies me with enough to survive the winters here, and I have a good store in the back of the lean-to. The soldiers didn't take any wood. However, they raided all my dried meats and tanned hides. They left the unfinished skins though; too bulky, I guess," she said. "Once a year, in the fall, I trade the leathers in Dienaté for those things I need to get me through the winter; that which the prairie does not provide for: honey, salt, dried fruits, a few spices. It irks me to step foot in Pendoria even one day a year, but I do what I must. I am careful not to be seen crossing the river, traveling far out of my way to avoid the ford at Dienaté. But the soldiers know I am here now. I don't think I shall stay here much longer either."

Kazareen felt very guilty. It was their escape that had roused the king's wrath and sent the soldiers to her home. Now she would have to abandon it.

"I'm sorry, this is all our fault," he said.

Leyrea understood where his regret came from, but despite her loss, she would have none of it. "Don't apologize for seeking freedom from tyranny. I did the same in my own time. And don't blame yourself for the evil that others partake in. That choice is theirs alone to make. You could not foresee what would happen to me. The fault lies with the king, and so with him I lay the blame."

Leyrea's words comforted Kazareen somewhat, but deep inside he felt he still owed her something. He turned his attention back to Florin, who lay in a restless sleep beside them. "What can we do for him?"

"Not much, I'm afraid." She handed Kazareen a small bolt of cloth. "Moisten this from the barrel outside. It is nearly full of rainwater now, and put it to his forehead. Keep him covered and warm. It will help a bit. I must leave for a while."

"Leave? Where?" He did not relish the thought of being left alone to defend himself, and Florin, should the soldiers return.

"We shall need more food. That small quarter hanging in the back will not last long, but eat it as you will. I fear your friend will not be eating for a while. I must go now in search of more game. Don't worry, I shan't be long—a day or two. Try to keep the fire going. If it should die in the night, use this." She handed Kazareen a sound piece of flint. "You know how to start a fire, yes?"

"Of course," he said. "Though we have flint of our own, in my pocket I believe." He went to the mantle and began to search his damp trousers. "But—"

"No buts. I have a favor to ask. My mount is small. I need to borrow the tall gray horse to bear back the burden of my harvest. The older beast I will leave here. If you should change your mind about moving on, or suddenly find you have great need to depart, then you will still have the means," Leyrea said.

Kazareen saw that in this he might repay some small measure of the debt he felt toward Leyrea, so he agreed. "Treat him well. I owe him

The Heart of the Graystone

much. He is named Wingfoot, but now I have taken to calling him simply Wings," he said.

"Thank you. Now I must be off. Fare well until I return," said Leyrea.

And she was gone. Apparently, she'd been readying the horses while Kazareen still slept.

For the next two days, Florin laid sweating and shaking in the cot. He spoke often, but Kazareen could make no sense of his fragmented thoughts and deranged mumblings. He did his best to comfort poor Florin, but felt impotent to help him in his fight to survive. By sundown on the second day, Kazareen began to doubt if he had done the right thing. Should he have so quickly placed his trust in one he knew so little? Had she simply played Kazareen for a fool, taken Wings as repayment for her troubles and moved on to greener pastures? If so, it was too late to do anything about it. Whatever the case, he knew he had had to stay with Florin, who held the only hope of finding Arpento in his tortured mind.

But by late that night, his hopes had begun to fade. Florin had lingered in a dream world for two days, and now seemed to be losing his battle with the fever. He had grown very quiet, and he lay motionless as the firelight danced among the droplets of sweat that covered his pallid face. Only the occasional flickering of his eyelids showed Kazareen that his new friend still clung to life.

He held Florin's hand and spoke soft words of encouragement to him, pleading with him not to give in to the fever, to keep fighting for his life. They had become friends, but deep in his heart, that portion that remains selfish even in the darkest of moments, he wanted Florin to live simply so he wouldn't be left alone to complete his task. If Florin died, all would be lost. Kazareen too, would most likely die here, abandoned and starving, or if he continued on to Bethë Khür, to die in the wilds or to be captured again. But his whispers of encouragement went unheard.

For hours into the night, he sat on the floor next to the cot. Then, as the first glow of dawn began to break through the window, it gave him and idea. Kazareen drew the Graystone from his pocket and as always, it began to burn with its silvery light. He placed it in Florin's hands and held it there for him.

"Look, Florin. A new day comes. Don't leave me here alone. Remember the Graystone? Arpento's home? Florin, I need you here with me," he said. But Florin did not stir; he was far away, wandering the black depths of his fragmented dreams.

As the soft shades of dawn grew into daylight, Kazareen continued his vigil at Florin's side, still clutching the old man's hands that held the Graystone, but he was locked in despair and hopelessness. He laid his head gently on Florin's breast. There was still life in him, but for how long?

Suddenly, from the silence that wrapped him in troubled solitude came a low rumbling, as if the earth itself were groaning. For a moment, he imagined he heard the passing of Florin's spirit from the world. But he realized the sound was a familiar one. What could it be? Then he recognized it: the sound of galloping horses!

"Leyrea," he said, as hope burst to life in him once again. "She's returned!"

He ran to the window, but what he saw made the pit of his stomach drop. Riding over the same ridge that he and Florin had traversed only three days earlier, he saw there a group of six riders, one bearing the royal standard of Pendoria.

His hope turned to panic in an instant. All he could think to do was hide. He pulled the skins over Florin's face and ran back into the deepest shadows of the dugout. There he took the remaining skins and covered himself. His heart was racing. This was it. There was no escape.

Kazareen tried to remain motionless as he listened to the riders approaching, but he was shaking with fear. The seconds passed slowly, painfully, as he awaited their inevitable discovery. Finally, he heard the horses pounding to a stop before the dugout and the voices of the soldiers as they called out.

"I hope your ready for another visit, wench!" said a gruff voice from the window. "Get up! There's no time for sleeping now, we've come to enjoy some more of your hospitality!" said the voice.

Kazareen heard the coarse laughter and taunts of the other soldiers in response. *They think Florin is Leyrea.*

"A little tired are we? Well lassie, I'm sorry to say you'll be wore out by the time we leave." More laughter rang out, but the voice was becoming impatient. "Not going to give us a fight this time? More the better."

The thought of these brutes and what they might do was more than Kazareen could take. To his surprise, all his fear retreated and turned suddenly to rage. He would not give in without a fight.

He stood up from his hiding place and grabbed his axe, which had stood in the corner next to Florin's sword for the last three days. When the door opened, Kazareen didn't hesitate. He hurled the axe with all the might and fury he could muster at the figure passing through the

The Heart of the Graystone

doorway. It buried in the soldier's chest and he stumbled backward and fell to the ground—dead.

The others were stunned for a moment at the sight of their slain lieutenant, but they quickly ordered themselves for battle. Kazareen heard them shouting for him to surrender as he picked up Florin's sword and braced himself for the end. He knew he was no match for five grown men: soldiers battle-tested and in a fell mood at the loss of one of their own. But Kazareen was now full of a wrath of his own and shouted: "Come in, and you shall receive more of my hospitality!"

Hearing Kazareen's voice, their courage suddenly blanched. The soldiers had been expecting a woman alone; instead they found themselves facing an unseen enemy, a man no less, and a deadly one at that. None now could muster the will to be the first to step through the doorway. The hushed sounds of whispers were traded outside, though Kazareen could not make out their words. They planned to set fire to the dugout and burn him alive inside, but all Kazareen knew was that he didn't have long before they were upon him. He stood defiantly with both hands on Florin's sword, unwilling to yield.

Kazareen had nearly readied himself to charge through the door when he heard a sharp twang, followed quickly by the shouts of one mortally wounded, then another. And another. His hope was reborn, for he knew that this time Leyrea had indeed returned. He rushed outside to find the last two soldiers in full retreat. Apparently, they had seen enough. As they tried to climb their mounts, Leyrea loosed another arrow into the back of one of the soldiers and he fell. But her quiver was now empty; too many of her arrows had been spent during the hunt.

The last soldier was atop his horse now, too terrified to consider anything but saving himself. Kazareen ran toward him and drew his sword back to slash at the soldier, but he was ready and swung his long blade down in a wild parry, catching Kazareen high on his left arm. He fell spinning to the ground. Still fearing Leyrea's arrows, the soldier urged his mount forward and rode off.

"Kazareen! Are you alright?" she shouted. He turned and saw her emerging from behind the lean-to.

His heart was still pounding from the heat of battle and for a moment he found he could not speak. The pain from his wound had not yet registered, though the sight of his own blood soaking through his shirt startled him.

"I'm fine," he said out of long habit, though he knew he wasn't.

She nodded in return, but she was still intent on the last soldier. Leyrea knew their tactics well enough. If news of their whereabouts reached the stronghold at Dienaté, more soldiers would come, and in overwhelming numbers. She ran to the body of one of the dead soldiers and wrenched the arrow from his back. Kazareen heard the sickening sound of his last breath being released. He turned away quickly, but could not erase the memory of that awful sound for the rest of his days.

Leyrea jumped onto one of the soldier's horses and rode after the last survivor at an amazing pace. As she rode away, Kazareen thought he heard someone speak his name. Drawing himself up, he turned to the soldiers lying on the ground and checked them one by one, but there was no breath left in any of them.

"Kazareen," the voice repeated. For a moment, Kazareen thought he was hearing the voice of Dien calling him again, as it had the day he found the Graystone in the forest. But it was not so.

"Kazareen" said the voice once more, and finally Kazareen knew from whence it came and his heart leapt.

"Florin!" He ran to Florin's side and pulled away the skins that covered his face. His eyes were open, though he seemed not to be looking at anything in particular. In his hand the Graystone still lay. "Florin. I am here. Florin?"

As if suddenly awakened from a dream, Florin's body jerked and his eyes drew focus. He turned to Kazareen with a terrible look of fear and puzzlement.

"It's alright," said Kazareen. "I am here. You're safe."

"Kazareen? Where are we?" he asked, looking around wildly.

"Leyrea's dugout. Do you remember? We were walking in the rain. She took us in."

Florin closed his eyes and exhaled slowly as his wits returned. When he opened his eyes again, he saw Kazareen's familiar face smiling down at him. "I saw it," Florin said.

"What?"

Florin spoke slowly. "I was lost. The darkness closed in all around me. Long I wandered." He closed his eyes, as if trying to recall events long forgotten. "Then I saw an awful light burning far away in the darkness. I could not look at it. But it drew close and I saw. I saw The Dragon, Kazareen. It was terrible. I felt as if it would burn me with its gaze or swallow me whole, but it turned away." Florin stopped and closed his eyes again.

"It was only a dream. You've been sick. Terribly sick, for days," Kazareen said, placing his hand on Florin's head. Indeed the fever had broken. "Now let me get you something. You need to build up your strength again."

Kazareen rose to put the last bit of meat to the fire. As he stood, he saw that blood had been flowing freely from his wound and had formed

The Heart of the Graystone

a puddle on the floor next to the cot. His shirt, which had once been nearly white, was stained red. The pain of his wound finally registered and he fell to the floor unconscious, so he didn't hear Florin finish telling his last memory of the dream.

"The Dragon. All it said...was your name," Florin said, and drifted off to sleep again.

"You should be more mindful, and tend to your wounds quickly, young man," said Leyrea as Kazareen opened his eyes. "You cannot help your friend, if you are yourself leaking all over my floor."

Kazareen saw her bittersweet face hovering over him. Not yet thinking, he tried to prop himself up, but felt the terrible pain in his arm and he cried out.

"Easy now. You've had a rough day," she said, carefully easing Kazareen back down to the floor.

Kazareen's first thoughts were of his friend. "How is Florin?"

"*You* are fine. Or will be, with a good deal of time and a bit more rest, for your injury is deep." she said, smiling gently now. "Your friend requires the same," she added, looking over to Florin.

Florin was still lying in the cot, sleeping soundly now. Kazareen breathed a bit easier.

"You've lost some blood, but you'll be alright, here drink." She passed him a deep ladle filled with rainwater. "You're lucky you passed out or you would have felt the sting of my needle and thread," said Leyrea.

When he finished the water he looked to his arm and saw it was wrapped with a thick bandage made from ragged pieces of cloth. And he was shirtless.

"But we'll have to find you a new shirt. It was the handiest thing at the time. Sorry," she said.

"How long was I out?" asked Kazareen, eyeing the ragged remains of his bloody shirt.

"Not long. Less than an hour, I think," she said.

"The other soldier?"

"No worries. I caught up with him quickly. I fixed him. Now the king has two patrols missing. Soon, he will begin to understand he has underestimated the ferocity of his prey. But I'm afraid it'll do little to deter him. If I know anything of this king, and I do, it will only stir his wrath. Soon enough, I'm afraid, he'll realize that he's hot on your trail. Do you think he knows where you two are headed?" she asked.

"I hope not. I don't even know why I was arrested in the first place," said Kazareen.

Leyrea gave him a curious look. "Just rest for now."

Kazareen laid back and found that Leyrea had slipped a thick fur under his head while he was unconscious. He looked at the remains of his bloody shirt nearby and he began to consider his actions of that day.

He had killed a man. Willfully. This was not a mistake, like the breaking of a dish, nor was it a harmless bit of mischief, but a real crime. His arrest had been unjust, so he felt no regrets for escaping, but today he had done something he knew was grievous in its finality. That man was dead because of him. The thought of it made his stomach curl up and he felt he was going to be sick.

Murro had raised Kazareen in the same manner as his father before him, teaching him the value of hard work, respect for the property of others, and above all, to treat others as he wished to be treated. Now he felt as if Murro's eyes were watching him from beyond the circles of death, and he felt the stab of shame pierce him like the horns of an angry bull. The strange fortune he had met in the last week was starting to pull him apart. A normal life, one of simple work and perhaps even raising a family of his own one day, had seemed to him boring and distant before finding the Graystone, but now he desired little else.

He wished he could go back to that day and simply turn around and run back to town with Talisa. Maybe then his life would be the same as before. Uncle Murro would be alive, and he would be home doing chores, as always. And none the wiser. But Kazareen couldn't go back. He turned away from Leyrea. Too much had changed too fast.

"Kazareen? What is it?" she asked.

Kazareen was silent. He could not speak the words to describe his feelings. He wanted only to be left alone now—to curl up and sleep until the end of time.

Florin and Kazareen rested for the remainder of that day, and the next. Florin's color returned with his strength, though Kazareen's arm was still nearly useless. He remained sullen and quiet. Always his thoughts returned to the simple life he had left behind and the blood of the soldier he'd killed that would always stain his hands.

Leyrea busied herself first with stripping and burying the bodies of the soldiers and later with the butchering and salting of the meat from the three antelope she had harvested on her hunting trip. She didn't bother preparing the skins—there was too little time. Soon, they would all have to leave this place. Inevitably, more soldiers would come upon the dugout seeking their lost comrades; it was too near the old north road.

Soon Florin was up and around again, and he came to Kazareen when Leyrea had stepped outside. He held out the Graystone. "I found this in my hands the other day when I awoke, I thought you'd like it

The Heart of the Graystone

back. I believe Leyrea still knows nothing of it and I think it best kept that way," Florin said.

But Kazareen did not reach for the stone. Here was the heart of all his troubles.

"Take it," said Florin, opening Kazareen's hand and placing it in his palm. But Kazareen let it drop to the floor. He wanted no part of it anymore; it had brought him only sorrow and regret. Florin had noticed that Kazareen had not been himself the last couple days and he believed it was his wound that bothered him; now he saw it was not so. Florin picked up the Graystone and quickly stuffed it in the young man's pocket.

"Kazareen, as much as you would like to, you cannot hide from yourself. Troubles find us all in the course of our lives. Open your eyes. You are not the only one here in distress. And you should remember your uncle's words as he lay upon the road. You have—"

"I have what? I'll tell you what I have. Nothing! I have nothing."

"You still have life, do you not?" Florin scolded. "You have love for your uncle still, do you not? If so, then you must carry on with hope if you can muster it. Or without hope, it makes no difference to me. But maybe it would make a difference to your uncle."

"You know nothing of Murro," said Kazareen.

"Of that, at least, you are correct. But you do. I cannot hold you to the promise you made to your uncle. It is your decision—and yours alone—whether to break faith with your kin and dishonor the memory of his sacrifice. I promised to see you through to Arpento and I'm prepared to live up to my vow, even at the cost of my life, for I will not return to Geraldi's dungeons to rot away. I won't do it! So you must ask yourself one question: What are you going to do?" said Florin, and then he turned away. "I'm going to see if Leyrea needs help," he added, walking to the door.

Florin's words cut Kazareen as deeply as had the soldier's sword. He thought they had become friends, but now he was not so sure. "Florin?"

Florin stopped at the door, but did not look back. "It's about time you grew up," he said and left Kazareen alone with his thoughts.

Kazareen put his hand in his pocket and drew out the Graystone. It no longer appeared the same to his eyes. Before, it had burned with a brilliant light, now it lay dim and lifeless. Once, it was beautiful, almost perfect, now it seemed dull and flawed. Was it the stone or his eyes that had gone dark? He couldn't tell. Here was the bane of his life. He stuffed it in his pocket and sighed.

He couldn't deny the wisdom of Florin's words. Despite his doubts and regrets, Kazareen had no choice but to carry on, unless he wanted to waste away in the king's dungeons, as Florin had for so many years. Or worse. Slaying the king's soldiers had only one punishment, and that was death. But he felt something far worse than death awaited him at the hands of the king. Who knew what plans Geraldi's twisted mind might be laying? The memory of Murro's warning about the king and his men would never leave him, nor would the memory of Murro lying in his arms; dead on the road to Pente Kaleán, and the vow he'd made to seek out Arpento.

About all he knew of being a man was that men kept their word, and like it or not, he knew he was bound to do just that. He set aside his guilt for the slaying of the soldier and turned his mind to that which was most important to him, all that remained to him: keeping his promise. And standing there alone, he took a new vow onto himself. He would never forget it was Geraldi's foul will that had led to Murro's death.

Florin and Leyrea were happy to see Kazareen emerging from the shadow of his doubts, for soon he came out to labor at their side. After an hour or two, his natural cheerfulness began to return and they saw in him a new strength that surprised them both. Perhaps his wound was not as bad as Leyrea had thought. When he worked up the nerve to speak seriously with Florin again, Kazareen apologized and told him of his decision to go on. And Florin forgave him with a glad heart.

"Good. For we leave on the morrow," Florin said.

Kazareen turned to Leyrea, curious as always, "You are coming with us?"

"For a while at least, our paths lie together. So we shall ride together. For how long, I cannot say. I do not seek a road leading back into the realm of Pendoria, but I will lead you to a safer crossing over Laché Dien. We shall go to a crossing farther east; the one I use on my trips to trade at Dienaté. Few know of it and even fewer use it," said Leyrea.

They continued working well past sunset, and it seemed to aid Florin's healing a great deal. They didn't have sufficient time to wait for the meat to dry much, so they cut it thin and pressed it with as much salt as it would take, in hopes it might be preserved in the summer heat. When the salt ran out, they still had more than a full side of antelope left over. Not wanting all the meat to go to waste, that night they treated themselves to a feast more befitting Blessingsday. Even so, they had to leave much of their bounty behind.

The Heart of the Graystone

Their mood was lightened as they ate, and they spoke only of the good memories of days long past. The trio found that they were even in spirits fair enough to sing a song or two. But the night closed in around them and their bellies were full and soon sleep overtook them for the final time in the house of Leyrea.

Voices in the Night

Dawn broke on the prairie, and they rose with a sense of purpose, as all were anxious to be away. The stars faded away leisurely into the indigo sky while Florin and Leyrea readied the horses. Not a single cloud interrupted the endless expanse that hovered above them. They loaded three of the soldier's horses with as much as they could bear, and set the rest free. They had enough supplies now for weeks and were a good deal better equipped than when Kazareen and Florin had arrived. They took with them many of the implements and tools of hunting that Leyrea had and some well-made clothes Leyrea had stripped from the slain soldiers for Florin and Kazareen—though none bearing the royal livery. They even had some proper riding boots and cloaks now. If they were caught in the rain again, they would fare far better than before. Leyrea had also collected the fine swords the soldiers had carried; good steel was expensive and hard to come by. They could be traded for a fair amount, so they would be of value to her when she set up her new home. Just where and when that might be, she couldn't say.

Kazareen's arm was still tender and weak, so he had to reassure Florin he could ride without too much pain. Getting on and off of Wings presented the only real problem for him. Leyrea helped him atop the tall stallion and they set off to the east, a slow caravan of six horses and three souls surrounded by an endless sea of grass. As they crested the ridge above the dugout, Leyrea paused for a moment to look back at the home she was leaving behind, but her will did not falter and she urged her pony, which she called Sirius, onto the uncertain road that lay before them.

As the prairie rolled slowly by, they found they still carried with them the fair spirits of the night before and so the journey seemed to them more like a pleasure ride in the country than a flight from imprisonment and death. Around midday they came upon a small brook, still cloudy from the rains, and stopped to water the horses. Kazareen wished they could build a small fire to cook some of the meat, but they could not risk sending up a white flag of smoke for any to see in the great emptiness of the prairie. They let the horses graze for a while as they gnawed on the half-cured meat.

The afternoon wore on much as the morning had, but with a little less talk. Florin and Kazareen were not as accustomed to riding as Leyrea, and they found themselves becoming saddle-sore once again. Florin still rode atop old Vala; he had refused to leave his new friend behind at the dugout in favor of one of the soldiers' bigger warhorses. So it was Wingfoot, the tallest of the three beasts, that led the way with his proud, elegant gait, even when traveling at such a leisurely pace across the prairie. Soon Kazareen found himself leading the others by a fair distance, so he halted to wait for the others. Leyrea was the farthest behind, for she led the string of bearing horses behind her.

As Florin approached, he seemed a little anxious. "Have you seen something?" he asked.

"No. Just waiting for you to catch up," Kazareen said.

Florin looked around anyway. He saw nothing out of the ordinary, and they could see for miles.

"Kazareen, may I ask you something?"

"Certainly," Kazareen responded. His bottom was sore, but he was still in fair spirits.

"I am not implying anything, but I must ask." Florin paused, trying not to sound too accusatory. "Was Murro really your uncle?"

"Why do you say that?" said Kazareen, suddenly aware that Florin already knew the answer.

"Because it seemed to me that you were, perhaps, a bit too quick to give up your vow," Florin said, finally looking up into Kazareen's big brown eyes. "Blood vows are not easily abandoned by most folks, especially the young, whose passions burn hotter than most."

"I thought I'd hidden it well," Kazareen said, smiling in wonder at the perceptive nature of his aged friend. "But you're right. He wasn't really my uncle. But I always thought of him as my kin. And I fully intend to live up to my promise."

"Then why...?"

Kazareen understood Florin's meaning, even if Florin couldn't find the words to finish his question. "The soldier. The one I...killed. I've never taken a life before. The worst thing I ever did before that was to steal a pear in the marketplace. I don't know. It's just that...I felt like Murro was looking down on me...and I was...ashamed."

Florin paused for a moment in thought. "Then why did you do it?"

"To save you. They were going to—"

"Would you do it again?"

"Of course."

"Then you have nothing to be ashamed of. If your decision to act is the same in the peace of the day as in the heat of battle, then your choice was probably a wise one. And I thank you for it. You put yourself in mortal danger on my behalf. If you had not acted I would be dead, or with you again in the king's dungeon. So think on it no more. I now owe

The Heart of the Graystone

you now my life as well as my freedom," said Florin, as Leyrea finally rode up.

"What is it?" she asked, scanning the horizon.

Kazareen nodded slightly to acknowledge Florin's thanks. Florin's stare turned into a slight smile, for he saw he had reached deep into the young man's heart.

"Have you ridden enough for today?" Leyrea asked.

"I'm fine. What about you Florin? Can you go on?" asked Kazareen.

"I can," Florin replied. He gave Kazareen a wink as they turned their mounts and continued on under the cloudless summer sky.

The rest of the day passed quickly and they saw no sign of enemy patrols. Their only company on the prairie had been a small gathering of antelope. They stopped grazing just long enough to consider them cautiously as they rode by at a distance. Later, they made camp in a shallow dell as the sun crept below the horizon. And the night passed as uneventfully as the day.

The next morning, they struck their camp well before sunrise in hopes of covering more ground.

"We should turn to the southeast today," said Leyrea. A look appeared on Florin's face as if he were about to protest. "Don't fret, the river takes a bend south as well, so we shan't draw much closer to it."

By the late afternoon, they had already traveled as far as the day before. Florin showed no sign now of the weakness that had nearly ended his life, and Kazareen's arm felt a little less painful and a little bit stronger with each passing hour.

They crested a high ridge and were greeted with a grand vista: the vast emptiness of the plain fading away beyond the edge of vision in every direction. Coming there had been no accident; it was this high place that Leyrea had sought out.

Kazareen squinted. Far to the south and a fair distance below them, he could just make out the meandering path of Laché Dien, like a tiny blue-gray thread cast carelessly upon an endless bolt of brown cloth.

"About ten miles lie between us and the river, but we still have to ride east another full day before we come to the crossing. It should be safe enough for us to draw farther south now, as the town of Dienaté lies more than forty miles to the west," said Leyrea.

Kazareen looked west along the river to see if he could make out Dienaté, but it was too far, even for his young eyes. The only town he'd ever known was Feria, so he was a little disappointed not to a catch a glimpse of Dienaté, even if it was teeming with soldiers with orders to kill or capture him. He was no longer sure whether the king wanted him alive or dead, but it didn't matter to him any more. One thought stood foremost in his mind: find Arpento.

Then, like a thief that returns to steal from the same home twice, dark thoughts crept back into Kazareen's mind. *What if Arpento can't help me? Or won't help me? What if the task he requires is one I cannot accomplish? What if he's dead? Florin said he had seen his home, but that was many years ago, and he was already an old man.*

The thoughts left him with a chill, but he refused to dwell on them. He would not step aside from chosen path; one he had vowed to tread no matter what dangers might come. No longer would Kazareen abide his own doubts or grant them sanctuary in the only home he had left: his own heart.

The party rode down from the summit, continuing to the southeast. They were still more than a week's ride from the western slopes of the mountains of Atan Beruth, but the hills were already beginning to grow wider and taller as they traveled eastward. Ever so gradually, they were showing signs of growing into foothills. Kazareen had never seen true mountains before, only the small hills that surrounded Feria, and he longed to see them for himself. Perhaps one day, when all his troubles were put behind him, he would make his way to Murro's birthplace: Beruthia, and gaze up at the majesty of Atan Beruth in remembrance of the one who raised him.

They rode on until dusk painted the sky with a rainbow of delicately blended pastel hues. The magnitude of such a brilliant kaleidoscope of color filled Kazareen with great awe, and made him feel small, and his troubles unimportant; both were dwarfed in the presence of such a sight. As the sky eased into deeper and deeper shades of blue, they found themselves riding down into a small, protected valley, traversed by another trickling brook. A sparse grove of stunted trees lined the edge of the stream, like a tiny oasis in that desert of grass.

Having found an ideal spot, they rode down to the edge of the creek to make camp for the night. Florin, always mindful of prying eyes, had decided to take a better look around and steered Vala to the top of the next ridge to see what he might in the last remaining embers of sunlight. While Florin was away, Leyrea had built a small fire from the dead twigs and branches she and Kazareen had collected. Florin came riding back about a quarter of an hour later.

"There is a large camp near the river with many fires already alight," Florin said, still atop Vala. It didn't appear he was going to dismount. "Put out the fire," he said, looking at Kazareen.

"Soldiers?" Kazareen said.

The Heart of the Graystone

"Which side of the river?" asked Leyrea.

"I can't say. It's too dark to tell. It could be a trade caravan or a hunting party, but I doubt it is either, given the size. I counted twelve fires," said Florin.

Florin's furrowed brow underscored the grave concern burning in his eyes and Kazareen became alarmed. Immediately he ran to the brook to draw water to extinguish the fire.

"Twelve? That sounds more like a small army than a hunting party. But this place can be no closer than eight miles from the river. The light from our small fire is well hidden in this dell. We should be fine here for the night, don't you think?" asked Leyrea, as she extended her arm out to stop Kazareen from putting out the fire.

"Perhaps. But they may have sorties out on patrol. We cannot afford to draw them close by foolishly keeping a lit fire. It would draw them to us like moths," said Florin.

Leyrea considered Florin's words for a moment before lowering her arm. Kazareen dumped the water on the fire and it squealed, hissed and then finally died. Another night on the prairie without a fire made for cheerless company in the cool night air, but Kazareen thought soldiers would make even worse company, so he drew his cloak in around him to ward off the coming chill.

Once the fire was out, Florin climbed down from his horse. Kazareen was glad that at least they didn't have to keep riding through the night—his wound was throbbing and his legs, back and bottom were aching for a respite from the saddle. Despite his pains, he was too anxious to sleep, so he volunteered to take the first watch. They ate some of the salted meats quietly, all of them put off by the presence of nearby soldiers.

Florin and Leyrea lay down to sleep soon after, as Kazareen kept watch. As always, his attention was soon drawn to the stars. They shone above him like fiery diamonds, suspended by invisible strings. But their brilliance dimmed at the rise of the half moon. The wonders of the sky, the beautiful sunset, the stars, and the glory of the moon, reminded Kazareen of the boundless miracle of nature, and again he felt small. And his problems seemed to shrink again. His troubles were real, this he knew. They would not drift away like a puff of smoke in the wind of a fanciful daydream; the kind he'd become all too enamored with during his afternoon jaunts to Bethë Dien; no, his problems were all too real. But he wondered if they really mattered to the stars. If he lived or died, would it change the course of the sun or moon? These thoughts were at the same time both consoling and disturbing, and he pondered them long into the night. When at last he heard the mournful call of exhaustion dragging him down, he woke Leyrea to take over the watch. The sweet embrace of sleep found him quickly.

Kazareen opened his eyes and saw Florin hovering closely above him, his finger to his lips. "Shh! Quietly now. We must be off, and quickly," Florin whispered, rousing Kazareen from a dream he could not remember.

Kazareen saw it was not yet dawn, though the sky was slightly lighter in the east. Leyrea was already leading the string of horses away.

"What is it?" asked Kazareen.

"Strange voices. Carrying down though the dell. Quickly! Come!" said Florin, barely audible. He handed Kazareen Wingfoot's reigns as soon as he stood.

They crossed the brook heading east and hustled off through the brush as quietly as they might, but Kazareen heard no voices. They emerged from the low trees and bushes that surrounded the stream and mounted their horses.

"Be ready to fly. It may be a trap!" he whispered. Florin went to help Kazareen up, but he was already atop Wings. He was glad to see the strength returning to his injured arm.

They rode slowly out of the hollow, making as little noise as possible. When they cleared the ridge, Kazareen paused for a moment. Looking back, he saw no movement anywhere. "Are you sure you heard voices?" he asked Florin.

"Of course I'm sure. I am old, but not yet doddering," he said.

"I see nothing."

"Good," said Florin as he too scanned the small valley for any sign. "Then perhaps we'll escape without notice. Now come!"

Kazareen kept looking back down into the dell. Still seeing nothing, he turned to follow his companions. If he had waited just a few more seconds, he would have seen the two small figures emerging from the cover of the low banks of the stream, and following after them.

They rode on quietly until sunrise, looking back often. But seeing nothing, they soon felt confident they'd had no more than a close call. Kazareen thought that perhaps the voices Florin heard belonged not to soldiers, but other travelers seeking shelter in the dell as they had. Either way, he was glad to be away undetected.

"The voices you heard. Could you make out what they said?" he asked Florin.

"Very little. They spoke haltingly, as if giving orders. But when I heard one of them say my name, I realized only the soldiers seeking us

The Heart of the Graystone

would say such a thing. We were lucky to escape. We should add one to the blessings we count," Florin said.

Kazareen nodded in agreement.

Florin gritted his teeth. "I made out one other word," he was loathing what he felt he had to say next. "I heard one of them say...Graystone."

Kazareen's jaw went slack. "What? That's impossible! They couldn't possibly know of it!"

Florin watched as Leyrea kept riding on ahead of them. "I'm afraid there is a way, Kazareen," he said, stabbing a quick glance toward Leyrea.

Kazareen caught on immediately. "No, I don't believe it."

The thought of Leyrea betraying them to the soldiers seemed impossible. His thoughts turned to her story of grief, the loss of her family, and the courage with which she had slain the soldiers that waylaid them at the dugout.

"Hear me out. She was gone many days on her hunt was she not? You told me of the lone soldier that rode away from the dugout. Did you actually see him slain?"

"No, I guess not. But she knows nothing of the Graystone either," Kazareen said, still not wanting to believe Florin's theory.

"Perhaps not. But on the rainy night, did we not remove our clothing? You didn't remove it from your pocket, did you?" asked Florin.

Kazareen shook his head.

"Then she could have come across it while we slept, but said nothing. Of her hate for the king's men, I have little doubt. But consider this: she is now without a home or means. She had ample opportunity to both find the Graystone and make secret dealings with the king's men for our capture. Also, there was her desire to keep the fire going last night. It could have been a signal to the soldiers. I am afraid she may have traded our freedom for her amnesty—and that treasure in your pocket. She means nothing to the king. It is you and I who are wanted," Florin said.

Kazareen saw the logic in Florin's arguments, but he still didn't want to believe. He was unsure whether to listen to his heart or his mind. "What should we do?"

"Bide our time. We narrowly escaped this morning, and I do not think they will attempt another ambush until night falls again. I will take the first watch this evening. Then, I think we should leave her behind while she sleeps. And if she wishes to light another fire tonight, I think we should let her. It's risky, but..."

They had lingered too long and their absence caught Leyrea's attention. "Are you two coming?" she shouted back.

Florin waved at her and they left their conversation hanging.

Kazareen thoughts turned to the battle at the dugout. Leyrea's bow singing. The fire in her eyes as she rode off after the last soldier. The skill with which she had attended to Kazareen's wound. It all seemed too much to reconcile. In the end, he decided to place his trust in Florin once more. He had not yet steered them wrong. Kazareen had no great love of Florin's plan, but he would follow it. And if they were wrong about Leyrea, and she was not plotting against them, they simply meant to leave her behind. When she woke, she would find herself alone and confused by their absence, but they will have done her no wrong. She would simply be on her own again.

They rode on without stopping until past midday. Kazareen didn't like playing this game with Leyrea and the more he thought on it, the more it grated on his nerves, like a pebble lodged in his boot, one he didn't have time to remove.

Kazareen noticed they now rode over stretches of bare rock that dotted the landscape. In late afternoon Kazareen spied ahead of them an outcropping of sandy colored rock. It emerged from the prairie like the head of a leviathan breaking still water, rising some seventy feet or more above the plain. Its ancient seams of layered stone appeared to have been twisted into an intricate pattern of interlaced arcs by the hands of some powerful giant. Here, it seemed drastically out of place.

"I call this The Knot. From here, we turn due south," said Leyrea, as they halted at the foot of the giant rock formation. "We are less than ten miles from the crossing now. I wasn't expecting to arrive here until sundown, but our early start has put us a bit ahead of schedule. The crossing may be dangerous midday, so I think it would be better to camp here for the night and make the crossing at dawn."

"That seems wise," said Florin in his most agreeable voice. He had no intention of rousing suspicion, but his eyes could not hide his doubts about her.

They rode round to the southeastern side of the rocks to get out of the prevailing west winds. There they dismounted and made camp. The horses sniffed around curiously and were disappointed at the lack of a water source, so they set about to grazing. In time, they came upon small puddles of water left over from the rains that had collected in shallow depressions in the rocks.

The rest of the day passed slowly with little to do and only thoughts of distrust and betrayal to keep Kazareen's mind occupied. He tried not

The Heart of the Graystone

to let suspicion take over his thoughts completely, so he scrambled to the top of The Knot to watch the sunset.

Soon, Leyrea followed after him.

Florin watched as she trailed after Kazareen. He hoped Kazareen was wily enough to deflect any attempts she might make at discovering their plans for tonight.

Kazareen came to the top of The Knot and seated himself on its wide, sloping summit. The rock was cool and hard, so when he leaned back and let his feet dangle over the edge, he closed his eyes and tried to imagine himself reclining in the soft leafy beds of Bethë Dien with Talisa at his side. Remembering her smile, he suddenly found himself longing to see her again. He was struck for a moment by a fanciful notion: that merely seeing her freckled face and glowing red hair again would make his problems disappear, but he knew it was not so. Better for her that she should never lay eyes on him again. He could only bring trouble to her now.

Below him, he heard Leyrea struggling up the rocks. He felt his stomach tighten, so he took a deep breath. He sat up and scanned the horizon as Leyrea reached the top and sat down beside him.

"Whew! That was more difficult than I thought," said Leyrea, half out of breath. "How did you manage with your arm?"

Kazareen gave her an odd look as he realized that it hadn't bothered him at all. "Fine. Surprisingly." He put his hand to the wound to reassure himself.

"Here, let me see if you have pulled my stitching loose," said Leyrea. She helped Kazareen with his cloak and shirt and began unwinding the dressing from around his arm. She gasped as the bloodstained cloth fell off.

Kazareen's arm showed no gash, no scab, and no sign of a scar at all; not even a hint of a scratch in the smooth, taut skin of his arm. Tiny loops of thread fell into his lap, and not a single stitch was torn or broken.

Leyrea's eyes grew very large and she drew back from Kazareen. "How is this possible?"

"I don't know," he said truthfully, though he already had his suspicions. Kazareen thought of Florin sprawled across death's threshold just a few days earlier. Was it the placing of the Graystone in his dying hands that had brought Florin back? Surely, in his state, he should have passed away. And now, with his wound so quickly and flawlessly healed, could there be any other explanation? Still, he wasn't ready to say a single word of the Graystone to Leyrea.

93

Her expression hardened and her gaze began to cut into the façade of his silence. Kazareen could not bear the weight of it, so he looked away, then went about closing his garments.

"Why is it the king wants you two so badly? What magic surrounds an old man and a young boy that they should escape death with such ease and find healing so quickly? What is it you are not telling me?" she asked.

Kazareen could not look at her. He truly felt he and Florin owed Leyrea their lives. And his silence was nearly choking him.

When Leyrea saw that Kazareen would not answer, she looked away. She took a small stone and threw it over the edge. "Don't think I haven't noticed the secretive glances you've tried to hide and the private conversations that stop suddenly when I draw near. I know you are keeping something from me. But I would remind you of who it was that took you in and gave you food and shelter and care and..." but her voice trailed off. She turned to the setting sun and sat quietly for a while at his side.

"When I realized you and Florin were not soldiers or bandits, I was glad to have you in my home. I spent too many lonely days in that place. And I don't believe I would have made it through another winter there, especially after the raid on my stores. The emptiness of my soul would have consumed me as it did my mother, long before starvation; of this, I have no doubt. But your presence kindled within me memories of friendship and simple gestures of kindness I thought I'd lost forever. Even thoughts of family. I felt a zeal for life again...a kind of...healing, as sure as your own. Perhaps greater." Leyrea paused to consider her own words.

Kazareen swallowed hard. And he believed he was beginning to unravel at least a little bit of the mystery of the Graystone by himself.

"If there is something you feel you cannot trust me with...then I will endure your doubts, if I must," she said. "Nevertheless, I wish to thank you for waking me from that slumber of spirit, from which I believe I would not have awakened without you." She rose.

Kazareen was yearning to share the truth with Leyrea. He was sure Florin would be angry with him, but he could no longer ignore what his heart was telling him.

"Wait," he said. Leyrea turned to him. Kazareen reached in his pocket and slowly drew out the Graystone, the full glory of its brilliance reflecting the light of the setting sun. "Have you seen this before?" he asked.

"No. I knew naught of it. But it is just a Graystone. Though, a rather large one at that," she added, drawing closer now.

The Heart of the Graystone

"Not just a Graystone. There is something very special about it. What exactly, I cannot say, but I think I am beginning to understand. The healing of my arm was as much a surprise to me as it was to you. I hadn't given it much thought before, but it is probably the reason Florin still lives as well. I put it in his hands when I thought he was dying. Not because I thought it could heal him, simply to remind him of our destination and his promise to show me the way. It was selfish." He kicked at the air. "If there is power or magic surrounding us, it comes from this jewel, not from me."

"Kazareen, no!" shouted Florin from just below their feet.

Florin's presence startled him, but Kazareen's voice remained pure and calm. "It's alright, Florin. I trust her."

"But—"

"Florin, you said you owed me your life. Well, I owe her mine as well...as do you, I believe. Would you have me show her less faith than you have shown me?" he asked.

Florin could make no reply.

"Trust me, Florin it'll be alright. Trust in Leyrea, as I trust in you," said Kazareen.

Florin seemed to want to continue his protests, but said nothing.

As the sun descended, Kazareen told their full story to Leyrea, filling in the gaps of their tale. She listened intently; at times asking questions about how they'd managed this or that. But Leyrea seemed particularly interested in the words of Dien's prophecy. "It seems that at least some of the prophecy has already come to pass. I think the real question is: What is your heart's desire, Kazareen?"

Kazareen hadn't given it much thought, their days having been filled with so many dangers and sorrows. "I don't really know." He looked at Florin, but his face looked as though it had been carved of granite. No one spoke for many minutes until the sun finally touched the horizon.

"We should get down before night falls," Florin said, already starting down.

Leyrea stood and put a hand on Kazareen's shoulder. "Come," she said softly. Kazareen looked into her eyes. No hint of lie or betrayal could be seen behind them, and he felt relieved he had enough trust in her to tell her the full truth. He nodded and they started their descent.

At the bottom, the two dark figures that had followed them from the hidden dale were already waiting for them.

The Marnalets

Florin was first to reach the bottom. Kazareen and Leyrea a little farther behind. He was still apprehensive about Leyrea's motives and had not yet fully abandoned the thought of leaving her behind in the night. It was the voices from the night before that still held sway in his mind, and there were still too many unanswered questions about her. A stern man would have a very difficult time surviving the winters on this barren, wind-swept plain, but a woman alone, accomplishing the same feat seemed unlikely to Florin. Maybe she had been planted as a decoy in that old dugout from the very beginning. Maybe the reason she had so few stores was because she had simply been dropped there only a few days before. The craftiness of Geraldi's men, when it came to planting the seeds of betrayal, could not be underestimated.

Perhaps they sought more than just their capture; perhaps it was their destination that interested them. If they had somehow divined that they sought out Arpento, perhaps they were biding their time, keeping the pressure of feigned pursuit upon them, in order to find Arpento for themselves. If the king's men could reach Arpento first, could it somehow tip the scales in Geraldi's favor? Did they know more about the Graystone than he or Kazareen? It seemed possible, at least. But they could not have known of the Graystone until after their escape. Kazareen had it with him in their cell in Feria; he had not been searched. Too many unanswered questions fed the doubt in his mind.

"Kazareen!" said a thin voice, just as Leyrea and Kazareen reached the bottom of The Knot. Florin thought the voice was that of Leyrea's at first and he turned to them, but he quickly realized it had come from behind a small rocky knoll to his right. He turned and drew his sword. It was the same voice he'd heard before dawn.

"They are upon us!" Florin shouted, but still saw nothing moving among the rocks. When he heard Leyrea drawing an arrow in her bow behind him, he felt sure he was about to feel her dart in his back.

"No—the eagle!" said the voice from behind the rocks. At first, Florin thought it was the same voice, but it had a slightly different timbre. There were at least two of them. Florin charged straight for the knoll, bellowing with the fire of battle.

He leapt over the rocks, sword drawn high overhead, ready to strike down with steely death. But he did not strike. Kazareen and Leyrea came running up from behind, weapons drawn. As they crested the knoll, Florin was slowly lowering his sword.

Before them, huddled together in a small crevice, sat two small creatures, their wide eyes peering up at the old man with the sword. They were nearly identical in coloring, white fur underneath and a dark brown above, though one seemed slightly larger than the other. Their coats of coarse fur were thick, and they were larger than rats, yet smaller than foxes. Their bright eyes shone with the light of awareness. They had sought cover, but did not seem terribly afraid. Still, they clung to each other with tiny hands that reminded Florin more of a baby's hands than the claws of an animal.

Florin turned away quickly, looking for the soldiers he thought sure must be nearby, but saw no one else.

When Kazareen stepped down from the rocks, the voice repeated, "Kazareen!"

"Eagle!" said the other voice.

Florin turned back to the little animals. "They speak?"

Florin and Leyrea looked at each other in amazement. "No," she said.

Kazareen's inexhaustible curiosity had already gotten the better of him, and he kneeled down in front of the furry creatures and smiled at them. If all that his curiosity had shown him through the years were added together, they would not equal this!

Kazareen laid down his axe and extended his hand in friendship, wishing he had something to offer them.

As if driven by a shared will, both of the creatures turned their head slightly to the right, as if pondering Kazareen's gesture. Slowly, they emerged from the crevice as Leyrea lowered her bow. They scampered to the top of the rocky knoll and sat up on their hind legs, their fragile forelegs hanging indifferently in front of them. Their eyes darted this way and that, taking in all. They turned their attention to Leyrea.

"Leyrea! Florin! Kazareen!" said the larger one. Kazareen was astounded. Not only could they speak, but they also seemed to know each of them by name.

The smaller creature responded only by saying: "Eagle!"

Kazareen looked at the smaller creature. "What is 'eagle'?" he asked, but neither creature seemed to consider his words. He repeated his question, but still they made no answer. They simply stared back at him. Kazareen turned to Florin. "Can it be...? Are these the voices you heard last night?"

"I believe so, yes. But..." Florin was too astounded for a moment to continue his thought. "...animals do not speak."

"No! Marnalet!" said the larger one.

"Marnalet!" said the smaller.

The Heart of the Graystone

"What's this?" asked Leyrea, stepping forward. "Marnalets?"

"Yes," said the larger one.

"Yes," repeated the smaller.

"What's a Marnalet?" Kazareen asked, but he had turned to her when he spoke and so missed the comical sight of the Marnalets pointing at each other with their tiny hands.

She chuckled. "A Marnelet, my young friend, is apparently what we have before us. I believe they are the Namers."

"Namers?" Kazareen and Florin asked together.

"Have you never heard the legend of the Namers?"

Florin and Kazareen both shook their heads.

"Men," she scoffed. "You don't pay enough attention to the old tales. Anyway, it is said that when the world was young and men knew little of it, two very wise creatures came and taught them the names of all the animals. I have heard them described in many different ways: that they appeared as wolves, or ferocious bears, or great cats twice the size of a man, even that they took the shape of giant men. But this...what I see before me, is something new and altogether surprising."

"Sounds like a child's tale, if ever I heard one," said Florin, scoffing.

"Then unless you disbelieve your own eyes and ears, I would say this children's tale is proven true," Leyrea said.

"But what is 'eagle'?" asked Kazareen.

"I know not," Leyrea replied.

"If what you say is indeed true, that these are the Namers, then it would seem an eagle is an animal, and one that is apparently nearby," Florin said.

They all began looking around for a creature to fit the name, but saw little of note in the fading light.

"Perhaps it is an old word for something we have since given a different name. Like a cricket or an ant," Florin suggested, looking to his feet.

"Locust!" said the smaller one.

"Ant!" said the larger.

"They don't have much use for idle talk do they? All they seem to say is the names of creatures," Kazareen said.

"So the story goes," said Leyrea. "But if you were listening closely you will note that one of them said no. It's possible they have a bit more vocabulary than is spoken of in the stories."

She drew a little closer to the Marnalets. "Let me try something. Are you Marnalets?" she asked.

"Yes!" they replied together.

"See?"

"Then perhaps we can get some information of a little more value from them," said Florin.

Kazareen was simply delighted with the whole event.

"Did you speak our names this morning in the dale?" Florin asked.

"Yes!" the Marnalets replied.

For the first time, Kazareen saw their tiny lips forming their words with as much dexterity as any man's, more perhaps. Behind their lips gleamed four sharp canine teeth, two each on the top and bottom, and ordered rows of tiny incisors. After they spoke, their noses twitched in unison. Kazareen was transfixed.

"Did you follow us this day, to this place?" Florin continued.

"Yes!"

"Have you seen the soldiers who seek us?"

"Yes!"

"Where? When?" Florin asked, but his question went unanswered.

They all thought silently for a moment. "It seems we've reached the end of their vocabulary. Yes, no, and the names of living things seems to be all they can say. I wish we could ask them why they follow us," Leyrea said.

"Graystone!" the Marnalets said in unison.

Kazareen raised his eyebrows and turned to Florin, then Leyrea. What this meant exactly, Kazareen was not sure. Then it dawned on him—the Marnalets named living things. "The Graystone. Is it alive?" he asked.

For the first time, the Marnalet's enthusiasm seemed to wane. They looked at each other momentarily, then back at Kazareen, as if trying to understand his question. Their heads cocked to the side again, but this time to the left.

"Yes," stated the smaller one.

"No," stated the larger.

"No!" chirped the smaller one.

"Yes!" squeaked the larger. Their words came in a quick flurry.

"Well, there seems to be some disagreement between them," Florin said.

"Not disagreement. Call it...confusion," said Leyrea. "You must listen to them carefully, Florin. Their ability to confound those who question them is as legendary as their very existence. Perhaps that is why they were described as such fearsome creatures. Ambiguity can be a frightening thing to simple men. They both said yes and they both said no."

Florin did not like the implication that Leyrea was making, but he took the slight in stride, it was the least of his due after doubting Leyrea's motives.

Kazareen thought of another alternative. "Perhaps it is both. Alive...and yet not. At the same time."

"I don't follow you, how can it be both alive and dead at the same time?" asked Florin.

"Not dead. Just...not alive. Like a stone, or water. Neither alive, nor dead," said Kazareen. As soon as he said it, he realized it made little sense and explained even less.

Florin stroked his tangled beard in contemplation. "Well, it makes no sense to me," he said.

"Nor to me," added Leyrea.

Kazareen just shrugged his shoulders. Still, it had given him more to think about. How could the Graystone be a living creature? Apparently, it must be alive in order for the Marnalets to name it. But it was mineral, was it not? Here was another riddle he could not wrap his mind around.

It seemed that new mysteries surrounded him with each passing day. He was becoming accustomed now to having his narrow ideas about the ways of the world torn away and replaced with a vision altogether new and wondrous; the recent turn of events had opened a window through which he had never gazed. He realized that with each step he took, he was not learning more about the world; rather, he was discovering that he knew almost nothing of it. But he also began to realize that that suited him just fine.

There is more in the world than I will ever know, he thought. If nothing else, his curious nature had taught him this. Once again, he felt older.

Regret was now coursing through Florin's veins. Leyrea's presence behind him vexed him like the needles of a prickly pear, its spines plunging to his very core. His regret was not for the caution he'd exercised, or for the dedication to his oath to Kazareen, only for his lack of trust in Leyrea. There was no doubt in his mind now that she had been true all along. The Marnalet's words had shown him his mistake. He turned to her. Already she seemed to sense his sudden disquiet, but she did not acknowledge it.

"Listen. I...I was wrong to mistrust you. I realize I now owe my life to both you and Kazareen. Tis another debt I will not forget. Forgive me," Florin said, extending his hand in friendship.

Leyrea looked at Florin's hand for a second, but only turned and walked away.

Florin felt a twinge.

"That's alright," she said to the sky, "I never really trusted you either." Finally, she stopped and turned to him. She had a devilish grin on her face. "Until now."

Florin shook his head as he returned her wry smile. He knew he deserved worse, but her smile exposed her jest for what it was, and he was heartened to see she held no grudge.

"Come, let's get something to eat," Leyrea said.

Kazareen had listened to Florin's apology with interest and it warmed his heart to know that they were now of one purpose. He stood up from his haunches and considered the Marnalets. "What of them?"

"What of them? Unless I am gravely mistaken, they have followed us for more than thirty miles. And if the legends Leyrea told us are true, and they certainly seem to be, then they are as old as the hills. I think they can look after themselves," Florin said.

"Yes!" said the Marnalets.

Florin shook his head and chuckled at the precocious little creatures. He put his hand on Kazareen's shoulder and they walked back to camp, their hearts a bit lighter.

The Marnalets watched as they walked away. But they viewed the world like no other animal; they saw beyond. The light of the Graystone in Kazareen's pocket burned as bright as the evening star to their eyes, and they scampered after it.

The Marnalets seemed content to sit quietly by as the party partook of the salted meats. Kazareen tore off a small strip and offered it to them from his hand. After sniffing it cautiously, the larger one said simply: "Antelope!" but they would not eat.

Leyrea took the first watch as they bedded down for the night and soon noticed that the Marnalets would not sleep. She heard them rustling around in the grass from time to time, though they never seemed to venture far from where Kazareen lay sleeping. Occasionally, one or the other would name a creature that drew near in the night. They spoke softly, as if quite aware Kazareen and Florin were trying to sleep, but Leyrea could never anticipate their next utterance. Just when she began to drift away on the monotonous song of the crickets, they broke its endless repetition with their sharp, tiny voices and always it gave her a start.

"Bat!"
"Rat!"
"Worm!"
"Antelope!"
"Finch!"

The Heart of the Graystone

As the night stretched on, Leyrea began to notice a pattern to their manner of talk. The smaller Marnalet named only those creatures that flew; the larger one named only those creatures that walked or crawled. She was delighted to find she could now add this tiny bit of knowledge to the legends of the Namers.

But her mind soon turned to other matters. That she was now playing a part in something that seemed to interest the king greatly, and that they had frustrated his efforts, at least up to this point, gave her a measure of satisfaction, which she relished. But there was something about this boy and his stone that resonated in her, like the pure ringing of the silver bells in the tower at Khürasé; their perfect pitch stretching out over the fields, calling to her, clear and true. Whether that call came from the boy or the stone, she couldn't say; she knew only what she felt.

For the first time in many years, Leyrea began to reconsider what she had vowed never to do: return to the lands of Pendoria. Her chance meeting with Kazareen and Florin had allowed a ray of hope to pierce the cracks in her broken heart. That she might find a way to repay the king for what he had done to her and her family began to fan the smoldering embers of vengeance inside her.

Leyrea sat on watch far longer than normal, because she knew she would not be able to sleep. Too much had happened to her in too short a time. She went over her options time and time again. Did she really want to risk losing all for a chance at revenge? She knew the odds were against her. But what was she really risking? Other than a slow descent into death, in a cage she had erected herself? It was only the chance encounter with Kazareen and Florin that had freed her from the bonds of despair and isolation.

In time, her words with Kazareen on the summit of The Knot came back to her and she felt her resolve begin to grow. By the time the stars began to fade in the east, she had made up her mind. She decided that if they would have her, she would carry on with her new companions.

She woke the others. After breaking their fast, they set off to the south to make the crossing back into Pendoria, and into greater danger.

"Will you be following us again today?" Kazareen asked the Marnalets, as he stroked Wingfoot's great flanks.

"Yes!" they said together.

"We will be crossing the river today. Can you swim?" he asked.

"Yes!"

"I hope you're strong swimmers. I've crossed that river before and it is treacherous," he said.

They just looked up at him with their bulging eyes.

"The crossing we make for is much safer than the one you took before," said Leyrea, as she hopped atop Sirius. "Shallower, narrower, and with weaker currents. You probably won't even get your feet wet, Kazareen. The same cannot be said for our new tag-alongs, however," she said, looking down on the Marnalets.

Kazareen smiled. "No need for that," he said, and he reached down to pick up the smaller of the two Marnalets. "You can ride with me, that way—"

But the Marnalet suddenly hissed and spat as Kazareen laid his hand upon it. It gyrated its body wildly, as if caught in a hunter's trap. Kazareen pulled away quickly, just in time to avoid the wild gnashing of its small but extremely sharp teeth.

"I don't think that is a very good idea, Kazareen," said Florin, laughing.

Kazareen had instinctively taken several steps back, as both of the Marnalets drew themselves up into a defensive posture. They were still snarling, hissing and baring their teeth.

"I am sorry. I meant no harm," he said to the suddenly ferocious creatures. He hoped they understood the meaning of his words.

"It seems that here is more truth in the legends," said Leyrea. "Now you see for yourself their wild nature. You best mount your horse quickly, young man."

Kazareen didn't argue. He jumped on top of Wingfoot in an instant. "They are no pets, that much is certain," he said. His heart was still racing. Their friendly appearance had lulled him into complacency. He would not let it happen again.

"No. They are ancients to be treated with reverence and respect. Would you, without permission, lay your hands on a king?" said Leyrea.

Kazareen shot her a dangerous glance.

"Bad example, but you take my meaning."

Kazareen frowned and turned away.

"Time is wasting," said Florin, still chuckling at his reckless friend. They turned their horses to the south and started off. Despite their brief fit of rage, the Marnalets calmed themselves quickly and followed after.

Florin remained amused. "Appearances can be deceiving, Kazareen. If I showed so little care around wild animals, I would have been torn to pieces long ago. Raccoons and otters have quite a friendly way about them—from a distance. But if I had tried to lay hands on a live one—whew! My hands wouldn't look quite the same today," he said, waving all ten of his fingers at Kazareen.

The Heart of the Graystone

Kazareen listened patiently, but did not like being made sport of. He dug his heels in and Wings cantered off ahead. He rode alone for a while, angrier at himself than at Florin. He knew he had acted foolishly.

"I don't think he took to your teasing well." Leyrea said

"He'll be fine. Nothing hurt but his pride. It was a good way to learn a valuable lesson. Next time, he'll not be so hasty to rush into something he does not fully understand. Anyway, look at this..." Florin rolled back his sleeve and pointed at a deep, jagged scar on his right forearm. "Otter." he said, imitating the Marnalets. Then he began laughing at himself.

Leyrea shook her head.

"Let's get moving. The earlier we arrive at the crossing, the better our chances of crossing safely," she said.

They quickened their pace as they made their way south. Behind them, the Marnalets scurried through the grass in an effort to keep up.

Bethë Khür

They arrived at the ford, and as they made their cautious approach to the river's edge, they saw there was little or no cover on either side of the river, so they felt there was little chance of an ambush. Kazareen was surprised to see that the river had shrunk to less than a third of the size it had been at the point where he and Florin had crossed nearly a hundred miles to the west. The water was much clearer here too, so much so that he could see the river's stony bottom quite easily. Still, they dismounted and watched carefully in the growing light for a quarter of an hour, just to be sure no one was around. By the time they felt confident enough to make the crossing, the Marnalets had caught up to them.

"I think tis safe," said Florin. Thinking that Leyrea would now part company with them, he turned to her and offered his hand. "Thank you for your help. I do not know if we shall see one another again, in this life or the next, but we owe you much, even our lives. If chance or circumstance brings us together again, we shall remember our debt."

She swallowed as she took his hand. "It is not yet time to part ways," she said, "If you will allow it, I would accompany you both to the house of Arpento."

"What? I thought...your vow," Kazareen said.

"I have come to realize it was a vow made in despair and...in fear. Since the night you came to my door, I began to see the error in it. I regret it now and so I cast it aside. Also, I would ask that you think no more on the debt you feel toward me, for I feel the same debt toward you, for my spirit is renewed," she said, giving Kazareen a warm smile. "What do you say? Shall we call our debts settled and go forward together?"

Kazareen and Florin eyed one another, each waiting for the other to speak. "Tis your decision, Kazareen. Of her, I have no more doubt. And I am still bound to my promise to see you to the house of Arpento. What say you?"

"You realize, of course, that by throwing your lot in with us, you put yourself in greater peril. If we're captured, the king will consider you his enemy as well," Kazareen said.

"I am already his enemy. He just doesn't know it yet."

"Then you shall accompany us," he said. He threw out his arms and embraced her warmly. Her arms were stronger than he'd imagined.

They mounted and made the crossing without trouble. Leyrea had been right about the ease of the crossing, for Kazareen's feet remained quite dry. The Marnalets too, followed easily, for they were more agile in the water than they were on land. They held their heads high and moved quickly and gracefully through the water. "Trout!" the smaller one managed to squeak in the middle of his swim. When they reached the far bank they shook the water from their thick coats with great vigor.

Kazareen turned and looked back. If there had been anything like safety on the other side of the river, he had just left it.

"Where now?" Leyrea asked, looking to Florin.

"Due south," he replied, shading his eyes from the light of the rising sun. "If we meet with no delay, we should reach the northern edge of Bethë Khür by midday tomorrow. From there...less than a day to the house of Arpento."

They turned their horses and left the great prairie and the river behind them. Kazareen started to feel a great anticipation growing in him. Soon, he would have his meeting with Arpento, and from it, he was sure, would come the burden of a nearly impossible task.

For some time, the lands south of the river were identical to those to the north: mostly grasslands, broken here and there by stretches of bare rock. Though as they rode on, Kazareen noticed that the land began to grow greener, the rocky stretches soon vanished and small groves of trees began to reappear.

By midday, they found themselves riding among the well-ordered rows of vineyards and huge orchards of olive and almond trees. They saw no one working in the orchards that day, only row upon row of gnarled trees and twisted, woody vines stretching into the distance, most looking as shriveled as the dried grapes Kazareen used to buy in the market at Feria. Later, they spied a whitewashed farmhouse through the sparse trees, standing some distance to the east. They steered clear of it and passed unnoticed.

As they rode, Leyrea finally told Florin and Kazareen what she had noticed about the Marnalets: that the larger one named only walking or crawling things, and the smaller one named only flying things. "And swimming things too," said Kazareen, recalling the trout that must have swam by them in the river.

"Ah...yes. Very observant," Leyrea nodded.

Kazareen looked back and saw that the Marnalets were still scampering after them. After a while, an idea began to form in his mind, one he hoped would help to make amends for angering the Marnalets. Finally, he stopped and waited for them. They seemed not to remember anything of it, for they approached with a cheerful manner and looked

The Heart of the Graystone

up at Kazareen no differently than they had the day before. Wingfoot kept one cautious eye bent on them.

"Do you have names?" he asked.

"Yes! Marnalets!" they said.

"No, I mean names like people have. When you first saw us in the dell, you called Florin by name; you could have just as rightly said 'man.' You called Leyrea and I by our names as well. Do you have names like humans have names?"

"No!"

"Well," said Kazareen, starting Wings forward again to keep up with the others, "I thought—if you don't object, I mean—I might give you both names of your own, like people have. Is this agreeable?"

The Marnalets stopped and looked at each other intently with their bulging green eyes, as if suddenly engaged in silent conversation. They looked back up at Kazareen who had pulled the reins in on Wings once again.

What Kazareen couldn't know was how perplexed and amazed the Marnalets were at that moment. They had spent all their long years on the earth naming the creatures, and now one of these creatures wanted to name them! They felt no offense, as Kazareen thought they might; in fact, they felt strangely honored that someone would wish to return the favor. In all their days, men had only sought information from them, but now they had found one who had turned their own ways back upon them in way they had never considered. Still, they could make no answer.

Kazareen, of course, knew naught of these feelings. Thinking they hadn't understood his question, he tried to think of a simpler way of putting it to them. He pointed at the large one. "I thought I might call you Zoot. And you" he said, pointing to the smaller one, "I would call Avery, in honor of each of you and your particular manner of naming the animals. What do you think?"

The Marnalets sat as if frozen solid, and still made no reply.

"Oh well, it was just an idea," said Kazareen, watching Florin and Leyrea ride off ahead. He tapped Wingfoot on the flanks and he started forward again. The Marnalets did not move for quite a while, but as the light of the Graystone faded in their eyes, they were again compelled to follow.

The afternoon passed slowly. The further they rode, the more farmhouses they came upon; so they zigzagged their way around them in their push to the south. Florin was determined to avoid detection, though there was little to fear from the simple farmers and growers of this region. The inhabitants met few strangers here, but generally, they were a hospitable folk, or so Florin said.

"They have no great love for the king, I can tell you that much," he said.

"Why is that?" asked Kazareen.

"It's difficult to say for certain. I have heard many conflicting accounts and stories. Some were exaggerations; some outright lies, no doubt. But it all stems from the fall of the Great Houses."

"Great Houses?"

"Surely you know of The Great Houses!"

Kazareen shook his head. Florin seemed more than a little surprised that Murro had never taught Kazareen properly of at least this much of Pendoria's history.

"Yes, well...there were four Great Houses. For ages, they co-existed in something like civility: the power of the throne passing from one house to the next, with little strife. But about twenty years ago, when I was still free, they began to disintegrate. For what reason exactly, I could never determine; too many people with too many different allegiances, don't you know. So, as their disharmony grew, the power of The Great Houses decreased. King Geraldi is of the house of Phenoa, whose lands lie in the west and the south. This area, where we now ride, was long under the protection of the house of Coraz, from which King Smidon arose. So perhaps you can understand their animosity for the king."

Leyrea spoke up. "You have missed much in your years of imprisonment. The Great Houses have fallen, yes. But the Council of Patris, that is, the council of the elders of the four houses, survived until about ten years ago." She thought for a moment. "Perhaps a few years longer. Anyway, it was Geraldi who finally brought them to their end."

"Disbanded?" asked Kazareen.

"Murdered. There was no proof that it was Geraldi's doing of course, but the assassination of the Council of Patris could only have been orchestrated by the king," she said.

"But why?" Kazareen asked.

"It would seem he has no intention of ever giving up the throne. But fortunately for the rest of Pendoria, he won't live forever. Who does?"

Kazareen had never heard of any of this. Perhaps this was the reason Murro had never trusted the king either. Surely, Dien's warning about the king was the main reason for his wariness, but Murro's homeland was far in the west, in Beruthia. He must have lived under the protection of a different house. Kazareen had never given much thought to the political wranglings of the wide world around him, but now he

The Heart of the Graystone

could see that Murro's distrust of the king probably had deeper roots than he'd imagined.

And what of himself? Kazareen knew not from where he had sprung. Could this political infighting be at the heart of why the king sought him out? Maybe it had nothing at all to do with the Graystone. It was a riddle he couldn't answer.

As they rode through the afternoon, the sky slowly cast over with a gray pall of clouds, hovering low over the land like a shroud. A very light rain, barely more than a mist, drizzled down upon them. They welcomed it at first, for it was a relief from the oppressive summer heat of the last few days' ride. The light of the sun was dim among the mists and so they stopped for the night in a thick grove of trees that stood at the edge of a wide, green meadow. They had seen no farms or dwellings for the last hour, so it seemed like a safe place to camp. The trees provided a measure of shelter from the rain, but the ground was already uncomfortably damp. Combined with the chill that came in the night, it would make for a long and cheerless watch.

Kazareen sat on a log, wrapped in one of the soldier's cloaks, while the others tried to ignore their discomfort long enough to find sleep. The mist subsided after a while, but his bottom was already soaked from sitting on the half-rotten log. With only the Marnalets for company, his watch passed slowly, for they were quiet also. It seemed few other creatures were willing to brave the damp night.

They rose later than usual the next morning; a soupy fog still clung to the earth, and so it was difficult to tell when dawn approached. Kazareen had slept poorly after passing the watch to Florin; he was becoming more and more anxious as his date with Arpento drew near. What would be his task? Would he be up to it? Could this Arpento really help him?

As they broke their fast, Kazareen tried hard to put himself at ease. He must have his wits about him if he wished to make the most of his encounter with the wise man. Leyrea and Florin both seemed to sense the apprehension he was feeling, and they spoke little.

They broke camp and Florin led them off in their quiet march toward the forest he had called home so long ago.

For Kazareen, the morning passed slower than any he could recall. Try as he might, he couldn't dismiss the nagging questions swirling around his mind.

Finally, Florin stopped and pointed into the thick haze. "Bethë Khür!" he said, unable to disguise the delight in his voice. The dark trees of his long home now broke from the mists, as if silently brooding in the dead calm before them, a wall of darkness floating like a ghost ship in the midst of an ocean of gray vapors.

A shiver ran down Kazareen's back. This was not what he expected.

A telling look swept across Kazareen's face and Florin read it correctly. "Buck up, Kazareen. Tis not as bad as all that! There are dangers to be found here, yes, as there are in any wild place. But lest you forget completely, I grew up here and I know its ways well. I'll not let it get the better of ye. Come! You will find it friendlier than its looks," he said. His voice was high and proud, like a father boasting of his son.

He led on, and when they passed through the dense foliage of the forest's borders, Florin drew a deep breath, sighed and said, "I am home."

Their journey through the forest was dreadfully slow; even dismounted, they were hindered at every turn by thick, tangled brush. Florin drew his sword and began hacking a narrow way through.

"Watch out for these," he said, pointing at a large, bushy plant whose leaves looked like the serrated edge of a saw. "Nettles. If you touch them, you will itch terribly. If you do happen into one, whatever you do, don't scratch! And don't touch your eyes, you'll be blinded for hours."

Kazareen and Leyrea gave it a wide birth as they passed, but they soon found themselves surrounded by the itching plants on every side. The horses took the worst of it, for their bodies were too large to avoid them.

The deeper they ventured into the forest, the darker it became. The fog had begun to lift, but the clouds were still thick, and the cover of the forest made it almost impenetrable to what light seeped through. The air of the forest seemed stagnant and old. Soon, just breathing seemed to become a tiresome chore. Kazareen stopped to remove his cloak.

"Leave it on," said Florin, "or you will soon be covered in burrs and ticks...or worse."

Worse? Kazareen didn't want to know what worse meant, so he left his cloak on. As he pulled the hood over his head, he saw next to him, suspended between the branches of a tree, a drop of dew, seemingly in midair. Then he realized the droplet clung to the delicate strand of a very large and intricate web. His eyes followed it upward. Above him he saw it's maker, poised motionless in its center; a green and yellow spider bigger than his hand, its legs outstretched symmetrically, two by two. He

The Heart of the Graystone

pointed it out to Leyrea, who followed behind him and they passed by unscathed.

"Did you see that spider, Florin?" Kazareen asked.

"I did. But it cannot harm you...much. If you are bitten, it will hurt, no doubt. But no worse than a bee sting. Those tree spiders are large, but not very aggressive— unless you are a fly. Tis the small, black ones you need to avoid. They can take off a grown man's limb, or kill him outright," said Florin.

"You jest," said Kazareen.

"I'm afraid not. They are one of the few creatures that can kill a grown man in these woods."

"But if they are so small, how can they take off a limb?" said Kazareen, watching his surroundings even more carefully now.

"Tis not their size, it's their poison; rot your arm off in a day—if it doesn't kill you. But they are shy creatures. And they don't like the damp. Watch for them in dry places, crawling upon the ground, for they spin no webs," said Florin, still hacking through the underbrush.

Kazareen was suddenly glad for the rain and fog. "What other creatures can kill a grown man here?" He was almost afraid to ask.

"Bears," replied Florin, matter-of-factly.

"Bears!"

"Yes, though they are fewer now. Mostly, they range in the eastern and southern stretches of the forest, beyond the river Laché Khür, which runs right through the forest. But we shan't be venturing that far south. Arpento's home is less than ten miles from where we entered the forest."

"Are there any other creatures to watch out for?" Kazareen asked.

"Isn't that enough? Anyway, that is all you need worry about. You should have your mind on other matters right now, I should think. But if I see any bears or black spiders, I shall let you know."

Their passage was slow as Florin was forced to continue to hack out a path. Before long, he grew weary of swinging the heavy sword. Seeing this, Kazareen took his turn at the front, hacking and slashing, but always Florin stayed near him, pointing out the easiest way and which plants to avoid.

After clearing their way for half an hour, Kazareen too became winded. He stopped to catch his breath. "If we have to cut our way for ten miles, it will be days before we reach Arpento. Is the whole forest like this?"

"Much of it, yes, but not all. We shan't have to hack out the entire road. We make for an old path that runs north from The Great Road. There is a great labyrinth of foot trails through this forest. Many are old deer paths and they run this way and that. It's quite easy to get lost here.

113

You're lucky you have me as your guide, or you would never find Arpento. We should come upon the path soon. Then our way will be easier...and faster," said Florin.

Kazareen was glad to hear some good news; too much of what he'd seen of Bethë Khür was frightful, irritating or exhausting. He took a deep breath and went back to work hacking at the underbrush. He cut and slashed at the thick weeds and vines for only ten more minutes when Florin said, "Here we are."

Kazareen looked around, but he saw nothing different about his surroundings. "What?"

"Look, here," said Florin pointing to his right.

Kazareen saw a narrow clearing in the undergrowth, no wider than himself. It led off into the distance like a snake winding through tall grass. Kazareen had cut through it without even noticing.

"That's it?" said Kazareen.

"What were you expecting? The king's road? Give me the sword. And follow me."

The party turned right with Florin leading once again. Despite it's humble appearance, Kazareen soon found that the way was indeed easier. The path wiggled this way and that, around obstacles and vines, away from the low areas where the itching plants grew together in large patches. Florin swung the sword from time to time, to cut back the occasional impediment, but they were making much better time now, and leading them was much less tiring than before.

Now Florin looked around often, stopping to touch the trunk of a particular tree here and there, feeling for lichens and moss. They walked along the path for quite a while, but seeing no sun, Kazareen could not tell the time.

Then Florin stopped and looked around carefully, "Do you smell that?"

"What is it?" asked Leyrea, scrunching her nose.

Florin turned. "Peat. Burning peat. Follow me, for I follow my nose." Suddenly, Florin plunged into brush to his left, but cut no path. They hesitated. "Trust me," he shouted back.

They followed him into the wall of undergrowth. They had gone no more than ten steps when the scrub completely fell away, and they found themselves standing at the edge of a large clearing.

A small pond stood to their left, mirroring the image of the forest behind it and a bit of sky, which they saw was now beginning to clear. A small pier, made of cleverly pieced together branches, jut out from the shore, nearly reaching the middle of the pond.

The Heart of the Graystone

Directly in front of them, the clearing was filled with growing plants, not the untamed growth of the forest, but the well-ordered furrows of an immense vegetable garden. Their eyes followed to the right. Not a hundred yards away, stood a large cottage with a steep, thatched roof and whitewashed stone walls. The wooden door was painted bright red, almost as if to stand as a warning. A thin ribbon of white smoke rose from the chimney.

"The house of Arpento." Florin's thin chest seemed to expand just a fraction.

Kazareen feared that Florin might suddenly turn and leave, but he stood next to him, tall and proud. Kazareen felt more fear now than he had confronting the soldiers that attacked Leyrea's dugout.

"Go ahead," said Florin. "That is why we came all this long way."

"Aren't you coming with me?"

"Not I. I have no business with him," he said, shaking his head. He turned to Leyrea. "I would suggest you stay here too. Arpento is a peculiar sort, to say the least, and not one to be trifled with or bothered needlessly. Go, Kazareen. Your time has come. But be wary; he is a strange man, wily and clever. We shall await your return."

The Marnalets stood nearby, but said nothing.

Kazareen took a deep breath and walked toward the cottage. This was it. He tried to prepare himself for the challenge that lay ahead.

Keep your wits about you. Speak carefully, listen closely and think clearly.

Kazareen hesitated when he came to the doorstep. He looked back and saw the Marnalets had followed behind him; they seemed to have no fear. Taking another deep breath and closing his eyes, he knocked on the door.

"Come," said a calm voice from beyond the door. Had he been expected?

Kazareen opened the door and stepped inside. A portly man was seated at a large dining table with his back to the door. The table appeared to be readied for a great feast. There was roasted pheasant, fried fish, and fricasseed squirrel. Wooden bowls filled with boiled potatoes and carrots and beans. A glass bowl of cherries and a small pyramid of apples. A large raspberry tart and a pie of mulberry and rhubarb.

"Come in. Sit. Don't be shy," said the man, but he neither rose nor turned to face his visitor.

Kazareen slowly rounded the table until he could see the man's face. He did not appear as old as Kazareen had imagined. He had no beard, no graying hair, nor any line upon his face, except where his double chin folded over, for the man was quite fat. He wore tan trousers and a green waistcoat over a white ruffled shirt. The shirt looked like new, made of a material Kazareen could not identify. It held the light in its smooth, shiny fibers. His curly brown hair was cropped very short, in a rim round his bulbous skull and his flat nose covered the majority of his face. His thin eyebrows curled up at the ends, giving him a rather sinister air. And long black hairs poured from his nostrils and ears.

Kazareen pulled out the chair opposite the fat man and sat down. There was indeed a great deal of food on the table, but only one place had been set.

The man stopped eating long enough to glance up at Kazareen for the briefest of moments. "Who are you? What do you want?" His attention immediately fell back to the pheasant wing he was pulling apart.

Could this glutton be the same wise man Murro had urged him to find? "I seek the wise man Arpento. I have ridden far, through great dangers to find him. Are you the man who tales speak of, the trader of wisdom for deeds?"

"I am Arpento," said the man.

The Marnalets stood at the door, unwilling to enter, but watching attentively. "Arpento!" they said together.

Arpento turned around to see who else was at the door. He turned back to his meal, almost as quickly. He didn't seem much surprised by the presence of the Marnalets. "I ask again, who are you? What do you want?"

He felt a little more comfortable now that the Marnalets had confirmed Arpento's identity, but the aroma of the feast before him soon had his mouth watering and it became difficult to speak.

"I am Kazareen de Pendi...of Feria. I seek your advice...and counsel...on a strange matter. I have traveled far with a tight belt and two friends. Not the ones you saw at the door, but a man and a woman, who have helped me on my way. We are weary and hungry from long days of travel. May we share in your meal?"

Arpento stopped chewing. Slowly, he looked up at Kazareen, and a scrap of meat fell from his mouth. "Kazareen de Pendi!" He said this as if he knew the name. "Kazareen de Pendi, well, I'll..." His words trailed off for a moment. "I've seen many things by day and by night, but I've never seen ale brewed in the shell of a hen's egg!"

Kazareen puzzled at this odd expression, but the lilt in Arpento's voice did not last long.

"I see much, but I do not see all. Certainly, I did not see you coming." These words he seemed to speak more to himself. "As for you and your friends, I did not invite you here. So don't presume to think

The Heart of the Graystone

you are a welcome guest. Besides, I do not have the means to feed every ragged and weary traveler that passes through," he said, wiping his greasy fingers. "Now tell me, what is it that you want? And be quick about it."

No means? Kazareen looked at the feast covering the table. Murro and Florin had certainly been right about this Arpento. He was a queer sort. Best he just got down to business.

Arpento continued at his feast. Occasionally his eyes would leave his plate long enough to catch a glimpse of Kazareen's face while he spoke.

He told Arpento of the finding of the Graystone, of Dien's prophecies, of his arrest, Murro's sacrifice, their flight, and their strange meeting with the Marnalets. As Kazareen spoke, he became more annoyed with the inattention Arpento showed him. This man would not be a friend to him, that much was clear. Kazareen did not trust him; nor did he care for his ill-mannered way. He moved his chair closer, trying to hold Arpento's attention. Finally, he began moving the plates and bowls on the table from in between them. Perhaps, he could make his tale more interesting to him than his meal.

"I've heard rumors that you are the wisest man in all Pendoria. If you are what folks say you are, then I could put your advice to good use. Can you help me? Can you see what to me is hidden? I've heard tales about the price that must be paid for your help as well. I'll do what you ask of me."

Arpento continued to eat. "Yes, yes. I am always willing to help those who are willing to help me. I see much that is hidden. And I will tell you all you wish to know, all you need to know, that is, if you will help me with a little...how shall I put it? Uh...chore," Arpento said with a sudden gleam in his eye. "If you perform this task, I will look into...your situation. Is this satisfactory?"

"It is."

"Good. Then we have an accord," he said, picking up a thin fillet. Then it seemed that Arpento finally noticed that Kazareen had moved the bowls of food around to suit himself. "I would appreciate it if you did not help yourself at my table."

"Fine," Kazareen replied sarcastically. He leaned back in his seat.

The lack of respect or reverence in Kazareen's voice only worsened Arpento's mood. "Foolish boy, know you nothing of me? Behave yourself in my presence. Now pass that bowl of potatoes back over here."

Kazareen raised an eyebrow at this; he tried to hide the private delight he got from Arpento's request. "Very well, I'll do as you ask," Kazareen replied carefully.

117

"Good! See if you can remember that!" Arpento was now glaring at him; he seemed to sense that he had something up his sleeve. He took the bowl of potatoes and slammed them down next to his plate. A couple jumped out of the bowl and rolled around helplessly on the table. Arpento made no move to clean up his mess. "I have lost my appetite now because of bothering with you," he said as he took the napkin from his collar and threw it on his plate. "This is what I want you to do for me—"

I have him. "Am I to perform two tasks for you now? I do not agree to a change in our bargain."

"I have not yet named my task."

"You asked me to perform a chore for you. I have done so. You asked me to pass the potatoes, and I did. My part of the bargain is fulfilled, now if you are man of your word, fulfill your part."

He glared back at Kazareen. This was unexpected. Yes, the boy was clever, but not clever enough. "If you wish to gain by thievery that which I promised, there is little I can do about it," he thundered, "for I at least, am a man of my word."

"I am no thief. A bargain was struck, and I have upheld my half. Now uphold yours." Kazareen was feeling quite pleased with himself, in his mind he had gotten the better of the strange Arpento.

"This is your last word?"

"It is," Kazareen said rather proud of himself.

"Very well, if it is my advice and counsel you seek, then here it is: Leave my home. Now. And never return. Now good day to you!" Arpento went to the door and picked up a sharp spade that stood next to it. Kazareen was afraid to move as Arpento hovered menacingly behind him.

All the blood left Kazareen's face as he realized what a terrible mistake he had just made. The memory of Murro dying in his arms came back to him. He needed a second chance. "Forgive me sir, I should not—"

"Your last word was given. Leave now! Or would you like to see what this can do to your skull?"

Revelations

Kazareen rose slowly and left the cottage. The bitterness of regret rose inside him like bile. What had come over him? Why had he been so rash? As he'd feared, his wits were no match for the wily Arpento. His attempt at cleverness had only succeeded in squandering his chance to unravel the mystery of the Graystone. Or who he was. What he might do next.

He felt a black cloud descending upon him as he approached Florin and Leyrea. How could he tell them what happened? He was too ashamed. Not only had he destroyed his only hope for answers, he had dishonored his promise to Murro. He'd put his friends in mortal danger and now he had failed them all.

Florin and Leyrea looked at Kazareen as he stumbled back toward them and they saw clearly his failure written upon his face.

"Leave this place!" shouted Arpento from the door of his cottage. He was planted firmly in the threshold like a squat pig, still clutching the spade in his pudgy hands.

Florin put his arm on Kazareen's shoulder, but Kazareen couldn't bear to look at him.

"Do not be ashamed. Few, if any, were ever able to meet Arpento's expectations for the help they sought. He may be wise, though of this I have my doubts. This much is certain: he is no friend to the people of Pendoria. If indeed he has a wealth of wisdom, it has not been enough to teach him that wisdom should be shared, for true wisdom is its own reward. A wise man aids those in need and expects nothing in return. Then, when the wise man finds himself in tribulation, he will have friends to help him; but Arpento has no friends. When the roof of his own problems caves in on him, he will be trapped and alone, and no amount of hoarded wisdom shall avail him. Let us shake the dirt of this place from our boots and seek solace in our own, stronger form of wisdom—our friendship."

Florin's words were wiser than Arpento's, but Kazareen didn't feel any better. He was still without answers to the questions that plagued him. He was utterly lost, and knew not the path his feet should seek.

Leyrea hugged him and tugged at his black locks. "It'll be alright," she said, kissing him lightly on the forehead.

The company left the clearing, refusing to look back. It was a place Kazareen wished to forget, and the sooner the better. They returned to the path and paused there; none now knew where they might go.

Without a word, Kazareen simply set off blindly down the path, with no particular destination in mind. He just had to escape that place. Florin and Leyrea followed silently.

The clouds had parted while Kazareen was in Arpento's home and the rays of sunshine that broke through the leaves made the forest seem friendlier. He'd missed much of the beauty of the forest before, in the dim gray; now he could not escape it and it seemed to mock him. No longer able to hold back the pain of his failure in the face of such beauty, he fell to his knees and wept, thinking only of Murro.

Florin and Leyrea stood by as Kazareen made his murmured prayers of apology to his memory of Murro. They waited patiently as he emptied himself of his grief for they knew no more words to stay his pain. Darkness and uncertainty filled his heart. Then, almost as if Kazareen could hear his voice, he remembered what Murro used to tell him when he was down.

Life goes on Kazareen, as it always does.

Slowly, he quieted. After a few moments, Leyrea helped Kazareen to his feet.

"I know of a place we can shelter this evening," Florin said, "an old haunt of mine, if it still stands. But the daylight is passing quickly, and we have a fair way to go. Take heart. What you need is some sound sleep. Things will not seem so bad in the morning. Come."

They trudged on quietly until well after sunset, making turns down paths that intersected and wound round in a dizzying maze none but Florin could have navigated. Always the Marnalets followed after, naming spiders and beetles, mice and sparrows. The darkness was complete, except the few places where the light of the full moon managed to find its way to the forest floor, and still Florin led on.

At last, they came to a small hut built round a pit filled with ash and the charred remnants of burnt wood. The walls were rickety and falling apart in places, but it would provide a bit of shelter nonetheless. There was just enough room to allow the three of them to lie down inside. They soon had a small fire going, the first they'd built since their last night in Leyrea's dugout. A large round hole in the center of the roof funneled out the smoke.

"Did you build this place?" asked Leyrea.

"No, not this one. There are many hunters in these woods. Over time, we built a fair number of these hovels in places near good sources of meat and fur. Simple shelter for a night or two. They belong to all," said Florin, seating himself by the small fire he'd built. "This forest is the largest in all of Pendoria; there are at least thirty of these shelters, spread

The Heart of the Graystone

out across the woods. No one ever called them home though, too small and too weak."

"At least one calls it home," said a voice from beyond the walls.

Kazareen and Leyrea sat up.

"Who is there?" said Florin. He motioned to the others to stay low, but did not draw his sword.

"Why don't you ask your furry friends?" said the voice, now drawing nearer the entrance.

Kazareen looked around and saw that the Marnalets were nowhere to be seen. "Zoot! Avery!" he called, but there was no response.

"I have quieted the Marnalets," said the voice.

Kazareen did not like the sound of that, and he feared the worst for the Marnalets.

An old man of slight build, wrinkled and short, stepped into the light of the doorway. His hair was white, as creamy as sea-pearls, and hung lightly round his shoulders in gentle waves. He wore a black robe with a red sash tied at the waist. And he bore no weapon, not even a walking stick. His eyes went straight to Kazareen. After a moment, he chuckled.

"No, my young man, the Namers are not dead. I sent them on a little errand. One, I think, you'll be glad of later." His voice was thin and reedy.

"You live here?" asked Florin.

"At times. There is a small cave to the west of the cottage you visited today. I shelter there in winter. This is my summer home...my vacation home, if you like. You could say I am a fabulously rich man." The old man smiled.

"Rich, eh?" said Florin. "Then you should be able to afford better accommodations than this. And a rich man should have better things to do with himself than to follow a wayward family through the woods as they seek simple shelter for the night."

The old man eyed Florin carefully. "There are different types of wealth. You said so yourself. 'A great wealth of wisdom should be enough to teach one that wisdom should be shared,' you said. Or something to that affect. Tell me, Florin, what family do you speak of? No family has passed this way in many months. Falsehoods do not become you."

"Who are you? How do you know my name? Why are you following us?" Florin asked. He was already past impatience.

The old man ignored Florin. He sat down by the fire and warmed his hands as he shifted his gaze back to Kazareen. "If my eyesight has not gone dim, and it has not, I assure you, then I believe it was the young man here who entered the house of Arpento. It is he who seeks answers. And it is he, I believe, who is most prepared to do Arpento's bidding in exchange for those answers." He eyed Kazareen carefully, waiting for him to speak.

"If you wish us to leave—" started Florin.

"Let the young man speak...please." The old man's voice was firm.

Kazareen was hesitant. "I sought out Arpento, yes. But I don't see how that's any business of yours. Besides, he was no help," said Kazareen.

"Small surprise there. The man who dwells in the cottage has a gift, no doubt. Yet he is...a disappointment to you, is he not?"

Kazareen nodded, but his disappointment came more from his own foolishness.

"Ah, to me as well. Your friend Florin was near the mark when he told you that few, if any, have been able provide payment to Arpento for his services, but not wholly correct. None! None, I say, have ever fulfilled Arpento's requests."

"How would you know?" Florin asked.

But the old man said nothing; his attention was given fully to Kazareen.

"How do you know this?" Kazareen asked in proxy.

"I am glad you asked, young man," he replied, giving Florin a rebuking glance.

It was apparent to Florin now that the old man would only speak with Kazareen. Leyrea sat listening and watching silently.

"Because none of them were you."

"I don't understand," said Kazareen.

"Of course you don't understand!" he said with a laugh. "Let me share with you my wealth of wisdom. Perhaps I shall make a friend who will help me when my time of woe befalls me," the old man said, echoing Florin's words at the clearing.

"Why do you mock my friend? Speak plainly. Who are you? Why do you follow us? How do you know so much of Arpento?"

"Sorry, I meant no offense; rather, I intended to honor your friend. His words were true. But your questions are sound and to the point; they bring us to the heart of the matter—so to speak. Good. All you need do is ask, and I am at your service. Who I am will become apparent to you soon enough. I follow you because I see what the Marnalets see—"

"And what might that be?" Kazareen asked.

"The Graystone, of course."

"What? I don't—"

The Heart of the Graystone

Arpento held up his hand. "Allow me to continue. Please. You asked how I knew so much about Arpento. The reason is..." the old man stopped, holding Kazareen in his gaze.

Kazareen peered into the man's eyes and felt the world he knew suddenly melting away. For a moment nothing seemed particularly odd, but soon an unnatural burning took shape there, and it exhilarated Kazareen, frightened him a bit, but he could not look away. The light grew into a swirling conflagration, the consuming fire of boundless knowledge, tempered with wisdom, wrought in the forges of countless passing ages. Time seemed to stand still, becoming nothing at all, until Kazareen could not recall how long he had been sitting by the fire. Finally, the old man shifted his gaze away, and Kazareen was released. He felt as if he hadn't breathed in eons, and he gasped as he drew a deep breath.

Kazareen spoke slowly, deliberately finishing the old man's thought. "...is because you are Arpento," said Kazareen. He knew it without doubt.

"Very good, young man. Your vision has become keen."

Florin could not hold his tongue. "If you are truly Arpento, why did you send away the Marnalets? They could have told us who you are, without delay. I do not believe him, Kazareen. He does not live in the house of Arpento, he said so himself. I have known of the dwelling place of Arpento for many years!"

Kazareen gave the old man a questioning look, but said nothing.

"I can see that doubt has taken root in you once more," said the old man, shaking his head. "How quickly we turn from what we know in our hearts to be true! It grieves me."

"How do you explain it?" asked Kazareen.

"Explain what?"

"All of it."

The old man smiled again. "Listen closely, young man, and I shall tell you all—all that concerns you, that is. But if you wish to hear all that I have to say, if you wish to find the answers to the questions that leave you no peace, then you must agree to perform a service for me. You know how this works, I think. What say you?"

Kazareen was quiet for a long while as he considered the old man. It seemed backward to him; that he should receive that which he had sought, even before hearing what his task might be, and it frightened him. But he had nothing left to lose. If this were the true Arpento, then he would not squander a second chance—his last chance—to discover the truth of the Graystone. Or himself. "Speak, and I shall do as you request," he said.

123

"First, tell me more of yourself, and more importantly, tell me why you seek my help," he said politely.

Kazareen told the old man the same story he'd told the fat man in the cottage only a few hours earlier.

The old man nodded when Kazareen finished. "I am Arpento. I see the past clearly. Of the future, I can tell only what may be. It is not mine to determine; that is the providence of men. I have walked the earth since time untold, before the ways of men, and so I have learned much. If you had lived as long as I, you might also be as wise as me, but my eyes see differently than yours. I see much that is hidden in the hearts of men—but not all. And I see what you carry, young man. I see the Graystone. I feel it. It calls to me, but fear not, I will not, I cannot, take it back—at least, not yet. For the time has not yet come. If ever it does."

"Take it back? This is yours then?" said Kazareen, reaching into his pocket.

"Leave it where it is!" Arpento shouted.

Kazareen stilled his hand.

"Thank you. In a manner of speaking, yes, it is mine. Then again, not really," he paused to consider Kazareen's blank expression. "I see by your face this is a but another riddle. Allow me first to tell you the story of the Graystone you carry. The story of all Graystones really—from the beginning."

"Long ago, in the land once called Farak, by a spring-fed pool in a forest long since turned to desert, dwelt the great counselor of men: the Dragon; in fact, the only dragon that ever was. The Dragon was the helper of men, a bringer of wisdom and healing, and he required nothing in return for his aid to men. It was in his nature to spread only peace and prosperity, despite his size and somewhat ferocious appearance.

"But seven centuries past, the sixth king of those lands, who was called Bellian, became jealous of the Dragon. He magnified himself in his own eyes, and seeing how the people revered the wisdom and power of the Dragon, even above his own lordship, his heart became darkened with jealousy, and Bellian began to lay plans to slay the Dragon.

"Now Bellian had two sons, whose lust for power over the minds and lives of men was exceeded only by their father's. But Bellian was foolish, and unwisely as it turned out, he trusted his sons and shared with them his plan to slay The Dragon. Now the sons saw an opportunity to be rid of the iron yoke of their father's will, so they made a secret pact. They would work together to betray their father, see him fall and take the kingdom into their own hands. They agreed that when the deed was

The Heart of the Graystone

done, the older brother would become king, and the younger brother would become general of the armies of Farak.

"The brothers set out in secret to seek the Dragon's counsel. They came under the guise of friendship, but spoke only lies. They warned the Dragon that a faction of rebels had arisen in the kingdom and there were rumors that the rebels would try to slay the Dragon in an attempt to deprive the true king of the Dragon's aide in his efforts to quell the uprising.

"'What would happen to a man if he drew up his sword against Thee?' asked the older and more learned son. Now the Dragon was wise enough to hear the deception of his words, though he was unable to discern that it was the king who sought his destruction. He assumed, incorrectly, that it was the brothers who sought to slay him. So the Dragon told them, 'Any who rise up against Me shall surely die.'

"Knowing that the Dragon spoke only the truth, and seeing that Bellian's plan was completely without hope of success, they were secretly satisfied. They spoke words of thanks and again warned the Dragon against the fictitious mob that sought his destruction. The Dragon, thinking he had cowed the princes into inaction, ignored their false warnings of an uprising.

"So the son's plot against their father was well laid. They encouraged their father to go and slay the Dragon, saying it would surely make him the most powerful man in the world. They bowed down to him, praising his courage, but told him nothing of the Dragon's warning of the fate he would surely meet.

"Finally, Bellian came to the Dragon to execute his plan, but the Dragon had no fear of the king, his thoughts were on the lies of the sons. So the king drew up his sword and fell upon the Dragon at unawares. With a lightning stroke, Bellian's sword pierced the Dragon's vulnerable breast. Realizing he was within a split second of his death, the Dragon attempted to shed his earthly mantle before the king's sword could touch his heart and slay him for all time. When his spirit retreated, the Dragon's body was transformed into something like stone, but the king's stroke had been swift. The sword touched the Dragon's heart at the same moment it transfigured, and what remained of the Dragon's form exploded into countless shards. The fury of the power released that day was immense. It laid waste not only to King Bellian, but the forest in which they stood. All the lands were consumed by fire for many miles. The spring was dried up, and the land remains an accursed desert to this very day. The only remnant of the kingdom that remained intact after the tempest of fire was the capital city of Aruthe, on a small strip of land far to the south, for it was shielded by high mountains.

"The brother's plan had come to fruition, and they received what they sought, their father's death, though not in the manner they expected. The inhabitants of Aruthe survived that terrible day, but their kingdom was laid low as its fertile lands were burnt to cinders.

"The remains of what had been the Dragon's body fell widely upon the earth, mostly in the wastelands of what had been Farak, but some fell also in the lands of Pendoria. Men came to call them Graystones, and they were prized among the men of Pendoria for their sudden appearance from out of the heavens. Though none knew their true origins, the Pendorians thought them gifts from heaven, made in repayment for all the long troubles of war they had endured at the cruel hands of Bellian, who had long bedeviled the southern borders of Pendoria with his plans of conquest."

Arpento became silent.

Kazareen was amazed at the story, but as curious as ever. "So this Graystone I found, it was part of the Dragon itself?"

"Not just part of the Dragon. As I said, Bellian's sword touched the heart of the Dragon, at the very instant it transformed. The heart of the Dragon is what gave it its power...its will...its very life. No, young man, what you have there is more than just a Graystone, *that* was the heart of the Dragon; and the source of its will. It is filled with the greater part of what yet remains of the Dragon's power, though even the tiniest of Graystones carries some small portion of that power."

"How do you know that this is indeed the Dragon's heart?"

"You spoke of wondrous healing: your arm, Florin's fever, Leyrea's spirit. This type of healing could only come from the heart of the Dragon. There is no doubt. And it awoke the spirit of the woods where you found it, this Dien you spoke of. The wood spirits passed into slumber ages ago. When their work of setting the forests in order was completed, they fell into silence in the bosom of the earth, though at times men can hear—or even see—their dreams. But the power of the Graystone woke Dien from his long rest, giving him renewed strength. Little wonder there. And Dien will fall back to sleep again soon, no doubt, because you took the Graystone from his woods."

"But...who was the man living in the cottage? Why do you suffer him to impersonate you and befoul your name?"

"He befouls his own name, though we share the same one. He is the son of this flesh," he said, patting his chest, "and I passed my mantle on to him not so long ago. And he has a gift I do not. It must have come from his mother more than from myself, or some curious and unexpected mingling of our blood. On this I must ponder more. Whatever the case, he is able to discern shadowy glimpses of the futures

The Heart of the Graystone

of men, though he is not always right, despite his pride. Alas, for I grow weary of this world. Too many have sought my help through the slow passing of years, and yet none were willing to heed my counsel. I do not ask for anything in return for my aid, not for myself, as most believe. But I do require that those who seek me do something difficult. These tasks are designed to benefit the lives of all men. That is why they are so dangerous. Men shrink from their duties, and from me. Nothing worth doing is easy."

"As I began to realize that there were few left in the world willing to do the hard things that must be done, I too began to lose hope for the world of men. So I taught my son as best I might, and bade him to take over the family business, as it were, in my stead. A decision I may come to regret. While his manner is poor, his advice has led none to harm, until recently, and none who have come to him seeking me, has sought to heal the wounds of this world. Their intentions have been small, or selfish, and unworthy of my aid. I know, because despite my retirement, I have always watched from afar those who enter the house of Arpento. I can see what is in their hearts, and I have allowed my son to deal with all comers in his own way, until now. He does not see as I do, and he knew not the history of the Graystones, until recently, and that not fully so. But that was not my doing. Still, I am sure your story interested him greatly. Did he look you in the eye?"

"Yes, but only briefly, once or twice," said Kazareen.

Arpento laughed. "You should feel honored. That is more attention than he pays to most visitors." Arpento mused quietly on his son for a while as he stared into the fire, shaking his head almost imperceptibly.

"You said that recently he has caused harm. Does it have anything to do with me?" asked Kazareen.

Arpento tilted his head. "I am afraid so. The king's counselors came to visit more than a month ago. And it wasn't their first visit. They took great pains to arrive by stealth, but they cannot hide their shadow from these eyes, old though they may be. I do not know exactly what they discussed, or what visions my son shared with them, but it is clear to me now that it must have led to your arrest. He must have foreseen the dark day and somehow warned them. But their goal in all this..." Arpento shook his head and sat silently once again.

Kazareen wasn't sure if this was all Arpento had to tell him, so he broke the silence. "Surely, this Graystone is a great treasure and I am honored to carry a thing of such great power and healing. But, what of me? I do not even know who I truly am. Murro was not my true uncle, only a surrogate for my true father. Who am I? Where are my parents?

127

Where is my home? What should I do with this...Dragon's heart? Help me, Arpento, this burden is too great for...one such as me."

Arpento smiled wryly at Kazareen, but his eyes appeared sad. "One such as you...yes. I am afraid I cannot tell you much about who you are. It is beyond my sight. Though I might be able to discover more later. There is at least one promising clue: Dien. Even with the Graystone to empower him, he could not have traveled far from his home. That he made it all the way to Feria carrying you quite surprises me. So when he took possession of you as an infant, your home must have been quite nearby. Certainly, your parents lived within a few miles of Feria...or the forest. I think I'll go and have a talk with Dien soon, before he tires and settles back down to sleep."

"For now, at least, you must try to discover more on your own. And it is of the greatest importance that you do so. I feel the king's interest in you is because of who you are, not what you carry. Otherwise, the one who had you arrested, this Du Fe, would have confiscated the Graystone immediately. And he let it slip that he had his eye on you for some time, so certainly they were seeking you before you found the Graystone. The simple fact that Murro had a child, and yet no wife, would have been cause enough to throw you into the light of suspicion. How could Murro adequately explain your coming to the folk of Feria? Surely they would have thought it queer: a widower blacksmith suddenly charged by a stranger into raising an infant. Word would eventually spread through the village, especially if one had an ear for idle talk."

"Before Murro told me the truth, he told me I was brought to him in the night by a traveling merchant, for a price, after being orphaned in the east when his sister died, though I never heard him tell this story to any other," said Kazareen. "He would've said something to our neighbors when I first arrived. He couldn't conceal my existence. Murro was not one for idle talk though, and he cared little for those who did. I often heard him tell people to mind their own affairs if they asked him prying questions. Being so tight-lipped about me would not seem strange, he was tight-lipped about everything."

"Then it would have taken many years of careful watching and listening on Du Fe's part to focus his attention on you. Therefore it can be only one way. The eclipse. Somehow, the eclipse was the sign they had awaited and it must have given you away."

"Eclipse?" asked Kazareen.

"Yes. The darkening of the sun is called eclipse. It is a fairly rare occurrence, but completely natural in the circles of creation; there is nothing to fear from it, I assure you. But it is often taken as an omen of doom by the Necromancers."

The Heart of the Graystone

"Necro- what?" said Florin, again unable to hold his tongue.

"The Necromancers. The living dead. I myself have often been accused of being in league with them, though none could ever offer any proof of such a claim," Arpento said.

"They utilize the dark arts. The Necromancers can see what lies beyond, in a sense. But true hearts cloud their vision, though they do not realize it, so they often misinterpret the true meaning of what they see. And they cannot be persuaded to turn from their ways; the power they obtain intoxicates them, blinds them to the error of their ways. And I am sorry to say that the king's counselors are just such men."

"However it was accomplished, the king now has his mind set on you, and while good fortune and the help of your friends here has allowed you to evade capture, eventually he will track you down. If they ever learn of the Graystone you carry, then I am afraid matters will be worse, not only for you and your friends, but for all men. When they learn of its powers, and they certainly would, then they will put it to evil use. That must not happen. It must never be sullied by their hands!"

"The Dragon is gone from this earth, and cannot return, but the greatest remnant of his power still burns in the Graystone. If it falls into the hands of the Necromancers, they can turn its power to evil. An evil so great that in time the wisdom the Dragon shared with mankind will be completely forgotten and war will engulf the world in a firestorm so unimaginable it will make the destruction of Farak look as small as your little fire here. And there will be no healing, no escape from this doom." Arpento closed his eyes, and a shadow seemed to settle over him, even in the light of the fire.

When the shadow passed, he gazed into Kazareen's eyes once again. "But this fate is not inevitable, not while the pure of heart protect the Graystone. I see that vengeance has taken root in your heart, young man. Do not let it grow. Detest the actions of the wicked, but do not imitate their ways. Hatred only tears apart those who indulge in it. Do what you must to protect the Graystone and those who are beloved to you, but do not give in to the lust of revenge. The evil that men do comes back to them tenfold, in this life or the next. If you seek to add to the suffering of the wicked, you will only hasten your own destruction. Beware!"

Kazareen tried to push the thought of avenging Murro's death into the corner of his mind, where it might not flower. But once again, he began to feel small and inadequate, unprepared for what fate had brought him. "What am I to do now? The more you speak, the less I know how I will be able to bear such a burden," and without thinking, he pulled the Graystone from his pocket. It filled the little shack with a light so brilliant it blinded them all. "Take it!" he said as he held it out for Arpento.

Florin and Leyrea covered their faces, but still they could not escape the light of the Graystone.

Look at me, young man, Kazareen heard, but Arpento's voice sounded different now: deeper, as if he spoke from the hollows of a great cave.

Kazareen looked to where Arpento was sitting, but the old man was gone. The shack, the campfire, even the forest itself, had all vanished. A white light that seemed to have no source surrounded him, penetrated him, and filled his whole mind. Then, before him, the Dragon appeared; its wings outstretched to the sky, its eyes burning brighter than the coals in Murro's forge, and in its chest, a jagged wound, deep and wide.

Do you see? asked the Dragon.

"Yes!" Kazareen cried.

Then put it away. I cannot take this thing. What is done cannot be undone, the Dragon said, though its mouth did not move.

Kazareen watched the light fade when he put the Graystone back in his pocket. As he did, the world he knew returned. Now, before him sat Arpento, holding his robe open. Kazareen saw a deep red scar across the chest of the old man. Before Florin and Leyrea uncovered their eyes, he pulled his robe shut. "Do you see?" Arpento asked, his voice as thin and reedy as before.

Kazareen sat gaping in astonishment, his eyes transfixed on Arpento. "Yes. I see."

Good. Keep this vision to yourself. Arpento's words came to him, but like the Dragon, his lips did not move. *None need know of it but you.*

When Florin and Leyrea finally opened their eyes, they too were astonished. They had not beheld the vision of Arpento as the Dragon; but they saw a figure they did not immediately recognize. "Kazareen, are you alright? What's happened?" Leyrea asked, reaching for Kazareen.

"What do you mean?"

"Your hair. It's gone...white!" said Florin. Leyrea leaned over to Kazareen and placed her hand on his head; she had to touch his hair to believe it.

"What?" Kazareen pulled his bangs down in front of his eyes and saw that it was so. His eyes darted to Arpento, but knew he could not reveal the truth of the vision he'd just seen.

"There is still some power in these old bones yet," said Arpento, suddenly laughing with a carefree smile. He snapped his fingers. "Do you not see? I have given the young man a disguise. It should come in

The Heart of the Graystone

handy for the road ahead. The king will be harder pressed to capture you now."

Florin and Leyrea looked at Arpento with amazement. There was more to this old man than they had ever dreamed.

"Arpento!" said a voice from the doorway. Kazareen looked up to see that the Marnalets had returned. Arpento turned quickly and held up a finger before the smaller one could speak. It uttered no name.

"So, my friends, how went my little errand?" Arpento asked.

The Marnalets chattered and squawked while Arpento listened closely. It seemed he understood them perfectly.

"Very good. I thank you," he said, nodding politely.

"You understood them?" asked Kazareen.

"I understand all the tongues of this earth. There was a party of soldiers on patrol and heading this way when you first arrived in my home. I asked the Marnalets to play a little game of find the fox with them. They called out after the soldiers, by name of course, and the soldiers chased after them. By now, the soldiers are on a different path, far away, and hopelessly lost." Arpento smiled brightly.

"Thank you, Arpento," said Florin.

"At your service," he replied, nodding in deference, not to Florin, but to Kazareen.

"But there are still many unanswered questions," continued Florin. "How is it you came to possess this thing? Why won't you take it back? And these Necromancers—"

"Silence, Florin of Bethë Khür!" Arpento shouted. "Who seeks my aid? Be it you or the one you call Kazareen? Remember your place. I will suffer no more questions from you, lest you be willing to pay the price for your intrusions."

Florin scowled at the old man, then turned to Kazareen. But he already knew the answers to Florin's questions.

"You have answered my questions," Kazareen said, "all that I came here to ask that is, and I will ask no more, save one. What would you have me do?"

"Of this, I would speak with you alone."

"It's alright. I trust them."

"It is not a matter of trust," said Arpento. And he would say no other word until they were alone.

Kazareen didn't relish the thought of asking his friends to leave, but they saw that Arpento would not speak until they had gone. They were good enough to leave without being asked and waited some distance away in the shadows of the wood. The fully lit moon was hanging low in the sky now, for they had been listening long to Arpento's tale.

When they were a safe distance away, Arpento drew close to Kazareen and took his hand. "You know what I was. But you do not know what I am. I am less than a man, for I have no heart. I am more than a man, for my knowledge and wisdom is greater than any man's. Yet I grow weary of this world. It has outgrown me. But as long as the Graystone exists, I am bound to this world and yet, of little service. Except for the help I am now able to offer you, I have been of no consequence for seven hundred years. Even my son does not heed me. He will live longer than most mortal men, but he shall pass away naturally some day, for his mother was as all women are. She died more than a half century ago. I thought I could bear living as a man, if I had companionship, but alas, she too passed away...and still I linger on. She loved me, and so I gave her a son. When she died, I understood like never before, what men must endure: the pain of separation, the loneliness. I understood it, but I could not feel it." Arpento squeezed Kazareen's hand. "Do you take my meaning?"

Kazareen nodded. He knew those feelings well; since Murro's death, he had been fighting them all.

"I know, I know," said Arpento, patting Kazareen's hand. Something warm passed between them in the long moments he was silent. "And those feelings will continue as long as the Graystone is in your possession. It has the power to heal, yes. But that is not its greatest power. I sent your friends away for their own protection. They must not know what I am about to tell you, though they may still help you on your way, if they wish it." Arpento paused as he looked over his shoulder. They were far away; they would not hear.

"The Graystone is, for want of a better word, desire. All that you wish, all that you will, shall come to pass, sooner or later, while you possess the Graystone," Arpento said. "If you touch it, if you hold it in your hand, and especially if you keep it next to your breast, touching your skin, its power to make your will indomitable will only increase.

"If you wish for death, it shall find you. If you seek revenge, it shall be yours. If you hate, you will be hated. Power...riches...even love, all these you may obtain easily, with the power of the Graystone. Other things too...terrible things...unimaginable things, of which I will not speak. This is why it must not fall into Geraldi's hands, or worse yet, the Necromancers.

"But beware! This power was not meant for you either Kazareen. Fortune has brought it to you, yes. But do not seduce yourself with what it can do. The Dragon was sent to aid mankind and that was its only desire; it knew no other. And its heart gave it the power to fulfill that desire. If you fill your own heart with selfish desire, you will become as

The Heart of the Graystone

wicked as those you despise. Keep your intentions pure. Reflect on what you really seek, what you really need from this life. If your desire is to remain pure, the Graystone will aid you in this as well. So it is not as bad as one might imagine." Arpento sat back.

Kazareen stared at the ground between his outstretched legs. "But I still don't know what it is I am to do. Tell me plainly."

"You must do as your conscience dictates. I cannot force you to do anything. You know now the true power and origins of the Graystone. You could keep it, and hope the king never finds you, or raise an army of your own and become king yourself. You could cast it into the sea or bury it and hope no one else ever finds it. Or..."

"Or what?" Kazareen asked, sensing Arpento's reluctance.

"Or...you could...destroy it."

"Destroy it! Why?"

"In doing so, you would free me from this mortal coil, end my long years of effort, that have, alas, been in vain. And you would help me take the next step..." His voice drifted off, and for a moment he seemed lost in some hidden vision.

Kazareen puzzled at what the 'the next step' might mean, but said nothing.

"If you did this, you could spare all the generations of men that come after you from the temptation of the power of the Graystone," Arpento said.

Kazareen raised his head and looked Arpento in the eye once again. "It seems like a terrible waste of such an awesome power. How would one go about doing such a thing, if he had a mind to, I mean."

"Find Bellian's sword. The work it began so long ago was interrupted, but now the time is ripe for its work to be completed. Carry the Graystone and Bellian's sword to the place called Kara de Sten Yah, in the deserts of Farak; the very place where Bellian and The Dragon stood on that terrible day seven centuries past. A valley it is, but in the fashion of a great bowl, dug from the land by the hand of the creator. Take the sword, and pierce the Graystone. If your intentions are pure when you do this, you will be spared Bellian's fate, and the great healing power of the Graystone will be released into world, and I shall be released from this flesh to take a new form; a form that will allow me to find peace, to inspire men, and to be of some use once more. But if your heart were black with corruption or malice, then the Graystone will seal your destruction. And then, even in your hands, it would be no different than if it fell into the possession of the Necromancers, and the doom of the world will be sealed."

"Bellian's sword?" Kazareen was incredulous. "How could a sword survive the fires that destroyed half of his kingdom?"

Arpento's face drew a bit more grave and pale. "This blade was not forged by human hands, only altered by them. It was Eldrimor who plundered the armory of Erub, an age ago or more..." His voice faded for a moment and his fingers pulled absently through the earthen floor. "But that is a long story; one for another time...perhaps. You need only worry about finding the blade for yourself now."

Kazareen was curious about the strange names, but intent now on his purpose. "Then where is this sword? How shall I recognize it?"

"Seek out Bellian's sons," said Arpento.

Kazareen's brow furrowed.

"Yes, they still live, even after all these years. You see, from the moment they succeeded in deceiving the Dragon, they brought upon themselves a terrible curse: to walk the earth under a shadow so great that death itself flees them. They sought out the king's sword for themselves in the wastes of Farak, during their long years of wandering, and there efforts were not in vain."

"A long sword it is, as black as night. Its hilt and pommel were inlaid with jasper and topaz. A single diamond was encrusted into the steel, just above the hilt. About the diamond, etched into the blade with powerful acids were the words: Morta, Média an Vité, which means 'In the Midst of Life, Death.' But they call it simply Morta."

"And where should I seek the sons of Bellian?"

Arpento was loath to answer, knowing the distress and burden his answer held for Kazareen. "Pente Kaleán. Alerien and Gueren, the sons of Bellian, are now King Geraldi's closest advisors and he is in league with them. They are the Necromancers."

Kazareen's heart sank. "I...how will I be able to do this thing? How can I face the king, who wishes me dead; and the brothers who do not die, or storm alone the strongest fortress in all of Pendoria? It's impossible."

Arpento leaned forward. "Nothing is impossible, not while you carry the Graystone. The whole realm of possibility is at your feet. Do you still not realize what has happened and what is happening?" He took Kazareen's hand. "The Graystone was once the heart of the Dragon, but now you—Kazareen de Pendi—*you* are the heart of the Graystone."

A New Day

The silky fragrance of the forest wafted through the hut, mixing with the sharp aroma of smoldering coals. The young man's dream retreated into forgetfulness and he began to stir. Arpento stood at the door, humming gently to himself, his gaze shifting back and forth, up and down, as he watched the subtle activities of the forest unfold in the growing light. Despite his small frame, he seemed to fill the entire doorway, immovable and proud. Kazareen wondered if Arpento had slept at all. Or had he watched all through the night while sandy clouds of exhaustion overtook the rest of them? Did he ever sleep? Kazareen wasn't sure, but after last night, nothing else would surprise him when it came to Arpento. Florin and Leyrea were nowhere in sight.

"Good morning."

"And good morning to you, young master," Arpento replied, not bothering to turn.

"Where are my friends?"

Arpento pointed to his left. "Just there. Readying the horses. It seems they do not wish to dally here."

Kazareen peeled himself from the ground and stretched. His body felt like a damp cloth that had been wrung too tightly, and his mind still reeled from all that had been revealed to him. He didn't want to think about it. He just wanted to feel normal again, but it struck him that normality had, for him, taken permanent leave. He rolled up his wool blanket and yawned.

Florin tugged on Vala's saddle strap. "Good and tight."

Leyrea was off searching for Sirius who had wandered off in the night.

Florin had no idea what new path he might now follow. He had fulfilled his part of the bargain: he'd seen Kazareen to the house of Arpento, and now...now, he yearned to see his old home again and to see if...somehow...she—he shook off the thought. His home wasn't as grand as the cottage they'd visited the day before, but his heart ached to see it once more. Did it still stand? Had someone moved in and taken it over as their own? Would he try to take it back, if someone was there? Or would he be welcomed home by a familiar face?

Despite the long years he'd been dreaming of his home and the tugging desire he felt to return there, Florin felt an even stronger pull now. He had made a friend in Kazareen. And he couldn't abandon him—not yet. Not until Kazareen found something like safety. Or a home of his own. Florin's home, if it still stood, could wait a bit longer it if it had to.

Then a strange thought came at him. Was he feeling the powerful magic of the Graystone...or his own dedication to a newfound friend? For a moment, he wondered. In the end, Florin decided that he didn't particularly care if the Graystone was influencing him or not, he would not abandon the friend who had won him his freedom.

Leyrea led Sirius by the bridle through the brush, whispering gentle words of admonishment in his ear. She began loading his burden. As she did, she felt doubts of her own creeping in. Where would they go from here? How much longer could she stand to breathe the same air as those who had slain her father and brother? If she were going to leave Kazareen and Florin, it would have to be soon. She was growing too fond of them both. If she didn't make a clean break and find a new home of her own, away from all these strange dealings, she might find herself too tempted to do that which Arpento had warned Kazareen to avoid: seeking revenge on the king.

What disturbed her more was the thought that Florin and Kazareen had started to become like family to her, even after such a short while, and the longer she stayed with them, the more difficult parting would become. As she secured the last pack onto Sirius, she began to realize that caring for Kazareen and Florin really wasn't what she feared; rather, it was the very real possibility, given their situation, of having to go through the torture of losing those she cared for all over again.

The horses were packed and readied, and Kazareen stood in front of Arpento, his head bowed. Whether it was in reverence for him or fear of his future, he didn't really know. "Where shall I begin? Where shall I go? I just..."

Arpento lifted Kazareen's chin.

"That is for you to decide, young man. But if one last word of advice is what you seek, then I say this: trust what your heart tells you. And trust those you now call your friends." Arpento looked at Florin and Leyrea standing nearby. He smiled and nodded to them.

Florin had a funny feeling that Arpento had been reading his thoughts.

Leyrea felt it too.

"Your road shall be shown to you—in time," said Arpento, shaking his hand. "Farewell, Kazareen. Remember the power of that which you carry, it can see you through, even when all seems lost."

The Heart of the Graystone

Kazareen shrugged at the mention of the Graystone, there'd been enough talk of it to last him a lifetime. "Shall we meet again?"

"Perhaps." Then with a smile and a wink, he turned and disappeared into the forest.

Delasur

Kazareen watched as Arpento slowly melted into the forest. A chill rolled through him and for the first time in his life, he truly felt like an orphan. Growing up with Murro, uncle or not, had been all he'd known, and now looking back, he began to realize how safe and content those days felt to him. How he missed Murro's quiet reassurance.

Kazareen took a deep breath and turned to Florin and Leyrea. And he realized he was not really alone at all. The path ahead of him would hold no peace for many months, perhaps even years to come, of this he was certain, but he drew a measure of comfort from knowing he wasn't really alone.

Then a new thought struck down that comfort as quickly as he'd found it. Florin and Leyrea had fortunes of their own to seek now, and they owed him nothing more. How could he heap any more misfortune on them? His own path was uncertain, but how could he truly call himself their friend if he imposed such danger on them, after they'd already risked so much on his behalf? Yes—it was time to find his way— by himself now. His hand tightened around the Graystone in his pocket.

"I...ah...want to thank you both for your help...but our company must now part. Florin, you have kept your word, and our arrangement is at an end. You're home now, and after seeing your woodcraft firsthand, here I believe you could hide forever from the eyes of the king. Good luck to you."

Florin moved to speak, but for the first time in his life, he could find no words. His hands opened suddenly, grasped, but found nothing.

"Leyrea, I don't know what you seek, be it revenge on the king's servants, or a quiet life, or something between, but without your aid, I would've been taken prisoner or killed long ago. Farewell," said Kazareen. A forced smile quivered upon his face.

Leyrea also found herself unable to speak. An odd sensation, as if being muted by some unseen hand, restrained her. She looked to Florin; his eyes were sharp with expectation. Still, he could not speak.

They stood silently and looked at the figure of the young man that stood before them. How his appearance had changed over a single night! It wasn't just his new pale locks that seemed out of place, but he seemed older now, his eyes deeper, his body fuller and his face a bit grimmer.

Kazareen took Wingfoot by the bridle and slowly led him away. Releasing them to their fortunes was the right thing to do, but in his heart, he wished it were not so.

Florin finally found his voice. "Kazareen!" the name seemed to pop from his mouth like a cork from an aged wine bottle. He could breathe again. "Wait!"

Kazareen stopped, but did not turn. The weight of all he bore began to lift, if only slightly. If they chose to follow him on his path, they would have to declare it now, free of any bond.

"I...I don't know what words were spoken to you in private, or what task now lies before you. And I do not ask you to reveal such secrets to me. But I heard Arpento's last words to you, and they were wise. You can trust in my friendship. My eyes are old, but not yet dim, and my body is growing strong again—stronger than I would have believed possible just a few weeks ago. If you count yourself as my friend, as I do you, then let me help you on your way. Allow me to guide and aid you still," said Florin.

Kazareen turned to him. Florin was no longer the image of the starving wraith he'd first beheld in the cell in Feria, but a man again, still thin and disheveled, but a man nonetheless. Had the Graystone been working its healing power on him from the first moment they met?

Now a smile was beginning to appear on Kazareen's face. "If this is your wish, I welcome your help, my friend." He ran back to Florin and threw his arms around the old man. "Thank you," he whispered.

Florin released Kazareen and held him at arm's length; he didn't seem comfortable with such a physical expression of fellowship.

Kazareen looked to Leyrea, but she remained silent.

Her head was bowed as if lost in prayer. "You speak of vengeance? No. It's beyond my means. The chance to repay the king for the injury upon my family may come, but I will not seek it."

Leyrea surveyed her surroundings. "The forest hems me in. I've dwelt too long on the open plain and now I miss the sky. I seek a new home, but not in this forest, so I'll come with you if you'll have me. At least until Florin can show me a way out of this maze he calls home," she said.

"Arpento said to trust in my friends, and so I shall. Where you lead, Florin, I'll follow. For a while, at least," Kazareen said.

Florin returned Kazareen's smile. Now they were free to seek out his old home. Kazareen agreed that it was as good a destination as any, for the time being. So they started off.

Before they had gone far, Kazareen cried out, "Wait! What about the Marnalets?"

Florin stopped and scanned the area.

Leyrea looked only at Kazareen as she stroked Sirius' mane. "I think they follow another now. That Arpento is filled with a strange

The Heart of the Graystone

power, perhaps stronger even than that which you carry. Or perhaps they have gone off on their own again. Either way, I wouldn't worry for them. They are ancient and powerful. If the tales of The Namers have truth to them, then nothing can harm them. Anyway, I think the shape they took in our presence was to put us at ease. I believe they could have just as easily appeared as ferocious bears or great cats, if they chose to. Come."

"I'll miss them," said Kazareen, resigning himself.

"I will too. But what cannot be helped must be suffered." she said.

Kazareen nodded and they set off again.

For hours they trampled through the dense thickets, following Florin's lead. Always the thought of what lay ahead pricked at Kazareen, and he warded himself against it as best he could.

As they marched into the heart of the forest, the thick layer of underbrush began to thin and finally recede. Soon, no path could be seen at all, and they found themselves wandering through damp, misty barrens beneath the dizzying heights of the tall pines of Bethë Khür. Except for a sparse layer of pine needles and cones, their way had become clear, almost empty, save the occasional cluster of fern. The trunks of high firs stretched up, higher and higher, like great columns supporting a roof far above them, the very tops of which were hidden from their sight. They had reached the oldest part of the forest.

For a while, the powerful smell of pine had been refreshing and soothing, but soon a stale and acrid odor fouled the air, overpowering the sweet fragrance of the forest.

Florin stopped, looked at Kazareen, and found himself still surprised by his pale locks and the subtle changes in his face. He shrugged it off. "We draw near to the Great Road."

"What is that smell?" asked Leyrea.

"Delasur. What wind there is, is from the east now and it carries the scent of the town our way. I was wondering when you would smell it."

"Why is it so foul?" asked Kazareen.

"'Tis the odor of mankind, and smells the same as any other place where men gather in great company, though Delasur is smaller than most of the cities of Pendoria. We've all wandered long in the free air of the wilderness, especially you, Leyrea, but tis not an unusually foul odor—for a city. Come, we make for its gate."

Kazareen took a step backward. "We can't go there! We'll be captured."

"You forget how much your appearance has changed."

Kazareen suddenly felt self-conscious. Indeed, he'd all but forgotten what the vision of Arpento as the Dragon had done to him.

"And we are far from where last we were spotted. Also, we were only a pair at the time, and now we are three."

Florin paused and scratched his head in thought. "Father, daughter and grandson we shall be, traveling east to Barése to dwell by the rejuvenating hot springs there, for I am old and weak." He turned to Leyrea. "There, you and your son seek refuge from your patriarch's endless complaints of his aging bones," said Florin, who, while spinning his yarn had bent over with a pained look on his face and put his hand to his back.

Leyrea smiled and shook her head. "When did you invent that tale?"

"Only now, as I spoke. How sounds it to your ears?" Florin said, straightening up.

"Well, you certainly look the part. And now that Kazareen's locks are as fair as my own, he may just pass as my son," she said, mussing his hair.

Kazareen was not so enthusiastic. "I see no need to go into a town, we still have supplies enough for quite a while. It seems an unnecessary risk. We can just as easily go round and be relieved of having to face the king's men."

"I'm afraid not, Kazareen. The river Laché Belen now lies between; tis impassable for more than thirty miles in either direction. There are great rapids of white and churning water that only a fool would try to cross. If we are to seek my old home, as we agreed, then we must follow the Great Road and take the bridge that connects the west with the east. Not far beyond the bridge lies Delasur—and we will not be able to elude the eyes of her watch once we make the crossing."

Kazareen pursed his lips and swallowed. "Very well."

Leyrea mussed his hair again.

"Will you please stop that!" he said, pulling away.

"Why, *my son*? Are you too old now to let your mother show her affection for you?" Florin and Leyrea had a good laugh and though he fought it, Kazareen found he could not completely hide a growing smile.

As they made their way south toward the road, they came up with some likely aliases for themselves and decided they would say they'd left from Khürasé, Leyrea's home, just in case anyone became a bit too curious.

Soon they came upon the wide and well-worn track of the Great Road and began following it eastward. The sound of rushing water was echoing through the forest and swelling to enormous proportions as they approached the river.

The Heart of the Graystone

The road led them to a great stone bridge, that was itself a wonder to behold. In the bright sunlight that funneled down through the rent in the trees where the river flowed, Kazareen saw the white stones, precisely cut and placed, without an ounce of mortar to hold them together, spanning the yawning gorge below. The roaring river made the horses skittish and they would not approach the bridge until their masters reassured them. With the horses finally calmed, they started across.

When they reached the apex, Kazareen and Leyrea paused to peer over the edge. The wild river, some forty feet below, coursed over giant boulders and jagged rocks between sheer, craggy banks. Kazareen had never seen such a violent torrent, nor heard such a din, which drowned out every other sound. Leyrea was next to him, but he had to shout to be heard. They marveled for a while at the sight, but soon Florin urged them forward. Down the cobbled stones of the bridge and back onto the road they led the horses, who seemed glad to be back on solid earth and away from fearsome growl of the river. They nodded and swooshed their tails in relief.

Just as the sound of the river had begun to fade behind them, the walls of Delasur began rising in a clearing ahead of them. They were not what Kazareen expected, but he knew instantly he should have. These were not walls of stone, but high palisades of timber, fashioned from whole tree trunks, each log ending in a sharpened spike, sealed over with pitch. The nasty odor crept up from a deep ditch that surrounded the palisades; it was filled with stagnant water, befouled with filth and rotting refuse. Watchtowers, a bit higher than the palisades and manned with archers, stood on either side of the gate. Two soldiers stood guard on the road, festooned in the royal livery, eyeing their approach warily. These soldiers looked sharp and alert, not relaxed and passive, like Kazareen remembered Feria's guards.

Kazareen's pace began to slow. Florin noticed it immediately. "Hup, hup, Kazareen. Just act natural. Like you really are Esperio."

Kazareen ran over their story and aliases in his mind again as he matched their pace.

He needn't have worried. Seeing Kazareen, the guards posed a few probing questions, but he didn't fit the description they'd been given and they were allowed to pass. The gate closed behind them with a lurch.

Kazareen was taken aback by how different Delasur was from his hometown. The houses and shops were huddled close together, crowding the town's narrow, muddy streets. Not a single stone edifice did he spy, as all were made of wood, and erected in a way far different from what Kazareen knew in Feria. They were fashioned from logs stacked one upon another, and the gaps between were filled with a dark cement, that Kazareen assumed was mud or clay. Their roofs were made of bundles of thick thatched grasses or heavy mosses, some of which still seemed to be alive and growing. Many of the buildings had heavy patches of vines and ivies covering their walls. It was almost as if the city had sprouted from the forest itself, without the aid of man.

Along what Kazareen supposed was the main avenue, he noticed that a few people had stopped to stare at them as they passed. It seemed that unlike Feria, with its constant stream of traders, strangers here would not go unnoticed.

"I don't know, Florin. I don't like it here. I feel like we're being watched. Can we move through quickly?" Kazareen asked, keeping his head low.

"Don't worry. The folk of Delasur see few outsiders and so they are naturally curious, but they can be as hospitable as any folk in Pendoria, if shown a measure of civility."

"Florin, please. I don't want to be here long."

"Do you still have the coin you took from the—" Florin stopped short. "Do you have the coin?"

"Yes." Kazareen dug for his small purse in the saddlebags. He'd almost forgotten about the silver he'd taken from the soldier Murro had slain on the road to Pente Kaleán.

"We could do with a bit of creature comfort. My tongue and belly grow tired of meat, day after day. I knew of a baker's shop not far from here. If it still stands, I'll secure us a supply of loaves. Perhaps even a few sweet roles or cakes."

Kazareen nodded and handed over the coin. His mouth had already begun to water at the mere mention of something sweet and he thought of the apples they'd long since devoured.

"Wait for me here, I'll return as quickly as I may."

"Why don't we just come with you?" asked Leyrea.

Florin seemed unsure of what he might say. "T'would be better if you two were seen together, rather than Kazareen and I, should the governor or magistrate happen by. Less chance of being recognized. Heed me now, I'll be back presently."

Florin turned onto the side street and then disappeared down an unseen alley. Kazareen and Leyrea waited uncomfortably by a hitching post near what passed as the main square. A tall wooden carving of something that looked vaguely like a bear stood in its center, casting a long shadow.

The familiar alleys of Delasur drifted by. Except for the aching of his aged joints, it was as if no time at all had passed since last he walked

The Heart of the Graystone

them. Florin turned down another muddy street until he came to the bakery. He tied Vala to the post in front and rang the bell. The face of a tired old woman appeared in the small window that faced the street. Seeing Florin, she drew the latch and he stepped inside.

"What can I do ye for, stranger?" she asked, stepping back behind the counter.

"Stranger? Do you not remember me woman?"

Her eyes darted back to him quickly, surveying the rangy figure before her, but all she saw was an unseemly man with a lined face, a long beard and matted gray hair. When, at last she looked to his eyes, the light of recognition illuminated her own.

"My stars! Can it be?"

Florin smiled.

"Florin? Is that you?"

"In the flesh."

"Lords, but it's been ages! I thought you dead," she exclaimed, rushing out from behind the counter. She poured herself into his arms, and he held her close. Instantly, the scent of her awoke memories in him he'd long forgotten. Florin kissed her on the forehead, then held her at arms length.

"Not dead. Not yet, anyway. But I see the years have been kinder to you, Solia."

She brushed the flour from her apron and pulled a stray lock of hair behind her ear. "Oh! I must look a sight!"

"A sight for sore and aged eyes."

"I can hardly believe it. Florin, what happened to you?"

"'Tis a long story. And a strange one as well. One I haven't the time to tell just now. I have to be on my way, and I need provisions. A dozen loaves should do. And some tarts or sweet roles if you have any," he said, suddenly business-like.

"Is this why you have come back? To say hello, buy loaves and disappear all over again?"

"It can't be helped. But I will not *disappear* again, as you say. Not immediately. Do your job, good woman, if you are still able, and I will tell you a bit more. I cannot linger in town long."

Solia blinked and wiped her apron again, then went about filling his order. "You have coin, I hope, as my charity for beggars has long since departed me." Her voice became suddenly as cold and stony as Florin's.

He expected it, he knew her too well. "Though I may look the part, I am no beggar." He slapped the silver pieces on the counter.

Solia raised an eyebrow. "Sure enough, you are not without means. Do you intend to stock up or buy my whole lot with that trove?"

She placed the smallish loaves on the counter, stacked them neatly and began wrapping them in cheesecloth. "Three silver for the loaves. I have four blueberry tarts left, but they are two days old I'm afraid. Do you still want them?"

"If you have not lost your talent at baking, then certainly," he said.

She shook her head. "Another silver for the tarts. Tis four total," she said, pulling the coins one-by-one from the small pile on the counter.

"And one for your service, as sweet as the tarts, no doubt," Florin said, pushing one more coin toward her and pulling the rest back.

Her eyes softened. "And what of you, Florin? Tell me, please."

He wanted to tell her all, but there was no time. "I am on the run. I was imprisoned...for many years. But I have found my freedom again, and I do not wish to risk losing it a second time by delaying here. We are heading back to my old home. Do you remember where it is?"

We? Who is 'we'? Solia's stare bore into Florin as he spoke. "Of course."

"I'll be there for a few days at least. Come if you can, and I shall tell you more. There is much I would say to you as well."

"I'll try, but—"

"Try. I'll be watching for you. Say nothing to anyone that you saw me. Especially the Guardsmen."

"No, of course, not. You have my word."

"Farewell, my sweet. See you soon?"

Solia nodded.

And like that, he was gone again. She watched from the small window as Florin disappeared down the alley, but she knew she was bound by a far deeper oath to tell the Captain of the Town Guard of her unexpected visitor.

"Any luck?" Kazareen asked.

Florin patted the full pack on Vala's hindquarter, nodding.

"Good, then let's get out of here. People have been talking and pointing," said Leyrea.

Florin led them through the shadow of the carving of the great bear, and toward the eastern gate.

As they approached the gate, they were greeted with a different stench—the stench of rotting death—and then it's grim sight. The bodies of two men hung lifelessly from both sides of a tall wooden gibbet, just short of the eastern gate. Their hands were bound above them, and their bloated bodies rocked back and forth slowly in the breeze. The air was thick with death and Kazareen pulled his shirt over his mouth and nose.

Leyrea looked away, but Kazareen, try as he might, could not.

The Heart of the Graystone

Florin had seen the bodies, but ignored them as he approached the guards, who pulled opened the gates just wide enough for the small party to pass through. Florin paused near the younger of the two guards to pay the toll and whispered, "And what, pray tell, were their crimes?"

The guard looked at his cohort, who turned his head away as if he had not heard Florin's question. "They were found guilty of refusing to aid the general in his search for fugitives from the king's justice," he said, unable to meet Florin's gaze. Though the guard was trying to hide his eyes, Florin saw they were full of guilt. Florin put three silver pieces in his hand.

"And this is a capital crime? What is happening to our land?" asked Florin, though he expected no answer.

"Shh! Keep your voice down, lest you meet a similar fate," said the guard. He looked around furtively. "It was General Gueren's idea, not ours. If I were you stranger, I'd just keep moving." The guard waved them through and said loudly, "Move along! Move along!"

He heard Leyrea gasp behind him at the mention of the name, but Florin only stared at the young man. "This Gueren, he is here then? In Delasur?"

The guard nodded slightly as he ushered them through the gate.

The large iron latch clanked behind them as the gate lurched shut. Florin led them away down the road, slowly at first, until the guard towers were out of sight. Then he darted from the road, almost running.

Solia's Word

Kazareen was almost numb with fear. The thought of the son of Bellian so hot on their trail pierced his courage, and his stomach squeezed with an icy pang.

"Did you hear that? Gueren! Here! How could he have tracked us here?" said Leyrea.

"I don't know! But for right now, we must keep moving," Florin said, keeping up his hurried pace.

"Why don't we ride?" asked Kazareen, his voice cold with desperation.

"Would you have us discard all our provisions? Besides, galloping horses make an easily read trail. Better that we walk. But we should leave Gueren behind us, and quickly!"

Suddenly, it struck Kazareen odd that the others were showing such fear at the name of Gueren. They had been sent away when Arpento had told him the names of the Necromancers. He puzzled on it for a while as they hurried away north, then, like a flash, he remembered. It was Gueren who had slain Leyrea's father and brother. Of course!

After pressing through the wide barrens for more than an hour, Florin at last allowed them a rest. Kazareen was exhausted from their great pace, but he was still coursing with adrenaline from the thought of Gueren nipping at their heels.

"Are we nearing your home? It's getting late," said Leyrea.

Kazareen looked up and saw that the light was indeed growing dim.

"We still have a few hours before us. But Kazareen was looking a little flushed and I could use a rest myself. We just needed to get off the road. If Gueren is based out of Delasur now, there's no telling how many patrols are out," said Florin.

"It would seem luck has favored us once again," added Leyrea.

"Dumb luck is more like it," said Florin, with a sarcastic grin. "I don't suppose they would expect a pair of fugitives to show such hubris, walking right into town as we did. But we had to cross the river. And trying to bypass the town would have been very unwise. Surely, we would have been spied by their lookouts. Only a fugitive would bypass a town; innocent travelers seek them out."

Solia stepped into the constabulary and gently closed the door behind her. "What can I do for you?" asked one of the guards.

"I would speak with Cathio."

The guard turned and knocked lightly on the door behind him.

"What is it?" came a voice from behind the door.

"Solia is here to see you."

After a short pause, "Send her in."

Solia appeared in the doorway. Cathio, the tall, strapping Captain of the Town Guard sat behind a humble wooden desk, littered with maps and letters. He stood as she entered. "What is it? I've a great deal to see to just now."

Solia closed the door behind her. "As usual, no time for an old woman. Why should I expect anything different?"

Cathio seated himself, and tried to hide the scowl that had suddenly appeared on his face. "What is it?"

"He's returned."

"Who's returned?" he said, turning his attention back to the maps.

Solia waited patiently until Cathio looked up before she answered him; she would have his full attention. "Florin, the hunter."

Cathio's eyes flashed.

"He says he escaped from prison and that he is now a wanted man. I thought you would want to know."

His face flushed a deep crimson. "And where is he now?"

"Said he was heading to his old home again. Tis some twenty miles northeast—"

"Yes, I know where it lies, we have it under watch," he said cutting her off.

Solia suddenly looked much older as the blood drained from her face. "Watched? Then you—and the general—knew?"

"The General had his suspicions. Was there a boy...or anyone else with him?" Cathio asked, leaning forward expectantly.

"No. He was alone when he came into the bakery. But when he told me where he was heading, he said *we*."

Cathio stood up straight for a moment, turned and grabbed his cloak and helmet and strode to the door, a determined look etched upon his face.

"I am coming with you, Cathio," said Solia. "and I *will* have my way in this."

Cathio caught and held her eye, but made no protest.

The forest was black as pitch; still, it was little hindrance to Florin. He knew these stretches of the forest too well. Little had changed in the fourteen years since last he walked the paths near his home. And they were close now.

The Heart of the Graystone

Kazareen reckoned the time as an hour or two past midnight. He'd grown footsore on their hasty flight and longed for rest and some peaceful sleep. But they were too close to shelter to stop now. According to Florin, only a mile or two more. Kazareen just hoped the house still stood.

"My home lies just over this hill," said Florin. Kazareen could hear the near-giddiness in his voice. He hadn't known Florin long, but it was the first time he'd seen him like this.

The party crested the small ridge and Florin halted them with a raised hand. It should have been too dark to see his gesture, but off in the distance a healthy fire illuminated the trees around his old home and Florin's figure was cast into silhouette.

Florin turned and whispered, "Lead the horses back down the ridge, while I take a closer look."

Both Kazareen and Leyrea seemed about to protest, but Florin would have none of it. "Heed me. I won't take any action, I just want to see what we're up against."

Kazareen and Leyrea turned and led the horses back below the crest of the ridge and waited impatiently for Florin to return.

Florin fell to his knees and crept slowly, quietly toward the fire. They had left the barrens behind them and the underbrush of the younger edges of the forest hid him well. His breathing seemed too loud to his own ears, and he held his breath as he drew within a few yards of the fire. He peered around the trunk of a wide pine and saw a single figure standing nearby.

He smiled and rested his cheek in the cool grass.

Solia seemed not to be touching the ground at all, but hovering weightlessly amid the golden embers and dancing flames. Florin marveled at this vision of her, clad in a white dressing gown of the most delicate finery, her hands extending, drawing in warmth, an inner light surrounding her, embarrassing the pitiful effort of the fire to outshine her. The aging of her face over the long years of their separation had melted away, and before him now stood the purest vision of Solia as he remembered her: young, beautiful, full of life, glowing with a ethereal light impossible to describe to any who could not see it for themselves. A gentle and placid smile caressed her face like the loving hand of a benevolent goddess, wrapped in a complete and private reverie.

His only love had come. And Florin felt young again. So young.

He wanted to hold on to this moment forever, lock it in his heart, and relive it every idle moment of his life. He closed his eyes and burned the image into his mind. Then, from the darkness behind him, came the distant sound of a horse neighing, and he opened his eyes.

Solia had heard it too, and she walked toward the commotion, her eyes attentively searching the night.

The moment was over, but Florin had imprisoned the vision of Solia in his memory and for the rest of his days, it would not escape him whenever he closed his eyes and thought of her. Now he could see that her clothes were plain and dark, her face lined with age once more.

Then she saw him. "For goodness sake! What are you doing hiding down there?"

Without a word, Florin rose and came to her. He took her in his arms, and she buried her head in his breast. He held her close, taking in her warmth and her smell. And for a moment, he felt dizzy.

"Look at me," he said, regaining himself.

Their eyes met. But she could not bear his gaze for long.

"What is it?" he asked.

While in his embrace, she'd gently laid hold of his sword with both hands. Suddenly, she tore it from his scabbard and tossed it over the fire behind her.

"Solia?" Florin's eyes were both questioning and piercing.

"Don't move!" came a voice from behind him. "We have you in our sights."

Two figures emerged slowly from the shadows behind Solia. Archers bearing the royal livery stepped into the light. Their bows were bent and fixed squarely on Florin's chest.

How could she have betrayed him? His heart was breaking and he couldn't bear to look at Solia any longer, so he turned to see to whom the commanding voice belonged. A tall figure strode out of the shadows, flanked by two more soldiers, their swords drawn and at the ready. The captain had drawn a long poniard, but kept it lowered. As he approached, he searched Florin's face for long moments before he spoke.

Florin returned his gaze without flinching. There was something familiar about his face. Had they met before?

"Bring the others!" the captain shouted over his shoulder.

Four more soldiers led Leyrea and Kazareen from the shadows, already bound and gagged. Florin's heart continued to sink.

"Bear you any more arms?" the captain asked.

"None," he replied.

The captain's eyes narrowed. "Do not forget—my archers have you in their sights," he said, sheathing his weapon.

The captain approached Florin cautiously and searched him for a hidden dagger or blade. Finding none, he stood up straight and met Florin's gaze from mere inches. Finally, seemingly satisfied that Florin

The Heart of the Graystone

would make no trouble, he turned to the near-ruined shack Florin had once called home and ordered the captives brought inside.

Gueren paced the swollen floorboards of the captain's quarters. As had become his custom wherever he traveled, he commandeered the ranking soldier's billet, for it was usually the most comfortable. Cathio's was no exception, but hardly the type of luxury he'd become accustomed to in the major cities of Pendoria.

He loathed this place, with its muddy streets and thick, mossy stench, but that was not what had kept him up well into the night—it was the thought that the captain might, this very second, be taking hold of the fugitives he'd chased half way across Pendoria. He'd wanted to savor that moment for himself, and the jealousy rose within him like a wretch of burning bile.

There was little cause not to trust Cathio in this errand. Still, he was uncomfortable with the thought of these Easterners executing his plans without his guidance. Gueren was well aware that Geraldi's influence over the peasants was stronger in the west, where the heirs of the House of Phenoa had long ruled, but here in Delasur, the people had an independent and stubborn streak, as they had once been under the protection of the House of Orgul. Old allegiances died hard, and only a single decade had passed since Gueren had personally overseen the slaughter of the Counsel of Patris.

Knowing their nature, and wishing to instill the fear of the his wrath into the hearts of these peasants, he'd ordered the execution of the first two peasants he'd laid eyes on the day he'd entered Delasur. He would have savored doing the deed himself, but it was more important that he make his presence felt in Delasur—not just for the townspeople—but to test the measure of the allegiance of the royal guard here as well. While they seemed hesitant at first, they performed his bidding dutifully when he drew Morta from his hip.

It had been Gueren's idea alone to revisit the Seer. He was never fully trusting of his brother's intentions, despite his own willingness to capitulate the throne of Farak to Alerien. But as his brother grew stronger in the practice of the darkest arts, Gueren had become wary that his brother might use his powers to control him, influence him in ways he could hardly comprehend. Alerien had always been more interested in his study of books when they were growing up, and his command of magik had grown far stronger than Gueren would ever know. Sure, Gueren could lay a protective ward on himself if he knew he would be going into battle, but this was a mere pittance compared to the vast knowledge Alerien had amassed over the years.

When Gueren was young, he had never foreseen the profit in studying the philosophies, and so focused himself on the arts of war, hardening his heart, in hopes that his bravery might overshadow his brother's wit. Only centuries later, when it was far too late to correct his oversight, had he realized the weakened position he held. But he still held Morta and that he would never relinquish to anyone, especially his brother, for it was the symbol of his ancestor's strength and held a dark power all its own.

His trip to the Seer had not been fruitless. Kazareen de Pendi had visited only two days before. Whither he went, the Seer could not say. While that was welcome news, it was not why he'd sought the Seer's counsel. He was beginning to worry about Alerien almost as much as the boy. But in this, the Seer was of no help. Either he could not pierce the fog of Gueren's future because of his own lack of talent, or Alerien had woven a tapestry of shadow around the Seer's eyes where it concerned Gueren's fate.

When he'd returned to Delasur, just after sunset, he'd gotten word that the captain had taken a sortie of soldiers after the fugitive Florin, who'd been spotted by a local baker, though none could say exactly where they were headed, other than east along the road after leaving town. Gueren wished to follow after them, but he would have to wait until dawn. While the boy in Florin's company did not match the description of this Kazareen de Pendi he sought, it was likely him just the same.

Gueren finally decided there was no bad out to the situation. If the old man had parted ways with the boy, then at least he would have the satisfaction of torturing him for information himself. If the boy seen with him were indeed De Pendi, then he would lay claim to the glory of recapturing him as well.

He looked out the window and considered the stars for just a moment, not noticing the newest dim star rising among the rest, then returned to pacing the creaking floor until dawn.

Cathio had ordered the prisoner's gags removed, though their hands were still bound behind them. Kazareen, Florin and Leyrea were seated next to one another on a dusty wooden bench behind the rotting remains of a pine table Florin had fashioned with his own hands long ago. A small lantern burned nearby, showing the state of ruin into which Florin's home had fallen over the years. Cobwebs as thick as burlap covered everything. Only the table and bench had been hastily cleared of the thick spider netting.

The Heart of the Graystone

As the captain ordered the guards out, Solia slipped in silently and stood behind him, all the while staring at Florin. He could not return her gaze.

Cathio stepped forward. "Florin of Bethë Khür, I presume. I am Cathio, Captain of the Royal Guard at Delasur, and *you* are a fugitive from the king's justice."

Florin mouth fell open. "Cathio?" The captain nodded slowly. "Are you—?"

"Silence!" He thrust the point of his dagger into the table and stared Florin down, but Florin turned his gaze to Solia.

Cathio turned to Kazareen. "You, young man, present a bit of problem. If I were to venture a guess, I would say you are Kazareen de Pendi of Feria, also a fugitive, though you do not match the description brought to us by General Gueren. But if I were to lay a wager, I would bet that you are him."

Kazareen said nothing.

Cathio turned to Leyrea. "And you, m'lady are a complete mystery. By what name are ye called?"

Leyrea said nothing, but her eyes held daggers of their own for Cathio.

"Come now, m'lady. Show some decorum. I have introduced myself politely, and if you are civilized, then you might reciprocate," he said, smugly flicking his fingernails.

"Cathio, please. Just—" pleaded Solia.

Cathio held up his hand to her. "I am coming to it, but introductions are in order." He kept his eyes on Leyrea. "Your name matters not," he said, now turning his back on the prisoners, "for you shall all meet the same fate."

Seizing the opportunity, Leyrea burst upward with all her strength, her hips heaving the table forward. In an instant, Cathio turned and slammed himself against the table. Leyrea was thrust back onto the bench and she cried out as her head slammed into the wall behind her.

"Patience," he said softly, "we'll be out of here soon enough."

"Cathio! Stop it! Tell them now," Solia said, stepping forward and taking his arm.

Cathio looked into Solia's eyes and gently cupped her cheek. "Very well. Tis enough of this game. But they should know, a taste at least, of what might have been. Gueren would have been less kind."

Cathio looked around and pulled a stool free from the grip of the murky cobwebs and seated himself in front of the prisoners. "I am Cathio, Captain of the Guard of Delasur...Cathio, son of Florin and Solia of Bethë Khür."

Solia's trembling hand gripped Cathio's shoulder. Her eyes glistened in the dim light as she pleaded silently with Florin to believe that this was indeed their son. The ethereal light that had surrounded her as she stood by the fire returned to Florin's eyes and he knew this was no ruse.

Kazareen and Leyrea looked to Florin, their mouths agape, but he said nothing.

"The General seeks your capture fervently. Especially you, young man, if you are who I think you are." Cathio said. "But as I said, your fates shall all be the same. It is my intention to see you all safely away this night—as far from this place as we can manage before the coming of dawn. Gueren will have no prize here. I shall lead you to a place where he shall ne'er find you, while men of good faith still abide."

Kazareen's heart was still pounding hard, but beginning to slow with the captain's reassurances. He looked to Florin again, who seemed unable to speak; he only stared at Solia. Kazareen looked to Cathio. "Why? Why would you do this?"

"You are Kazareen de Pendi?" Cathio seemed intent on knowing.

Kazareen still wasn't fully sure if he should trust this man, but he was already captured, so how could he possibly make things worse? "I am," he said.

"Good. And m'lady?" Cathio said, looking to Leyrea.

"I am Leyrea of Khürasé," she said sharply. "Even if you are Florin's son, why should we trust you?"

"I don't see that you have any choice in the matter. If I were loyal to the general, I would simply take you to him now. And as I am unwilling to do so, then I would say your situation is infinitely improved," he said, with a mischievous grin.

Leyrea showed him a face of granite.

"But why would you do this? Because of Florin?" Kazareen asked.

Cathio's face became suddenly sullen. "Blood is thicker than water, they say. It is." Cathio took Solia's hand from his shoulder.

"It is," he repeated, feeling the warmth of his mother's hand in his own. "And though I remember little of my sire, for his absence has been long, I see now that he did not abandon us, as I long believed. And I would turn from my long held bitterness and know my father once more."

"But tis not the reason I turn now from the king's service. Long have rumors of his foul nature been whispered among the peoples of the East—and in this, Delasur is no exception. For many years, I chose to ignore their grumbling for the greater good—but no more. I have seen with my own eyes the folly of the king. For Gueren slays at will, and his

The Heart of the Graystone

foul will corrupts others to do likewise. Perhaps you saw some of his handiwork at the gate, yes?"

Kazareen and Florin nodded. Leyrea did not stir.

"So now I deem these whispers to be true—in part, at least. Whether the king has so little vision as to see Gueren for what he is, or whether he has intentionally chosen this...madman, this...monster as his General of the Armies of Pendoria, then I call him my king no more. And my host with me. We all swore to serve the king, yes. But for centuries, the king's charge has been to serve and protect the people of Pendoria. In this he has failed utterly, so we reckon ourselves released from the bond of servitude we swore."

Cathio seemed to grow taller as he spoke, and hearing the conviction in his voice, Kazareen had little doubt he spoke from the heart.

"Then why this ruse? What purpose is served by binding us, if you seek to protect us?" asked Leyrea, still in doubt. "Release us!"

"Patience, m'lady—all in good time. I did not rise to my station by accident, I assure you. I have the lives of the men with me under my protection as well. Tell me, would you have laid down your arms to treat with the royal guard? Or would you have fled?" Cathio smiled again. "I think not. Seeing the fire in your eyes, I believe you would have fought— and fought bravely, no doubt. Perhaps some of my men might, this very moment, be lying dead in the cold grass. Or myself...or my mother perhaps. I could not allow that. Not given my intentions...and my responsibilities, which I take most seriously."

Finally, Leyrea's fiery will began to recede. "Then free us. My hands have gone numb."

"On one condition. I must have your word of honor, from each of you, that you will tell no one what has transpired here tonight, nor reveal to anyone, without my consent, the former posts my men and I held. For as you are, we have now become."

"And what is that?" asked Kazareen.

"Fugitives, of course."

There was no more need for discussion. Once Florin had given his word, Kazareen and Leyrea too gave Cathio their oaths of silence. Cathio cut their bonds, purposely saving Leyrea for last. She massaged the deep, red imprints on her wrists, flexed her fingers sorely and waited for the tingling in her hands to dissipate, all the while still glaring at Cathio.

Florin walked over to Solia. "He has grown strong. I did not recognize him. But I see we have much more to talk about," he said, barely above his breath.

She nodded gently. "Aye, we do."

He stood in front of her, as tall and proud as ever he had, but his eyes narrowed to slits. "You lied to me. And you gave me your word."

"Nay, I kept my word. I told no guardsman...I told our son," she said.

Florin's eyes searched her face for a moment. Then he nodded slightly and closed his eyes.

Into the East

As the first hints of dawn began to glimmer in the east, Gueren had his party assembled at the gate, ready to make for the old hunter's home. He sat astride his tall black steed, its nostrils blowing heavy jets of steam into the cool morning air. Despite his façade of dark confidence, he had an inkling that things had not gone well in the night. If the fugitives had been captured, then surely the party would have returned to Delasur by now. Perhaps they had simply eluded his grasp once again, but he had a deeper suspicion: that Cathio had betrayed him. It was no mystical foresight that brought this thought to him, but a reasonable deduction. The boy had eluded him far too long—he *had* to be receiving aid. From whom, he could not say, but now he saw that it was quite possible all the East would soon turn against him.

Gueren had warned his brother that raw military power was the only real way to ensure the king's rule over Pendoria. Alerien had seen it differently, and as usual, his counsel held sway. The system of appointing the king's most loyal lackeys as the magistrates and governors over the cities and regions of Pendoria was built on a foundation of greed. Their loyalty had been bought for a price, and Gueren feared it could be sold just as easily. Already, the creeping strands of rebellion were taking hold—and at the worst possible time.

If there had been a better method of concentrating the wealth of Graystones into their hands, then Gueren had not been able to provide it. The magistrates were ordered to hoard every gem that came their way. They in turn passed them on to the governors for cascading measures of gold and silver, and then finally to the royal treasury were they delivered. A bureaucracy was a flimsy system for controlling the people, but it was a chance Alerien was willing to take.

"We need only bide our time, until the flow of Graystones into the treasury wanes to a trickle," Alerien had pointed out. "A decade or two at the most, and we shall have enough. Let these peasants do as they will; the internal strife of Pendoria does not concern us, as long as the flow of Graystones continues. When our stores grow large enough, then no one, not even the king and all his armies, will be able to stop us."

His brother's words had placated him then, but that was long before the Seer had spoken the prophecies of this boy. A boy who had it in his power—though it was not known how—to bring all their plans down, destroy them even, if he were not dealt with. How exactly the boy might accomplish this feat, the Seer could not, or would not, say.

The treasury was nearly full now, and their moment of triumph was drawing near, as long as they could stop the boy from bringing all their plans crashing down. It was up to Gueren to see to it, and so far, his efforts had been in vain. Not even the Seer had been able to aid him much in this quest. When he told Gueren of Kazareen's visit, Gueren became excited and impatient with the fat and gluttonous Seer and demanded to know only where he went. The pride of the young Arpento was bruised, so he held back the story of Kazareen's Graystone in defiance of the general. Gueren rushed back to Delasur in his haste none the wiser.

Gueren drew Morta from its sheath and urged the company of soldiers forward through the east gate. The trackers rode out ahead, searching the ground for signs of the fugitive's trail in the morning light.

As their pursuers were passing through the gates of Delasur, the party of fugitives, now a dozen strong, had already left the great forest of Bethë Khür in their wake. The going had been tediously slow at first, for the paths were narrow and thick underbrush enveloped the younger edges of the forest, but now they rode hard over open ground.

The sun shone brightly on the wide expanses and endless orchards of the east, and Kazareen struggled to maintain his grip on the mighty Wingfoot. The long strides of the gray stallion outpaced all, even the soldier's seasoned warhorses. Wingfoot flew over the open stretches with wild abandon, in what seemed—if Kazareen could have read his mount's mind—the first time in ages. Time after time, Kazareen had to reign Wingfoot in, to keep him from leaving the others far behind. His coat took on a brilliant, silvery sheen as the sweat of his efforts glistened in the late morning sun.

They'd come to a small riverbank, so Kazareen stopped so the others could make up the distance. He turned back to see Cathio approaching. The others were not far behind, except for Florin, who was little more than a dot in the distance, Vala being far too old to keep up. Solia rode slowly beside her love.

"Tis one fast mount you have, Kazareen. Ne'er have I seen its match! Does the beast have a name?" asked Cathio, trampling to a halt.

"He is called Wingfoot. Though I have taken to calling him Wings," Kazareen replied, patting the beast soundly on the neck.

"Aptly named," Cathio said. His expression turned suddenly. "Not the same Wingfoot reported stolen from Feria's magistrate?"

Kazareen blushed and said nothing.

"Ah well, such are the ways of rebellion," said Cathio with a nod and a grin.

The Heart of the Graystone

"I am no rebel," he said sharply. "And I want no part in your rebellion, if that is what you seek. I was wrongly imprisoned, as was Florin, and so we managed to escape. So what? It does not mean we seek a path that leads to open war with the crown." He was surprised he had spoken the words so boldly, so defiantly. Kazareen blinked and looked away.

"As you see fit," Cathio replied. He did not sound surprised.

Leyrea and the rest of the soldiers began to arrive one by one. Little Sirius had proven himself quite fleet of foot, especially compared to the larger warhorses on which the soldiers rode. Solia and Florin were still nearly a mile behind.

"We rest here. Heragis, Anton, see that the horses are watered." Cathio still seemed to believe these men were under his charge. Kazareen realized that at least technically they were not. But their personal allegiance to their captain still held them in obedience.

"The rest of you may refresh yourself at your leisure, but I want you posted there and there," he said pointing. "And keep a sharp eye to the flanks."

Leyrea bounded from Sirius, still out of breath. An expression of annoyance and distrust was firmly entrenched on her face. She strode immediately up to Cathio. "When do you plan on telling us where you're leading us?"

Her words could not rattle him. "It is said that patience is a virtue, one I see you are not blessed with," he said, keeping his back to her. He removed his water skins from his saddlebags and turned to the stream to fill them. But then he stopped and faced her. "Why is it you trust me so little? What have I done to be plied so? Other than rescue you and your friends from Gueren's trap, I mean."

His sarcasm cut deeply, and Leyrea turned away. She began walking back to Sirius, then collapsed and was suddenly ill.

Cathio looked about ready to go to her aid; instead he turned and went down to the stream.

Kazareen went to her and held her forehead as she wretched, just as Murro had done for him so many times. "Are you alright?"

Leyrea rose to her knees. Her face was flushed and beads of sweat covered her face. Whether it was from the hard ride, the onset of illness or simply her dislike of Cathio, Kazareen couldn't say for sure, but he supposed it was the latter.

"I'll be fine. Thank you," she said, drawing a kerchief from her pocket and wiping her face.

Kazareen tried to remove any accusatory tone from his voice. "Why do you dislike him so much? Florin vouches for Solia, and she for Cathio. I believe he is trustworthy."

"It's the way he looks at me. I don't like it. He's an arrogant man, too accustomed to giving orders and having his own way. Well, not with me!" Her anger was growing again, and so she struggled to her feet and left Kazareen kneeling alone in the dirt.

Then it began to dawn on him. Her distrust, her dislike—perhaps even her hatred of Cathio was not brought about by his manner alone. It must be the uniform, the armor, and most likely of all, the royal livery that bedeviled her. It was the same livery worn by the men who'd killed her father and brother. The same livery worn by the men who'd stormed her house on the prairie, stolen her supplies and...done what?

Kazareen had only the most vague notion about how a man might dishonor or violate a woman. Murro had never gotten around to speaking to him on the subject. His fourteenth birthday had been far too extraordinary a day for Murro to burden himself with that age-old custom.

But thinking now about the tawdry words the soldier had shouted that day when they'd returned to Leyrea's dugout, Kazareen began to believe that perhaps that was exactly what they'd done on their previous visit.

From his knees, Kazareen watched as Leyrea fetched her water skins from Sirius, and his heart began sinking slightly, then aching for her, but he said no more on the subject.

They rode on for three more days, paralleling the Great Road's northeasterly path. Wherever possible, they kept to the long rocky stretches that littered this land in order to hide their trail. Cathio regularly sent two of the soldiers off to scout the road. If Gueren had indeed followed after, their efforts at stealth had been successful, for they saw no sign of pursuit.

Leyrea kept her distance from the soldiers, especially Cathio. She seemed sullen and withdrawn. She spoke little to anyone.

Florin and Solia rode side-by-side, and when they stopped to rest or water the horses, they separated themselves from the others and spoke privately in hushed voices, but with hearts that seemed to grow closer with each passing day. Cathio seemed too intent on his responsibilities to join them often, though from time to time they could all be found huddled together. Slowly, the bonds of family were growing back.

The rest of the soldiers mainly kept to themselves. It seemed to Kazareen they had a strong tie between them, as they often made coarse

The Heart of the Graystone

jests to one another and yet laughed heartily after. Kazareen had noticed this strange camaraderie among the soldiers of Feria, and he wondered what happened to a man when he came under arms to form such a curiously strong connection with others of his ilk. It would remain a mystery to him forever.

Strangely enough, the few conversations he had on their journey were with Cathio. Kazareen began to see he was much like Florin in many ways: his manner of speech, his dogged stubbornness. Kazareen tried many times, as skillfully as he might, to wheedle some information out of him about their final destination. But Cathio would say nothing, no matter how subtly Kazareen disguised his query. Truly, this was the son of Florin.

Many times, Kazareen felt the urge to ask Cathio more about his family, but something held his tongue in check. Asking something so personal of a man he barely knew seemed out of place. In this way, at least, something of Murro lived on in Kazareen, and musing on this fact, he was both slightly saddened and gently warmed.

Since they'd left the fields and orchards around Bethë Khür behind them, the land had been rising and falling in steadily more rugged and steep terrain. When they turned north, away from the more easterly path of the Great Road, long valleys began stretching out before them, each one marking the passing of another tiring trek and a full day's ride. The jagged and craggy escarpments they traversed grew ever larger and more numerous, each one dwarfing the one that came before.

Low sage and scrub oak grew unchecked, hugging the contours of the land to escape the persistent winds that blew in these high steppes. Huge patches of brambles and thorn bushes covered endless acres, slowing their progress.

On the morning of the fourth day of their flight, Kazareen was treated to one of the most awe-inspiring vistas he ever beheld. As they crested the lip of the high plateau that had been looming before them for most of the previous day, Kazareen saw mountains, true mountains, for the first time. The dizzying heights of Atan Beruth stood proudly before him like gray sentinels, extending upward, ever upward, each row in the distance higher than the one at its feet, the loftiest scraping the very edge of the sky itself. The jagged summits were draped in blue-white capes of ice and snow. From horizon to horizon these hulking masses stretched in an endless and unbroken chain, until they faded into the misty edges of the world.

Kazareen stopped and tried to take it all in. He was completely unaware that the others had halted as well.

"There. That is our destination," said Cathio suddenly, breaking the moment.

Kazareen saw him pointing, not to the mountain peaks that had so distracted him, but due north, down into the last long valley that lay in the shadows of Atan Beruth.

"Finally," whispered Leyrea, as sarcastically and as quietly as she was able. Kazareen found himself wanting to chuckle suddenly, but held it back as he rode up next to Cathio.

"Where exactly?" he asked, straining his eyes. He saw nothing but more empty land.

"Look closely," said Cathio, pointing again. "Do you see that ridge, there?"

"Yes."

"Follow its edge down into the valley. There, at its end, along those cliffs. Do you see?"

Kazareen shaded his eyes from the morning sun that had just broken over the top of the mountains. He saw a small gray speck in the distance, slightly lighter than its surroundings. "What is it?"

"Tis the sanctuary we seek. That...is the seat of the Great House of Pendi," Cathio said proudly. "And there we may find sanctuary and rest."

Leyrea could not contain herself. "This is where you have dragged us? Have you no sense at all? The Great Houses fell over a decade ago." She could not hide her disdain for Cathio, or the feeling that she'd been duped after all. "That's it! I'm sorry, Kazareen. But this is where I must part ways—"

"Tis what you think?" Cathio interrupted. "That I would drag you here for no purpose? As Captain of Delasur, I have heard many rumors and seen many reports. There are intelligences I've had access to, far beyond the means of common men." He sighed and checked his frustration. "You have come all this way. Will you not at least see for yourself if I speak the truth or nay?"

She said nothing.

"Or are you afraid, for some reason, that I am right in this?" added Cathio.

She looked to Kazareen.

He knew what she was thinking. "Come and see," Kazareen said. "If you still wish to leave after, I won't try to stop you. You owe me nothing."

Leyrea's face was red, though whether it was from anger, embarrassment, or the long days of riding in the sun, Kazareen could not

The Heart of the Graystone

tell. She swallowed hard and nodded. "Very well. But only for you, Kazareen."

Cathio shook his head.

Kazareen soon lost sight of their destination as they snaked their way down the long slope of the valley, for in this place, the fir trees grew tall and proud, if somewhat sparsely. It wasn't long before he began to feel the cool, stinging winds that swept down from the mountains. The wind whispered eerily as it blew through the trees, and its cold bite sent shivers down his spine. Kazareen saw that gooseflesh began to appear on his bare arms. The wind flowed easily through the light shirt he wore, so he went through his saddlebags and put on his leather jerkin. Surveying the snow-capped mountains whenever they appeared between the gaps in the firs, he imagined that summer must come to an early end here.

For the first time in ages, he tried to think of the date. How long had he been running? Could summer really be coming to an end already? Or was this bitter wind normal in the highlands, even this time of year? It felt like forever, a lifetime's gathering of strange events, since he'd found the Graystone. He'd become so consumed with traveling, hiding from soldiers, seeking Arpento, so many strange and confounding things, that time no longer seemed to have much meaning. He couldn't even remember the last time he'd bathed.

For hours they rode down the gentle slope into the midst of the valley, which seemed much larger than it had from the top of the plateau. When they finally came upon a well-worn trail, something less than a road really, Kazareen noticed they were now climbing upward again and he became anxious.

"Are we almost there?" he asked Cathio.

"It shan't be much longer, an hour or so."

Cathio had no more than spoken when three men, bearing an unfamiliar livery on their helmets, rode out from the trees onto the road before them. The livery looked like a tangled knot or a wreath of thorny brambles. Each of them wore a fine purple sash across his chest, the only bright color over otherwise ordinary-looking coats of mail. And they bore great spears, the like of which Kazareen had never before seen. They were fashioned entirely from a single piece of forged metal, as bright as polished silver, and twice as long as a man. Much to Kazareen's relief, they stopped and lowered the points of their spears to the ground, in an act of obvious deference and salute.

"Greetings," said the hardiest and darkest of the three men. His black, bushy beard and long flowing moustache hid his mouth, but his voice boomed. "What aid might we render to the king's servants?" he said, bowing his head to Cathio.

"We wish merely to pass," Cathio replied cautiously, as he eyed the devices on their helmets. But the men did not yield the trail.

"If you seek Beruthia, then you are sorely lost and on the wrong road. It lies to the southeast. Only three days ride from the fork of—"

"We are not lost, friend. We seek the House of Pendi."

The man laughed heartily. "It may be news to you, *friend*, but the House of Pendi fell long ago—"

A determined look appeared in Cathio's eyes. "And it has risen once again, or you would not be wearing its devices and colors. We seek to—"

Cathio stopped short. The man had raised his spear and planted its butt to the ground. When he did this, twenty or more archers, each bearing purple ascots, suddenly materialized from out of the wood. Their party was suddenly surrounded and outnumbered. Kazareen's heart began pounding like the drums of war. All he could think to do was to grasp the Graystone in his pocket.

"Foolish one. You should have taken my advice and made for Beruthia. Instead, here you shall die, your bodies left for wolves and carrion. And your mother shall learn not the manner of your passing, but be left only with lingering doubts in her dark hours of grief. Think you we so foolish as to allow the passage of the king's men? The livery you bear has become an anathema to all we hold dear. Besides, it would take more than your pathetic little band to bring down our Great House once more."

"We do not seek the fall of the House of Pendi, we come to treat with the Patri of Pendi for protection and sanctuary," said Cathio quickly. As Cathio drew his sword, Kazareen heard bowstring bending all around him, then Cathio let if fall to the ground. "We are no longer in the king's service, despite our appearance. Will you not bring us before your Patri? I bear him a gift."

The look of surprise that had appeared on the great man's face vanished when Cathio dropped the sword. "The Patri has no need of gifts! Silver, gold and Graystone mean nothing to him in this hour...only blood." The knight's eyes shrank to slits.

"Tis the very gift I bear. The Patri's own blood." Cathio kept his eyes on the man, this knight of the House of Pendi, but motioned with his left hand for Kazareen to come forward. "I present Kazareen de Pendi of Feria."

The knight stilled his spear and held up his left hand. Kazareen heard the bows go slack all around him, so he gently urged Wingfoot

The Heart of the Graystone

forward until he stood at Cathio's side. The blood rushing through his ears drowned out nearly every sound and he had to strain to hear the words that were spoken.

The knight eyed him carefully, slowly. "Is this true? Tell me of your sire."

Kazareen thought quickly and spoke the first words that came to his mind. If this didn't work, they would be slain here, now, and he knew it well.

"It is true. My name is Kazareen de Pendi and I hail from Feria in the western lands. My father was..."

Who?

"...Murro de Pendi, a blacksmith of some renown in those parts." As Kazareen spoke the words, the Graystone suddenly grew hot in his hand. Instinctively, he let go of it before he was burned.

Kazareen did not see Florin blanching at his lie.

The light of recognition shone in the knight's eyes. "Murro, the blacksmith? Yes, I remember him! A distant cousin he was, but blood of my blood nonetheless. And if memory serves, Murro indeed had a boy named Kazareen, and you would seem to be of the correct age." Then his eyes drew to slits once again. "But I seem to recall that Murro died, along with his family, at the Siege of Beruthia, for after that, he was never heard from again."

"No! We fled the siege when I was but an infant, though my mother died on our journey into the west. My name is Kazareen de Pendi!" Kazareen hated lying, especially when it was mixed with the truth, but what other choice did he have? They would certainly all die if he didn't.

The truth of Kazareen's lineage was unknown to him, and he had lived most of his life under the guise of another lie, that he was Murro's nephew. Yet had the lie not served a purpose? And when the time was right, had the truth not been told to him?

The knight searched Kazareen's face for long moments. On this, all depended.

"Give me your word that you are indeed Kazareen de Pendi, and I shall take you before the Patri. He shall judge further in this matter."

"I give you my word, I am Kazareen de Pendi," he said. In this, at least he did not have to lie.

The knight nodded. "Very well. Lay down your arms, all of you, and dismount." All did as he asked. "Lads, confiscate their weapons and beasts and follow behind!" he shouted to the archers.

The knights regrouped and turned up the path. The extra archers who bore no burden of weapon or horses formed a loose circle around the fugitives. Kazareen stole a few quick glances at them as they walked

167

and noticed that many were indeed merely lads. Most appeared slightly older than him, though not by much. A few were markedly younger. The stocky, dark-haired archer-boy who walked beside him scowled when he caught Kazareen looking at him. "Keep your eyes to the front," he said. Kazareen did as he was told.

After nearly two hours of trudging up the long slope, Kazareen's lungs began straining to find breath; his heart began pounding faster and harder than he'd ever known. The toll of his seemingly endless days of flight seemed now to be sapping his strength in whole.

His knees began to quiver and shake, and at last he fell. His vision shrank and all he saw was a distant light, framed in an ever-shrinking field of black. He could still hear voices, faint and distant, and he had the vague notion someone was speaking to him, but he felt he was no longer within himself, but hiding under the guise of some new identity, some other life than the one he knew. As the light drew to a mere pinpoint, Kazareen thought he heard the great wings of the Dragon beating the air above him, then all went dark.

The House of Pendi

Something cool lay upon on his forehead and he felt a firm yet tender hand warming his own. His stomach ached, his mouth was matted and dry, and his body felt completely drained of blood. It took a great effort to simply open his eyes. He saw Leyrea sitting beside him, holding his left hand. Her face, as full, round and fair as the moon itself, though still smudged with streaks of dust mixed with sweat, seemed sweeter and friendlier than he remembered.

"It's alright. You're alright. Take this," she said, lifting a large clay tankard to his lips.

"What is it?" he asked, but his mouth was so dry and foul, his words came out muffled and distorted.

"Just water. Drink. You'll feel better."

He drank, slowly at first, then after a quick breath, more greedily, until it was emptied. He began to feel better almost instantly.

"What happened?"

"You have mountain sickness. Don't worry. They say it is easily and quickly cured. This will help. Here, take of this what you can." Leyrea handed him a large heel of bread.

The bread was dark and tough, less sweet than the loaves he was accustomed to. Leyrea refilled his tankard from a large pitcher that sat on the table next to her.

As his eyes cleared, he began to notice his surroundings. He was in a small plain room with walls fashioned from large irregular stones of uncut granite, mortared sloppily together, as if laid in great haste. Kazareen saw no window or decoration of any kind, and little in the way of furnishings, only a plain pine table on which sat a lit candle and the pitcher, a single bench on which Leyrea sat, and his armchair.

"Where are we? And where are the others?" he asked between mouthfuls. It seemed the more he ate, the more ravenous he became.

"We are in the Great House of Pendi, of course. If you had lasted another ten minutes on the march, you would have seen it all for yourself. The others are in the main hall. Don't worry. They're fine. We are being treated as guests rather than prisoners. But they still haven't returned our weapons. We've already taken a good meal and some rest." She took the cloth from his forehead and gently wiped the grime from his face. "The Patri awaits you. He said there is no hurry, but to come when you are able." Leyrea smiled at him softly, and as much as from the food and drink, he drew strength from it.

Soon Kazareen had finished the entire loaf of bread and nearly emptied the pitcher. His stomach felt better, if a little bloated, and he was soon anxious to rejoin the others. When he stood, he still felt weak and a little dizzy, but with Leyrea's help and guidance, he was able to walk. They passed a short distance through an arched alcove and into the wide, smoky gulf of a large hall.

Kazareen was first taken aback by the sight of its lofty ceiling, perhaps twenty feet high, suspended by eight gargantuan beams, unpainted and unadorned, that ran down the center of the hall. A great many torches, along with four simple brass braziers standing in each corner, lit the hall with a constantly flickering golden light. Four rows of tables and benches were arranged in parallel fashion down the length of the hall, two on either side of the supporting beams. These tables were much longer, but of the same simple construction as the one in the small anteroom where Leyrea had tended to him.

At the head of the hall another large table of like construction sat perpendicular to the others. On the wall behind it hung the only decoration of any sort Kazareen had yet seen. A great bolt of purple cloth draped the wall entire, and it shimmered like sunlit water. Kazareen had seen a great variety of tapestries and textiles in the markets of Feria, but nothing as exotic and brilliant as the magical luster of that which he now beheld. On either side of the tapestry, four great spears, such as the knights had carried on the road, stood crossed in pairs, held aloft by heavy rectangular stands of brass, fitted firmly to the floor.

At the front of the hall, their companions sat chatting among themselves. Several of the boy archers were also seated at the table next to them, though they did not seem to be in a festive mood. At the head table sat five men. Three of which Kazareen immediately recognized as the knights they'd encountered on the path earlier, despite the fact they had shed their mail coats and helmets. After pausing for a moment, Leyrea led him to the others.

Florin stood when he saw them shuffling slowly toward the front of the hall. "How are you feeling? Better, I hope." He took Kazareen by his free arm.

"I'm still a little weak."

Florin saw Kazareen to the bench and sat next to him, Leyrea seated herself across the table. A hush fell over the room. Kazareen's eyes drifted inevitably to the knights at the head table.

The bearded knight who'd spoken to them on the road stood. "I am glad to see you feeling better, young sir. Marching in the highlands of Locnomina can sap the strength of even the hardiest of men, if they are unaccustomed."

The Heart of the Graystone

He motioned to a servant who'd been standing in the wings. The servant brought forth a simple silver goblet and placed it on the table in front of Kazareen. It contained a small amount of a dark liquid he didn't recognize.

"Drink. It will return you your strength faster than mere bread and water, but is too strong to be taken on an empty stomach," said the knight.

Kazareen lifted the glass, but hesitated.

"Go ahead, Kazareen. It tastes much better than it looks. We have already partaken," Florin whispered.

Kazareen put the goblet to his lips. He'd only hesitated because his stomach felt on the verge of bursting. When he took a drink, he found that the liquid was cool and sweet like cider, but heavily spiced with rose hips, sage and mint, along with a bevy of other delightful flavorings that he couldn't quite place. It had a thick, viscous consistency and it slid down his throat almost without effort. His eyes widened with surprise, and he greedily emptied the goblet.

A couple of the young archers snickered at the expression on his face.

Kazareen didn't mind though, he felt a tingling energy coursing through him immediately, from his scalp to his toenails. He imagined it was something akin to lightning in a bottle, because the quivering weakness left his body immediately and the fog lifted from his eyes.

Kazareen gave the cup back to the servant and nodded politely.

The knight cleared his throat. "Decorum demands that introductions are in order—again. To my left, my nephews: Dregis and Demu." They rose and nodded as they were introduced. "To my right, my sons: Romath and Benedicio, my first born." They also rose duly. "And I am Raízo, Patri of the Great House of Pendi, reborn in Locnomina."

"Hail!" shouted all, save Kazareen. Their voices shook the hall and reverberated like thunder.

"Hail," Kazareen added, sheepishly. Raízo nodded to Kazareen in gratitude.

Kazareen imagined a smile under the Patri's bushy beard.

"Now that that is taken care of, once again, we have more important things to discuss. I trust you are feeling better by now, young sir?" Raízo and his kin reseated themselves.

"I am. If I might ask, what was in that— "

"Do not ask," he replied quickly, "you may not want to know." Many of the archers and knights laughed openly now. "Besides, it is an old recipe and we hold it close. We call it *tomporian*, but we are not here to discuss recipes for ancient elixirs."

"Your companions and I have had ample time for discussion as you made your recovery, and I have already learned much of your situation and intentions. Captain Cathio has provided this House with a good deal of information we shall find of great value in the coming months. In addition, both he and his small host have offered to pledge their service to this House, and I am taking their offer under consideration. Your friends, however, have declined to treat with me until you graced us with your presence. This is queer to us, considering your youth. Do you lead?"

"No. But we have shared many hardships together. And I count them as my friends." Kazareen prayed the subject of the Graystone would not come up.

"Very well. But you are among them now, so tell me, young sir, what is it you seek?"

Kazareen could answer that question in so many different ways that he was momentarily befuddled. What was it he sought? An end to the Graystone? A place to call home again? An allegiance with a Great House, which seemed as bent on rebellion as Cathio and his men? Or was it rest? Simple rest and a respite from his seemingly endless flight?

Kazareen stood. Unconsciously, his hand had slipped into his pocket again and grasped the smooth form of the Graystone. He felt a great weight lifting, and his words came to him without effort or thought.

"Rest...and an end to flight. I was wrongly arrested and Murro gave his life to free me. Since the day Florin and I found freedom again, we have traveled far, enduring long days of toil, illness, and many sleepless nights, seeking shelter from the long arm of the king. But we knew naught of the rebirth of this Great House. It is Cathio who coaxed us here with his hints of sanctuary. Though I see now it was not his to provide."

Cathio shifted uncomfortably in his seat.

"And those of you who traveled with him, is it sanctuary you seek as well?" Raízo asked. "Speak your intent."

Florin answered "Aye," and Solia, still clutching Florin's hand, spoke the same.

Raízo's gaze fell on Leyrea. She seemed reluctant to answer for a moment. Finally she looked at Kazareen and said softly. "I do."

"I see," he said. Then his gaze fell back on Kazareen. "Come here, Kazareen. Stand before me and allow me a closer look."

Kazareen stood before the grizzled Patri and met his gaze without fear. Raízo searched the line of his face, attending to each subtle curve,

The Heart of the Graystone

the bend of his nose, the length of his brow, the breadth of his jowl. But in the end, he was captured by the gleam in the young man's eyes. And for a fleeting moment, Raízo witnessed in those dark pools a miniscule but brilliant flash, a stiletto twinkling of bright silver light that shook him to the core. He wavered slightly, but quickly steadied himself. Only his eldest son, Benedicio, took note of it.

Kazareen had not yet released the Graystone from his grasp. For some reason, he knew he should not. Not yet.

"We shall hold counsel on your requests." Raízo turned and left the hall and his kin followed after him. The young archers remained in the hall, and a few of them rose and stood at the exits.

Kazareen sat back down and Florin put his hand on Kazareen's knee. "We need to talk," he said as quietly as he could.

"Later," Kazareen replied, knowing that Florin would be uncomfortable with his false claim that Murro was his father.

They sat in the hall for over an hour, awaiting the pronouncement of their fate. Cathio's men chatted quietly. They seemed confident their service would be accepted. The others spoke little, as their own fate seemed somewhat more in doubt. What good would two women, an old man, and a young lad be to these proud men, who seemed intent on raising arms against the king? They could not tell.

They floundered in their doubts until the Knights of Pendi returned. "Rise for the Patri," said one of the archers. All obeyed as a hush fell on the wide hall once again.

Raízo looked to Cathio. "Captain Cathio, we have great need of men at arms. Gladly, do we accept your offer of aid. By your own words, your allegiance lies in Locnomina now, and so here you shall serve." Someone exhaled softly in relief.

"Kazareen de Pendi, your fate we debated long. And though some still have their doubts, I accept you. I have seen in your...face...the likeness of nobility, so I offer you the shelter and protection of this House." One of the knights behind him grunted slightly, though which one, Kazareen could not tell. Raízo's voice raised a notch to quiet the sound of dissent behind him, "And as we share the same blood, you have a rightful claim to it! You are welcome here."

"As for the others, we have little to spare for idle hands and hungry mouths. So tell me, each of you, what service can you provide this House, in exchange for our protection?"

Solia spoke quickly. "I am a baker and cook," she said. "I have done so for thirty years in Delasur. I will work in your kitchens as tirelessly as I did in my own."

Raízo nodded, but said nothing.

Florin thought for a moment. "I am skilled in the arts of hunting and tracking. I will provide food for your board, and teach others of all I know."

Raízo nodded again, and turned to Leyrea.

Leyrea hung her head, searching the floorboards quietly.

"Well, young lady, what talents do you bring to this House?" asked Raízo impatiently.

"I would offer my service, if I thought you would accept it," she said.

"And what service is that? Now is the time to speak it."

Still she seemed reluctant. "I would serve with your archers, as long as I am treated the same as any other, without regard to my sex. And I will fight for this house, but only against the king's men. And though I am not counted as a fugitive from the king's justice, with him I have grievances of my own."

A few archers snickered openly. The absurdity! Fighting along side a woman?

Raízo gave them a sharp glance and they quieted. He thought quietly for a moment and turned to Benedicio. He shrugged at his father. Raízo frowned at him and turned back to Leyrea.

"I do not know the customs of the western lands well. But here, our women bear no arms. Still, our needs shall be great." Raízo scratched his beard and thought for a moment. "Show me that you will at least be no burden to my archers and I will allow it. Bring her bow."

One of the archers went to the corner, took her long bow from the cache of confiscated weapons, and brought it to her.

"You have one arrow to prove yourself." He squinted as he searched the hall. "Do you see that knot in the farthest column? Pierce it through from where you now stand and you shall be allowed to serve this house. Give her an arrow."

The archer drew a single arrow from his quiver and handed it to Leyrea. After examining the dart carefully, she said, "I desire an arrow of my own making. This one is poorly wrought." Evidently, the archers fashioned their own arrows, because several of them grunted and hooted in protest.

"Fire the arrow," said Raízo.

"It will go astray. The fletching is not bound correctly."

He stood with a grim face, waiting for her to obey.

Leyrea sighed and nocked the arrow. She drew it and sighted in her target as best she could in the dim light of the hall. "This arrow will bend wildly to the right as I have it nocked. I will try to adjust my aim." She shifted her aiming point three feet to the left of her target and let it fly.

The Heart of the Graystone

The arrow sang as it left her bow, straight at first, then just as she'd predicted, it sailed to the right, missing the beam altogether. A sharp crack echoed through the hall as the arrow ricocheted off the stone wall beyond the beam, then fell harmlessly to the floor.

"You see?" she said defiantly.

Raízo gave a disapproving glance to his archers for their poor workmanship. "Bring her one of her own making."

Another archer brought her quiver over to her. She sifted through them until she found the best of the lot. Carefully she nocked it, drew it back and let it fly. A couple of the archers gasped when they saw it land squarely in the middle of the knot.

Raízo pursed his lips and rocked on his heels. He glanced back at Benedicio briefly, but he offered no advice. Then he cleared his throat. "Very well. I will allow you to serve in my corps if, and only if, you agree to show my archers how to fashion an arrow *properly*." He sent the archers another disapproving glance. Shamed, they turned their eyes from the Patri.

"I will," she said, without even a hint of satisfaction.

The Patri took a step forward and clapped his hands. "Then all is settled. But beware, all of you, for our protection comes at a price. For any who would betray their word given to this House this day, in any manner, there is only one punishment, and that is death. We take no oaths here. Your word is your oath, as it has been for ages among the mountain folk of the east. That said; let me extend to you all my welcome. My archers will see to your needs. We may find opportunity to speak more on the morrow, but for now, take you all the rest you require."

The Patri spoke quietly with one of the archers for a moment, then he and his knights turned and left the hall.

Their weapons were returned them and they were promptly shown to their new billets. They wound through narrow corridors and up twisting staircases. Kazareen had no idea of the size or shape of Locnomina, having fallen unconscious before drawing within sight of it. None of the soldiers were quartered with the others, not even Cathio, as they were led down a separate corridor on what Kazareen supposed was the ground floor. Leyrea, though part of the archer corps now, was allowed to room near her friends.

Florin, Leyrea, Solia and Kazareen were shown to four small rooms adjacent to each other. Their hosts departed quickly after showing them to their doors. Kazareen stepped into his room and found it as sparsely furnished as the room in which he'd awakened.

Below a single torch, stood a small table and chair. On the table, a chamber pot and a washing basin. For his gear and clothes, wooden hooks were fastened to the wall. In the corner, a low frameless bed huddled beside a narrow, shuttered window.

Kazareen went to the window and opened the shutters, hoping to see the lay of this place, this Locnomina, as the Patri had called it. A gust of rapier wind, sharp and cold, stole through the room. Kazareen shivered, drew his collar close about his neck, and peered out, but there was little to see. Darkness had already fallen and no torch or lantern illuminated it. And there was no moon. He bent forward and looked straight down, but could not even see the ground below him, only rough walls of stone disappearing into shadows.

Kazareen sighed and closed the shutters. He would have to wait until morning to see. The strong elixir had masked the weariness in his body, brought on from long weeks of travel in the wilds, but the sight of a bed, however simple, called out to him. How long had it been since he'd slept in one? He couldn't say with any certainty, but it felt like years.

He disrobed and slid under a generous layer of warm quilts and woolen blankets. The cold of the room faded with his worries as he curled into a ball, and he quickly slipped into the world of dreams.

The Token Crucible

Florin pulled back the blankets and roused him. Kazareen rubbed the sleep from his eyes and saw Florin seated on the bed next to him holding a candle. "What?" He was annoyed at being woken. Clearly, it was still the middle of the night. "Let me rest," he said, pulling the blankets back over his head.

"We said we needed to talk, and we do. Now, before we get into this too deep."

Kazareen sighed and folded the blankets down again.

"Why did you lie to the Patri about Murro? I am sure he would have accepted you into his house even if Murro were only your uncle. You should tell him the truth in the morning. Lies beget more lies, and before long, you will lose track of what lies you have told and you'll find yourself in deep trouble."

"You know he was not my true uncle. Would you have me lie about that instead?"

"But you called him your uncle your whole life, and no one but us and Leyrea know differently."

"Arpento knows as well."

"Very well, but he will never venture to this place, I'm sure. If, by chance, someone should come to this house who knew Murro from Beruthia, or Feria for that matter, you might be exposed."

"Not Beruthia. Many were slain in the siege, and his son was little more than an infant then. I could certainly pass myself off as his son, as grown as I am now."

"Still, what of someone from Feria?"

"Those are the lands of the House of Phenoa, and the people's loyalty lies with the king. Do you really think someone who just happened to know me would come this far east, to a secret house few know of anyway, to pledge their allegiance to a rival house? The chances are small."

"You did."

Kazareen thought for a moment. "I'm willing to take the risk that I'll be the only one."

Florin glared at him.

Kazareen began to wither under his gaze. "Alright, I'll tell him. But in my own time."

"When?"

"When I feel the time is right. I didn't ask you to take part in my deception. Why does it worry you so?"

"You heard what Raízo said, we may have to pay for your deception with our lives. And the longer you wait, the greater his wrath will be. A Patri of a Great House is not to be trifled with!"

"Then you'd best keep your mouth closed," Kazareen said. He yanked the blankets back over his head. It was clear his mind was made up.

Florin stood, his face blank and expressionless. "Very well, young man. But I warn you; I will not take part in this deception. Not at the cost of my life. Though I will not offer the information freely, if any of this house ask me directly, I shall tell the truth as I know it."

Florin stood above him for a moment, then left.

Kazareen lay awake far longer than he wished before his weariness overtook him again.

Kazareen was standing in the midst of a vast emptiness. How long he'd been there he didn't know. He felt the sun roasting him, its fury beating him. His arms glowed bright crimson and were covered with thousands of tiny blisters. All around, there was nothing but endless stretches of hard, pale sand. And beyond that, a silvery ocean that trembled and shook at the edge of his sight.

Was he on an island? What is this place?

He turned. Wingfoot lie motionless just a few yards away, and Kazareen ran over and laid hands on him, but the great horse was not breathing. Flies buzzed around its lifeless eyes, which stared at nothing. Kazareen recoiled in horror as a scorpion crawled from its open mouth. He took a step back and looked away.

From above, he heard the familiar beat of the Dragon's wings on the air. But this time it was different somehow. He looked up and saw vast wings stretched against the cloudless sky. They beat furiously to keep the giant creature aloft. Kazareen covered his face to keep the sand from flying into his eyes. The ground shook as the beast lit near Wingfoot's carcass.

The Dragon gazed at him with empty eyes. There was no silvery light there as he'd expected, and it began filling Kazareen with a dread so profound his chest felt ready to collapse. Ever so slowly, the Dragon began to take on a new shape. Its brow narrowed and its eyes deepened and flashed a sickly yellow. Great horns sprouted from and curled round the crown of its head. Teeth like sharpened spikes of black iron grew in its mouth. Scales appeared on its body, bristled, stood on end, and then

The Heart of the Graystone

hugged its monstrous black form. It's wings thinned and became like leather.

Suddenly the beast tore a great piece of flesh from Wingfoot's hindquarters and began to devour the rotting flesh. But Kazareen could not force himself to look away.

"No! What are you doing?" Kazareen put his hand to his belt, seeking his axe, but his belt was empty. Only the Graystone would save him now. But his pocket was empty as well.

This thing, this monster, this horrible black beast, which only a second earlier had been in the shape of the Dragon, stepped over the carcass and closed on him. What could he do? He had no weapon, no ally. Surely this was the end. He wanted desperately to close his eyes, but he couldn't.

It was nearly on him now, and its foul breath nearly knocked him from his feet. The beast reared back and blew a great torrent of dark vapor from its gaping nostrils.

"No!" he screamed.

Kazareen bolted upright, but he saw only dim, unfamiliar shapes around him. It took him a moment or two before he realized he was still in his humble room in Locnomina.

Kazareen drew a deep breath as his heart began to slow. "Just a dream," he said to himself. Drops of sweat were running down his temples, and his bedclothes were damp with perspiration.

He fell back into the pillow, relieved.

Leyrea came bursting through the door. "Kazareen! What is it?"

She startled him, but not nearly as badly as his dream had. "Nothing. I'm fine. Just a dream," he said, his eyes gazing thankfully at the protection of the stone ceiling above him.

"You too, huh?"

"What?"

"It must be the air here. I also had a vivid dream last night. You're sure you're fine?"

"Yes," he said. His heart finally began to beat at a tolerable rate. He wiped the sweat from his brow.

"It looks like yours was more a nightmare than a dream," said Leyrea, stepping to the window. "You need the reassurance of sunshine." She pushed out the shutters and the room brightened, though the light of day was not yet whole. "Better?"

Kazareen nodded.

"Good. Ready yourself for the day."

Leyrea had just about closed the door behind her, when Kazareen said: "Thank you."

She made no response, but paused at the door for a moment before closing it behind her.

Kazareen got up, washed himself from the basin, and dressed. It was still early, as the sun had not yet risen above the mountains. He stepped to the window and took in the view. His window faced the west, this he knew, for not a single mountain was in his view, only the long, vast valley they'd traversed the day before. It was still quite a sight. He looked down, but saw little more than he had the night before; only the wall curving away from his perch, elevated some twenty feet above the rocky surface, stretching out of sight in a wide arc in both directions. Kazareen was anxious now to see the full lay of Locnomina.

After a few minutes, Leyrea returned and they waited together in his room, but it soon became apparent that no one would come to see them round. They checked on Florin and Solia, with light knocks on their doors, but they were already gone. So they wandered through the narrow corridors and back down the winding stair they'd ascended the night before and found their way into the great hall. Many of the archers and men they'd seen the day before were there along with Florin, Cathio and his men. Solia was nowhere to be seen. Off in the kitchens already, Kazareen assumed. There were only a couple of servants, so they were rushing around trying to get everyone their meal and out of the hall as quickly as possible. Kazareen and Leyrea had arrived at the tale end of breakfast.

As they went and seated themselves beside Florin, Kazareen felt somewhat uncomfortable, remembering his short words with him the night before, so he said nothing. Florin did likewise.

Raízo nodded slightly to Kazareen as he sat down and helped himself to some dried dates, bread with butter. He returned the Patri's nod quickly and averted his eyes. Under the great man's gaze, he felt naked. There was a glimmer of shame inside him, and he flushed. It struck Kazareen that perhaps the Patri already knew the truth about him. Had he been so bold as to question Florin on the matter this early in the morning? Had Florin kept his own word and told the Patri the truth about Kazareen? If so, he would find out soon enough, but for now, he was famished. If he kept his mind on that, his face would show nothing but the truth of his hunger.

After snatching a boiled egg from the serving bowl, for it passed quickly, Kazareen saw the Knights of Pendi take their leave, without ceremony or pomp. A few of the archers stood quickly as they passed, then returned to wolfing down their meals.

The Heart of the Graystone

Kazareen poured himself a mug of milk from the pitcher on the table to wash down the last of his breakfast and nearly choked. It was goat's milk. He'd grown up on cow's milk and the acrid twinge of goat's milk, though he'd tasted it once before many years ago, came as quite a surprise. He supposed he'd made a face more sour than the flavor in his mouth, but not wanting to insult his hosts, he swallowed it just the same. He left the rest untouched. No one noticed.

Soon the hall began to empty and Leyrea and Florin went and spoke with the archers, seeking a plan for the day. Kazareen stood and watched, but they drifted out of the hall with the last few stragglers.

What was he to do? The Patri had granted him sanctuary here because of his supposed bloodline, but no word had been spoken to him about how he might contribute. He sat alone in the hall for a while, hoping someone might come to him, but no one did. Finally, he decided to take the opportunity to see what he could see.

After wandering around inside the keep for a while, he found his way to a pair of lofty double doors. He pushed on one of the heavy doors and walked out into the courtyard. The sunlight had finally broken over the mountains and now shown down on the large, open space before him. Chickens were strutting here and there, seeking some tiny sustenance in the ground as they pecked randomly. A few goats were munching at grasses that grew along the high outer wall, but they'd already cleared most of it away and the pickings were slim. Hounds barked at the chickens if they passed to close to their kennels.

Kazareen strolled to the center of the courtyard and looked at the gatehouse; no one was guarding it. The place seemed mostly deserted. Walls of stone stretched away from the gatehouse in a somewhat circular, though irregular fashion. The walls were lower in some places, unfinished by the look of them, and a great deal of rubble and uncut stones littered the edges of the courtyard.

Many rag-tag structures, most as simple as a lean-to, were scattered here and there against the portions of the wall that seemed to be finished, some stabling horses or hounds, others with barrels and crates of supplies. One was filled with hanging tack, and in another, a forge lay cold and silent beside a small anvil. Hooks on its wall held a small array of hammers and tongs. Now all he could think of was Murro, and gazing upon the silent smithy, it struck him to the core. The awful feeling of loneliness poured over him once again. He turned away from the tiny smithy, and looked for the first time upon the high keep of Locnomina.

The walls surrounding the courtyard drew back, climbing gently higher and higher, merging with the great keep along steep rocky cliffs. Its tower rose at least ninety feet above the courtyard and stood above what was obviously the great hall. The façade of the great hall facing the gate was plain, but apparent. The tower seemed to blend imperceptibly with the mountainside from which it rose, for Locnomina's stones were hewn directly from the high cliff of gray granite.

No banner or flag yet flew from the tower's pinnacle. Small shuttered windows dotted the lower stretches of the tower, which grew narrower as it rose, and several small firs still grew from the steep rock around it. He began to understand why Locnomina had gone undetected by the king's men.

When Cathio had pointed it out to him from the across the valley, it was no more than a pale smudge on the multicolored backdrop of an amazing vista. No one could possibly discern the stronghold that stood here when faced with the majesty of Atan Beruth—it was too well disguised. The eye just naturally ignored such things, being overwhelmed by the spectacular view that lay around it.

Hidden in plain sight.

Still, the presence of the tower dominated the landscape for many miles around, and it would not be ignored, and could not be missed. Kazareen knew that must be why they patrolled the meadows, trails and fir groves with such vigilance. Their party hadn't even drawn within sight of it before the Patri and his archers waylaid them on the approaching marches the day before. Kazareen also supposed this was why there were no guards at the gate. Their sorties would range much farther out. If the enemy drew near to the gates, then all would have already been lost.

After marveling at the cleverness of its design for a while, he finally decided he'd seen enough, so Kazareen passed through the double doors in the façade, determined to find something constructive to occupy himself with.

Kazareen wandered the cavernous hallways for a long while, at times losing his bearings, until he was convinced he was going in circles. Always he seemed to be funneled back into the main hall. He ran into servants occasionally, but said nothing to them. Where were the kitchens? Surely, at least Solia would still be around.

He passed many doors, and at first, feeling somewhat shy in this new place, he passed most of them untouched. But as his curiosity began to get the better of him, he tried opening a few, but most were locked.

"There you are! I've been looking for you, Kazareen," said a voice.

Kazareen turned and saw the bearded Patri striding down the corridor toward him.

"Good morning, sir. I mean...sire. I...ah..." Kazareen had no idea how to address the great man.

The Heart of the Graystone

He laughed heartily as he drew near. "I am no king!" Placing his hand on Kazareen's shoulder, he said: "You may call me Patri, or Raízo, if you so desire. We do not stand on ceremony here, despite the formalities of last night. They were required at the time, but now that we have accepted you and your companions, we are one! So be not shy, this is your home now."

Home.

The word rang hollow. It certainly didn't feel like home. But standing so close to the Patri, he could see that he had a warm smile beneath his beard, and his eyes were sparkling with a welcoming he had not felt in some time.

"Come, let me show you the high rooms. You are blood of my blood, and you shall be shown all."

Kazareen averted his eyes once again. He wasn't sure how long he could bear to deceive his host. The Patri turned and Kazareen followed behind him, his insides squirming like festering maggots.

Raízo led him down the curving corridor and stopped at what appeared to be just another ordinary door. He drew a single key from his pocket and unlocked it. Inside was a dim spiral stairwell.

When they reached the top of the stairs, they passed through a high-roofed chamber with a long table of dark stained cherry surrounded by ornately carved chairs. Two closed doors stood behind the highest chair, which Kazareen supposed was Raízo's. Wide shuttered windows opened on the valley opposite the doors. On the far side of the chamber, an arched doorway.

Raízo led him through the archway. The anteroom was filled with furnishings of the highest craftsmanship, in places, stacked to the ceiling. In the center of the room, a stout pedestal of stone supported a large round tabletop fashioned from a tightly grained, but unfamiliar, black wood. Many rings, pendants, brooches and other trinkets, some of gold and silver, some inlaid with precious stones, were displayed neatly on a heavy brocade cloth that had yellowed with age. Hanging from the walls were portraits of many stern, bearded men along with their families, bound by elaborate frames. Tapestries with intricate embroideries also hung there, some depicting great battles, others with unfamiliar symbols or strange designs: long complex knots of colored ribbons that were certainly pleasing to the eye, but utterly meaningless to him. Kazareen had never seen a collection of such finery all in one place. And while marveling at it all, he almost forgot the Patri was still in the room with him, until he spoke.

"This is all that remains of the treasures of the Great House of Pendi, all we were able to salvage from the ruin of our House," said

Raízo. His face was blank as he spoke, and his eyes seemed transfixed onto some distant sight visible only to him.

"It is a fabulous horde," said Kazareen.

"Tis but a tiny fraction of what the House held before that black day. The wealth of many generations was lost to the king's greedy hands." The Patri's voice rose in righteous indignation as he spoke, but quickly sank back into a gray melancholy as he added: "and that which you see here is the last wergild for our lost brethren and families."

"Sir?" Kazareen had a confused look on his face.

"This is the reward for the member of this house who slays the king and returns this House to its rightful place of honor. It isn't much, I know. But we have little. Most of this house was slain the day Gueren fell upon the last Counsel of Patris. He showed no mercy upon man, woman, child, or beast. Barely a single stone was left standing of the keep of my childhood. I am the last of the old House that yet survives in direct bloodline, save my sons. And if they are blessed, they shall be the sires of the new House, if we are able to stand against the king and his foul hand."

"You mean General Gueren?"

"I do, though it took many years to add a name to the face I saw mercilessly cutting down my father and the rest of the Patris. I was fortunate to escape his wrath that day, but my young wife was not so lucky. When I realized what was happening, I went to my father's aid, but when I burst into the counsel chamber, someone hit me over the head with something hard, and I was a knocked from my senses. I guess they thought me dead. Poor judgment on their part, for I awoke before the fires consumed the upper levels, and I was able to slip away. May Gueren live to regret it. If ever we meet again, then his head shall be mine for what he did! But that day may yet be far off."

Watching the Patri's eyes as he spoke, Kazareen began to understand why the seeds of rebellion had taken such firm root in the east. They had suffered much under King Geraldi's rule.

"Come," said Raízo, leading him to the table with the great treasure displayed on it. "These are the last tokens of our House. Look on them and tell me which one you fancy. Take a moment to consider. For I sense in you the feeling that you are an outsider here. But we share the same blood. We are family Kazareen, and as I am Patri, it is my right to offer you a token of this House—to welcome you and reassure you of your rightful place among your brethren. Please, choose and it shall be yours."

Kazareen looked into Raízo's eyes, and his heart felt as if it were caving in upon itself. Florin had been right about his deception, and

The Heart of the Graystone

Kazareen knew it. And in the face of the Patri's generosity he was shamed. He couldn't bear to deceive this truly noble man—not for another minute. He thought he had an idea how Raízo would react, but he had to tell him the truth.

"I can't choose."

"Take your time and—"

"No. You don't understand. I have no right to a token of this House. Forgive me, please, great one, but I...I lied about Murro. He was not my father." Kazareen tried, but he could not look Raízo in the eye again, he was either too afraid or too ashamed of himself.

The Patri said nothing.

After long moments of staring at the floor, Kazareen finally looked up at Raízo. To his surprise, the Patri was nodding. There was even a hint of smile under that beard.

"I know, Kazareen. But I'm proud of you, you have passed the great test."

Kazareen could not speak.

"I knew Murro well; far more than I revealed to you last night. And I know for certain he lost his family at Beruthia. We spoke after Geraldi was crowned. It was I who counseled him to travel into the west. I thought he might find it easier to bear his loss if he was no longer surrounded by the familiar things of his home; they would only remind him of his dearest departed. Besides, you are far too fair-haired to be the son of Murro."

Kazareen winced. "Then you knew all along?"

"I did. And I shared this with my kin, which is why we were chambered so long in deciding your fate. They were all against you."

Kazareen felt small; all the Knights of Pendi knew him for a liar. He wanted to disappear. "Then why did you offer me a token of your House?" His voice was thin and soft.

"It was the crucible I needed to reveal your intentions. If you had chosen, I would have known your heart was comfortable with deception. But you did not. You chose to turn from your lie. That tells me you have a sense of honor—and a measure of courage."

"Then you'll allow me to stay?"

"That depends. I will not pass final judgment until you tell me the whole truth."

Raízo stood tall, his brawny arms folded across his barrel chest, listening closely as Kazareen told him all he knew of his lineage, which sadly, was very little. And though Kazareen said nothing of the Graystone or Dien or his dealings with Arpento, he felt a weight lifting as he spoke the truth now about his love and affection for Murro, whom he'd called his uncle, and the sacrifice he'd made for him on the road to Pente Kaleán. He'd tried desperately to put that dreadful day out of his mind, and he felt the loss all over again now that he was recounting it for the Patri. While he spoke, he began to foresee images of his own death, the certain consequence of deceiving the Lord of the Great House. When he finished, Kazareen stared meekly at the floor. Fearing now for his life, a strange panic began to mix inside him and he wanted to run.

"I thank you, Kazareen, for your honesty. I can see that you knew Murro well from all that you have said. And I understand your desire to find sanctuary from the king's so-called justice and the temptation to lie to find refuge from your long suffering. I really do, for I know what it is like to lose all, to be a homeless fugitive, wretched and alone. And so I forgo the punishment for your transgression," said Raízo.

At first he wasn't sure if he'd heard the Patri correctly. Kazareen looked up at the great man, his eyes searching for some clue as to how such a proud leader would turn aside from the promise of wrath.

"Last night you said...I thought...it would be my death."

"My father, may he rest, taught me many things. How to read and to write. How to hunt and fish. How to defend myself. But knowing that someday I would be Patri, for I was eldest, this he impressed upon me more than any other lesson: that a man, especially one who leads others, must learn to mete out mercy before wrath. That justice must always be tempered with forgiveness."

"He taught me to be humble while sitting in the judgment seat. He said that justice is a like a proud beast to be feared, and that pride will devour the merciless judge, even if the transgressor is guilty. I refuse to dishonor my father, so it is my place to do now as he instructed. Your lie is forgiven...and I remember it no more. Nor shall my kin. That said, I also refuse to stand in the light of Murro's sacrifice and shame his memory by standing before you more niggardly than he who took you in as his own. And as Murro did before me, so I too accept you into the House of Pendi. Once again, I offer you the token of our House. Now choose," he said, gesturing to the table again.

The chill in Kazareen's blood retreated. Twice in his life had members of the House of Pendi rescued him from certain death. He set his mind never to forget the love, the sacrifice, and especially the mercy shown him by Murro, and now Raízo. And though Raízo said it was forgotten, Kazareen still felt the shame of his deception, so as he looked over the trinkets and tokens, he searched the table for the most humble his eyes could find. He passed over the proudest jewels until he saw it. Lying near the far end of the table was a simple leather necklace, unadorned. The only thing remarkable about it was its many loosely

The Heart of the Graystone

intertwined laces of thin leather; tied in the same strange but beautiful manner as the hanging tapestry.

He picked it up with as light a touch as he could muster and looked to the Patri. "This one?"

Raízo smiled and nodded. "A humble choice. I see you have understood my father's lesson well. But a good choice. It was fashioned by my aunt Rosari, as a gift to her husband, Verdio, of the House of Phenoa, though he died at Beruthia before she could present it to him. Keep it well, Kazareen. And never forget by whose hand it was wrought."

"Rosari de Pendi," said Kazareen.

"Rosari du Phenoa," the Patri corrected. "May she rest."

The Days of Sanctuary

And so the days passed quickly, and by October, winter descended upon the high country of Locnomina. Kazareen spent many evenings with the Patri in the high rooms and as he got to know him better, his friendly way began to remind Kazareen of Murro, and he found a great comfort in the time he spent talking with Raízo. Often he spoke of the fair days before the siege of Beruthia, when the Great Houses still stood. After Kazareen's long weeks of flight and danger, the Patri's familiar manner made Locnomina feel more like home.

His first few weeks there were spent honing his skills with a bow in the company of archers—it seemed the most likely way for him to serve the Great House, not unlike the other young men his age. After learning their stealthy ways in the forest and proving his marksmanship with the bow—which he took to surprisingly fast—he was allowed to patrol the outer marches with the others—though not as often as he wished.

When he learned the House was without a skilled blacksmith, reluctantly, he volunteered to do what he could in the humble smithy. Raízo seemed particularly pleased with this, seeing Kazareen follow in Murro's footsteps. And while at first he rather dreaded the work that had proved such a bane to him in previous years, soon he realized that the heat of the forge was a comfort in the biting wind and frigid air of the highlands. And the ringing of hammer on iron, the roar of the fire, and the sharp scent of iron and steel brought back memories of simpler days.

Often he found his mind wandering while he worked, and the worries he'd carried so far and so long simply seemed to melt away. He would look up from his anvil, half-believing he was still in Feria, and half-expecting to see Murro standing behind him, pointing out the best way to work a particular piece.

Keep the hammer flat as it strikes. Shorten your backstroke, no need to pound it so hard. Hit while the iron is hot. Don't forget to set the metal in the bath once you've shaped it properly. Watch those flanges!

At times, it was almost as if he could hear Murro speaking the words aloud, like some ghost from a children's story, not a lost spirit cast with dread—just Murro—exactly as Kazareen remembered him. But he knew they were just memories. He began to feel as though a piece of Murro still lived on in the work of his hands. Before long, his skills improved and he became so deft with the hammer that it found his fingers no more.

Even with his work to distract him, the shame of deceiving Raízo lingered on inside him for many months, forcing him to muse on Raízo's act of tender mercy. When his feelings of disgrace tormented him, Kazareen would often go to his room and slip Rosari's necklace gently over his head, not to admire its craftsmanship, but to remind himself of the Patri's grace. Forgiveness was a gift difficult for him to accept, because he knew he didn't deserve it. Out of reverence, for this was a token of the Great House, he kept the necklace hidden away in his room for a long time, but when he did put it on, the roughness of its leathery knots against his skin comforted him. It was a great reminder to him, how tenuous was his existence, so one day he put it on, tucked it under his shirt and decided to leave it there. And there it would remain until King Geraldi passed from the earth.

The days of sanctuary were long and full, and brought many changes. Within a month of arriving, Florin and Solia renewed their vows to one another with their son Cathio by their side. The Patri presided over the ceremony in the great hall and a feast followed. The harsh words between Kazareen and Florin were forgotten when Kazareen told him he had revealed the truth to the Patri, but a distance had begun to grow between them since their hardships together on their long flight. Kazareen saw it mattered little to Florin, he had his one true love to fill his heart now, but Kazareen missed their little talks.

Leyrea also found love in Locnomina, though to Kazareen's surprise it was Cathio who snared her heart. The Patri married them privately in the high rooms because they did not wish for a public celebration. Everyone said that it was a marriage of necessity, as Leyrea's belly was already showing that she was with child. Kazareen thought differently. Though he said nothing of his suspicions, not to Florin, not even to Leyrea, Kazareen thought the real father was probably one of the soldiers who'd raided her home on the prairie. Kazareen didn't doubt that Cathio loved Leyrea, but he wasn't sure if the reverse were true. Perhaps she had accepted his proposal simply to avoid the stigma of raising a fatherless child. For a long time he was unsure, but after a few months, it became plain to everyone that they truly loved one another. She gave birth to a daughter on the fourth day of April, and they named her Mari.

So time began to pass more quickly. And as his days became filled with a comfortable routine, Kazareen's mind drifted far from the all the worries the Graystone had brought him. He rarely carried it in his pocket these days, there just didn't seem to be a need for it. He was safe here. He'd found a new home in Locnomina and his friends had found new lives. Though sometimes, when he was quiet and alone, he would

The Heart of the Graystone

ponder the words he'd spoken with Arpento so many long months ago, about destroying the Graystone, and he would feel the weight of his words returning.

But didn't he say it was up to me to decide what to do with it? Yes. I made no promise to destroy it. Besides, then I had no idea I might find a place like this—a place where I could be safe, far from the king's reach.

These thoughts comforted him, but he could never fully rid himself of the nagging suspicion that even here in this high strong place, the long arm of the king might eventually reach out to take hold of him. For now, he just wanted to live in peace.

The Patri and his knights, however, were always talking about their plans and desire to overthrow the king. But so far, it had all been talk. Still, this was their ultimate goal, and Kazareen knew that whether he liked it or not, he was now part of it, and sooner or later their haughty words would turn to action—he just kept hoping it would be later.

Months passed and seasons changed and before he knew it, more than a year had passed. Over time, the Knights of Pendi found their ranks swelling quickly—for Gueren had become the terror of the eastern lands and his tally of victims grew ever longer. Still, the existence of Locnomina remained hidden from the dark eyes of the Necromancers.

Many who fled Gueren's reign of terror brought their families with them, and the once-spacious keep became a place of bustling activity. Masons came to finish the walls. Carpenters came to provide more and better furnishings. A small group of minstrels, led by a bard named Jorg, also landed in Locnomina, their songs and music bringing a much-needed spirit of joy and recreation, and at times, lamentations of somber remembrance of the terrible carnage at Beruthia. And many hearty men came, offering their swords and service.

Another blacksmith also came from Beruthia, though his skills were not much greater than Kazareen's. Could it be that he'd grown quite skillful over the past year? Or was the newcomer as much a novice as he was? Kazareen wasn't sure. But it freed him up to serve with Dregis and his archers more often, and of this he was glad, for his soul had always found solace in nature.

He didn't mind working and living inside the great walls of Locnomina, as long as he could venture out on the marches from time to time to renew his spirit amid the wonders of creation. Though the marches around Locnomina were nothing like the eaves of Bethë Dien, he still found many moments of peace and fascination among the high firs and white aspen of his new home.

And so it went for Kazareen, and as time passed, he came steadily into the semblance of a man. His body grew strong from swinging the hammer, hearty from living in the thin air, and sure-footed from traversing the rugged terrain of the highlands. Thin patches of dark whiskers even began to sprout on his face.

With so many new arrivals, Kazareen believed he would become just another face in the crowd, which was fine by him, but there were few in the East with hair as fair as his own, and so he often drew stares from newcomers. His hair never returned to its former shade, though for a while he hoped it might, and at times, newcomers mistook him for an orphaned son of a barbarian Northmen, and for all Kazareen knew it might be the truth, but it never bothered him much—for he was ever held in the Patri's favor. This became evident to all over time, and so few were willing to give him much grief about his appearance for fear of drawing the Patri's ire. Still, he had to deflect the occasional inquiry about his lineage.

But much to his delight, Kazareen was accepted in Locnomina more than he had ever been in Feria, for lineage was important in all parts of Pendoria. He was known to be an orphan in Feria, and believed to be an Easterner to boot. For that reason, most of the boys his age in Feria would have little to do with him—only Talisa had seen past. Now all that was changing here in Locnomina. For the Patri had claimed him as a blood relative. And that, more than anything else, transformed Locnomina into real sanctuary. Here he'd finally found the acceptance he'd never known in Feria. It was as if he'd slid slowly into the reassuring envelope of a hot bath, ever soothing him with its warm embrace, an unbreakable cocoon to quiet his restless soul. And he reveled in this newfound peace of mind.

By the following December, after scouring the east for over a year, Gueren was beginning to wonder if the fugitives had fled Pendoria altogether, but the odds were low that they would, or could, traverse the treacherous passes of Atan Beruth; or flee to Farak for that matter. No, they had to be somewhere in the East.

His monthly reports to the capital had been met with silence, and he could feel his brother's impatience growing, though the breadth of Pendoria lay between them. No matter how many he tortured or slew, he could not discover the whereabouts of his quarry, and it seemed to him that the people of the East were resisting him at every turn. The seeds of rebellion were now taking a firm root, and Gueren contemplated retreating into the relative safety of the west. But it would not do. He had to find the boy—too much depended on it.

Alerien, though silent to his brother's reports, was by no means idle during those long months. Ever he toiled to find a way to locate

The Heart of the Graystone

Kazareen. If the eyes of men could not spy him, he would be sought by magik.

Alerien sat slumped at a small table in the royal treasury, amid the huge piles of Graystone they'd collected over the years. The treasury was but a dank grotto, hewn from the rock of the dark catacombs far below the high tower of Pente Kaleán.

By the flickering light of a single candle, his weary eyes strained as he poured over an ancient tome of dark magik. A thin trickle of tacky fluid seeped from his dark eyes; yet these were not the clear, salty tears of an ordinary man, but slim streaks of his own foul and accursed blood soiling his pallid cheeks.

The spells, first reckoned is some forgotten age, were written in a language that had long since withered away from the world. But it was not enough to simply intone them in the old speech—which was simple enough, given Alerien's long years of study—the caster had to infuse the words with a dark will and power. It was only through decades of painstaking effort that Alerien had translated the many spells: charms of warding and deception, spells even Gueren had learned to cast, despite his feeble skills. For years, the most powerful spells had resisted Alerien, but his efforts were not wasted. He had finally learned to decipher the complex metaphors, coax their meaning forward, and unlock the subtleties required to give them true power.

Over the years, he'd also discovered that sitting amid the frozen flesh of the Dragon imparted a focused power. Power to the heart and mind to do that which the will intended. To this, Alerien's dark will was no exception. And now that he had collected nearly every Graystone known to exist in Farak or Pendoria, the dank grotto throbbed with a vitality like the very wings of the Dragon itself.

His trembling hand hovered over the page as he spoke the final words of the making spell. The complex incantation had taken him several hours to recite. And as he uttered the last of those foul words, he was sapped of the force that kept his mind and body bound together.

As he uttered the final phrase, "Deya ez plat golem..." he collapsed. His head hit the table with a dull thud and the dark blood on his face smeared the ancient text.

When he opened his eyes, he saw a blurry gray image of a high meadow nestled among the foothills of a great range of mountains, blanketed all with snow. Then a long and sonorous howl carried far through the high country, echoing its lonely charms through the deserted dales.

The Golem Strikes

One fine spring morning, with the sun reflecting brightly off the last few inches of snow that still hugged the high marches, and when there was little work to be done in the smithy, Kazareen felt the familiar itch to venture out on his own again. The summer before, he'd discovered a high pinnacle of rock a few miles away that was fairly easy to scramble up. The view of the valley below and the mountains above was much better than from the high rooms of the keep. In fact, the highest peaks were all but invisible from Locnomina, for it was set directly into the cliffs behind and they blocked the view.

He sat atop the rocks of that high place, breathing the crisp, pine-scented air for some time, thinking of nothing in particular—for peace had come to reign in his heart once again, and soon sleep overtook him. When he woke, little more than an hour later, gray clouds had swept down out of the high country and enveloped the mountainside. The careful tutoring of the Knights of Pendi had taught him that vicious snowstorms could blow down from the mountains in no time at all—even when winter was all but over. So until high summer arrived, he never left the grounds of Locnomina without a light pack containing the barest essentials: mittens and a cap made from the fur of wolverines, flint and tinder, and a small flask of tomporian, the elixir he'd been given on his first night in Locnomina.

Kazareen had no more than reached the base of the pinnacle when the air began to fill with a light flurry. He pulled on his hat and mittens and started off. Within ten minutes, great clumps of wet snow were coming down so heavy he couldn't see more than a few yards. His heart began to pound. He already knew he was in bad way, though he had never been caught alone in what Dregis had called a blind snow.

One of Dregis' earliest lessons concerned itself with what one should do if caught in such a heavy snowfall, and that was to stay put and wait it out. If the snow got very deep, all one had to do to survive was dig a burrow and you'd be warm and safe until the storm ended—as long as you left a small opening to let in some fresh air. Dregis said it was pointless to burn up all your strength trying to plod through heavy snow if you couldn't see where you were going. But Kazareen had begun to panic and forgot what he'd been taught.

He hustled on. And the farther he marched, the less familiar his surroundings seemed to become. His quick step soon became a full-on sprint, though he could not tell exactly where he was headed. On and on he went, never pausing to collect his thoughts or he would have remembered his all-important lesson. He began to wish he'd brought Wingfoot with him. Maybe *he* could find the way back to the keep; horses were wily that way. At least they could keep each other company, and a little warmer.

Little did he know that his sense of direction was still very good, for he had drawn to within a couple hundred yards of the main gate, but he couldn't see it through the heavy curtains of snow, and he passed it by unaware. His breathing became labored from running in the thin air and he began to slow. It never crossed his mind to call out for help.

Surely I must be there by now.

But the safety and warmth of Locnomina was already a quarter mile behind him.

When Kazareen finally stopped, his head ached and it grew worse with every beat of his heart. He could stand no longer. Nearly two feet of snow had fallen since he'd left the high rocks and when he fell, it muffled every sound except his breathing. It was then that he remembered Dregis' lesson.

You fool. Just stay here.

But he knew that he'd already exhausted himself. There was little he could do now but wait out the storm. The endless fall of snow piled up around him while he tried to find some hidden store of energy. But he was almost completely spent. Despite his warm clothes, the wet of the spring snow soon penetrated them. His hands and feet were growing numb and his face tingled and burned in the freezing cold. Then he remembered the tiny container of tomporian. Kazareen drew it from his pouch and emptied it with two large gulps. He was so drained by now that even this simple act took great effort. It was dreadfully slow to take affect, hindered by the frigid temperatures and his pathetic state, but it gave him just enough energy to move.

How long he'd been lying there in the snow he couldn't say, all he knew was that the storm had raged on and on. When the sweet elixir's power seemed to have peaked, he began to burrow into the deep layer of snow. The work was frightfully slow, but he wouldn't stop. He couldn't— if he wanted to live.

When at last he had completed his snow shelter, he found himself once again drained. Exhaustion and cold made his body quiver uncontrollably, and slowly, fitfully, he lost touch with the world in his tiny burrow.

The lone wolf sniffed the ground, trying to discern the scent he'd come across in the snow. The scent was familiar to him somehow, but he

The Heart of the Graystone

couldn't quite place it; the familiarity tickled the recesses of his mind. He'd wandered far through the foothills for months now, and this was only the second time he'd caught wind of a human, so he convinced himself he did not actually know the scent. The only other human scent in his mind belonged to a hunter the wolf had waylaid in his sleep. He put up a bit of a fight, but not for long. His powerful jaws and sharp canines tore into the hunter's neck mercilessly and he was quickly silenced. The taste of human blood and flesh appealed to him, and he found now that he craved it. Besides, bouncing around and chasing after squirrels and rats took too much energy for the small bit of nourishment they provided.

The wolf trotted along, following the faint scent trail until he came upon the unmistakable odor of a well-traveled path through the firs. He stopped and looked around. There was no movement to be seen anywhere, but dozens, perhaps scores of different scents mingled together and lingered upon this trail—and they were all human. He knew of no settlements in these parts and perhaps there was none, but he was surprised to find such a concentration of human scents. A large hunting party perhaps.

Sniffing the ground, he could still detect the one particular trail he'd been following earlier. It was fresher than the rest—powerful and strong, and laced with fear. And it led down the path of the other older, fainter scents. It was then that the wolf realized he was heading in the wrong direction. He couldn't follow the scent trail down the path to where many humans might gather, for he was no match for a pack of men.

He turned around and followed the scent trail back in the direction from which he'd come. Then he began to notice that the snow was coming down much heavier now, so he picked up his pace. He didn't want to lose the trail in the gathering snow. The thought of a fresh meal so close started the wolf drooling.

Florin peered out from the main doors of the keep and a swirl of snow and wind stung his face. The heavy white shroud was so thick the main gates—a mere thirty yards away—seemed to have disappeared completely. Pulling up his collar, he ventured out into the courtyard and ran to the smithy. It was empty; its forge dark and cold. His stomach tightened. Knowing that Kazareen often ventured out into the marches alone in the afternoons, he began to fear the worst.

Finding his way up to Kazareen's room, he found it empty as well. Frantically, he raced around the corridors, calling his name. When he was quite sure Kazareen was nowhere inside the walls, he went to the high rooms, where the Knights of Pendi were holding counsel. He burst through the door without knocking.

"What's the meaning of this?" Benedicio shouted. Always on guard of assassins, he jumped to his feet and quickly drew a long dagger from his belt. The Patri stilled his son with a firm grip of his arm.

Seeing the dagger, Florin raised his hands and did not move. "Tis only I, Florin."

Benedicio lowered his dagger, but did not yet sheath it.

"It's Kazareen. I've searched everywhere on the grounds for him, but he is nowhere to be found. I think he may be caught in the storm."

The Patri stood. "Are you sure?" His eyes widened and his face paled.

Florin nodded.

The Patri turned to Dregis. "What do you think?"

Dregis rose, but spoke calmly. "I found Kazareen to be a fast and attentive learner. If he took his pack with him and remembers my lessons, he should have little problem enduring. It is fierce for a spring storm, but it will end soon I should think."

Florin didn't care for his matter-of-fact attitude. "We need to search for him! What if he did not take his pack? Then he will need our help...and soon."

Dregis said nothing. He looked to Raízo.

"Search his room and see if his pack is still there. If so, then I believe we should venture out after him," said the Patri.

Florin nodded and left.

Dregis shook his head as the Patri slowly reseated himself. "If he did forget his pack, then he's already as good as dead. And I don't think it wise to risk more lives blundering blindly through this storm looking for a body. To what benefit would that be?"

Raízo gave his nephew a sharp look, but said nothing. He turned to Benedicio.

"I agree," said his son.

The Patri sighed, but waited anxiously for Florin to report back.

Florin burst into Kazareen's room and scanned it quickly for his pack. A pair of light summer trousers hung from the hook on the wall— but no pack. A good sign. Florin noticed that the room was now furnished with a wardrobe, obviously a new edition thanks to the arrival of the carpenters from Beruthia. Florin looked inside, but saw it was mostly empty. A few oddments were scattered around inside, a few simple shirts hung limply, but there was no daypack inside. Then a familiar glimmer caught his eye from the dark recesses of the top shelf.

The Graystone.

Why Kazareen should leave this treasure unguarded and out of his possession, Florin couldn't say, but it seemed a foolish thing to do. The sight of it brought back many memories of their journey together—most of which he'd tried hard to put behind him. His heart and mind had belonged mostly to Solia since their reunion, but seeing the Graystone again reminded him of the hardships he and Kazareen had endured together.

The Graystone was an odd thing and he was loath to touch it. But remembering the power it had to heal, he grabbed it before heading back to the high rooms. Instantly his will began to steel: he would find Kazareen, with or without the Patri's help.

The storm was beginning to wane and the clouds slowly beginning to break up, but so much snow had fallen that the scent trail had become sporadic and hard to follow. But the wolf was close—very close now to his quarry. This he knew. He could almost smell the blood. He could almost taste the sweat. Fear was in the air and the hackle on the back of his neck rose instinctively.

Then, a streak of sunlight burst through an opening in the clouds. The wolf raised his head, and through an opening in the firs, it saw above him a great dwelling of men standing proudly among the cliffs, illuminated by the isolated rays of the sun. There were high walls surrounding a grand keep rising from the rock, and at its pinnacle, a purple banner fluttering in the sunlight.

What was this? He knew that banner. But from where? It was as if something he had seen in a dream, long ago—in some other life. Vivid flashes of colorful memories from long ago, seen through different eyes. Yet had he not always been a wolf? Would he not always be one?

Then, like a bolt of lightning, the truth of his existence dawned on him. I was a man once. Yes. I was...no...I am Alerien. Yes...the spell. It worked! The wolf's eyes narrowed and it remembered the whole of its true nature. Alerien stared at the banner as the break in the clouds closed, leaving Locnomina dim and gray once more.

The banner bore the livery of the House of Pendi, and he knew it well. The four banners of the Great Houses, empty tokens of Pendoria's past, still flew over the high tower of Penté Kaleán. But what was this place? Had one of the Great Houses been reformed in secret? There was no other answer. He had to get word to his brother.

His thoughts were interrupted by a muffled moan nearby.

The nature of the wolf seized him once again. His ears stood erect, his neck stretched, and he stood tall. Listening. Scanning the blanket of unbroken snow. His nose drew in a draught of brisk air. Fear, he sensed. And sweat he smelled. But he saw no movement.

Man. Yes, it was very near now. And weak. It would be easy prey. Then he could send word to his brother of this new threat. But there was time enough to take a hearty meal first.

The low moan came again, and in an instant, the wolf leapt high into the air and pounced on the sound. The snow gave way, and he tumbled into a hollow space.

The great commotion woke Kazareen from his restless sleep. White and cold all around him. He dug wildly through the ruin of his snow shelter and he saw it—a great gray wolf, already upon him.

The snarling beast bared its deadly teeth. Its ears were drawn back and its hackle stood high. Threads of thick drool hung from its mouth, and it stank. But then, just as Kazareen thought it was about to pounce, the wolf hesitated; almost as if it were gloating, wanting Kazareen to know he was about to die. But the expression on its face suddenly changed. Gone was the ravenous look of a wild beast bent on killing its prey, and it was replaced with one Kazareen could only describe as surprise.

But it was not an expression of surprise—it was one of recognition. Alerien knew the curve of that face. *This is the one! It's him!* Alerien tried to shout, but in his present form, all he uttered was a long and terrible howl. The wolf's lonely cry echoed through the snow-covered marches.

Kazareen seized the moment. Leaping to his feet, he tried to draw Murro's axe from his belt, but he was still too weak. His vision dimmed. The trees seemed to be spinning round him. His eyes fluttered and he fell back into the snow.

A moment later Kazareen felt the wolf upon him. Wrenching pain seized his mind. He cried out as deadly fangs sank into his leg. Again and again, the frenzied wolf tore into him. Its body shook, twisting and gyrating wildly as it began to render precious flesh from bone.

Then, to Kazareen's surprise, the pain receded and a great calm, a welcome but unexpected peace of spirit, fell over him and he closed his eyes.

He felt his body being shaken and thrown about mercilessly, and the warmth of his blood slipping away. But there was no more pain. No more sound. He felt suddenly far away; separated from existence; utterly detached from the violence being wrought on his flesh.

Then, while clinging to the last few threads of life that kept him bound to the world, the all-encompassing silence was broken with a

The Heart of the Graystone

sound that had become all too familiar to him: the slow crescendo of the Dragon's wings, growing louder with each beat of the air.

I am coming.

With his last bit of strength, Kazareen opened his eyes, but he saw no Dragon, only the bloodstained snout of the wolf hovering over him. The beast was panting from its efforts, but no warmth of breath could Kazareen feel, only its icy glare, as it hesitated one last time. It eyed his neck wantonly for the final strike.

But it never came, for just as the wolf seemed about to finish him, a dim figure fell down upon the beast, wrenching him away. A great yip went up as his rescuer fell upon the wolf with his full weight, pinning it in the snow.

Florin had come.

He rolled over on top of the wolf, trying in vain to get his hands round its neck. The wolf snarled and snapped with great fury, gnashed at Florin's hands, and so he found no grip.

The wolf squirmed from beneath his enemy, ran back a few yards, and then faced him. It saw that the man's sword was still sheathed. It took two cautious steps forward and readied himself to pounce.

Florin leapt to his feet, and meant to draw his weapon, but to his surprise, he found that his hand had gone to his pocket instead and he now wielded the Graystone. He held it forth as he would his sword, and in Florin's righteous wrath, it burst to life. Great rays of silver light shone through the gaps between his fingers, stopping the wolf dead in its tracks.

What kind of magik is this? Alerien thought. He couldn't bear the blinding light from the stone and averted his eyes. *Could it be? The very last piece of the puzzle? In the hands of this common fool?*

The wolf circled Florin, trying to find a way to pierce the light of the Graystone, but each time he drew near, he felt himself weakened and blinded. Feeling its great power, he quickly became convinced that this was indeed the Graystone he required to complete his nefarious plans. He had to get that stone.

The wolf jumped forward blindly into the light, jaws snapping. Florin sidestepped the attack and booted it in the rear as it flew by.

Seeing it had the desired effect, Florin kept the Graystone held high, shielding Kazareen from the fury of the beast. But the wolf would not retreat. It circled and stalked them from just a few yards away.

Florin drew his sword with his other hand. While the wolf could not see this through the blinding light, it heard the steel ring against the scabbard as he drew it. The odds were turning against him now. Perhaps it was time to retreat. *But the stone. I have to get the stone.*

The air suddenly filled with the sound of many voices echoing in the trees.

From somewhere behind the blinding light of the Graystone: "There! Watch your aim, now! Fire!"

The wolf watched several arrows pierce and then disappear into the snow all around him. None had found its mark. The wolf turned to run, but it was too late.

Leyrea came to Florin's side, and nocked an arrow in a flash. She loosed it and it found the wolf's hindquarter. Another great yelp went up.

The wolf stumbled forward, away from its pursuers. Heavy footfalls were pounding through the snow behind him as he tried to make his escape, but his hind legs were useless.

The Patri, his shining spear held high, fell upon the wolf with a mighty shout. Raízo's long spear skewered the wolf's skull, nearly cleaving it in two. This beast would breath no more. But to his astonishment, Raízo saw that the wolf had somehow slipped away. His spear still stood upright before him, pinned into the snow where he had thrust it just a moment before, but the carcass was gone. All that remained was a smelly pile of leaves and dirt surrounding the shaft of his spear on the snow's surface—in the shape of a wolf.

"Golem," he whispered, as he plucked his spear from the snow.

Turning, he saw Florin and Leyrea kneeling at Kazareen's side. All around them, the snow was splattered red, and the Patri feared the worst. The strange light still shone from Florin's hand as he whispered to Kazareen.

As he drew close, Raízo found he could not look directly at the source of the light, and he shielded his eyes. Then he felt a hand reach up and gently take his own. As he felt Leyrea's soft touch, the light dimmed, and he saw them kneeling in the snow beside Kazareen. He kneeled down with them.

Kazareen's face was as white as the snow. His eyes were open, yet looked at nothing. Florin whispered something inaudible as he curled Kazareen's fingers around the stone, but its light had gone out.

"He's lost a lot of blood. And his wounds are grievous. We need to get him back to the keep. Quickly now," said Raízo.

Finding Heart

Alerien awoke with a jerk. The darkness around him was complete. Something clung to his face and as he swatted at it, he heard the tearing of the brittle parchment. Groping through the black, he felt something smooth and shapely: the wax-covered candlestick on the table before him, but there was no candle left; it had long since burned away to nothing. He stumbled blindly through the grotto until his hands found the door. He pulled on the handle but the latch was down. How long his body had been locked away in the dark catacombs while his mind wandered the lonely foothills of the East, he couldn't say.

He lifted the heavy iron latch and stumbled forward toward the dim light far ahead. Finally he came to a single lit torch at the entrance to the catacombs. As he passed through the door, he was surprised and angered that no guard stood ready to defend it.

"Guards!" he shouted. His voice echoed down the long corridor and in the high hollows of the hall, but there came no reply.

Alerien ran to the end of the hall and found the door to the tower unlocked as well. He rushed up the stairwell and burst into the high turret. His muscles burned with fatigue. There was nothing and no one to greet him there. Geraldi was gone.

Gritting his teeth, he ran to the east window. There was little activity in the courtyard, only a few guards at the gate and one pacing the rampart above it.

Seconds later, the main doors of the hall flew open and Alerien found a single guard sitting at the top of the steps, more interested in enjoying the first rays of the spring sun than watching his post.

Hearing the doors crash open, the guard turned; his mouth fell open at the ghastly sight of the high counselor. His face was smeared with black ooze, the pale skin of his gaunt face hung limp about his jowls, and his eyes were framed in deep, sagging wrinkles.

"What is the meaning of this? Why aren't you at your post?" Alerien shouted, pointing at the guard shack.

The guard leapt up and ran to his post. "Where are the rest of the guards? Where is King Geraldi?"

The guard stuttered across his words like a dull plane on wood.

"Answer me!"

Finally regaining his bearing, he spoke, but could not bring himself to look at the horrid sight of Alerien's face. "Forgive me, my Lord. The king departed a week ago. And the greater part of the royal guard travels with him." The soldier was sure he'd feel the lash for his indiscretion.

Alerien's stark eyes narrowed. "Why? And to where exactly?"

The guard gave Alerien a surprised look; he thought that the high counselor would certainly know not only of the king's departure, but of his plans as well. "My Lord?"

"Are you deaf! Tell me where he has gone and why!" Alerien screamed.

"I don't know for certain, my Lord. Only rumors and scuttlebutt."

"Speak them now, or I'll see you strung up before the sun sets. Test my patience no more!"

The guard stood tall and straight and his eyes stared blankly forward again. "I know only that they travel into the East, my Lord. I believe they were to pass as far as Delasur, for my bunkmate was sent out before them carrying a message to ready supplies there in advance of their arrival. Of where His Majesty ventures beyond that, I know naught. There was rumor of a group of rebels forming in the east, but I know not if this be true either."

"True enough," said Alerien, speaking more to himself than the guard.

"How many still remain to guard the capital?" he asked, almost as an afterthought.

"Two score, my Lord."

Alerien turned away, but paused at the door. "See to it that *all* the posts are manned, including the entrance to the catacombs. And the next guard I find not at the ready will swing. Do you understand?"

"Yes, my Lord."

"And have a rider readied. I'll have an urgent message for General Gueren in a few minutes." Alerien slammed the great doors of the hall and made for the high tower.

The guard sighed in relief. His hand drifted to his throat and he massaged his neck in reassurance.

Raízo laid Kazareen's body on the table in the great hall. His clothes were torn and shredded along with the flesh of his arms and legs, but there was not as much bleeding as Leyrea supposed there should be.

"Fetch the healer, quickly," ordered Raízo. Hyrta, one of the older archers, disappeared down the corridor.

"I think the cold has retarded the bleeding," said Leyrea, dabbing her finger in a deep gash in Kazareen's leg.

The Heart of the Graystone

"Yes. It is so. We have seen it before," said Raízo, cutting away the tattered remains of Kazareen's breeches with his dagger. "When the body is chilled the blood is slowed."

Kazareen's eyes were still open, but rolling back in his head as he mumbled something unintelligible.

Florin put his hand to Kazareen's chest. He was still breathing, but he was frightfully cold.

"He's nearly frozen," Florin said.

Raízo pointed to one of the large brass braziers. "Bring that near, and add some more fuel. The cold has slowed his bleeding, but it could kill him if we don't get him warm soon."

Florin hurried over to the corner of the hall and began dragging the brazier across the floor. It rattled and thumped as it scraped across the rough floorboards.

Hyrta returned with the healer close behind.

After quickly surveying Kazareen's wounds and feeling his neck and armpit, the healer sighed and turned to the Patri. "There is little I can do for him, I'm afraid. He's lost too much blood and the cold has seized him from the inside. He will die."

"No!" Florin shouted. "He will not! Close his wounds and..." Florin paused as he peered at the Graystone in Kazareen's hand, "...and he will survive. He is young and strong."

"Nothing and no one can save him now. Even if I close his wounds, he will come to death in no more than a day or two. I've seen many heartier men with lighter wounds do the same," said the healer, shaking his head. "It is hopeless."

"It is not hopeless," said Leyrea softly. She drew close to the Patri and whispered: "You saw the light on the marches." She motioned to the Graystone in Kazareen's hand, but the Patri did not see. "There is a great power in it. Power enough to save him. Still, we must do what we can. Please."

Raízo gave her a puzzled look. He had no idea exactly what Leyrea meant, but with the appearance of the weird light and a golem wolf, he realized that a strange fate, rife with strong and ancient magic, was being played out around him.

The Patri turned to the healer. "Close his wounds. And give him the best care you might."

"But my lord—"

"I command it."

The healer was wise enough to argue no more. He ordered Hyrta to bring a tub of hot water, bolts of clean cloth and his sewing needle and thread. Leyrea left with Hyrta to help.

205

Raízo took Florin by the arm and led him into the front alcove while the healer began attending to Kazareen.

"'T'was no wolf that did this."

"What? I saw it with my own eyes."

"As did I, until I slew it. After I plunged my spear into it, it left behind no earthly body, only dirt and leaves. It was golem."

"Golem?"

"An unnatural familiar, a beastly manifestation of dark magic, devoid of true life. I believed them to be no more than myth—until today."

Raízo waited patiently for Florin to respond. He only looked around nervously.

"Tell me, Florin, what was the source of the light on the march? What art of magic do you wield to fend off a golem wolf?"

"I have no *magic*. And I would never have believed in magic—until I met Kazareen." Florin looked back to Kazareen and the healer for a moment before he spoke again. "It is not my place to say more. I have given Kazareen my pledge of silence on the subject. So once again, I must defer to my young friend. If he lives—and I believe he will survive this—then I believe he should be the one to tell you of this magic, as you call it. If he so chooses."

"Ye Lords! Where did he get this?" the healer exclaimed.

Florin knew immediately what had happened and he flew back to Kazareen's side. The healer held the Graystone. A small twinkling of silver light shimmered deep inside.

"That belongs to Kazareen," said Florin jealously.

The healer gave Florin a bitter look. "I am no thief, it is just that I have never seen the like of it before." The healer held it up to take a closer look. "Where do you suppose—"

Florin scowled. In a flash, he snatched the Graystone from the healer and just as quickly thrust it back into Kazareen's clammy hand. The light twinkled again faintly then went out.

"Let me see that," Raízo said. His voice was calm, yet forceful.

Florin turned and gave the Patri a pleading look. "I cannot."

"Step aside."

Florin suddenly felt trapped. He didn't wish to defy the Patri's will in his own House, but he couldn't allow Kazareen to be separated from the healing power of the Graystone either. He had to choose.

"I cannot."

Raízo did not stir, but the healer's eyes widened as he took a step back. The Patri considered Florin carefully for a moment. Without another word, he stepped around Florin and came to Kazareen's side.

The Heart of the Graystone

Florin leaned forward anxiously.

Raízo pried open Kazareen's hand and saw the huge Graystone, but he left it where it lay.

Florin's gaze shifted back and forth from the dark crystal to the blank expression on Kazareen's face. Why did it no longer shine? Was the healer right? Was Kazareen already as good as dead?

After a long silence, the Patri rolled Kazareen's fingers around the Graystone once more. Florin exhaled ever so slightly and his muscles wilted in relief.

Raízo turned to the healer. "This stone shall remain in Kazareen's possession. If it comes up missing, I will hold you personally responsible. Do you understand?"

"Of course, my lord," said the healer nodding. His eyes had grown to the size of saucers.

Leyrea and Hyrta came hustling back. An uncomfortable silence filled the hall and hung there like a stagnant mist on a bog. She placed the pot of warm water on the table.

Raízo seemed about to say more, but he turned quickly and left. A small crowd of curious onlookers soon began to gather at the far end, mumbling and pointing. They parted as the Patri strode through. "Benedicio!" he shouted, disappearing down the corridor.

Florin and Leyrea traded glances. His face was already etched with despair.

Leyrea shook her head at him and went to the healer's side. "I have tended wounds before, and am skilled with needle and thread. Let me help you."

The healer did not look at her. The young man was a frightful mess and though he thought his work was in vain, he would keep his word to the Patri. "Fine. See to the smaller wounds on his left leg, while I deal with this."

The healer cut away the rest of his clothes and Kazareen laid naked on the table now, save a tattered rag for modesty, and the full extent of his mauling became evident. The wolf had inflicted scores of puncture wounds all over his body, though most were clustered around his upper legs and forearms. The wounds dotted his body like red pox, and they bled not at all. His face had been clawed and red streaks ran across it like thin red ribbons, but the healer was intent on his right leg.

"Help me turn him over."

Kazareen groaned weakly as they placed him face down. The beast had done more than just snap at this calf; it was torn wide open. Florin winced. Layers of fat and muscle lay open, oozing with thick, gelatinous blood, a hideously unnatural orifice, mangled and torn. Inside, tiny fibers of what remained of the flesh of his calf twitched and jumped uncontrollably. The scraping indentations of the golem's teeth on the white of bone were easily discernible.

Florin had to turn away. Not because he was squeamish, he had skinned and gutted many animals in his day, but because he couldn't bear the sight of his friend in such a condition. He felt his stomach churning and his head beginning to spin, so he sat on the bench to catch his breath. His face disappeared into his hands, and a single pitiful sob escaped him.

"Florin!" Leyrea said.

He looked up. The on-lookers were growing bolder and had begun to encircle the table where Kazareen lay, whispering and gasping. Florin bolted to his feet.

"Step back, folks, please. Give them peace to work in. Please, step back. It is not a pleasant sight," he said, both as forcefully and as kindly as he could muster. Arms raised, he ushered the on-lookers back to the side alcoves, hoping they would disperse down the corridor.

"Who is that?"

"Is that the blacksmith?"

"What happened?"

"Will he live?"

"What did this?"

The flurry of overlapping questions came quickly, and none-too-quietly. Florin hushed them.

"Shh, folks, please. Quietly now. Let us attend to him in peace. Go about your business," he pleaded, but none seemed willing to leave until their curiosity was satisfied.

Florin sighed. "It is Kazareen, the blacksmith, yes. He was attacked by a rogue wolf, which our brave Patri has duly dispatched; do not fret. And he will live, but only if you give the healers time and peace enough to attend to him, now please, go about your business!"

Florin was nearly shouting. A couple of the onlookers turned the tables on him and shushed him back. But they seemed satisfied enough with his brief explanation, and slowly, they began to wander off. When the last few cleared away, Florin went back to Kazareen's side.

Leyrea and the healer worked feverishly for more than two hours, binding and tending his wounds as best they could. Kazareen did not stir at all, but the Graystone, still dark, remained wrapped between the fingers of his left hand. When all his wounds were sewn shut, save the small puncture wounds, which were too small for sewing, the healer began searching the sundry of supplies.

"Did you bring the brown salve?" he asked.

The Heart of the Graystone

"I don't know," she said, looking round the bloody mess on the table.

"Well, could you go..." his voice drifted off. "Never mind. You wouldn't know it if you saw it." He studied the wreck of Kazareen's body for a moment and then pulled a thick blanket over him. "Anyway, I believe I shall have to mix some more. I'll go." The healer dipped his hands in the water and wiped them dry, but they remained stained with blood. As he left the hall, he sighed and shook his head. He didn't seem to be in much of a hurry.

Florin looked to Leyrea. It was the first time they'd been alone together for many months. Their eyes met and each saw in the other's a silent desperation. "I think the healer may have been right," she said. "We may lose him."

Florin looked away, grunting. "No. We mustn't give up hope." But the cracking of his voice revealed the doubts he was trying so hard to reject.

Leyrea looked down at Kazareen, who now laid face up. He was the very image of death: cold, pale, torn and bloodied, and motionless but for the slight rise and fall of his chest, and that was shallow and irregular. She looked at the necklace round his neck and realized she'd never seen it before. Perhaps he'd worn it beneath his shirt since before they met.

But it was the Graystone that she was more interested in. Did it have power enough to pull him back from the very precipice of death, where he now teetered so precariously? Kneeling down, she pried open one of his fingers. The dark stone looked so impotent, so useless there in his hand. She didn't know why, but she began to grow angry.

Work! Save him! Heal my friend. Please.

But the stone remained dark. The sudden urge to smash the thing into a thousand pieces overtook her and she reached for the crystal. She touched it with her bloodstained hand, and it sparked to life. This caught her off guard and she pulled her hand back instinctively, as if to keep from being burnt. The brilliant light waned as soon as she withdrew her touch.

While she'd felt no heat from the Graystone, she naturally inspected her fingers. At fist she didn't realize what had happened as she eyed the fleshy pink skin and brown calluses on her hands. Then it struck her. She looked at her left hand; it was still stained with the drying blood of her friend. Her right was pure and clean.

The flash of light startled Florin from his inner struggles. "What are you doing?"

She held up her hands for Florin. "Look."

Leyrea leaned down with her eyes just inches from the Graystone, which was still twinkling weakly. Bringing her other, still bloodstained hand slowly, carefully down toward the stone, until it was no more than a fraction of an inch above it, she watched in amazement as the blood on her hands condensed into a sparkling blue mist, flowed quickly to the tip of her finger and then fell on the stone. Three quick drops of fully liquid blood dripped from her finger and her hand was as clean as the other. With the falling of each drop, the twinkling in the Graystone grew slightly brighter.

Kazareen's eyelids flicked, but his friends missed it.

"What do make of that?" she asked, holding her hands up for Florin.

"I do not know."

For a moment, she pondered, and then took the Graystone from Kazareen. It shimmered slightly. "I have an idea," she said.

She held the Graystone above a small pool of blood on the table, but nothing happened, so she dipped the tip of it in. Still nothing. Leyrea sighed.

"Give it back to him."

Leyrea looked at Kazareen's wounds. "Wait."

Florin squirmed, first one shoulder, then the next.

She pressed the Graystone gently to the skin beside the huge wound on his right leg. It was a horrid sight, and the healer had done his best to sew it shut, but too much of the flesh was torn away and a gap the size of her thumb still yawned dreadfully in the open air. This time, the misty blue-gray aura returned. At first it only evaporated the blood around the wound, but then suddenly the aura grew, and in a flash, it enveloped Kazareen's entire body. He seemed about to lift from the table; his back arched for a moment, his arms reached out with open hands. Then he fell limp. Every bloodstain on his body was cleansed, like he'd been given a hot bath and a good scrubbing, but the wounds themselves seemed little affected.

Leyrea smiled brightly, her eyes twinkled, and she felt a wisp of hope sweeping through her. The Graystone was a bit brighter still.

"Whew!" No matter how many times he saw the Graystone, Florin was always amazed at its power. Still, his rational side tugged at him, trying to pull his mind away from believing what he saw with his own eyes. He pushed the feeling back. He couldn't deny this, no matter what his long experiences had led him to believe—or disbelieve. So many times, in his those dark years of imprisonment, he entertained the thought of taking his own life, just to end the suffering, but his heart had led him through it, with a sliver of hope so scant it seemed not to exist at

The Heart of the Graystone

all. It was the image of a young and beautiful Solia that had sustained him, nourished him, and extinguished his self-pity when it seemed about to consume him. As a younger man, he had always trusted his eyes to show him the way through the dark recesses of the forest, and though it seemed backwards to him, he now had trouble trusting his eyes. But he had to.

Trust in the heart to believe the eyes.

The heart? The Dragon's heart. Yes! The heart!

Florin gazed at the necklace round Kazareen's neck. "Give me the Graystone."

Examining the necklace carefully, he thought it might just be long enough, yes—this might work.

Leyrea handed him the stone.

Florin began tugging at one of the knots; the wet leather kept a firm grip, but he managed to loosen it just a bit. He slid the pointed end of the Graystone through a tiny hole created by one of the finer knots and pressed it in. He was able to force the large bulbous end between two, then four, strands of leather of one of the more open areas of the design. He pulled and straightened and tugged, and though the leather was fighting him, he gradually worked the Graystone firmly into the intricate lattice of swirling, interlaced knots.

Pulling the necklace taught, Florin centered the Graystone directly over Kazareen's heart and stood up straight. It seemed right to his eyes. Almost too right, as if the necklace had been tied for that very purpose, a sturdy support for what its maker had never known or seen. The Graystone now lie twinkling on Kazareen's chest, bound perfectly in a handsome work of art, the missing centerpiece of an unassuming structure, the glory of which Rosari du Phenoa could only have dreamed.

"Do you think he'll be alright?" Leyrea asked.

"I do now." Florin took her hand absently and kissed it, not out of love for her, but out of the pure relief that seemed to be flowing through him. Kazareen would live. Somehow, he knew it.

And until the healer returned with the salve some minutes later, neither of them was able to either release their grip or take their eyes off the light that grew slowly but steadily in the Graystone at Kazareen's breast.

The Coming Storm

"Message for you General, sir." The soldier handed the parchment to Gueren. He checked the seal; the embossed figure of the dragon was still intact and stared back at him almost mockingly. He raised an eyebrow as he read. He had heard nothing from his brother, or the king, since leaving Pente Kaleán more than a year and half before. The message was short, and written in Alerien's scrawling, thin script.

It was good news, if not curious. His brother wrote that the boy was last seen alive, though barely so, many leagues northwest of Beruthia, beyond the ancient North Gate that barred the only known pass into the Northlands, in a newly built stronghold at the foot of the mountains. Gueren was to ready his troops for siege and battle, as soon as possible.

"Dismissed."

The soldier left.

Gueren stared out the west window of the tower of Beruthia. The plain that stretched out before him was starting to show some semblance of life again, growing greener with each passing day. He sighed.

How Alerien had come by this information he didn't know, but he had his suspicions. Had he visited the Seer again in his absence? Or had he acquired the power of long sight by dark magik? Did it matter? His suspicions had been proven. The boy was receiving aid, and open rebellion was imminent.

He read the message again. No word on whether Alerien, or the king, might come to join him in battle, or how his brother had learned the location of the boy. It didn't matter. Gueren didn't care if he came or not. He would have his prize—at last.

"Guard! Send for the captain, the magistrate and the governor, at once."

At last, there was an army to be raised.

The appearance of the golem had shattered the relative peace Locnomina had enjoyed since its construction began more than seven years before. The Patri became convinced, and his kin with him, that they would soon come under attack. The golem had been the first sign of the trouble to come, but not the only one, for even more ominously, the sign of the dragon had appeared in the crystal blue of the eastern skies, and as it often had in the past, it foretold of a great battle to come.

The bard Jorg had noticed it first, when the gray skies of winter had finally receded. A new star appeared: diamond-bright, following after the sun, sinking below the horizon in early evening, with long, wispy wings of silver-white trailing after. As the days passed, what folk called the dragonstar grew brighter, and its wings grew longer and wider, and eventually it became visible even in the light of day. When the hand, held at arms length, could no longer hide its gray streak across the sky, they knew the fateful day had nearly come.

Those days were not wasted. They used them to make all the preparations for war. For weeks, Locnomina was abuzz with activity. Hastily constructed hoardings of wood sprung up on the recently completed ramparts. The archers spent their time between patrols fashioning a great cache of arrows and practicing their marksmanship. Florin led the woodsmen on hunting trips, clearing the marches of as much game as they could find, in preparation of siege. Leyrea joined the far rangers, whose orders were to carry back word of an approaching army.

The Patri worried most about the siege engines that would certainly spring up when the attack finally came, and so he personally oversaw the carpenters and stonecutters work. Night and day he drove them in their labor: constructing catapults and ballistae on either side of the gatehouse, where the walls were widest. The stonecutter's work was the heaviest: gathering boulders from the cliffs, shaping them into deadly shot, and moving them into position on top of the walls.

Kazareen's able hands as a smithy were missed dearly as he recovered from his ordeal. The Patri ordered the lone smithy to reinforce the iron bars of the gate, but by himself, the work went dreadfully slow, and it would take time to re-hang the gate, at least a full day's effort by twenty or more men. But Kazareen was unable to help.

Kazareen healed slowly from the golem's attack and was unable even to rise from his bed for more than two weeks. The healer would not have allowed it even if Kazareen were able. He had tried several times to stand when he was left alone, and despite his efforts, he could not bear the pain. His right calf had been too badly injured and in his weakness, he would crumble to the floor. The healer walked in on him unexpectedly during one attempt, and finding him writhing in pain on the floor next to his bed, admonished him to rest, lest he pull loose the stitches. Kazareen hated to admit it, but the healer was right. He had to rest and heal.

The Patri made regular visits to keep his spirits up, at least once a day, though they were brief. He said nothing to Kazareen of the golem wolf or the dragonstar for some time. Mostly, he spoke of the bravery and loyalty his friends had shown on the marches. But Kazareen was

The Heart of the Graystone

silent when Raízo talked of Florin and Leyrea, and his eyes would wander away to some private place inside.

"What is wrong, Kazareen?" asked Raízo, "Are you in great pain?"

"No. It's not that," he replied, his gaze still directed out his window.

"Then tell me what vexes you."

Kazareen hesitated for a moment. "You say they saved me from the wolf, yet they have not come to visit me even once since it happened." He closed his eyes. "I don't understand...it doesn't really matter, I guess."

"Not true. Leyrea helped the healer to bind your wounds and both she and Florin sat at your side all through that first night, here, in this room, until I ordered them out."

"I don't remember that."

"Of course not. You were out of your head for a several days, thanks to the concoction my alchemist devised. Nicholas said it would relieve your pain and allow you rest. No, your friends would be here every waking minute if I would have allowed it, but they were needed elsewhere."

"For what? I've heard a great deal of commotion, hammering and shouting and the like through my window, but the healer won't tell me what's going on."

"He's a good man. I'm afraid he is also doing as I ordered. Kazareen, that was no wolf that attacked you. It was golem."

"Golem?"

The Patri explained to Kazareen all that happened on the marches, how he and his friends had saved him and slain the monstrous beast. But when the deed was done the wolf's body had disappeared, or rather, shown its true make-up, the decaying matter of the forests. He spoke of the old legends, kept alive mostly as children's tales now, of how dark magik could cause the forest itself to spring into unnatural and ferocious beasts. Finally, he told Kazareen of the sudden appearance of the dragonstar in the sky. All these things could not be taken as mere coincidence and they pointed to one thing: an evil force was taking shape and an attack on Locnomina would surely come soon. The sounds Kazareen heard through his window were the sounds of the House of Pendi readying Locnomina for battle. Against what dark power, he couldn't say for certain, but he believed the king and his advisors must have fallen under the spell of some ancient evil.

Kazareen didn't want to believe his ears. He knew well that the Necromancers were in league with the king; it was that they'd finally found him that he regretted most. He had found peace and a home here, and now it seemed that this too would be brought to a bitter end.

He knew that all this misfortune was coming about because of him. Of this there was no doubt. All because of what he now bore round his neck. Arpento had warned him of the dark arts of the Necromancers and so he knew only they could have conjured the golem wolf. After nearly two years, they were seeking him still. Kazareen had tried desperately to put the idea out of his mind, but it never fully left him. No matter how hard he tried to convince himself that he'd found a new home, deep down, in a place he wouldn't allow himself to visit, he knew it was all just an illusion. He had fooled himself, for a time, and now everyone around him would pay for it. He realized now he would never find true peace for himself, or for those nearest him, until he did as Arpento had urged. As long as he was alive and carried the Graystone, he was a threat to everyone, friend and foe alike.

And something new began to grow inside Kazareen at that moment, something he'd never felt as strong before in his life, something as hard as tempered steel being drawn from a forge, burning white-hot: his own will.

"That is why your friends have not visited. They are serving this House. I am sure they would visit you if they had time, but they are doing as I asked. And doing so in good faith," Raízo said.

"This is all my fault. I have brought disaster upon this House," Kazareen said in a near whisper.

The Patri could not force himself to take a breath. Every muscle in his body tensed. He sat down on a stool beside the bed. "You mean the Graystone?"

"You know of it?"

"I know of its existence, though little of its power. It was Florin who found it in your room, and he who reached you first on the marches. Wielding it like a burning flame, he kept the golem at bay until the rest of us caught him up and slew the monster. Though he has served this House well, he refused to tell me anything more of your Graystone. Just as on the day you came to us, he has deferred to your judgment. And though I desired greatly to quiz you on the matter, I thought it best to wait until more of your strength had returned."

Kazareen was listening, but staring out the window, his brow furrowing, his eyes narrowing. And his heart burning. "Then the golem saw the Graystone?"

"Yes. Myself, Benedicio and a handful of the archers beheld the glory of its magic as well. It lit the woods with a strange light too brilliant to go unnoticed and yet...too bright to see direct, if you take my meaning. Kazareen, tell me, what is this magic you carry? I must know...if this House is to survive the coming storm."

The Heart of the Graystone

Kazareen looked into the Patri's eyes now. He couldn't tell him everything he knew of the Graystone; of that much he was certain. Too many knew of its existence already. But he felt obliged to share what he could. All their lives depended on it.

"I found the Graystone in the forest of Bethë Dien, the day before I was arrested in Feria. After Florin and I escaped, I began to learn about its power to heal. And later," he wasn't sure if he should mention Arpento, "I discovered it has other powers as well. Powers that King Geraldi and his advisors, Alerien and Gueren, might put to evil use. They are responsible for the appearance of the golem. I am sure of it. I eluded them for a long time, but now that their golem has found me, then they too must know where I am. I'm afraid we may be facing all the armies of Pendoria before this over."

Raízo blanched and his face went pale. He stood up. There was much he still didn't understand, but things were worse than he'd imagined. If Kazareen was right and the king was bringing the full of weight of Pendoria's armies to his door, he knew they were not yet strong enough to defeat them.

The Patri turned to leave, but stopped at the door. "There is much that requires my attention, but I would speak with you more about this Graystone. According to my healer, you should not have survived the golem's attack, and I trust his judgment in this matter. Yet here you are. Tell me, can the magic of your jewel...save us from what comes? As it did you?"

Kazareen paused, wanting only to say that it could. "I don't know."

Raízo sighed. "We shall speak again soon," he said, and left.

Florin and the hunting party passed through the archway of Locnomina later that afternoon, as planned. They were ordered to return to the keep every other day with what game they had taken, in case they missed word of an approaching army while on the hunt. Their horses bore the carcasses of four heavy stags, a bevy of rabbit and squirrel, and a single mountain ram, all field-dressed, yet still bearing their coats. The four great hounds of the yard, smelling fresh meat, came sniffing about, looking for a handout, but they were trained well enough to know they were not allowed to help themselves.

Florin chased them away. "Sorry, boys. You'll have to wait for the bones." One of the hounds eyed him sadly, then shuffled away with the others, disappointed. Still, the scent of fresh meat kept them close.

Raízo shouted down to the hunting party: "Well done, lads. When you get your take unloaded, head back out. Still no word from the rangers." But he spoke too soon, for at that moment, Leyrea and Hyrta, came riding hard up the muddy path.

"Where is the Patri?" Hyrta shouted as he jumped from his spotted mount. Even in the cool spring air, their horses were covered with sweat.

"Here!" Raízo shouted back. "What word?"

"They are coming!"

Everyone within earshot stopped what they were doing and listened. Raízo slid quickly down one of the ladders, missing every riser, and ran over to them. "Report."

Benedicio, who'd been helping with the last of the hoardings on the opposite wall, hustled over to them as well.

The air in the yard stiffened.

"We spotted the vanguard before dawn," said Hyrta, still huffing and puffing from their frenzied ride. "To the southeast. I make it forty miles, as of daybreak."

"How many?"

Hyrta looked to Leyrea for a moment. "About four thousand," he said finally.

"I make it five," said Leyrea.

The Patri scowled, but he'd expected as much. "Riding hard?"

"No. Most were on foot. There were no more than fifty riders," Hyrta said.

"All the regular soldiers were mounted. The rest looked to be conscripts, as they bore no livery and no armor heavier than boiled leather. Most carrying bows, though some were armed with swords or axes," Leyrea added.

Raízo raised an eyebrow. "Anything else?"

"A caravan of about twenty wagons and thirty or so heavily laden mules trailed the column," said Hyrta.

"And they are led by General Gueren," Leyrea added.

Raízo took a small step forward. "You are sure of this? Not by the king?"

Hyrta shrugged.

"I am," Leyrea said, holding the Patri's gaze.

"Good work," Raízo said, patting Hyrta on the back and nodding to Leyrea. He looked to his son. "How long?"

Benedicio thought for a moment. "On foot? Narrow muddy trails. I would say two days at least, if they were hard pressed. No more than three."

"I agree. You hunters, when you finish with your loads, help the smithy. We must re-hang the gate. And the rest of you, back to work! No time to spare now! Long live the House of Pendi!" Raízo shouted.

The Heart of the Graystone

The host on the walls and in the courtyard answered with a great cry: "Long live the Patri!"

Raízo turned to his son. "Call the counsel. We must lay our final plans." Benedicio nodded and ran off in search of the rest of the knights.

As the small crowd began to break up, Florin gave Leyrea a look of gentle rebuke. "Did I not counsel you to leave? And to take your daughter with you?"

"We have nowhere else to go. My life is here, with Cathio...and with this House."

"Your life, and your daughter's, may come to an untimely end if you choose to stay."

"The choice is already made, besides, I don't see you running anywhere," said Leyrea, leaving Florin behind.

Florin shook his head; he was now well accustomed to her jibes.

The Patri turned and began to make his way toward the high rooms, but he paused at the doors to the great hall and looked up. In the deep blue of the afternoon sky, the dragonstar hung directly overhead. Once again, it had rightly foretold of a great battle, though as always, it left silent who might prevail in the end.

The next morning, the Patri ordered that all but five of the horses stabled at Locnomina be set loose upon the marches. They would be of little use in a siege. Better that they live free than perish unused.

Kazareen watched from his window as Wingfoot trotted off through the last few patches of snow still dotting the landscape. Sirius and Vala trailed behind. His heart ached. It didn't seem right to part this way, without even the simplest of goodbyes. Had Wingfoot's part in the prophecy been fulfilled? He supposed this good beast had served him well enough.

Kazareen had never grown as fond of an animal as he had this mighty, but gentle steed. And as the horses began to fade into the distance, Kazareen wished he could at least stroke Wingfoot's mane once more to show his gratitude and affection. He stretched out his hand to the last image of the gray stallion he thought ever to see, not waving goodbye, but trying in vain to touch him one last time.

Just before he disappeared from sight, as if he'd felt Kazareen's distant hand, he stopped amidst a thin patch of glistening snow and turned his head back to Locnomina. Then suddenly he threw himself to the ground and rubbed his back in the snow. Kazareen had never seen him in such a playful mood. His body arched and he rolled from side to side as his hoofs beat harmlessly in the air.

Kazareen couldn't help but chuckle at Wingfoot's final salute.

The horse paused for a moment and raised his head again. And even across the distance that separated them, their eyes seemed to meet. For a second, they were as one.

"Fare well, Wingfoot," he whispered. "Thank you."

The stallion rose quickly to his feet and then trotted out of sight.

On the following day, the last of the rangers returned and the gates of Locnomina were shut. Just before sunset and a scant hour after they'd managed to re-hang the heavy iron bars of the gate, a lone figure dressed in black, came waddling slowly up the path that led to the entrance.

"Halt!" shouted one of the lookouts as the figure approached within thirty yards of the gate.

The man stopped and raised his hands, showing them to be empty.

"I am unarmed!" the man shouted back. "I come in peace."

The man's voice rang with the charm of one beloved, and the lookout felt a strange urge to order the gates to be opened. But he caught himself and the words stuck in his throat. The strange rumors of the last few weeks were too fresh in his mind to ignore. Rumors of sorcery and dark magik had been sweeping through the House since the day the wolf had mauled the young blacksmith, rumors the worldly men of Locnomina found very difficult to believe at first, rumors of the return of the accursed golems from the ancient times. And tales of the aged hunter's own powerful magic on the marches, a brilliant white flame of power he wielded to fend off the golem.

And what of this man approaching the gate? Could he be weaving some spell around his voice to gain entry? If the rumors had any truth to them at all, then anything seemed possible now. Better to err on the side of caution.

"Stay where you are!" the lookout shouted.

The man stood with his hands at his side, palms upward.

"Who are you?"

"A friend in need," he replied.

The shouting had grabbed the attention of all the others upon the wall and they peered down through the narrow slits in the hoardings and wide gaps in the ramparts and listened.

"Tell me your name or we shall loose our arrows!" A few of the archers nocked arrows—those who were not captured by the soothing song of the stranger's voice—the rest only gazed at the lookout as if he must be mad.

"If the House of Pendi wishes to survive the coming storm, then you shall loose no dart upon me." Then the man pulled back the hood

The Heart of the Graystone

of his cloak and revealed himself. "I am the one called Arpento. I have come bearing aid and counsel to the House of Pendi."

The archers who'd managed to nock arrows lowered their bows. Hushed gasps of disbelief swept over the wall. There was nary a man in the East who had not heard tales of the infinitely wise, yet cruelly selfish Arpento.

The lookout stood silent. Were all the legends he'd heard as a child coming true, now, in his lifetime? The dragonstar. Golems. And now Arpento himself. His mind swam for a moment. When he regained his wits, he spoke again: "I shall fetch the Patri. He shall be judge in this. Wait there and do not move."

Arpento swung his hands behind his back and stood patiently before the gates, tapping his foot in the mud and whistling, as if he hadn't a care in the world.

The Patri was fetched straight away and soon stood upon the wall above the gate, Benedicio at his side. Word spread quickly through Locnomina of the arrival of the wise hermit and many dropped what they were doing to come see the stranger standing at their door, Florin and Leyrea among them. Still alone in his room, Kazareen sat restlessly on the edge of his bed, but no word came to him of Arpento's appearance at the gate; for the moment, he was forgotten.

"My men tell me you call yourself Arpento. But I know somewhat of him. He does not venture from the wood of Bethë Khür. So tell me, stranger, who are you?" asked the Patri.

He smiled. "I am Arpento. And you are right in what you say, for the most part. I have not ventured from my home for...a long time. But the time has come for me at last to play my part. I am Arpento. And I am here. Will you not show me a bit of hospitality?"

"How do I know you are not a spy for the approaching hoard?"

"I suppose you don't. But tell me, what good be a spy if you take him captive during the coming war? Still...I am no spy. And unless I am mistaken, there are some among you who can vouch for me."

"And who might that be?"

Arpento raised his voice. "Florin? Leyrea? Are you near?"

Florin pushed his way forward and stood next to the Patri. "I am."

Leyrea's voice came down from one of the hoardings far to the right. "As am I!" she shouted.

"And your friend?"

"He is—" Florin started.

"Silence!" the Patri ordered, as he took Florin by the arm. "I alone shall speak for this House!" He loosened his grip on Florin's arm slowly. "You know this person to be Arpento?"

"I do."

Leyrea jogged up to them. "This is truly Arpento. We have met him before. With Kazareen," she said.

Raízo stood silently for a moment. Turning to Benedicio, "What do you think?"

"Perhaps he has come to help. But there is always a price to be paid for his aid. And the cost is high," said the Patri's son.

As the Patri contemplated his decision, someone on the east wall shouted: "The vanguards! The vanguards approach!"

All turned their gaze toward the marches. And they saw there now, breaking through the tree line, the bright crimson of the royal banners fluttering in the breeze, borne by tall riders. The muffled sound of horses neighing drifted up to the walls as they halted.

"I say! If you wouldn't mind, might you let me pass? I am afraid those approaching might find my presence here...uh, rather distressing." Arpento said a bit more anxiously.

He hesitated no more. "Let him pass!" Raízo shouted to the gatekeepers. "Quickly!"

"It seems he has come too late to provide us any useful counsel. But I allow him passage on your word. So he is your responsibility. If he turns against us, I shall hold both of you responsible!"

"Don't worry," Florin reassured. "He is true."

The gate groaned as it was opened just enough to allow Arpento to pass through. He smiled kindly at the gatekeepers as he slipped in. "Thank you, my good men." The loud clank of the gate closing behind him was their only reply. The gatekeepers gave Arpento a wide berth.

The Patri, Benedicio, Florin and Leyrea hurried down the ladders and surrounded the old man.

"Search him!" said the Patri to Leyrea. She did not move. "Do it!"

Arpento nodded slightly to her in reassurance. "It is necessary for his peace of mind."

Leyrea searched him quickly, though gently. "He bears no arms."

Raízo explored the old man's face, though kindly as it was, he could find no reason to trust him yet, despite Florin and Leyrea's words of reassurance. "My guard reports you have offered aid and counsel. Well, now is the time. Already, the king's army encircles us! So speak."

"I would speak with you, and the one called Kazareen—in private."

"There is no time for delay. And Kazareen is not well. He was gravely injured not long ago by— "

"A wolf?"

Raízo's eyes flashed. How could the old man know such a thing? "No, it was no wolf."

The Heart of the Graystone

"Then you are aware it was...something else?"

"We believe it was golem," the Patri said softly.

"Ah. I see the old tales have not been completely forgotten. Good! Then a bit of wisdom has found sanctuary in the House of Pendi as well," said Arpento. "Enough I hope to take advantage of the opportunity of the help I now offer, but only if you and I speak with Kazareen. He is well enough to converse with us at least, is he not?"

Raízo bit his lip. There was little time to spare. He had hoped the enemy's first stroke would not come 'til the morrow. Yet the feeling that Arpento might actually provide some valuable information, some bit of knowledge that might turn the tide of battle in their favor was too tempting to pass up. He turned to Benedicio. "See that the archers are readied and the full supply of arrows are upon the walls. Then check on the right catapult. The triggering pin is still sticking. Oh, and the pitch has not yet been set. See to it while I see to...our guest."

Benedicio frowned, but did as he was bid. "Yes, father."

"Come with me," said Raízo, and he led Arpento into the keep.

The Patri and Arpento were sheltered in Kazareen's room for more than two hours. All the while Benedicio saw to the preparations, his eyes continually checked the doors of the Great Hall, wondering how long it would be before his father returned.

The men were becoming restless. They were put off by the appearance of Arpento, and especially by the Patri's absence, as the enemy's great host took up positions around Locnomina. They were outnumbered by at least five to one, and their spirits were fading.

When darkness settled over the highlands, and the gloom of the men's spirit seemed as black as the night that surrounded them, the Patri emerged from the keep holding a lit torch. It was a welcome arrival, and the men cheered his return.

The Patri stopped in the middle of the yard. Alone he waited there, bearing his torch high overhead, until they quieted and he felt the eyes of every warrior in the House upon him. Then he cast the torch at his feet.

"House of Pendi, listen while your Patri speaks! Remember now your word is your oath of fealty to this House! For there is something I must ask of you all. Something great and terrible. But fear not! For I have seen our victory borne upon the wings of the dragonstar. Victory for this House. And perhaps for all of Pendoria! If you hold to your word!"

The men shouted out for joy. The Patri's mere mention of victory seemed to override the caution they heard in his voice.

The Patri waited patiently until they quieted themselves.

223

"For this is my command to you! Come down from the walls! Leave your arms behind. Extinguish the fires. Leave your posts and come down. Our nightly sup awaits us in the Great Hall. Come down and break bread with your Patri. Come down!"

A gasp stole through the courtyard, followed by a long moment of stunned and silent disbelief. Not a single soul moved from its station, and the men began to grumble and hiss in defiance of their lord.

Benedicio held his right hand above him as he stepped forward. The men, seeing their trusted captain, quieted once again. "Father! What spell has that old wizard wrought to make you turn away from your own blood? Wake up, I say! The enemy is at our doorstep! We must fight! We must defend the last Great House!"

A few of the men cheered, but were torn between their devotion for the House of Pendi and the their personal allegiance to Raízo.

"No spell, only good common sense. Now come. All of you! While we may."

Still, none moved.

Suddenly, the deadly hush that had fallen over the courtyard was shattered with the bright wailing of royal trumpets outside the gates. Many heads turned to see General Gueren riding forward, flanked on either side by two of his lieutenants. They bore the royal standard of gold and crimson and their banners fluttered gently in the cool breeze. Tied hastily below each was the white flag of truce.

"My lord! A small party approaches!" a guard shouted.

Most turned to see the sight, and so few noticed as Arpento and Kazareen emerged from the doors of the Great Hall. Kazareen was hobbling weakly on his injured leg, and Arpento lent him his left arm for support.

"They bear standards of truce!" another shouted.

Raízo sighed and turned slightly to his right, where he saw Kazareen and Arpento making their way up slowly behind him. All around, he heard the stretching gut of bows.

"Lower your weapons! For I mean to treat with them," said the Patri. A few of the bows went slack, but most remained bent, ready to repel any act of treachery on the part of the dreaded General so many had fled.

The riders halted before the gates. Gueren was smiling as he surveyed the men of Locnomina. "House of Pendi! I am Gueren. High General of the Armies of Pendoria! Come forth and hear the terms of your King!"

Hisses and taunts rained down upon them, but Gueren only smiled, as if he reveled in their hatred. "Will you not treat with the

The Heart of the Graystone

representative of your king? Or has the House of Pendi taken leave of all its wisdom? Come forth now! Or no mercy or quarter will be shown to those who defy the king's just rule of this land."

More cruel words and jeers floated down from the ramparts, but they soon faded into silence. Finally, one of the heavy wooden inner doors to Locnomina swung open, creaking and groaning. And the Patri stepped forward, standing proudly before the General. The reinforced iron of the outer gate was not raised, and so yet barred the threshold. Gueren dismounted and stepped forward, a sick grin spread across his face.

"That's far enough!" Benedicio shouted from above.

Gueren stopped short. He knew a hundred arrows were bent on him, but his air of confidence did not falter. He eyed Raízo with contempt. "So this is what passes for rebellion?" he scoffed.

The Patri was silent.

Gueren said loudly: "You are dreadfully outnumbered. You shall all perish—"

The Patri cut him off. "Speak your terms!"

Again, Gueren chuckled to himself, but lowered his voice. "Not quite as foolish as I thought. Very well. The terms are simple. Hand over the one called Kazareen de Pendi. He is a fugitive from the king's justice, escapee from the royal guard of Feria, and murderer of more than twenty of the king's soldiers. Hand him over now, and my forces shall be withdrawn...for now." Gueren's eyes drifted up into the dim shapes above. There, the gray silhouettes of archers were barely visible.

"For now?" queried the Patri.

"The king will not stand for the raising of a hostile force within his own borders. You understand, of course...a house divided upon itself. Yet he is mindful of the old rivalries between the Great Houses, and therefore offers you a measure of amnesty. By his wisdom and grace, the king grants you two weeks to redeem yourselves, before the situation becomes untenable. In that time, you must lay down your arms, disband your forces, and forever open the gates of this stronghold, which I must say, is of a far better construction than I had thought possible by a group of..." Gueren would not finish the thought.

Raízo stood silently at the iron grating. He seemed moved to unleash a torrent of defiant words, instead he curled his lip under his beard and bit.

Florin stood next to Leyrea atop the wall above them, straining to hear the words of parlay being spoken below, but their voices were lost in the murmur of the guardsmen and archers around them. "What's he saying?"

"I cannot hear all. Something about amnesty. Shh, listen," she whispered back.

"The king is mistaken in more than one matter," began Raízo. "If there is a hostile force upon this land, then it the one that now surrounds Locnomina. His betrayal of the peoples of Pendoria, of the Great Houses, and of the Counsel of Patris has not, and shall never be forgotten—nor forgiven—for the King is held to the highest standard. And the one called Kazareen is no murderer. By his own admission, he has slain one soldier in the king's service—a single man. And that was just, for in doing so he saved his friend's life from Geraldi's tyrannical hand. Indeed, the act was justified. No, if anyone is guilty of murder, then it is Geraldi himself. This much is plain enough to see, by merely looking into the eyes of the wretched beast that now stands before me—"

"Enough!" Gueren's shout nearly shook the walls. His eyes blazed with a murderous fury and the armor he bore suddenly bristled with an unearthly sheen of dark power. "If death is what you seek, then greet it now, for it draws neigh."

Gueren turned his back on Raízo.

"One moment, General. I have not yet given you my answer to the king's terms."

Gueren stopped. He was fuming from the Patri's insult and his brow seemed about to ignite.

"Raise the gate." Raízo said.

As the iron bars slowly lifted, Kazareen and Arpento stepped forward. They ducked under it before it was fully raised and presented themselves to Gueren.

"Drop!"

The great weight of the gate slammed down with thunderous finality.

Florin looked down at the figures leaving the safety of Locnomina. For a moment in the darkness, he could not tell who had gone forth. Then seeing Kazareen's limp, he realized who had been handed over.

"NO! KAZAREEN, NO!" shouted Florin.

"I believe we have met the king's terms. For now," said Raízo calmly, ignoring Florin's protests.

"Raízo, what are you doing? Kazareen, no!" Florin shouted down once again.

But neither Kazareen nor Arpento looked back.

Leyrea paled to a sickly gray; and she found herself unable to utter a single word. Her knees buckled and she fell unconscious. No one, not even Florin, noticed in the dark.

The Heart of the Graystone

Gueren's face drew blank. He had not expected them to capitulate. Then the devilish grin reappeared on his face. "Seize them," he said. His lieutenants dismounted and quickly bound the prisoners.

"And who is this?" Gueren asked, approaching the old man.

"You know who I am." Arpento said.

Gueren studied the old man's eyes for a moment. "Ah yes! I believe I do! Unexpected this is. But welcome enough. We have killed two birds with the same stone," he said, suddenly laughing.

Now filled with pride for having cowed the Great House so easily, Gueren pushed out his chest and remounted his black steed. Head held high, he rode off into the comforting darkness and safety of his own battle lines, with the two most valuable prizes he could have hoped for marching weakly before him.

Florin's lone voice wailed repeatedly in the dark. "Kazareen, no!" Kazareen kept his eyes shut as he hobbled on, because he could not prevent his ears from hearing Florin's cries.

Gueren's party had no more than disappeared into the darkness and shelter of the tree line when the first of the red-hot boulders came sailing through the air, seeking the high walls of Locnomina.

The Battle for Locnomina

A light breeze blew through the turret and King Geraldi was struck by the vague notion that something had changed. Exactly what, he couldn't say, but the easterly winds seemed to bear it to him. Fresh and scintillating it was, pouring through the window like a splash of cool water to his face on a hot summer day. Somewhere unknown to him, a veiling fog burned away, and the last of the gray tentacles of winter were cast aside.

Geraldi stood at the east window, yet ignored the panoramic vista of the kingdom before his feet. With eyes shut, he took a deep breath. Yes. Spring had indeed arrived. The land seemed to breathe with him, then summon him with the rejuvenating scents of life renewed. He could not remember the last time he felt like this: so young, so alive.

With each passing moment, the color and vigor of the world, that had long appeared to him dark and threatening, stirred up hazy memories of better days, the days of his youth, those carefree afternoons atop spry Deneb, riding like a swift gale through the emerald glens of his home. Geraldi opened his eyes and grinned at the thought of trusty Deneb, aged though he had become.

He turned away from the window, scratched his crownless head and pawed at a beard that suddenly seemed much longer than he remembered. He tried to think of when last he'd gone riding, if only for its simple pleasure.

He couldn't recall.

Had it been so long? Casting his mind into the murky past, he found he could no longer remember when last he'd ventured beyond the walls of Pente Kaleán, or the confines of the high turret for that matter. What was he doing in this dreary place on such a fine spring day? No good reason came to him.

"I am going for a ride," he said to the empty turret. The words fell limp in the musty gloom, yet even this simple notion lifted his heart.

Geraldi fit his finest riding boots to his feet, twisted a hearty cape about his neck, took one step toward the exit and stopped. He went back to pick up the royal scepter from the small table, though he wasn't sure why, slid it in his cloak, and walked back over to the door leading to the stairwell.

That door. He eyed it cautiously.

Geraldi extended his hand to the latch, but his hand was stilled. It was as if the door were staring back it him. Its gaze was cold and hard and blank. Like a dull, artless statue he stood, face to face with a deadly enemy, locked in motionless battle, each awaiting the other to make the first furtive move.

The mournful groan of the sea crashing into the rocks below faded to white.

Go through the door.

What held him back?

Another gust of east wind stole through the turret, and he began to realize how silly he must look. Unlocked from his absurd fear, he reached out and raised the latch.

Nothing.

Geraldi exhaled in relief and opened the door, but paused before stepping over the threshold. Then, as he passed over it, like a flash, he realized where the hazy fog had gathered, and from whose hands the gray shroud of permanent winter had been woven.

His eyes widened. "Kazareen!"

By the afternoon, King Geraldi was leading the greater part of his Royal Guard into the east.

A week passed, and Alerien sat at the table in the high turret, scratching out the message to his brother as quickly as he could—yet choosing his words carefully. He knew where the boy was and they had him cornered now. Even if he had somehow survived Alerien's golem, he wouldn't be going anywhere soon. They had to make sure he was dead. Alerien paused to consider the wording of his message. All his brother need know was where to find the whelp. Gueren had his uses, but in Alerien's estimation, taking possession of the most powerful Graystone was not one of them, so he left the matter silent.

If a common fool like the one who had wielded the Graystone against his golem self could tap into its vast reservoir of power, then it was a potent piece indeed! And how much more so it would be in the hands of a true sorcerer like himself. He would mention nothing of it to Gueren. Who knew what treachery might take shape inside Gueren if he held both Morta and this most powerful of the Graystones at the same time?

Alerien had seen through his brother's masque of feigned loyalty long ago. It was a feeble disguise at best, for Alerien's keen vision recognized every guise born of malice. As the years passed, Alerien watched his brother's ambition and lust for power grow, and how he tried to bury it away—in some hidden chamber of his black heart. But he could hide nothing from Alerien. The sorcerer's eyes penetrated the depths of his brother's will far too easily—it was only the depths of a pure

The Heart of the Graystone

heart he found difficult to plumb. Still, he was uncertain how long his binding spell would hold Gueren, especially since they had been apart for so long now, for despite his growing knowledge of the black arts, he knew his spells would grow weaker over time and greater distance.

As he finished writing, he found it was not his brother's will that vexed him, rather it was the unexpected departure of the king from the protective walls of Pente Kaleán. What had happened to send him out?

The guard appeared at the door. "My lord?"

Alerien dusted the ink, rolled up the message and sealed it. "Take this with all speed to General Gueren in Beruthia. You have three days."

"Three days? Forgive me, my lord, but that is simply not possible."

"I don't care if you have to drive every horse in the kingdom until they drop, but get it to my brother! Do you understand?"

"Yes, my lord," said the guard, taking the message.

"One more thing. If you should come across the king's party in your travels, say nothing of this message. It does not exist until it reaches my brother's door."

The door creaked shut as the messenger left.

Alerien eyed the door carefully, puzzling on how the king had evaded his powerful ward. He touched it with the back of his hand, but felt nothing but its swollen wood.

"Come down! Down from the walls! All of you! Now!" Raízo shouted. The air crackled and filled with a spray of flying shards as the first of the enemy's shot found its mark upon the wall.

"Into the hall! Come down!"

Whether the men of Locnomina finally decided to heed their Patri, or they were overcome with fear brought on by the enemy's sudden onslaught, Raízo could not say, but at last they began hurrying down the ladders. As the assault continued, some became over-anxious waiting their turn and jumped. In the dark, no one noticed Leyrea's dim shape lying in a heap in the shadows of a ballista.

Now only Benedicio still stood upon the parapet above the gatehouse, not as some proud figure defying his father's will, but a ghostly shape of indecision, stilled by the uncertainty that tainted him. Would all come to an end like this? His father seemingly unwilling to fight, the treachery of Gueren, the handing over of hostages, and for what?

"Come down, my son! Trust your Patri and come down!" Raízo shouted.

Benedicio scanned the darkness beyond the walls, but in the moonless night saw only shadows. How could the enemy have constructed their siege engines so quickly? Where were the fires that heated the shot?

"Benedicio! Do as I say!"

He turned to his father again. In the courtyard, men scurried to and fro like a jostled nest of termites, trying frantically to force their way into the great hall. Only Raízo remained motionless in the center of the courtyard, lit by the torch at his feet. Benedicio's eyes found him quickly, but still he did not abandon his post.

Florin, filled with rage for the delivering of Kazareen into the hand of the enemy, ran to the Patri and took hold of him by the shoulders. "What have you done? Why?"

Raízo struggled to break Florin's grip.

"Father!" Benedicio cried. Seeing Florin's assault, his indecision vanished and he raced to his father's aid, but before he made it to the ladder, another flaming bolder came hurtling over the wall. It slammed directly into Benedicio. He was hurled to the courtyard below, limp and bloodied.

Raízo tore himself away from Florin, tossing him aside like a child's doll, and ran to his son. He fell to his knees. "My son!"

Benedicio did not move.

The Patri took up Benedicio's mangled body in his arms and stood.

Florin could only look on in disbelief. Everything seemed to be falling apart.

Raízo carried his first-born to the doors of the great hall. He said nothing as he passed Florin, his face as gray as the granite of the cliffs of Locnomina. Pausing at the threshold, he turned to Florin. "Get inside," he said weakly, and then disappeared into the hall.

Florin, his chest heaving, could not force his legs to move. He looked to the gate, but knew he couldn't open it himself. Even if he jumped from the walls and made his way to Kazareen's side, he knew he couldn't help him now. He would be slain on sight.

No.

The deed was done.

The betrayal complete.

Torn between his rage at the Patri and his contempt for Gueren, he found himself frozen into inaction. The urge to fight both sides began pulling him apart.

Suddenly he realized that the deluge of flaming shot had ceased. Were the enemy forces now marching on the walls? He had to see.

Florin made his way up to the ramparts above the gatehouse. Without a moon to light the marches, he saw little, not even Leyrea, still lying unconscious just feet away. The dragonstar, bright though it was,

The Heart of the Graystone

provided only the dimmest of light, and he could barely discern the outline of the nearest trees. Beyond lie only blackness until the starry sky met the dark of the land below.

"Florin! Florin!" Solia's voice echoed in the courtyard.

He turned away from the gloom to the thin ribbon of light pouring from the doors of the great hall.

"I am here!" he cried back.

"Come in! Now!"

Her voice trembled with pleading fear. It touched his heart like the cold tip of a sword. And he found himself running to Solia's side.

"Are you alright?"

"I'm fine. But you must come in," she said, pouring herself into Florin's arms.

"The Patri has betrayed Kazareen. Betrayed I say! Handed him over to the enemy, and for what?"

Solia pulled herself from his arms and made a point of capturing his eyes with her own. She seemed not to hear his words. "You must see this. With your own eyes."

"See what?"

"I...I cannot say," she said, confounded.

Florin's brow furrowed, he'd never known Solia to be at a loss for words.

Solia took him by the hand and began to lead him in, and grudgingly he allowed it.

Florin stopped to close the door behind him. He nearly had it shut when he heard a great clamor. But it did not come from the walls. This was far beyond, in the marches. The fractures that echoed through the valley of Locnomina were not of stone being undone, but like the crack of lightning far too near, or the shattering of the very bones of the earth.

Florin began to push the door open again. He had to see what was going on outside.

Then he felt Solia's hand squeeze his own. "No, Florin. Do not turn aside. Come, and in the hall you shall see a greater sight than war."

With one hand on the door, the other in Solia's, he stopped.

"Come," she said.

Florin bit his lip as he gave into the wishes of his only love, and he pulled the door to the great hall closed.

He turned from the strange din coming from the marches, and allowed Solia to lead him slowly into the great hall. When they passed through the alcove and into the main space, as all the others had before him, he gaped in awe at that which stood within, and he heard nothing more of what transpired on the marches.

233

Kazareen hobbled on, his right arm now slung over Arpento's shoulder. As they trod through the mud before their captors, each step became more torturous. His calf prickled and ached as if he'd fallen on a bed of thorns. He began to groan. Try as he may, he couldn't prevent the tears from welling up in his eyes.

"Courage, young one," Arpento whispered, taking on a bit more of Kazareen's weight onto himself. "Lean on me. Not much longer now, and you may—"

"Silence, curs!" Gueren shouted from behind. "Or I'll have you gagged. The time for words shall come soon enough."

Arpento shot him a glance of disdain, but turned away quickly.

A minute later, they were crossing slowly through the enemy lines. Even in the darkness, Kazareen felt the weight of thousands of eyes glaring at him. The soldiers stood in dead silence, moving not at all, except to make way for Gueren's returning sortie. Kazareen loathed the weight of unfamiliar eyes upon him, and so he tried hard not to look upon any face, but they were unavoidable. Looking about, he saw that this was in truth no army of hardened soldiers. Only a few regulars, wearing their mail shirts and bearing the royal livery upon their helmets, stood proudly in the front ranks, the rest were poorly equipped and poorly clothed.

Here was an army of conscripts and little more. Many old men and young boys were among them, their faces gaunt, their clothes mud-splattered from a long and thankless march, many bearing weapons no more lethal than a stout cudgel. He kept his gaze low to avoid their stares. And he saw that many were the feet that had no proper shoes or boots; some even stood barefooted, and those were caked with a vile fusion of blood and earth. His heart began to sink, and still he felt their eyes weighing on him.

Kazareen heard a few quiet murmurings among the commoners, barely audible above the ghostly whispers of the wind as it stole through the firs. And he found enough courage to look one of them in the eye. A young man he saw, not much older than himself, as thin as twine, his cloth meager and tattered, a small, crude hunting bow dangling limply from his hand. Yet he saw in those eyes no malice or hatred, no veracious appetite for battle or blood—only the blank gaze of deprivation and hunger. When he realized Kazareen was returning his gaze, the young man turned away. And Kazareen saw that his bearing spoke not of pride, but of degradation and deep-seated fear, fear of his own ruinous end.

Kazareen looked to Arpento, but he shook his head.

The Heart of the Graystone

When they reached the rear areas, Gueren halted them and dismounted. He came and stood before his prisoners until he held their gaze. The air bristled for a moment with expectation as a smile grew upon the general's face.

"Commence firing!" Gueren shouted into the darkness. Immediately, the jerk and groan of flexing wood filled the air as the enemy siege engines began to loft their deadly shot toward the walls of Locnomina. In the darkness, Kazareen could not see where the great machines were hidden, but by their sounds he knew they were not far.

"You liar! You—"

Kazareen felt the back of Gueren's hand smash into his temple and he collapsed headlong into the mud. Arpento fell to his knees and pulled Kazareen's face from the earth. Kazareen coughed and spat, trying to clear the putrid mud and slime from his mouth and nostrils.

"The reign of your pride is nearly at an end general," said Arpento.

Gueren drew his hand back to wallop the old man, but this time he did not strike. "We shall see. Take them into my tent. I'll deal with them later," then he looked Arpento in the eye and an evil grin spread across his face, "I have a rebellion to put down."

The captains that had ridden out with Gueren immediately dismounted and led the prisoners into a large tent; on a small table in the center a lantern flickered. They stood guard, silently watching their captives as Gueren's voice echoed in the marches, ordering wave after wave of shot to be lofted from the catapults.

Arpento and Kazareen huddled close together on the ground, one of the few grassy places the army had not churned into mud. Still, it was damp from the spring thaw and a chill shuddered through Kazareen's body. He was thankful at least to get off his feet. His leg throbbed with pain, and it wasn't long before it cramped up into a frightful knot. He pulled up the leg of his trousers and tried to massage it without disturbing the wound.

"Are you alright?" Arpento whispered.

Kazareen nodded in the affirmative, though he wasn't. He looked to their captors. They stared back at him blankly; they didn't seem to care if they spoke. Arpento exhaled deeply into his hands for a few seconds, then laid them on Kazareen's leg. The warmth they imparted was deeply soothing, and as his cramp subsided, he lay back in the grass and exhaled in relief.

"Better?"

Again, Kazareen nodded.

"Good. Rest while you can. We'll be safe here—for the moment," Arpento said.

When Kazareen seemed freed from his pain, he heard Arpento's familiar voice again, this time ringing clearly inside his head. *Cover your ears, and do not fear. And no matter what happens, do not leave my side.*

Kazareen had no idea what might happen next, but the voice in his head was beyond mistrust, so he covered his ears and huddled in the damp grass. Arpento stood slowly and faced the guards, but his eyes were shut.

"Get down, you," said one of the captains, and they both drew their swords.

Arpento opened his mouth, but his words were not of this earth. What came forth was like the roar of a flood, loosed from some deep gorge, a low rumbling of ancient authority that seemed to rattle the earth from its very foundations. Both of the captains fell back, their faces painted with astonishment and disbelief, changing quickly to uncontrollable fear. Their terror overtook them, and dropping their swords they fled. Arpento's cry lasted only a moment, but it sapped him wholly and he collapsed to the ground in a heap.

When Kazareen opened his eyes, he was amazed, for his leather bonds had crumbled to dust and fallen away. He crawled to Arpento's side and took his hand. "Arpento?"

He didn't respond.

Kazareen ignored the growing commotion outside the tent as the army's fragile discipline was shaken. Shouts of fear and panic filled the marches, but he stayed where he was, holding Arpento's hand, hoping to revive him.

Then, at last, he heard that which Arpento had surely summoned. Thunderous growls rolled through the glen, punctuated with intermittent shrieks, like the terror of a woman set afire. Something unimaginable was closing in. The pounding of colossal feet upon the earth rolled over the land like the troubled waters in a tempest. The air bristled with shouts of panic and the sharp splintering of mighty timbers. What horror approached was beyond Kazareen's imagination, but it seemed to him they bore his death upon their shoulders.

Kazareen buried his head in Arpento's breast and squeezed his ancient hands, and they seemed to him cold and lifeless. He tried to comfort himself in the thought that all would soon be over.

The utter silence in the great hall seemed only natural to Florin. There was a peace about it, like the moment before kissing Solia. He wasn't even sure if silence was the best way to describe the blanket of serenity that insulated him, for there seemed to be the slightest hint of

The Heart of the Graystone

music wafting over all, a trickling brook of tranquility flowing from...could he believe his eyes?

Nary a soul in the room could compel itself to stir, for in the center of the hall stood three golden figures, burning with an unearthly glow, commanding the attention of all. Benedicio's body lay broken at the feet of these strange figures, and beside him his father knelt, head in hands, yet weeping not. He seemed the only one in the hall capable of ignoring the presence of the three strangers.

Florin strained to see their faces, but the harder he focused on them, the brighter they shone in his eyes. Should he be frightened? It seemed likely to him he should, but somehow it was impossible, the cocoon of stillness they wove was impenetrable to the gray miasma of fear.

How long they stood gaping at the strangers Florin could not later recall, but it seemed only a few sweet moments. The moments that lasted a lifetime, yet passed all too quickly, like the cherished memory of his stolen glances of Solia standing beside the fire outside his home in Bethë Khür.

Solia.

He did not yet turn, but he knew she was still beside him, still clinging to his arm. He felt her warmth. The thought of her finally broke the spell—no—it was a seamless, integral part of it, and he turned to look at her. The loveliness of her face had never been more evident, more real to him. He felt as if they were floating weightless there and all the others in the hall had vanished.

And he looked into Solia's eyes. Florin expected to find the familiar attendance of his love in those eyes, but she was elsewhere, drifting along on the peaceful eddies that flowed through the hall.

As Florin searched those deep gray pools, he became aware there was something else there. His focus was drawn far beyond—and he saw the unfettered image of the golden strangers reflecting in the glint of her eyes. Somehow, the reflection allowed him to pierce their veiling glow. Florin squinted at the tiny image.

And he saw there a man and a woman standing hand in hand, dressed in fine clothing, but he could not recognize them, the image was too small. Behind them stood another man, by appearances a soldier, facing away. As Florin looked, he found he was no longer caught up in the rapturous fugue that entranced the multitude in the hall. These seemed to be ordinary people, at least their reflection suggested they were ordinary—looking upon them directly was something else entirely.

The strangers seemed as curious about the rest of them as Florin was of the strangers. They searched the faces of the host of Locnomina and their lips moved as if they were speaking to one another, but Florin heard no words, only the constant hum of some ethereal music. Was this the sound of their voices?

Finally, the third stranger turned toward where Florin and Solia stood. The portly man's gaze drifted among the faces, swaying slowly back and forth, like the beam of a lighthouse on a foggy night. This face seemed familiar to Florin, he was sure he had seen this man before—but where? Then finally, the light of recognition flashed in Florin's mind.

He took a step back from Solia, as if she were the source of this vision. When he turned to look at the strangers directly, he became aware that they were no longer bathed in the eerily pleasing light. He saw them plainly, but still he could barely believe what he saw.

Florin released Solia's hand and made his way forward through the mute masses huddled around the strangers. He pushed them aside with no gentleness, but none were roused from their reverie.

When he stood before the strangers, his mouth fell open. "It cannot be!" he said.

In his astonishment, he'd not noticed he now stood beside Raízo, who still knelt beside the lifeless body of his son.

The Patri looked up at Florin. "Do you see?"

"Yes. But I don't believe it...I..."

"Believe it," Raízo said softly.

The portly stranger, arrayed in bright armor bearing the royal livery, seemed intent on Raízo's words at first, but then suddenly took notice of Florin. For a moment he stood motionless, then when it seemed he recognized Florin, he took a step forward and a look of relief washed over the man's face.

To Florin's surprise, the man captured him in a hearty bear hug. "Thank you," he said.

Florin was speechless. He stood limp in the huge man's arms until he released him and held him at arm's length. "Bless you for helping Kazareen."

"Murro?"

In the face of the furious attack, the conscripts broke and ran. Few even of those in royal service stood up to the great beasts; those who did were mown down easily. Gueren screamed at his men to stand and fight, but as panic and fear overtook them, most dropped their weapons and ran for their lives. Victory was slipping away.

With the dark glory of Morta to protect him, Gueren felt no fear. "Fight, you cowards! Stand and fight for your king!"

The Heart of the Graystone

But their fear of the great beasts tearing through their lines was greater even than their dread of Gueren, and they would not be rallied.

In his rage, Gueren began to swing Morta at anything that moved. In only a few seconds, the bodies of six men lay strewn about him, and Morta throbbed in his hands, awakened from long slumber by the power of the blood that sullied it.

Soon Gueren found himself alone, cursing the bodies and souls of his victims. In the distance, the cries of panic and fear of his once strong army echoed weakly through the marches until finally falling into silence.

He may have lost this battle, but he still had the most important prize. Or did he? "The boy!" Would the captains of Beruthia and Barése abandon him too? "No!" Gueren turned and dashed back down the slope toward the tent.

As he ran, he did not perceive the growing pale light that now illuminated the marches. His mind was afire at the thought of the cowardice of his army. None would escape his wrath if the boy escaped. As he crested a small ridge, he saw that the tent still stood, no more than a hundred yards distant. Then it struck him. It should be far too dark to see it.

Looking up, Gueren saw the dragonstar burning in the sky above him, brighter than a full moon, and to his horror, seemingly within his grasp. It's brilliant glow swept across the heavens, nearly from horizon to horizon. Ignoring the ominous sign above him, he hustled on. He had to get the boy.

Gueren threw back the flap to the tent and saw that the captains had indeed abandoned their post. He screamed in his rage, but it caught in his throat. By the light of the small lantern within he saw it was of no consequence, for inside the boy and the old man still laid, clinging to one another on the ground, motionless.

Gueren knew he should bring them both back to Pente Kaleán, but a frenzied bloodlust had seized him, and he felt Morta thirsting for more. His army had abandoned him, but he still had the boy. He grit his teeth and decided to put an end to the only real threat left to him in Pendoria—now, while he still could.

Gueren stepped into the tent, his deadly intent etched upon his face.

Kazareen raised his head just in time to see the dark silhouette of Gueren appear at the flap. Then he heard the faint sound of hoof beats, still far off, rumbling through the glen. Kazareen bolted upright.

Gueren shook his head. "None can save you now," he growled.

He drew Morta back, but he froze when the tent suddenly disappeared from around them.

Gueren stopped and cocked his head.

Just feet away stood the great beasts that had sent his army into full retreat. They towered over him. To his left, the heavy cloth of the tent hung in an enormous claw. The beast tossed it aside with a nimble flick. It caught on the branch of a nearby fir and hung there like a wet rag.

In the gray light of the dragonstar, Kazareen caught a glimpse of the creatures from the corner of his eye. Then once again, he buried his head in Arpento's breast.

Gueren stood gaping at the two great beasts. Their faces were like those of lions, with snarling mouths and long ivory teeth, and their bodies were like those of bears, but colossal in size, and from their heads seven horns sprung, like the points of a terrible crown. And their eyes burned through him, shining with a light he could not bear. The ground shook as they stepped between Gueren and his prey.

"NO!!" he cried, and he slashed at the leg of the beast nearest him. It found its mark, but not even Morta was able to pierce the thick hide.

In a flash, Gueren felt himself rocketing backward through the air. He slammed into something hard and his lungs were emptied. He gasped and coughed seeking breath, and when he looked up, the beasts were gone.

"Morta!" he called out, but he had lost his grip when the great beast struck him. He couldn't see it in the dim light, for it lay in the grass some thirty feet away.

Suddenly Kazareen felt Arpento stir beneath him. "Arpento? Arpento! Wake up!" Kazareen lifted his head gently, and the old man opened his eyes.

"I'm alright," he said. "Where is he?"

Kazareen pointed to where Gueren knelt, still doubled over and gasping.

"There," said Arpento, pointing to Morta. "Take it. Now!"

The dark blade, bloodstained and menacing, lay only a few feet away. He didn't really wish to touch the thing, but he rose and gathered it up as quickly as he could. As he held it out, he felt a wash of fear pour over him, for Gueren saw him take it up and began crawling toward him.

"Give me that! Morta is mine and mine alone!"

Kazareen kept his eyes on Gueren and he pointed the dark blade at his enemy as he limped back to Arpento's side.

"Do not touch the blade of my fathers! It is mine, do you hear me!"

But his words held no sway in Kazareen's ears.

Gueren stood. Ignoring the shooting pains in his back, he advanced.

Then, on the edge of his vision, Kazareen caught sight of movement. Something small and dark scurried through the grass to his

The Heart of the Graystone

left. Then he sensed its mirror image doing the same on his right. The dark figures leapt through grass, came quickly to rest between Gueren and Kazareen, and then joined tiny hands.

They were both small, but the larger of the two turned and said in a high voice, "Kazareen!"

"The Marnalets!" Kazareen cried. His old friends, having shed their most terrible shape, had returned in their familiar guise.

Gueren eyed the small creatures with contempt. Slowly, he began to laugh, but it was hollow and false. "See what happens to your mighty beasts when the power of Morta works against them. Give me that blade. I alone have the right and the power to wield it. Now hand it over!"

Still, Kazareen held Morta at the ready, and it's dark power held even Gueren at bay, despite his haughty words.

Arpento's face became stern, almost sad, then he looked down upon the Marnalets and spoke softly: "My friends?"

Together, the Marnalets turned to Gueren. A haunting stillness settled over the glade, as if nothing but their voices could be heard in all the world.

"No one!" said the larger in a booming voice. The sound of it hurt Kazareen and he clutched his ears.

"No thing!" echoed the smaller.

Then together: "No name!"

A great peal of thunder clapped and tore through the heavens. All was lit by white bolts of lightning that stretched not from the sky, but leapt forth from every sinew of Gueren's body. He fell to his knees, his mouth wide with cries of terror, but his screams went unheard amid the rolling thunder. The lightning that enveloped this ancient undead shape of a man did not simply flash and then fade, but built up around him, swelling slowly to uncontainable proportions, until it consumed him wholly and completely, and then at last, the frightful sphere of energy ruptured, and when the deafening din of his undoing subsided, Kazareen looked and Gueren was no more.

Broken Circles

Kazareen stood in the darkness with Morta still in his grasp, but he knew its power to craft dread had not diminished, for the hand that held it had already begun to grow unnaturally cold. The only hint that the Necromancer had ever existed was the neat pile of his traps on the ground. Arpento stood silently as Kazareen hobbled over and sifted through the sundry clothes and armor lying in the dewy grass. Then, pulling Gueren's belt and scabbard from the pile, he stood, girded it round his waist and sheathed Morta.

Instantly, the warmth began to return to Kazareen's hand. He flexed his fingers in relief and peered at his hand in the darkness. The darkness? Indeed, all seemed darker to him than before. Had he fallen under some spell? A curse perhaps, left as some final act of revenge upon the articles of Gueren's long possession? No, his eyes told him it was truly darker than before.

Kazareen looked up. To his surprise, the dragonstar had completely disappeared from the early morning sky, but there seemed to be twice as many stars as before. He looked and saw that the stars themselves seemed to have been upset, for the greater number were gliding wistfully across the firmament, and all to the west. They seemed closer. Some raced across the sky with great speed, flashed brightly, then died. Others drifted by more lazily.

"Arpento? What's happened?" Kazareen asked, looking toward the heavens.

"The great circles have been shaken," he replied.

"Circles?"

"Yes. You see, there exists a balance to all things, and when Gueren was removed, the equilibrium of the..." Arpento's voice faded off.

The muffled pounding of hooves began rumbling through the marches again, and Kazareen sensed they were closing in quickly. Was what remained of Gueren's army returning to fight? He couldn't say.

"I think it would be wise for us to continue our discussion elsewhere," said Arpento.

"I agree," said Kazareen.

Arpento wrapped his arm around Kazareen's waist and they began making their way slowly back up the slope toward the gate.

Florin still could not believe his eyes. "Murro?"

243

The man looked at him curiously for a moment, and then, as if he barely recognized his name, he began to search the faces in the crowd again. "Where is he? We need to speak."

Murro seemed confused, elsewhere.

"How? How is this possible? I saw you...forgive me...slain...on the road to Pente Kaleán," Florin asked.

"I am here...for a very important reason," he replied rather absently, and then as if the meaning of Florin's words began to take hold, his eyes widened and he gave Florin a puzzled look. "Slain? No, I...what is it you're saying? What is this place?"

Florin felt Raízo's hand on his shoulder. "Say no more," the Patri whispered in his ear. "They remember little of their passing." Raízo pulled him aside.

"Specters?" Florin took a step back.

"I wouldn't put it so. But I sense there is no reason to fear them."

Florin didn't seem convinced, but he was still amazed. "Who are the other two?"

"My kin. They are Verdio and Rosari du Phenoa."

Florin recognized the names vaguely. "Not..."

"Indeed. The king's brother, and his wife, my aunt."

When Leyrea finally opened her eyes, she found herself alone on the wall. She doubted her senses when she saw the stars wheeling overhead. Had she been knocked senseless? She sat up slowly, shook her head and looked again. Everything seemed normal enough, except the stars—at least, most of them—which were indeed drifting slowly into the western sky, retreating from the first blue embers of dawn creeping up from behind the mountains.

"Where is everyone?" she said aloud. Slowly, she rose, still unsteady, and looked through the narrow slits in the hoardings. There was no sound of battle coming from the marches, nor from the courtyard below, only the first lonely calls of whippoorwills and doves to the coming dawn. Not a soul was in sight. Had all been slain save her? She saw no bodies.

Then it came back to her. "Kazareen!"

Her last memory was of Kazareen and Arpento being led off into the darkness before Gueren, and she began to burn with anger again at their betrayal.

Then she paused with the thought of little Mari, her chubby hands reaching out to her with her first few steps—cautious and unsure. Leyrea looked to the keep, but not a single light shown in the high rooms.

The Heart of the Graystone

Was this all just a dream? Perhaps. If dream it was, then it mattered little what she did next.

Finally, the silence was broken with the neighing of horses from beyond the walls. She turned back to the marches and strained her eyes, but it was still too dark to see clearly in the dim veil of dawn; the long shadows cast by the mountains of Atan Beruth still ruled. And then, ever so faintly, she caught a shadowy glimpse of the outline of two figures moving among the trees, and the shapes to her were unmistakable.

"Kazareen!"

Leyrea slid down the ladder in her excitement. When she saw the gates were still closed, she knew she could not open them herself, and she realized there was only one way out, only one way she could reach Kazareen and that was over the wall.

"What is happening here? This is all too mad to believe. Why did you surrender Kazareen and Arpento to the enemy? We must get them back—"

"Patience! Do you not see that I have lost in this as well? Look here! Look at my son!" Raízo pointed at Benedicio's body at his feet, and he took hold of Florin by the shoulders.

"You must tell me what is going on. I am sorry for your loss. But there is no time now for grieving. We must save Kazareen from this Gueren. He'll kill him. He is evil, this I know, as surely as I know my own name."

Florin seemed to have gained Raízo's undivided attention, for he returned his piercing gaze with bloodshot eyes. "Think you I a fool? I know of this Gueren. And of what he is capable. Kazareen should be returned to us very soon."

"Returned? How do you know this? And how have the dead come back to walk among the living? Keep me in darkness no longer!" Florin's face seemed suddenly withered and drawn, as if the torture of his long years of imprisonment had returned.

"Come here," he said, leading Florin to the edge of the hall. They passed through the crowd, unnoticed, unrecognized.

Raízo kept his voice low. "Do you not trust me? Have I not granted you sanctuary here, in my home, when you were homeless? Did I not feed you when you were without means? Have you so little faith in my judgment?"

Florin's voice rose. "How can I trust you, when you have betrayed Kazareen?"

"It was the only way we could win this battle. The only way this House, you and I, our beloved, could survive this night. Nevertheless, my firstborn lies dead. And why? Because even he did not have faith in my judgment! What have I done to deserve such doubt?" he asked, his voice suddenly cracking.

Raízo's hands closed around Florin's shoulders, not in anger, but in a pleading attempt to connect with him. "Honor my son's sacrifice, in vain though it was, and place your trust in me now. You said you have met Arpento before. So you must know of the depth of his wisdom."

"Aye."

"It was Arpento's counsel to hand themselves over to Gueren. I protested, of course. But his powers of persuasion are...undeniable. And very...old." The Patri's voice drifted off for a second.

"He said that they could fulfill the prophecy, put an end to Gueren forever, and save this House, and perhaps all Pendoria, now, this eve, but only on this night, while the dragonstar was at the full height of its glory. He said that this was the only way to achieve victory. He spoke of some ancient power that both Gueren and his brother possess, but would say not how they acquired it, though I pressed him."

"Then Arpento gave a warning. No one, not a single soul of this house, was to witness what must take place when they gave themselves over to Gueren, lest they be caught up in the fury of his undoing. I knew that would present a problem, getting the men to withdraw from the walls while the enemy were at the gates, perhaps impossible, for the House of Pendi is proud and does not cower from a fight, and I told Arpento the men's pride might cause them to defy even their Patri. But he left it to me."

"He said that if I did as much it would be enough, for they would return to this hall by morning's first light and there would be much rejoicing, and a glorious reunion. I thought he meant between us and Kazareen, but I see now that is not what he meant at all. The appearance of Murro was one I think no one could have expected, save Arpento himself. I see now that it is Kazareen who will have the great reunion."

"I think I understand why Murro is here, but why the other two?"

"I don't know, exactly. Certainly they have some interest here, for Rosari is my aunt." Raízo paused for a moment in thought. "Perhaps they know something of Kazareen's true linage and have come to share that knowledge with him at last. I cannot be certain."

Florin watched as the three strange visitors continued to look expectantly among the faces of the crowd. "Then they are watching and waiting for Kazareen's return as well?"

"It appears so," Raízo said absently. He turned from Florin and went back to his fallen son's side. As he took up Benedicio's lifeless

The Heart of the Graystone

hand in his own, it suddenly struck him that, as the stories portended, there was indeed a high price to be paid for Arpento's counsel.

Seeing he would get no more information from Raízo, Florin drifted back to Solia's side and with nary a glance, she took his arm. He stood waiting for Kazareen's return, but the young man would never see the inside of Locnomina again.

As the sound of approaching horses bore down upon them, Arpento urged Kazareen forward, but his mangled leg was becoming more useless with each passing step. Kazareen felt a warm stream of blood now trickling down his calf and into his boot. Though the wound had closed, it was not yet healed fully, and his exertions were too much for the tender flesh, and the gash in his leg re-opened.

At last, Kazareen collapsed. Arpento took him up in his arms, but he was of slight build, and Kazareen was nearly a fully grown man now, both taller and heavier than Arpento, and he struggled mightily to lift him. The burden was too great for him, for his strength was not measured in raw might, but in deep wisdom. Arpento managed to stumble forward a few yards before they both toppled into the mud, well short of the tree line.

The old man took a moment to catch his breath and began to help Kazareen up, but it was too late. As they stood, their pursuers, numbering more than thirty, sloshed through the mud and formed a loose circle around them.

Arpento called out, though he knew it was in vain; there would be no one left upon the walls to hear his cries for aid.

"Halt!" shouted one of the riders.

Kazareen looked past the mounted soldiers, hoping for the reappearance of the Marnalets in their most terrible form, but there was no sign of them anywhere; he knew they had done what they'd come for this night. Resigning himself now to this unforeseen fate, he raised his eyes to the rider before him. As he looked up, the first rays of morning broke over the high peaks of Atan Beruth and crowned the rider with a halo of brilliant rays of golden light. Kazareen shielded his eyes, but could not see the rider's face.

"That's him. I would recognize that face anywhere. At last! My search is over," said the rider.

Arpento stood and poised himself defiantly between Kazareen and the rider, and for a moment, he seemed at a loss for words. His stance drew grumbles from those surrounding him. He spat upon the ground. "So, the murderer king arrives! Too late to save his general, or his army. Small surprise! And in typical cowardly fashion, he waited in the rear, riding forward only when the battle was done, just in time to claim the spoils."

"Silence!" shouted one of the king's company. "On your knees before King Geraldi, High Sovereign of Pendoria!"

Arpento made no move, save to raise his head in defiance. It was too much for the Captain of the Royal Guard, proud as he was of his station, and he drew up his lance. "On your knees!"

Geraldi stared back into the face of the old man and spoke with the uncertainty and shame of one who had been caught in a lie: "No. It is—" but his words came too soft and too late.

The proud captain, meaning to cow the old man into humble stance, rushed forward, but he moved too fast and his lance pierced the old man squarely in the chest. Arpento gasped as the air was forced from his body. And through a turn of ghastly fate, the captain's mount lurched forward in the unsure footing of the muddy terrain and in a flash, Arpento was impaled on the lance and pinned to the ground.

"NO!!" Kazareen cried.

"Stop!" Geraldi shouted. And he hopped quickly from his mount.

The captain, suddenly aware of his terrible mistake, jerked the reigns hard to his chest, and his mount reared up in response, tearing the lance backward, freeing the old man's flesh. Arpento's body spun round in mid-air, almost weightless, and then fell to the earth.

Kazareen rolled Arpento over, pulling his face from the muddy slop. Arpento's eyes were wide, and though there was no breath left in him, Kazareen heard him speak.

The circles...No, not yet!

His eyes seemed intent upon the heavens, and as Kazareen watched, the familiar silver fire ignited there once more.

Arpento's hands clutched at Kazareen's arms.

The prophecy...not yet...Kazareen? Not yet...

The words faded with the vanishing light in his eyes. Arpento went limp.

A slow rumble began, like far off thunder meandering over an endless sea. The east wind was stilled. All seemed to rise and fall, and Kazareen's head began to spin. He held Arpento to his breast, clutching this shell of a man desperately for any sign of life, but he could feel there was nothing left inside him. His ancient spirit had departed.

Kazareen let Arpento's body fall gently to the earth.

The wind turned suddenly and the land was shaken. Words and shouts surrounded him, spun through his dizzying mind. The din forced him into a distant corner, beyond the realm of earthly senses, and a faint array of lights filled his thought.

The Heart of the Graystone

Then Kazareen heard, as it were, the call of the wind and the pull of the sky above.

You still have a choice to make! One thing yet remains!

Kazareen felt no more grief, only the burning in his heart and the hurrying wind.

Tongues of fire erupted from the blue-gray morn as the circles of heaven were shaken once more. A hail of screaming stars tore through the air, and then slammed into the earth. Showers of dirt and splintered wood fell all around.

Riders fleeing in terror.

And fire. Everywhere, fire.

Kazareen shut his eyes. Instead of darkness, he suddenly found himself facing something that looked like a violent whirlpool of pure light in the sky above. The Dragon stood guard before it, unmoving.

What do you seek?

Kazareen was silent as a stronger will than he'd ever known rose within. His body heaved and shook with this new, indomitable force.

"Only to help," he said.

With that, The Dragon disappeared and the doorway opened.

Kazareen's chest bounded, and with a terrible crack, this heart, so long imprisoned by doubt and loneliness, now rose above all. He felt as though he were being torn apart and put together all over again. And his voice cried out screaming, but his ears heard only the far away screech of some lonely bird of the mountains, long undiscovered.

Danger! Fly, now!

Suddenly, he felt no weight, no burden at all.

With a gentle leap, he rose above the firestorm. Wither he fled he did not yet know.

Further and higher he rose, carried away by the wind, but he could not escape the burning that filled his nostrils. The acrid scent of scorched wood mingled with the foulness of searing flesh.

The wind was stronger—or he had become lighter—and now he detected a different, fainter scent of burning, the last wisps of an ancient fire, borne on the southern wind. And as if by instinct, he followed after.

A Hard Rain

Since Alerien sent word of Kazareen to his brother, the days passed in a slow, tedious march. Ever he paced in the high turret of the tower in anticipation and growing doubt; at times straining his vision to catch a shadowy glimpse of what transpired in the east or a fleeting glance of the renegade king, or in the dire stretches of the creeping hours of night, to ponder the omen of the dragonstar as it loomed ever larger, and bringing with it, no doubt, a hidden doom, veiled even to Alerien's dark magikal vision.

Time was running out, and his shadowy hopes began to fade. What might ultimately come to pass, or what play might be left him if this boy and his precious stone once again slipped through his fingers, he knew naught.

When at last he received word from his brother that an army was being raised and the secret rebel stronghold would be assailed before month's end, he was reassured. Yet doubt was not fully driven from him, as no word had come of the king's whereabouts. It wasn't long after he sent word to his brother of Kazareen's location that he sent out another message: this one ordering any magistrate, soldier or citizen in the realm who crossed the king's path to send word to the capital of his whereabouts. Whether Geraldi moved by great stealth or held personal sway over those from whom Alerien sought his intelligences, he could not say. But even the king's disappearance seemed of little import to him, in light of what would soon come into his grasp. Then Geraldi and his small band would matter not at all.

The warming days and cool nights dragged on in his impatience, until the winds finally changed, and in his favor. The light chill winds of the east that had for the last weeks obscured his dark vision, and apparently washed away his warding spell upon the door, suddenly turned. And now, from the south an ill wind blew, and brought with it the warm, dry air of his long home, renewing his strength and determination with each passing moment. He peered out the east window and saw at last what he'd long sought, Gueren's great army bearing down on that far rebel fastness. Far beyond that of mortal man he drove his sight and watched in growing anticipation as his brother's army assailed the fortress of Locnomina.

The hands were in motion. The final thrust had come and he felt it was time for him to set out, perhaps past the time. He thought this likely, but blinded as he was for so many days, he'd had to bide his time until the east wind abated and his dark vision was fully restored.

Alerien was sure of one thing. He could not allow the power of the last Graystone to work long in his brother's possession, lest Gueren, yes—even he—grow too bold, and at last throw off the yoke of Alerien's dominion over him. For little faith he had in Gueren, and even with his insatiable lust for blood, and an enemy far outmatched in number, the omen of the dragonstar stood against them, and it vexed him.

He wrung his hands for slow hours, sweat beading on his head and arms in the warm southern wind, peering out the high window, and watching in anxious impotence as the assault at last began. But the distance was too great for Alerien to see the two small prisoners being led through the gate before the first blows were ever struck, and ne'er would he hear of how they were handed over without so much as a single arrow being loosed.

But when the army of the east broke and fled, and his brother fell not long after, there was no mistaking the signs. How exactly such a thing might be managed he could not say with certainty, but he believed now that the power of this Graystone was great enough to destroy even him.

The boy had to be stopped. Already half of the Seer's prophecy of their doom had come to pass. He was growing powerful indeed. Mastering the will of the Graystone with such skill as to defeat entire armies, the sword of his fathers, even slaying one who could not be slain, made Kazareen de Pendi his most deadly foe. He would not allow the rest of the Seer's vision to be fulfilled.

But where now would come the power to overthrow the young De Pendi, master of the Graystone, and his chief deadly foe? For the first time in centuries, Alerien began to feel real fear. Then it struck him.

"The Graystones."

Alerien reasoned that while this chief of all Graystones might hold a great power onto itself, he had now in his possession the greater store, nearly the complete remainder of that accursed dragon's cleaved and lifeless flesh. If he were to somehow harness their power together, even without the greatest stone, the chief keystone, Alerien, with his depth of knowledge in dark magik, could exceed the power of the one the boy wielded, and obtain for himself the final piece of the puzzle. Then no one in Pendoria, or in all the world, could stop him.

"How could I have been so blind?"

Alerien peered out the window once more and he was amazed. For it appeared to him that all the stars of heaven were falling from the sky, and across the length and breadth of Pendoria, fires were springing up in various places, though mostly in the east. For a moment, he thought his

The Heart of the Graystone

end was at hand, and that the boy, empowered so by the slaying of his brother, was hurling flaming shot at him from across the wide expanse—assailing him even from the foothills of Atan Beruth.

But he quickly realized it was not so. For even as he felt the powers of darkness diminish with his brother's passing, and with it, his dread and doubt wax, so too he felt something else now, something far more unexpected, like the opening of a curtain or the sudden clearing of a dense mist, he felt that great spirit that had forever opposed him, though he knew little its earthly guise, weaken, stumble and finally fall silent.

His mind suddenly cleared and his vision sharpened as the ancient veil lifted. The foul reek of iniquity in his soul grew unchecked. And in that moment of evil clarity, he knew how he would infuse himself with the power of the Graystones locked away in the dank catacombs of Pente Kaleán. Alerien turned and left the turret, intent on putting his plan into action as soon as may be, and so missed the most important vision he could have beheld that night: the manifestation of the Dragon, long absent from the circles of the world, rising above the fires, just yards from the gate of Locnomina.

Leyrea climbed over the battlement, carefully slung her body over the edge until she hung from the wall by her fingertips, pausing for a moment only before releasing her grip. There were no rocks visible below, only a stretch of soft mud, or so she perceived it in the shadows of the wall. Leyrea fell the short distance to the ground below. Her feet pierced the thin layer of mud, but hidden just below were the hard bones of the mountains. As she struck, she heard a loud crack. Searing pain shot up her right leg and she cried out in agony.

Wrenching her foot from the mud, she saw now her ankle bent sideways in a terrible misshaping of its natural form, the frightful mingling of blood and bone and mud, and she turned away from the sight of it before her rising sickness could take hold.

Even with the whirlwind of misery beating down on her, her thought was still on Kazareen. The light of morn grew and she turned her gaze to the marches. Out beyond, in the deep valley to the west, she saw the line of sunlight creeping up the long slope, illuminating the firs, and the remaining shadows of dawn retreating before its steady advance.

So set she was upon reaching Kazareen, she ignored her terrible injury and tried to rise. She placed but an ounce of weight upon her right foot, and she crumpled to the ground in unimaginable anguish. Still, her will did not falter. If she had to drag herself to his side, she would. Perhaps it would be enough to simply get within bow range. Ignoring the searing pain, she pulled herself through the sloppy mud at the foot of the wall.

She was little more than half way to the edge of the wood when the sun finally broke over the high summits of Atan Beruth. Looking out in the clear morning light, she now spied the shapes of many tall horsemen, and the royal banners they bore, standing some thirty yards to her left and roughly the same distance into the trees. They had their backs to her, and she hoped she would not be seen. Frantically, Leyrea pulled herself forward, sliding easily through the mud, until she came to rest with her back to a young fir. She heard Arpento speaking, and though she could not make out the words, his voice was full of distress.

She drew her bow and nocked an arrow, then rolled out from behind the tree and rose to her knees. Pausing for a moment to survey the situation and take aim, she saw Kazareen kneeling beside a shadowy figure on the ground, yet between her and Kazareen stood a tall armored man, now dismounted. The fire of vengeance was upon her, and deep in the bitterness of her soul, she prayed it was Gueren who stood between them.

"This is from my family," she said gently, and loosed the arrow.

But in that moment, the earth groaned and suddenly shook, and her dart went astray, flying harmlessly over the left shoulder of her target. Geraldi knew naught of it, for he was astonished at the suddenness of the world's quaking.

Then a great burst of brilliant light filled the marches, like the pure burning of the midday sun, and none could bear to look upon the sight of it. The stars came tumbling down, and a loud cry—like the shrieking of inconsolable grief—went up. Those nearby could not tell whether they should shield their eyes or cover their ears, for their senses were caught in an onslaught so great that their wits abandoned them.

When the light and terrible cry subsided, Leyrea looked out again, and saw that Kazareen was gone. The party of riders had vanished as well, borne away on their mounts, which had panicked and fled. Two figures now lay on the ground, yet only one moved, clutching at his ears and writhing. Ignoring the hail of stars and the fires they brought with them, she rose to her knees once again and nocked another arrow, for she was consumed with a fell spirit of vengeance.

Geraldi finally opened his eyes. The lifeless body of the old man lay in the mud, but Kazareen was gone. Where had he gone? Destruction rained down all around him, and he knew only that he had to get away. He rose slowly.

"Gueren!" Leyrea shouted. She wanted to see his face when he fell.

The Heart of the Graystone

Turning, he saw a small gray figure behind him, backlit by the morning sun. And the point of an arrow coming straight for him. At the last moment he tried to dodge it, but he was too late. Surely it would have pierced his heart had she not called out. Still, it punctured his bright mail and bore into the soft flesh between his left shoulder and his highest rib, knocking him to the ground.

Overcome with the desire to gloat over the one responsible for the death of her family, Leyrea forgot her injury and stood. But as she set her right foot beneath her, the shattered bone made a sickly crunch. The flood of pain was beyond bearing, and she was overcome. With a weak cry she fell, and just before all went black, she beheld the figure of the Dragon rising high above the trees.

Geraldi clutched the arrow that jutted from his chest and gritted his teeth. Thinking now only of flight, he tore the glove from his right hand, put his fingers to his mouth and blew. A high, sharp whistle echoed through the trees, rising even above the din of the falling stars crashing into the earth.

Deneb was at full gallop, already a full furlong away, fleeing the ruin that came all around. But it knew Geraldi's call well, and being a faithful beast with long memory, it stopped in its tracks. He held his head high and turned his ears behind. The whistle came once more, and his simple love for his master overcame all fear and he dashed back to Geraldi's side.

Ignoring his pain, Geraldi managed to mount Deneb, skittish as he was from the hail that fell all around, and they rode off. He took a scant moment to marvel at the falling of the sky, and looking up through the boughs, he caught a glimpse of something high above. Though he'd never seen such a creature before in all his days, he knew its shape well, for it was the very image of the Dragon that graced every royal standard in Pendoria. He watched in amazement as it hovered for just a moment, as if stalled by indecision. Then it turned decisively with a beat of its great wings and headed south.

Geraldi urged Deneb forward.

It wasn't long before the storm of burning rock subsided, though fires grew in many places, choking both man and beast with a great pall of gray-white smoke. The once pristine highland woods were being laid waste.

Soon Geraldi caught up with what remained of his company, who after regaining control of their horses, reassembled in a clearing that remain untouched, so far, by the raging fires. Yet only six had escaped with their lives. They took a few moments to see to the king's wound, though as there was no healer among them, they did no more than brake off the long shaft of the arrow and wrap the wound in a clean dressing. It was decided that they should leave the arrowhead be for the time being, lest they aggravate the bleeding, making matters worse. And so they rode southeast toward Beruthia to find shelter and aid for their injured king.

Geraldi left quiet his sighting of the Dragon. Though from time to time as they rode, he thought he could see, between the high wispy clouds and low blankets of thick smoke, a dark speck soaring in the heavens high above; heading southward.

As the House of Pendi stood enchanted in the great hall, there came at last a low rumbling of the earth, and it shook them from their reverie and they became afraid. Some shouted out in distress as the roof of the great hall creaked and groaned. A thin cloud of dust fell on their heads, and soon filled the air with fine splinters of wood and chips of rock. All seemed ready to crumble. Folk were dashing into the alcoves and down the corridors in a great crush. But the fastness and strength of Locnomina held and did not buckle in the end, and so the earthquake passed.

Florin did not run, but led Solia to Raízo's side. They looked, and before them, the three golden figures began to slowly fade.

"Murro?" Florin wanted an answer to a question he could not form.

Raízo said nothing, attending only to the faces of his lost kin.

Murro, Verdio and Rosari all seemed to be watching something beyond their reckoning. Their gaze was fixed over his shoulder, rising slowly, and they seemed to notice not at all the presence of the others before them. Their images faded slowly, but their mood seemed to have changed; they seemed contented. Murro's eyes remained fixed beyond, and he stood more erect, his chest rising in growing pride. Verdio took Rosari's hand, gazed into her eyes and they shared a bittersweet smile.

"Murro?" Florin asked again, but the strange visitors slipped away into nothingness before his eyes.

A moment later, the sound of boulders crashing into rock came once again to their ears, shaking them from the last remnants of the strange and silent calm that had only moments before ruled in the great hall. And it seemed that Arpento's plan had failed. The onslaught of Gueren's siege engines on the walls of Locnomina had not abated. They would have to fight after all.

Raízo looked down on the body of his fallen son. Had his sacrifice had come to naught? The fires of rage and vengeance filled Raízo and he ran through the halls shouting, "To arms, to arms! Rally upon the walls! To your stations, all!"

The Heart of the Graystone

His men, still confused by these strange events and their Patri's sudden change of counsel, were divided once more, and for long moments many stood unmoved. But the Knights of Pendi, and those of stout heart like Cathio, were quickly swayed, and turned to man their posts once more. Seeing their lack of doubt, those who seemed less inclined took heart and went also, not wishing to be shamed into dishonor when the battle was done.

When they rushed into the courtyard, they beheld an even stranger sight than they'd seen within. For the flaming shot was not coming over the wall from the west, but falling from the sky above. And once again, the men's confidence was shaken.

"What is this?" they cried. "All is coming to an end!"

Raízo knew something had gone terribly wrong with Arpento's plan, yet the look upon the faces of the three visitors as they faded, their gentle expressions of peace, gave him hope that all was not yet lost.

The Patri strode forward unafraid. He set the men to quenching the three small fires that had broken out in the lean-tos that lined the courtyard.

Raízo climbed to the high parapet above the gate. There he stood alone for a while, gazing out upon the flames and billowing smoke. No sign of Gueren's army did he see, only burning and destruction. Then, for a brief moment he thought his eyes deceived him, for rising to a great height above the fires was the image of the Dragon, his huge wings spread wide to catch the wind.

Raízo's mouth fell open. He blinked twice in disbelief. But the image was lost in the rising clouds of smoke. Had he really seen what he thought he'd seen?

A moment later, Romath, Dregis, Demu, Florin, and Cathio came to stand at his side above the gate.

For a moment, no one spoke.

Suddenly, Cathio cried out: "Leyrea! NO!" He pointed to where her body lay, just beyond the tree line. "Open the gate!"

Cathio and Florin went down from the wall, and with help from several others, drew open the heavy gate. Cathio sprinted out with Florin trailing not far behind.

Seeing her lying motionless there, Cathio thought her dead. "No!"

Florin followed after his son. He kneeled beside Leyrea, and placing his hand over her mouth, felt her breath. "She lives still."

His hope restored, Cathio composed himself and took Leyrea's hand. She was still warm. He took Leyrea up in his arms and bore her swiftly away from the approaching fires and into the great hall.

Cathio had no more than laid her down inside the first alcove, when she opened her eyes. But her mind's eye still beheld that which she'd last gazed upon. "The Dragon!" she cried. Her eyes were set elsewhere and filled with wild disbelief.

Then seeing her husband's face hovering over her at last, she threw her arms around him. And he held her tight.

Slowly Cathio released her from his embrace. Then cradling her head in his lap and gently stoking her hair, she began to gather her wits. And when the wild look had left her eyes completely, she looked up at Cathio, "Kazareen...he is gone."

For weeks, the markets of Pente Kaleán were abuzz with the talk of some approaching doom. For with each passing day, the dragonstar loomed ever larger in the sky. And when the Day of Fire, as it came to be called, finally dawned, many hid their faces in fear of death, or cried out in their terror when the terrible rain fell upon the land. Despite the scattered fires and untimely deaths of a few, they had not yet witnessed the worst that would befall Pente Kaleán.

Six days after the terrible Day of Fire, when a tenuous calm had finally begun to fall over the great city, the black beast suddenly appeared overhead. Some would later swear that it rose from within the great keep itself, others, thinking this impossible, would reason that it must have soared unseen across the stretches of the great sea, until it fell upon the keep in its wrath, a curse upon the land unleashed by the fire from the sky.

But those who had their eyes turned toward the keep at the precise moment the beast appeared were not mistaken, only dismissed by the masses that could not fathom their own blindness to such an evil in their midst. Indeed, only three pair of eyes beheld the truth: the monstrous black beast, rising from the ruin of the once-great hall it left in its furious wake.

Alerien had once again descended into the dark grotto, and there in the presence of the hoard of Graystone, he poured all his dark will and evil force into this final spell. Casting himself atop the throbbing power of the collected shards, the frozen yet fiery remains of the Dragon's flesh, he exiled himself from his mortal shell entire, never to return. For the power of the Graystones in the treasury could not be tapped in any half measure.

The black beast opened its eyes. Looking around, it saw that the mountain of gems that had once nearly filled the grotto were gone. Alerien now inhabited them, fused them together, tapped their latent

The Heart of the Graystone

power for his own black purpose. When he realized there would be no return from this golem, in an abominable act of pure malice, the black beast tore apart the still warm, but lifeless body he'd inhabited only moments before, consuming his once-native flesh with ravenously evil delight.

For a moment, the beast believed itself to be trapped in the narrow spaces below the castle. But folding back its wings and crouching low, it found it could just squeeze through the dank tunnels of the catacombs, pulling itself slowly forward with a great effort, until finally it emerged in the main hall, and with a great leap, burst through the high roof, laying it waste. The beast rose high over Pente Kaleán, its scaly wings beating the air furiously to keep its huge bulk aloft. Dark, rancid fumes lingered in its wake.

Seeing the banners of the Great Houses still fluttering in the breeze, the beast circled around and fell upon the high tower again and again. With each strike of its mighty claws, stones shattered and fell, until at last fatally weakened, the turret of the great edifice toppled and fell into the jagged rocks and churning sea below, dragging half of the tower down with it. The majesty of the tower and the hall had been laid to ruin, and the protection of Pente Kaleán's high walls had availed it not.

Rising higher, the beast left behind his desire to lay all the capital low, for there was something more important to be done. Was he too late? Ignoring the shouts of the panicked masses below, he strained his yellow eyes to the east, but it saw there nothing of great import.

Then a shudder ran through the beast's spine. Could the boy possibly know? Know the only way to render the Graystones forever powerless? It had taken Alerien centuries to piece together the truth from a thousand bits of lore collected from hidden hermits and accursed hags, all those who remained of the few practitioners of dark magik that still troubled the earth. Even then, it was little more than a guess. If the boy did know, how could he have discovered it so quickly? Did the Dragon itself retain a way to speak through the Graystone directly? Did the boy have Morta as well? This, at least, seemed likely, now that Gueren was gone.

It didn't matter. He would put an end to this. And now he had the strength and means to do so. Even in this awesome and terrible shape, his existence depended entirely on the power of the Graystones. He could not allow the boy to live. As he'd always suspected, he would have to accomplish himself what his fool of a brother could not.

Turning into the wind and peering south, he saw now unmistakably what he sought. Unlike the misty images he obtained through dark magik, he sensed with the utter clarity granted by his new form the ethereal burning of Kazareen's Graystone, far in the south, already nearing what the Pendorians had named Kara de Sten Yah, which in their ancient tongue meant loosely: The Valley of Lost Spirit.

The Great Desert

Kazareen pried himself from the earth, his head feeling as heavy and battered as an anvil. He blinked several times, until his vision came into focus, and he found himself in a world far removed from the one he'd come to know so well. The cool, spring air had become hot and arid, there was no wind on his face, and there were no mountains, hills or trees anywhere.

He wiped the grit from his face and tried to regain his bearings. Then he heard behind him the gentle trickle of water flowing over rock. Turning, he spied a wide meandering brook, not far behind him. It was the tender whispers of running water that refocused his thoughts and brought it all back to him.

Arpento! He stood tall and looked all around.

"Hello!" he shouted. "Arpento!" He waited for a reply, but he knew there would be none. The strange old man was long gone.

"Anyone!" Kazareen's voice went out, but no echo returned to him. It was as if his words were swallowed whole by the vast emptiness of this place.

Wherever he was, he was alone. He felt as if he should want to weep for the passing of Arpento, but he could not. After living among the proud men of Locnomina for so long, crying seemed childish to him now. True, none would see him in this moment of weakness—there was no one else around. He swallowed the lump in his throat, and it seemed too easy to do so.

Arpento. There was something ambiguous about the man. Kazareen thought he cared about him, and he did really, in his mind, at least. But there was always something hidden about him, some part Kazareen couldn't touch or fully understand. He had seen him for that brief moment in the Dragon's shape, but couldn't quite digest the idea that he felt anything like love for the man. It was something else, something more elusive than love, as he understood the meaning of the word.

Kazareen had always thought of love as a deep and moving feeling, that one couldn't resist, even if one were foolish enough to try. He had no feelings like this for Arpento, even at his passing. It was a terrible thing, and it disturbed him, but he didn't feel like he thought he probably should.

His face flushed. Was he just growing colder in his age? Was his ability to love abandoning him? The icy thought stilled him. He didn't want to become like so many hardened folk he'd known in Feria. Calloused traders who, it seemed, cared for little more than riches. Was it something inevitable, something that happened to all, as they grew older? Or was love something else entirely?

In that quiet moment of reflection, his thoughts turned to Murro.

Scattered images came to him in a flash. Murro holding him when he was sick. Sitting in his lap beside the fire as he spoke of the majesty of the mountains in the east. Murro with his huge arm around his shoulders as they watched the parade of the Royal Guard through the streets of Feria on midsummer's day. Murro riding hard, like a gilded knight in some ancient tale, coming to free him.

Murro as he lay dying in Kazareen's arms.

A tear rolled down his dirty cheek and fell to the ground. And whether it was the earth that shivered or his own body, Kazareen could not say.

Yes. He could still feel love.

Kazareen sniffled and wiped his face with his sleeve. And his mind began to turn back to his present situation. Where he was exactly, and especially how he'd gotten there, he didn't know. The last thing he remembered was holding Arpento's lifeless body. When he opened his eyes, he was here.

Looking back across the wide brook, he thought he could just make out, on the hazy edges of the horizon, splotches of green grass, and beyond, a row of high trees standing. Looking up now, it seemed to him it was already past midday, and the sun was a bit to his left as he faced the river. He closed his eyes and stilled his mind.

Think!

Desert to the south. Seemingly, a forest some way off to the north. And a river dividing. Was he? Could he be in Farak?

Slowly, he turned to the south.

This is it. How you got here doesn't matter. No more excuses. You know what must be done.

His hand drifted to his side and touched the hilt of the sword that still hung there. The bite of bitter cold shot through his fingers and he pulled his hand away quickly. Instinctively, his hand drifted to his neck, seeking the healing warmth of the touch of the Graystone. It had hung in the leather necklace that Rosari had tied since the day of the golem's attack. In his long and lonely days of healing, his fingers had sought it out more and more, seeking solace.

Kazareen gasped, for his fingers found only leather. The Graystone was gone.

The Heart of the Graystone

He ran all around, searching the ground for his lost treasure. Kazareen leapt atop some nearby rocks for a better view of his surroundings, but saw that the land around him was completely undisturbed. He could not even see his own footprints where he must have crossed the river. As a wave of panic washed over him, he began sifting his fingers through the sand, kicking over stones and even pushing over some small boulders.

Then he took a step back as if suddenly in fear. Kazareen shook his leg.

There was no pain. No weakness at all.

He sat down and rolled up the leg of his breeches.

The wound was now closed. And completely healed. There was a large, faint scar, one he would carry for the rest of his days, but already the wound appeared almost as if it had happened years ago. Could that possibly be? How long had he wandered in his empty dreams?

And once again, his hand instinctively went to his chest. Still, it found no Graystone. His hand lingered over his heart as he shouted: "I must find it!" His hand now clutched at his chest.

Then a great warmth, one far different and far deeper than the heat of the desert, began filling him. And his fingers began to tingle as they always did when he held the Graystone.

He tore open his shirt and saw there upon his chest a new scar: thin and faint, as fully healed as the one on his leg, just beneath the lowest loop of Rosari's handiwork. And his chest held a faint glow of flesh illuminated from within. Could it be?

He fell to his knees.

As Kazareen withdrew his hand, incandescent trails of blue and white lingered for a moment between his fingers and his chest, and then faded away like steam on a morning breeze. He closed his eyes and tried to take a deep breath, but found it impossible.

No one could take the Graystone from him now. It was never truly his own, but now...

Suddenly, the full price of what Arpento had asked him to do became clear.

I would have been a fool to believe otherwise, he thought.

His heart pounded like a war drum in his chest. But it brought to him not fear of death, nor faint spirit, nor blanching will, but an inflexible determination to complete that which he knew must be done. If not for himself, then for all that he loved: for Murro and his sacrifice, for true and noble men like Raízo, for his friends Florin and Leyrea, for his memory of Talisa, Pendoria itself, and for the endlessly interwoven circles of the natural world he'd loved all his life. For if he refused now to do what he must, he knew the consequences were far too grave to contemplate. Everything depended on him now that Arpento was gone.

Something hardened within him as Kazareen stood and brushed himself off. He felt like one forged of tempered steel.

He went to the river and took his fill of water as he peered back at Pendoria one last time. Then he took a deep breath, wiped his mouth with his sleeve, turned and began his long, lonesome trek into the southern desert, with only his heart as his guide.

Kazareen walked on, always keeping the sinking sun to his right. A high ridge stood before him, and it was at least two hours before he reached its summit. Time was difficult to judge, for there was little to look at, little to break the monotony of walking in this barren place. There was no grass or trees or bushes of any kind, only scattered boulders, the occasional outcropping of rock, and short, round cactus covered with spiny thorns. His only company was the occasional snake or scorpion, and they fled his footfalls whither he ventured.

At the top of the ridge, Kazareen felt a great temptation to look back across the river, but he held himself in check. Something told him not to look back, because if he did, he might not be able to go on. He had no food, no water, no hood to keep the sun off his head, nor any clear idea if he were headed in the right direction. He took a deep breath, and resisting the temptation to glance backward, he forced himself on—toward certain death.

When dusk fell, he was many miles south of the high ridge. And it seemed to him the air became thicker and more stale as he continued on. Was it because of the traces of the death and destruction wrought here so long ago by Bellian's hand? Or was it just how a desert felt naturally?

Finding a nook in some rocks, Kazareen settled down to rest, and he found his mind returning to the puzzle of Arpento's passing. How could one who had lived for so long be taken so easily? He wracked his mind for an answer. It didn't make sense to him. So he retraced all he could remember from the events of that strange day. Before long, his thoughts turned to the other he'd thought immortal: Gueren. He was one of two who could not be killed, at least by mortal hands. One who should have lived on under the curse of the Dragon. An unnatural life, beyond death.

Unnatural? Yes. He was a Necromancer. The dead whose body and spirit continue on, against all the laws of nature.

Nature. Was this the key?

The Heart of the Graystone

He thought of his vision of Arpento as the Dragon. Was not the Dragon itself part of the natural world? A unique part, yes, but certainly it was not *un*natural. The Dragon had been slain once before, in a sense, at least. Yet its memory and spirit had survived, in Arpento. Now Arpento's body too had been slain. It followed that the Dragon's spirit would survive once again. Yet in what form? He couldn't say.

He closed his eyes, and suddenly he remembered the words Arpento spoke to him in the hovel in Bethë Khür. *You would free me from this mortal coil, end my long years of effort, that have, alas, been in vain, for in this form, I have been of little aid to men. And you would help me take the next step.*

What had he meant? What form could he possibly take now? His passing was brought about not by the destruction of the Graystone, but by the slaying of his mortal body. Was he really gone? Kazareen decided he couldn't be, not with the Graystone still intact. Though in what guise he might now roam the circles of the earth, Kazareen could not imagine.

Realizing after a while that there was no use in trying to answer these questions, a calm resignation overtook and seemed to shelter him. He was sure the Dragon's spirit would not depart the world forever. Not completely. It was in this thought that he was comforted and Kazareen soon drifted off into a deep sleep.

Kazareen woke before dawn, shivering from the cool of the night air. He opened his eyes to the eastern sky, glowing in shades of pale indigo. Looking out in that strange and fleeting light, he beheld the brilliant reds and golds of the desert transforming into a dazzling array of vividly luminous colors. They seemed to shift hues with each passing moment. But Kazareen found he could derive little joy from a sight even as beautiful as this, for his stomach twisted and growled at him, crying out for food to break his fast. His tongue felt like a dry sponge, glued to the roof of his mouth. Would he find water or anything to eat in this barren place? If he didn't, he had little hope of reaching his goal. How far south the valley lay, or in what direction, he had no idea. But he knew he wouldn't last more than a day or two without food or water in these endless wastes.

But he would not turn back. His will was already set. And so in the cool of the morning, he set off to the south once again.

Soon, the sun broke over the horizon and brought with it soothing warmth for which Kazareen was initially grateful. The night had been far cooler than he would have imagined, and it took some time before the chill in his bones receded. But as the sun rose higher and the day grew hotter, he found himself once again facing the dire straits of the desert.

His stomach continued to growl. He hadn't eaten in nearly two days. A light sheen of perspiration appeared on his arms and face for a while, but he was soon robbed of even this small measure of comfort, for the dry desert air evaporated it quickly.

With each passing minute, the forge of the desert intensified.

Though he couldn't see it, the skin on Kazareen's head began to turn bright pink, then almost a blood red, as he roasted slowly in the sun. And his mind began to wander.

No clear thought occupied him, just vivid memories of his past, visions of faces—both familiar and strange—flashed quickly in and out before his eyes, speaking randomly, making little or no sense. Images of ghostly shapes walked on an endless sea of water on the edges of the desert; edges that retreated as ever he made his approach. The desert sang to him, he thought, humming a strange and mournful tune, without melody or coda. The voices of the desert spun 'round him wherever he went, sometimes before him, sometimes behind. And always his mouth burned with an unquenchable thirst.

His mind was swallowed whole by the dizzying whirlpool of the desert. Every moment became as the one before, until he knew nothing of the passage of time. There was the merciless sun, and the endless wastes, and the image of the merciful silver sea he could not reach.

He became lost in a maze without walls, followed familiar faces around unseen corners, and reached out for something always beyond his grasp.

Suddenly, he saw Leyrea running away before him. Recognizing her face, he ran after her. She stopped and looked back at Kazareen, but it wasn't Leyrea anymore. It was Talisa. Still he chased after her, but the faster he ran, the further behind he fell. When she seemed about to disappear into the wavy distance, she stopped and looked back at him again, but this time he couldn't add a name to the ghostly face. Still, she looked familiar to him somehow.

He tried to call out, but made no intelligible word.

She turned and walked off again, but he could follow no more. The figure kept walking until she became lost in the silvered sea. Kazareen fell to his knees, spent.

What was he doing here?

As he kneeled in the sand, his hand drifted absently to his chest out of long habit, and his fingers slid along the thin layer of salty grime until he felt the hard leather knots of Rosari's necklace. Then he remembered.

When he felt the familiar tingle of the powerful Graystone, all his thoughts and hopes and dreams for the life he'd once sought after, one

The Heart of the Graystone

of peace and simplicity, of home and family, even of enjoying a simple afternoon in the woods, were at once burned away. And he was left with nothing but the constancy of the desert, and the finality of his decision to destroy the Graystone that he bore now inside his flesh.

All that remained for him to do was to take the next weary step.

He rose slowly and stumbled on, raising his feet deliberately, and then setting them down. Each step was followed inevitably by another. And another. And another.

When the bizarre theatre of faces flashing before his eyes ceased, and their images faded, he thought he'd been relieved of their torment, but their mournful cries and wailing voices only grew louder.

Undecipherable words.

Howling anguish.

Shouts of terror and bitter anger.

Pitiful whimperings of slow and painful torment.

Children crying out.

He ran now to escape them, hands over his ears, his mouth agape in a wretched and silent cry for silence.

How they plagued him!

"Stop!" he cried.

Then as if in answer to his plea, a stabbing bolt of pain in his foot silenced the din of phantoms and Kazareen stumbled to the ground. For the moment, he was thankful for the silence, and for the pain, for his head was suddenly cleared. He lay motionless in the sun as his foot throbbed. Finally gaining the strength to look, he saw that he'd stepped on one of the many spiny plants that littered this land.

A particularly large thorn had entered the leather on the side of his boot and pierced the soft flesh of his instep. A large portion of the ear-shaped plant still clung to the long, hard thorn embedded in his boot. Reaching down and grasping it by the base of the spine, he yanked it out and tossed it aside. He did this quickly, for he knew that the pain would be less. And for a moment he thought the ghostly, tortured cries had returned to haunt him once again. It took a few moments before he realized it was his own voice he heard crying out.

After the pain in his foot began to subside, he took off his boot and his stocking to examine the wound. There was but a very small puncture in the soft of his foot. It felt worse than it looked, for only a tiny dot of blood appeared on the opening of the wound. Kazareen shook it off easily, and pulled his stocking back over his foot.

He was lacing his boot back up when he noticed a diamond-sparkle, a flash of sunlight caught in a glittering drop of water nearby. Water?

Kazareen picked up the broken ear, careful to avoid the other, smaller spines, and saw that a few droplets of what looked like clear water had appeared on the yellow-white, broken flesh of the cactus.

Dare he? It could be poisonous. If it was, even a few drops could kill him. The thought made him hesitate, and he nearly set it back in the sand. But it looked too inviting. Surveying the vast emptiness around him, he came to the realization that he would surely die in this place without some way of replenishing himself. It was a tremendous risk. In the end, the peril of poison was outweighed by his burning thirst.

Kazareen held the ear of cactus to his mouth and three or four drops of the liquid fell onto his dry, matted tongue. It was wholesome, beyond praise for its wetness, and even surprisingly sweet. Only time would tell if it was poisonous, but given its agreeable flavor, it seemed unlikely. Ignoring any hint of caution now, he tore the spines from the ear and squeezed its fibrous green flesh as hard as he could. It was a scant trickle that flowed out and into his waiting mouth, but to Kazareen it felt like a river. His head spun in relief and joy. More!

Again he squeezed. He got a few more drops, but it seemed he'd already drained it of its precious treasure. Kazareen threw the broken ear aside, licking his lips greedily.

He crawled over toward what remained of the cactus he'd stepped on and saw there were three more ears, bigger than his hand, still standing undisturbed in the sun.

"Praise you!" he said, and soon began to bathe his mouth in the sweet water he extracted from their flesh.

When he'd drained the last ear, he found himself suddenly coursing with renewed energy. The strange plants seemed to have been put here for this very purpose: to sustain life where life was seemingly unsustainable. Yes, he was tired, hot, dirty, smelly and generally miserable, but at least he was once again able to go on. All his fears of being poisoned had dried up, and with renewed hope and slightly rejuvenated body, he pressed on.

With this new-found source of water to sustain him, he carried on, sometimes with relative ease, other times drudgingly, stopping at every opportunity to pull apart the cactus and partake of their precious lifeblood. All the while, his stomach growled for something more substantial. But the cacti's thick fibrous flesh was unpalatable; he would just have to make do with the sweetwater, as he began to call it.

For four days he marched on, sometimes finding great patches of the cactus, so many in fact, he found he could pass many of them by, for harvesting them began to slow him down. At times, he even found his

The Heart of the Graystone

belly aching from the sweetwater, just as it had back in the Feria market long ago, when he'd partook in one too many of the fresh jelly pastries the bakers sold at week's end. But taking the extra time was only delaying the inevitable, and it wouldn't do, because Kazareen was starting to get the feeling that the further he penetrated this desert, the more urgent his errand was becoming; he wouldn't survive long here.

The ghostly voices never returned to haunt him in his lonely trek and for this he was thankful, but the mournful song and low hum of the desert never ceased. Nor could he escape the ghostly image of the silver sea, retreating in the distance, wherever he went. And while the sweetwater sustained him, he found himself growing a bit weaker with each passing day, for without substantial meals, he was slowly wasting away. Already, he'd had to tighten his belt a notch to keep his trousers up.

The pangs in his stomach were so sever at times he wanted to cry out, but by the fifth day of his march, the feeling of hunger left him completely. He thought this a bad sign; even it was a bit of a relief. How close to death by starvation must he come before the feeling of hunger itself could no longer be felt?

When he began to fear he might not be able to complete his errand for lack of strength, he tried once again to consume the flesh of the cactus, even forcing himself to swallow a stringy mouthful of the stuff, but this caused his stomach to ache worse than before, and Kazareen abandoned the idea.

And still he marched on.

To his dismay, he found himself sleeping a bit more each day, and that getting up and moving about took more effort, for his bones and joints were plagued with a terrible ache. Often his temples pounded with the beat of his heart, his neck and back were becoming as stiff as tree trunks, and he felt constant pressure in his teeth.

The patches of sweetwater cactus had become sparse by the fifth day, until finally they disappeared from the desert altogether. On the whole of that day's march, he only found three plants, one of fairly normal size in the morning, followed by one with two small ears, and the last, a single ear not much larger than a coin, which he took just as he settled down to rest for the night.

Kara de Sten Yah

Kazareen woke on the morning of the sixth day and thought that at first he'd risen rather early, for the sun was still hidden. But he soon realized it was not so, rather, the land was covered by storm clouds as far as the eye could see. The distant rumble of thunder rolled over the dunes and far barren stretches, giving Kazareen pause before he started off, for there was no shelter for him anywhere. There was no helping it. So he drew his bearings from his own tracks in the sand from the previous days march, and started off. But the nagging feeling that he was being watched left him unsettled.

By midday, he saw strokes of lightning beginning to flash in the north, and drawing nearer all the time. He tried to hurry on as best he might, for if the clouds broke and loosed a great torrent there would be nowhere for him to escape the coming storm.

Kazareen stumbled on, constantly looking over his shoulder in his hasty retreat from the ever-deepening brew of clouds that blotted out the sun. And because the sun was hidden, he soon became confused and was no longer certain which way was south. But he carried on with his best estimation, for the clouds had taken on an evil cast, beyond the dark gray of the worst storms he'd ever stood witness to—no—these were far worse: a broiling mass of unnatural blackness mixed with a sickly brown sludge, that seemed intent on hunting him down and doing him harm.

Kazareen saw no more of the sweetwater cactus on his march, and his reservoir of strength was nearly emptied. He doubted he would have had the courage to stop and harvest them, even if there were any left here, so great had his fear grown of the coming storm.

Then, as if waking from the mists of a dream, he saw with his own eyes the hazy outline of what he sought, appearing slowly from the hazy edges of his vision. And it was just as Arpento had described it: a great yawning abyss. Kazareen could not decide whether this was a sacred place or an accursed one, but he was sure he'd come at last to the valley of Kara de Sten Yah.

Then a very strange feeling came to him. He felt like he was no longer inside himself, but like a bystander, a mute witness to a strange dream, unable to help himself, or even to speak. But he shook the feeling off and made for the edge of the valley, which was farther away than first he'd thought, and it took him more than a half hour before he stood at the precipice.

The valley was surrounded on all sides by a high lip of jagged rocks, which he scrambled atop with some difficulty. His hands and feet had become adept at rock climbing during his time in Locnomina, and his skill had not abandoned him, but without the sweetwater to rejuvenate him, he was beyond weak. He peered out on the valley and judged its width to be two miles or more, and it was at least five hundred feet deep. In the center of the great crater, Kazareen thought he saw small wisps of smoke or steam rising a short height before being consumed by the desert heat. But in the dim light, he could not be certain if his vision was true. Could there still be something left of the great fire here, after all these centuries?

He had to find a way down, but the sides were steep and covered mostly with small rocks and pebbles that looked to him loose and treacherous. There didn't seem to be any sure footing anywhere. And Kazareen hesitated. For how long, he could not later say, for the strange feeling of separation from himself, of being cleaved painless into two halves had returned, only much stronger this time.

It was the sound of approaching hoof beats that returned him to his wits, but far too late. For when Kazareen turned, only a few scant yards away, his eyes drew in on the same face he'd seen moments before Arpento's passing on the marches of Locnomina: the face of King Geraldi—but this time he was alone.

What was Kazareen to do? Stand and fight? And risk all and everyone—for all time? Or jump? And give himself at least a chance of doing what must be done? Kazareen looked back and forth, from the king and to the abyss before him, but he could not force himself to choose between what seemed to him two equally dreadful alternatives.

A great bolt of lightning flashed behind Geraldi. A near-deafening clap of thunder followed it immediately, shaking Kazareen's teeth. Panicked, Geraldi's horse reared up and bucked the king from his saddle, and then galloped off in great haste. Geraldi cried out in pain as he hit the ground. "Deneb!" he shouted, but his mount paid no heed.

Kazareen's nerves seemed to be shredding.

You must not come before the king.

He readied himself to jump.

Then with a weak groan, Geraldi rolled over slowly, and finally spoke. "Kazareen!" he shouted. "Wait."

Kazareen ordered his legs to propel him into the abyss, but nothing happened. He looked to the king and realized that while this was indeed Geraldi lying before him, he bore no weapon, no scabbard, and no armor whatsoever. He was clothed simply, like a common peasant of the east. And he bore no hint of livery.

The Heart of the Graystone

"Listen to me. Please. I mean you no harm." He lifted an empty hand to Kazareen.

It's a ruse. It has to be. Yet Kazareen sensed something genuine in his voice, and saw something familiar in those dark eyes, something—what was the right word for it—friendly? *No.*

"I know what you have come here for. And I want to help you," said Geraldi. "But there is something—"

"You...shut...up!" Kazareen shouted. Geraldi dropped his arm and rested his head in the sand. "Why should I trust you? You have sought my capture, and more likely, my death, for years now! You are in league with the Necromancers! You are a murderer! Now leave me!"

Geraldi closed his eyes. "Am I?" A small chuckle escaped him, but there was neither malice nor joy in it, only resignation. "Perhaps. I have certainly chosen to do...evil things. Yes, in this you speak the truth. I have done those things...and worse."

"Then leave me alone, or I'll—"

Now the king's eyes were piercing. "You'll what? Murder me with that sword that hangs at your side? Yes, I know it well. Long has it held me at bay."

Kazareen didn't know what to make of this statement.

"Would you strike me down, unarmed as I am, and become what you abhor?"

Kazareen's face flushed for a moment, and then quickly went pale. He thought of the soldier he'd slain in the house of Leyrea, and his oath to himself never to take another life. But what if he *had* to, to destroy the Graystone.

He stood frozen on the precipice, his long pale locks flaying in the wind, unable to release himself from Geraldi's gaze. The storm was nearly atop them now, and its gales kicked up sheets of biting sand. There was another brilliant flash and rock of thunder, behind them now.

"No, I thought not. Besides, you have yet to hear my most grievous act. Listen," said Geraldi calmly. Then very quietly, he added: "or I will forfeit all...forever."

But Kazareen heard even these softly spoken words and a wave of anger broke over him. What did he care if Geraldi lost his crown? "I am not your confessor...why don't you turn to that dark counselor of yours, and see how much pity you can squeeze from him?"

He'd made up his mind. He turned to jump.

Geraldi finally stood up, groaning, but did not advance on Kazareen. "Because I know who you are."

Kazareen's knees went weak. Arpento had suggested as much. That it was *who he was* that brought the king's attention to him, not what he carried.

"Do you wish to hear what I have to say?"

Kazareen could not move, even as every nerve in his body sprung to life, urging him to jump into the abyss.

"You are the son of Verdio du Phenoa and his wife Rosari, from the House of Pendi." the king said.

Rosari? His mother? Kazareen reached for the necklace and felt the rough knots fashioned by his mother's hand. *My mother.* He fingered the empty knots that once bound...his heart. And did once again, for the first time.

For a moment all seemed still to Kazareen, yet the wind still blew and thunder still clapped, but he noticed them not at all. Then his heart began to sink.

"They are dead." Kazareen said. It was both question and answer.

"And I am responsible," Geraldi replied, nodding. "For the death of your parents. The fall of the Great Houses. It is all my fault."

Kazareen tried to hold back the rising fury of his soul, but his hand crept slowly to Morta's hilt.

"Verdio was my brother you know," Geraldi said, his face suddenly darkening, "and so I...I am your uncle."

Kazareen wanted to shut his ears. "No!" he shouted. But as he stared at Geraldi in disbelief, he understood what he'd first recognized in that face: his own. There was no denying it. The resemblance was strong, especially in the curve of the nose. And the straight jet-black hair was of the same fine grain as his own.

Had Murro known this all along? What about Raízo? Surely they must have known. And they said nothing. Nothing! Was he the victim of a great deception? Now Kazareen couldn't stop the tears from streaming down his face, but they were not tears of sorrow, but of rage.

A hammer blow of sudden anger twisted his hands into fists, his eyes shone with a gleaming fury, as dark as the skies above, and a loathing for all those who he thought he loved poisoned his blood with bitterness. In a flash, he drew Morta from his side, and held it aloft, but this time he felt no icy pang, but throbbing heat running up his arm. He leapt from the rocks and approached the prostrate king. His heart pulsed cold and thin.

The king spoke with a quiet patience. "Would you slay the very last of your own?"

Kazareen only smiled in an uncontrollable lust for the king's blood.

The Heart of the Graystone

Geraldi fell to his knees. "I do not come as your king, nor do I seek your destruction. I come as a beggar, seeking mercy in place of wrath. And to help you in your quest, if I am able. But if my appeal does not speak to you, then do what you must. For I know this penalty I deserve. Try to find it in your heart—if not now, then some day hence—to forgive me for what I have done." And King Geraldi bowed, offering Kazareen his neck.

Kazareen was ready to strike, but his hand was suddenly stilled, for Geraldi's words were ringing in his ears. Had he not heard them before? Then as if all the time between then and now fell away, he saw clearly Raízo's kindly face in the high rooms of Locnomina.

Mercy in place of wrath. He heard the words clearly in his head.

A striking pain shot through his chest and he faltered. Was not Kazareen only standing here now, but for the mercy Raízo had shown him?

But I only lied about Murro, he told himself.

Then another voice, one he thought never to hear again, spoke. *Yet the penalty for either transgression is death.*

All became still, and as his wrath slowly melted away, there seemed to be nothing before him and nothing after him, only this one moment. And he felt suddenly like a blank slate, a plug of raw metal, ready for the blacksmith's hammer, and from his grip Morta finally fell. And with total disregard for all the warnings he'd heard about the king, he laid his trembling hand on Geraldi's crownless head, and felt he was about to speak, though he truly did not know what words he might at the last moment utter. And then he closed his eyes, for he thought he heard above him the familiar beat of the Dragon's wings upon the air.

"I am—" he began, but all the air was suddenly driven from his body.

The black beast had come, and it was the beat of these foul wings that Kazareen heard. Diving from the cover of the fume of its breath, it bore down on the glaring light of the Graystone that only a few moments before had nearly faded into nothingness. When its light shone anew just below, it streaked downward with its great claws extended for the kill. But as it drew closer, the Graystone's brilliance grew like never before, and the beast shut its eyes to the blinding light. And so it closed its claws too late and missed its mark—barely.

The hard scaly palm of the black beast's claw hit Kazareen squarely in the chest, the force of it knocking him through the air before it could close. His body flew a full thirty feet, up and over the rocks upon which he'd stood, until he landed in the loose scree that covered the steep slopes of Kara de Sten Yah. He careened down the side of the crater, stunned. The loose rock rolled and tumbled around him, growing stronger as he fell, pushing him further and further down, until he came to rest, half buried, at the floor of the valley.

Bloodied and shaken, Kazareen tried to find his breath. After several empty gasps, his lungs finally caught air. What had happened, he couldn't say, for his eyes had been closed at the moment of impact. His head spun and his chest cried out to him in anguish. He opened his eyes, but his vision was blurred and doubled from the mighty blow of the black beast. Finding his hands free, he rubbed his eyes, but they would not clear. He felt a warm liquid running down his face. The world was spinning out of control. His head lolled back and forth. He tried to move, to crawl away, though to where he had no idea. Knowing something terrible had happened, though not yet what, his instinct was to find shelter, but he didn't have the strength to free himself from the prison of fallen scree.

When Geraldi felt the warmth of his nephew's hand upon his head, he felt he knew. He felt all had finally been forgiven—if not yet paid for. For the first time in ages, he felt warmth of heart. In that pure moment of light, the icy fingers of his misdeeds released him and were replaced with a fire unlike anything he'd ever known.

Long ago, it was the thought of just such a rich fulfillment of heart that had driven him to usurp the throne. But he had been deceived by self, and by the evil brothers who had offered him aid in achieving his goal. For he'd long since realized it was the brothers' plan all along to hold him as their puppet. After disguising the last remnant of the people of Farak as barbarian Northmen and leading them to their certain death by laying siege to Beruthia, it was Alerien who had laid the dark ward on Geraldi, so that no Farakian could see his true face, nor raise a sword against him. For a while, his dream of taking the throne for himself and all the glory and power that went with it, seemed to be coming true. But when Alerien had suggested, and later insisted, that the Great Houses and the Counsel of Patri's be wiped out, he began to see the Necromancers for what they truly were. And with each step downward into the chasm of his obedience to them, the fear and isolation only grew stronger, more frigid upon his soul. He had allowed the Necromancers in, and as far as he knew at the time, they could never be expelled; no matter how strongly he wished it.

By the time he understood his folly, he knew it was too late for him, but years later, the prophecies of the Seer had restored his hope. He remembered well the moment he took it upon himself to defy them, to bide his time, hiding the last glowing nugget of his true intentions deep in

The Heart of the Graystone

his heart, where, he prayed, the very last shred of love left to him might hide it from their prying eyes: it was the day they had told him of their first meeting with the Seer. Hearing that there was even one soul in the kingdom who might one day rise and destroy the brothers had buoyed him every day since. And their regular visits to the Seer reinforced his slim hopes. For with each new prophecy they shared with him, thinking he was completely under their control, it became clearer to him who this champion was: the only other living remnant of his House. How Kazareen had escaped the death squad sent to Rosari's humble longhouse on the prairie north of Bethë Dien, he would never learn, but it was enough that Kazareen had lived.

Hope beyond hope was being fulfilled, for Gueren was now gone, and Kazareen was now with him. He felt Kazareen's rough hand upon his head.

I have found solace and forgiveness from the son of my brother. Together, we shall destroy Alerien and the long nightmare will end. What I fool I was! But no more. I swear it...

The peace of his reverie was shattered as the great beast slammed into Kazareen. Geraldi opened his eyes just in time to see Kazareen flying into the abyss. Morta lay on the ground before him. The shadowy figure of the black beast receding back into the mists above caught his eye, and in an instant, he recognized Alerien for what he had become.

It cried out in a cackling screech, flapped its leathery wings twice and disappeared back up into the soupy mass of churning black fume, leaving a swirling, stinking trail of dark mist in its wake. Geraldi knew that reek too well. A blinding stroke of lightning smote the high rocks as it passed. The thunder that followed left Geraldi's ears filled with a piercing hum.

Geraldi ran over, leapt onto the rocks at the edge of the crater and peered down inside. He groaned and clutched at his chest as he leaned over the edge. The dark mists were collecting quickly, even beginning to fill the uppermost rim of the crater now, and so he saw no sign of Kazareen below.

He was about to leap over the edge in his haste, but then it struck him: *Morta!* Geraldi jumped down and went back to collect it, for he knew that if left unattended, it would call out to the last heir of Bellian. The darkness was gathering quickly now, and he could barely see the ground before him. He searched in the gloom, first standing, then crawling, and would not have found Morta if he'd not placed his hand directly on its icy hilt. Long had he desired to draw the blade from

Gueren's belt, though not for the reasons Gueren had thought. But now that he touched it, he wished only that it had never existed.

Geraldi stood and held the dark blade out before him, using it as a blind man might use a cane, but to no avail, for after only two steps, he tripped over a low, hidden rock and fell headlong into the earth. At the same moment, he felt the air part just inches above his head, followed quickly by another piercing cry of the black beast. It had barely missed him. Thinking better of standing now, he groped along the ground in the darkness until he found his way back to the rocky rim of the crater. He did not pause; he just threw himself blindly over the edge.

Kazareen had given up for the moment trying to free himself from his rocky prison. He just couldn't gather the strength, and his efforts only made him dizzier. As he rested, bits and pieces of the last few minutes began to come back to him. Kara de Sten Yah. The Graystone. Geraldi. Morta.

Morta! Where is it?

He opened his eyes to look for it, but the world was still rocking out of control and he felt as though he would be ill. Quickly, he shut his eyes again, and felt the sickness retreat. *Think!*

And with his inner eye he searched his mind, until he remembered why he was here, and what had to be done. His hand searched for Rosari's necklace, and found the loose, empty knots where the Graystone had once hung. Slowly, his fingers sought out the thin scar upon his chest. He thought of the passing of the Dragon. And the empty hole in Arpento's breast. Is this what it would take?

Yes, he thought.

I must. The sound of wings beating the air came to his ears once again.

And I will. As he nodded his head slowly in quiet affirmation, he felt once again his chest heave, his heart leap, and the pull of the wind.

Geraldi reached the valley floor. When he'd leapt, he'd fallen only a few yards through the air, until his feet sank into the scree. Then, with Morta firmly in his grasp, he carefully waded through and slid along the top of the loose rock until he reached the bottom, where the dark mists had not yet gathered.

Geraldi spotted Kazareen, some fifty yards to his right, and he began running toward his motionless body. Was he dead? His pace slowed in his sudden dread, until he saw Kazareen's head nodding slightly. And for a moment he breathed easier. But the moment passed

The Heart of the Graystone

quickly as he saw the shadow of the black beast breaking through the dense mist, claws extended, making directly for his nephew.

"Kazareen! Look out!"

And just as it had on the marches of Locnomina, a brilliant silvery light shown forth, blinding him. When Geraldi looked again, Kazareen was gone.

The black beast slammed into the valley floor, tumbled across the rocky bottom, crashing head first into a great boulder. With an ear-splitting howl, it righted itself quickly, and looked to take to the air once more, but as it extended its wings, the image of the Dragon suddenly appeared behind, driving it hard into the valley floor.

The Dragon dug its talons deep. Its sharp beak tore into the back of the black beast, rending great shards of flesh from bone, flapping its wings furiously to keep its foe pinned down. So furious was the beating of its wings that soon the great feathers that gave the Dragon flight began to come loose, and then float gently to the ground like falling snow.

To Geraldi's amazement, he saw that as the bloody shreds of the black beast were tossed aside and lit upon the earth, the gruesome things instantly transformed into...could it be...Graystone? Yes! Yet as they hit the ground, their beauty faded quickly, and within a second or two they fell away into dust.

The black beast flailed wildly, and when it felt the sting of the Dragon's claws and the rendering of its flesh, it fought with a renewed fury. It freed itself with a great swing of its barbed tail to the Dragon's head. The Dragon tumbled over, stunned.

The black beast turned to the Dragon, it wings spread high, hiding the image of the Dragon from the King. Geraldi had stood frozen as he watched the great struggle unfold before him. But when he saw that the monstrous beast was ignoring him completely, he realized this was his chance, his one chance to right the wrongs of his youth. The tingling chill of Morta had crept slowly up his arm as he watched, but with the horrid beast intent on the struggling Dragon, Geraldi raced forward unseen. Leaping high, and with both hands firmly behind the blade to impart maximum force, he plunged forward, at the very heart of the black beast.

Kazareen heard a familiar voice calling him. The world had finally stopped spinning, and his head was clear. When he looked, he saw a great black beast only three feet before him, rising slowly. Was this what had launched him over the precipice?

But Kazareen felt no fear at all; for once again, it was as if he watched all from a dream. He noticed there was someone else there with him, standing at his side. The figure turned and kneeled beside him as the black beast continued its snail-slow approach.

Things are never really quite as we suspect, are they Kazareen?

There was silence for what seemed a long while, though the beast hardly moved at all.

Do you love your kin?

"You mean Geraldi?"

Arpento nodded.

Kazareen thought of the slain parents he never knew, of Murro, even of Raízo's pardon. But he could be nothing but truthful. "I can't really say I feel that, no."

Arpento seemed to laugh gently. *My dear boy, I thought you would have understood by now. Love, true love, is not a feeling...it is a choice.*

Kazareen face went pale. Arpento only returned his blank gaze. Then Kazareen felt a shiver in his body or a tremble of earth, and like before, he couldn't tell which it truly was.

Arpento finally blinked and looked around.

Well, I said I might need this back. And I believe now is the time. Many strange things have come to pass, and not always quite as I'd imagined, but as I said, I never was very good at seeing the future.

And then Arpento's hand reached forward and drew the Graystone from Kazareen's chest as easily as one might pick a daisy from the ground. And there was no pain, no blood. Only peace.

And to Kazareen's surprise, for he thought Arpento was going to reclaim it, Arpento deftly slipped the Graystone back into the knotted necklace round his neck.

"Don't you need it?"

Arpento only smiled at him, touched him briefly on the cheek, and then closed his eyes.

Thank you, Kazareen heard. And then, the form of the man called Arpento departed the circles of the earth for all time.

Geraldi thrust the blade forward, but at the final moment the black beast leapt aside, for it's sharp ears heard the king grunt softly, yet uncontrollably, from the pain of Leyrea's dart still lodged in his chest. To Geraldi's horror, he saw Kazareen suddenly before him. Unable to change his course in the final split second, Morta's tip closed in on the empty knot that hung over Kazareen's heart.

"No!" Geraldi shouted as he felt Morta make contact. But his voice was instantly lost in a far greater din, the ear splitting shriek of the black beast. For in that moment, Morta found neither Kazareen's flesh nor the

The Heart of the Graystone

empty knot at his breast, but the heart of the Dragon that had appeared at the point of the blade in the last possible moment.

The sword shattered into a thousand pieces in his hand, like brittle glass thrust against granite. Geraldi fell into a heap beside Kazareen.

The black beast wavered as the shriek caught in its throat. It froze in midair, became shrouded in a great shadow for a moment, then its shape began to fade and finally, it burst into a cloud of countless thousands of tiny Graystones. They shot up into the air, spun weightlessly for a moment, then fell to the earth and quickly became as dust.

Gathering his wits, Geraldi looked up and saw Kazareen standing over him, crowned with the light of the desert sun, for the dark mists had gone.

Kazareen extended his hand to his uncle. And when their hands touched, a great flock of majestic birds, never before seen on earth, rose out of the dust, leapt up, and filled the air with the sound of their flapping wings.

Thrice they circled overhead, rising slowly out of the valley, until, reaching a great height, they turned and broke to the north.

The Servant and the King

Geraldi and Kazareen watched in amazement as a fountain of water suddenly gushed forth from a great rent in the rocks beside them. Fresh water spouted high over their heads. They were overcome with a near-uncontrollable fit of joy as the waters poured down, drenching them like a cool summer rain. They refreshed themselves and took their fill in the gathering waters. But they saw that the mouth of the spring was growing quickly, eating away at the rock about their feet and that the waters were collecting quickly too, so they began their trek up the steep slopes lest they find themselves drowned in the forming lake.

When at last they made their way to the edge of the valley, they struggled for a while to catch their breath. Looking up, they saw the sky darkened, not by the foul mists of the black beast, but with the seemingly endless flock of birds that blanketed the sky, each likened unto the Dragon, though much smaller in stature. Still, they were larger than most birds Kazareen had ever seen or even heard of. And there were thousands upon thousands of them, far more than he'd seen rising from the valley floor, and all were making their way slowly to the north. And so they began following the birds back toward their homeland with lighter hearts, forgetting the long and weary trail they knew still lay before them.

An hour or so later they came upon Deneb, standing quiet and lonely in the sand. He eyed them carefully as they approached. "Here you are! I knew you wouldn't go far," Geraldi said, and scratched him on the forehead. "Good boy."

Geraldi turned and looked at Kazareen sternly for a moment, but said nothing as he began digging through his saddlebags. He pulled out something bright.

"I believe this belongs to you now," Geraldi said, turning to Kazareen. His hand held the golden scepter of the king. "I am proven unworthy to sit in the judgment seat. Besides, it should have gone to your father. I am sorry there is no crown; Alerien took it from me long ago and kept it for his own. Where it might be or if it still exists, I do not know."

Geraldi cradled the scepter with both hands and kneeled before Kazareen. "You should consider your choice well."

Kazareen's face flushed as he eyed the scepter; the gold shone invitingly in the desert sun. And he began to muse on the fact that his heritage was truly a noble one. His father should have been king, which meant he too might have been in line for the throne one day. It didn't seem possible. He'd never thought of himself as anyone special.

His thoughts suddenly turned to all the boys in Feria who'd scorned him for an orphan and all the pain it had caused him, though he long refused to acknowledge it. But he thought also of Talisa, who had never uttered a single word against him. She cared about Kazareen for who he was, not because of his lineage, or lack of one, or some vague notion of social status. Would she think differently of him if he were suddenly made king? All he had to do was reach out and take the scepter from Geraldi's hand and...

He looked Geraldi in the eye.

Here was a familiar face; so familiar that Kazareen thought at times he was gazing into a looking glass that showed him how he himself might appear in thirty years or so, if his hair ever returned to its former shade, that is. But it was also the same man he'd feared for years. What had really changed? He was still Geraldi, with the same past. He was still responsible for the death of his parents, and countless others as well. What had driven him to such a dark path? By his own admission, Geraldi had chosen to follow the Necromancers. But he had also chosen to do good, had he not? It was Geraldi who destroyed the Graystone, not Kazareen. And by Arpento's own words, he knew Geraldi could only have accomplished that task with a pure heart.

Was the dividing line between light and dark so narrow? And so easily crossed?

Kazareen blinked.

And what of himself? Would he have broken his oath and slain another man, his own blood no less, had he not in the last moment recalled the mercy shown him by Raízo? He tried to comfort himself with the idea that his wrath only stemmed from the dark power of Morta in his hand at the time. But Kazareen quickly realized he'd handled it before and it had held no such sway over him then. No, it had always been up to him. Neither the Graystone nor Morta had made his choices for him; he made them of his own volition.

Was not the same true of all men? In all choices?

Kazareen looked on the scepter, glowing so bright and so pure, but saw there only mortal danger. If great power and high position had done nothing to shield Geraldi from evil, Kazareen knew he too might fall into that deadly trap.

"No," he said, shunning the scepter. "My work for the kingdom is done."

Geraldi stared back at him gently. "Because you are young and unfamiliar, I ask you this: are you sure? This is a tradition as old as

The Heart of the Graystone

Pendoria itself, and the throne is never offered a second time to one who refuses it a first."

"For my own sake, I'm sure."

Geraldi nodded as if he understood all that Kazareen had been thinking. He rose and slipped the scepter back into Deneb's saddlebags. "For my sake, I hope we are able to find another with your wisdom and mercy, Kazareen. For as king, you could have pardoned me."

Kazareen's heart dropped.

"I don't think we shall," Geraldi said, hopping onto Deneb. "Come."

Kazareen took his uncle's hand and climbed atop Deneb. Geraldi grunted as he pulled his nephew up. "Are you alright?" Kazareen asked.

"Fine," he said, and though Kazareen barely knew this man, he knew Geraldi was hiding some discomfort. "And by the way Kazareen, if there is anything I've learned it is this: one's work for the kingdom is never truly done."

They rode off in uncomfortable silence, ever in the shadow of the great flock of strange birds.

Some hours later, Kazareen found he was not wholly surprised when he saw a great party riding out of the phantom sea. But he could not hide his surprise to see the two friendly faces of the Marnalets who scampered deftly through the sand, well ahead of the others. Kazareen and Geraldi dismounted as they approached. Ever was the Marnalet's appearance unexpected. And as usual, they were first to speak.

"Kazareen!" said the larger in its chirpy voice.

Kazareen bowed his head in deference.

"Eagles!" said the smaller one.

"Eagles?" Kazareen said curiously. "You said that before..."

The smaller Marnalet pointed his tiny hand skyward. "Yes. Eagles!"

And so the new birds received their true name, and were ever after known to men as eagles. And upon the Marnalet's word, as if they had been drifting along patiently for that very moment, the great flock suddenly broke; some turning east, some west, some even to the south, but by far the greater number continued on to the north.

The rest of the party stomped to a halt behind the Marnalets and shouted for joy at their reunion. Somewhere in his heart, Kazareen knew his friends would not forget or abandon him. As they approached, he saw many familiar and beloved faces. Raízo and Florin not least among them.

However, their delight in finding Kazareen alive was quickly soured when they recognized the ragged looking companion at his side, and

285

many began to burn with thoughts of revenge upon the king. But Kazareen stilled them, for a while at least, with his account of the great deeds Geraldi had done in the valley. Most were wary of him still, for their hearts were hardened by all the ills he had brought to Pendoria, in spite of Kazareen's sudden and unexpected defense of Geraldi. And because of their ignorance, none could comprehend the true importance of the destruction of the Graystone; they focused on Geraldi's slaying of the black beast, which they grudgingly admitted was a noble act, but only because it had spared Kazareen's life. Still, it was not enough to erase his misdeeds from their hearts and memories.

Kazareen was glad that for whatever reason, Leyrea was not among their party, for he doubted his ability to restrain her. When Cathio told him of her grievous injury, he felt a bit guilty, for she was again suffering for his sake.

In the heat of the day, when they settled down to rest, for now they wisely rode only at night, when it was cooler, Kazareen was ever forced to shield Geraldi from his accusers. And though they pressed him hard on the matter, Raízo in particular, they found that Kazareen could not be turned. He swayed none to his point of view, because even now he was unwilling to speak much about the true nature of Arpento and the Graystones. He'd promised to tell no one, and he was bound by his word. It was enough that he was able to restrain their wrath, at least until they passed over the river Laché Khür and back into Pendoria. For there, he knew the ancient and common laws of the land would take effect once more, and there was nothing he could rightly do to assuage their desire for justice.

"Kazareen, can you not see the evil he has wrought?" Raízo asked on many occasions.

"Can't you forgive him? As you did me?" Kazareen always asked in reply. Deep inside, he still wondered if he were able to do this himself.

"This is different."

"How?"

"He is king! Don't you understand?"

Kazareen would often shake his head to this, but he was growing tired of the same argument. "I understood when you spoke to me of mercy in place of wrath! When you spoke of forgiveness in place of justice!" he finally said, the day before they crossed the river back into Pendoria.

Raízo bit his lip and stormed off. It would be a long while before they spoke on the matter again.

The Heart of the Graystone

After the Great Fire and the destruction of the tower at Pente Kaleán, news traveled quickly across Pendoria of the fall of General Gueren and the disappearance of the both Alerien and the king. A spirit of renewal swept across the land as the web of malice spun by the sons of Bellian lifted.

Most of the governors and magistrates in Pendoria were slain in the general uprising, though some in the West found gentler souls to shield them from the revolting masses. For in the West, allegiance to the king's house, if not the king himself, was strong. In reality, few in the West were able to ignore the ill deeds of the king and his henchmen, but even fewer were willing to speak out, even privately, against the house of Phenoa, for fear of appearing disloyal. But in the end, those in the West were just as happy to be rid of the king's yoke as the rest of Pendoria. Those officials who escaped the rebellion with their necks intact found their plight not much better, for those who were spared were mostly thrown into the dark cells and dank dungeons they had once filled with the innocent. A scant few managed to flee Pendoria altogether; most making their way north, to eke out a living on the great prairie.

Nearly all of the common soldiers turned against their corrupted leaders as well. Those who kept to their masters were disarmed, stripped of their rank, and met the same fates as those they remained loyal to, though most were eventually granted amnesty. When the people's anger began to wane, the soldiers loyal to the ideals of Pendoria kept the peace as best they could. As word spread of Locnomina's victory over Gueren The Cruel, as he came to be known, soon all eyes turned to Raízo for leadership.

But Kazareen sought a different kind of leadership from Raízo. The kind he'd shown in the high rooms of Locnomina. Leadership that knew the value of mercy.

Kazareen's words had cut Raízo deeply, more so because they were true, and Raízo's failure to stand up for the king as he had for Kazareen cut equally deep. Kazareen still had great respect for the Patri; he couldn't deny it. If only this proud man could somehow forgive Geraldi, it would make it all the more easier for him to do so as well. It was hard to bear, the knowledge that Geraldi believed himself forgiven. Kazareen knew the measure of a man was not just in his words, but in his deeds as well. And he had not truly granted Geraldi forgiveness in either manner. Where would he find the strength and the will to do that which he knew he should, now that the Graystone was no more?

After crossing the river, a great counsel and court was called in the town of Khürasé. Riders were sent out across the breadth of Pendoria carrying summons to those of the Great Houses who had escaped the purge to come out of hiding, and to make their voices heard, for there was business before them. There was a kingdom to reorder and a king to judge.

It took more than a month for the last stragglers to arrive, for many were still wary that this too might be a trap, and they delayed in coming. But soon their minds were put at ease when they beheld a great sign: the sudden appearance of the eagles, that began settling down and building their nests and eyries in the forest groves and high places of Pendoria. And so soon all was set. A council of twenty-four was established, and Raízo was selected, as the last living Patri, as their chief head and speaker.

But no court was ever convened to judge Geraldi; he would pass away quietly before they got their chance. For when the king arrived in Beruthia after the rain of stars, he fled in secret not long after his arrival, to follow the shape of the Dragon into the south—for he knew it was his nephew—and so in his haste, the head from Leyrea's arrow was never removed. And the wound, which Geraldi had neglected in his haste, had turned septic. By the time they arrived in Khürasé, it had laid him low, and he began to fade in the dark cell where they held him prisoner. The healers were called, but they could do nothing—only wait for the inevitable to come.

No one was allowed an audience with the jailed king since their return to Pendoria, not even Kazareen, but when word spread that Geraldi was gravely ill, he went to the constabulary, his mind set to speak with his uncle—no matter the cost. He had not sought permission from Raízo to make his visit, for there was a distinct rift between them now. And as he walked past the rows of blossoming lemon trees and through the bright sunlit streets, he felt his heart sinking at the thought of not having a chance to speak with Geraldi once more.

When he arrived at the constabulary, to his surprise, he was allowed an audience without question. Had Raízo expected this and allowed it? It seemed likely.

A very old man greeted him as he stepped inside. He was wearing a kindly face, common dress, and yet a rather out-of-place-looking fancy red cap. After asking his name, he led Kazareen down a dimly lit corridor without delay. He pointed with his gnarled hand and withdrew. Kazareen saw a single guard facing the open door of a cell. He nodded to the guard, and it was politely returned. As he stepped inside, he was taken aback by the musty smell, and it triggered in him the memory of his first meeting with Florin so long ago. A healer sat in the corner, illuminated by a thin sliver of sunlight that poked through the high

The Heart of the Graystone

window, reading some tome, of healing perhaps, as Geraldi lay gray and fading in the damp embrace of a ragged cot. Whether he was asleep or already dead, Kazareen couldn't tell.

"How is he?" Kazareen's voice was not much above a whisper.

"He is dying. And the sooner the better, I say," replied the healer.

Kazareen curled his lip. "Leave us."

The healer rose and met his icy gaze for a moment, snapped the book shut under Kazareen's nose, and left.

Kazareen did his best to ignore this. He pulled the chair from the bright corner and sat down next to Geraldi's cot. For a long while he studied Geraldi's face in silence.

He took a deep breath. "Uncle?"

Geraldi did not stir.

He placed his hand on the king's; it was clammy and chill. "Uncle?"

The king's eyes fluttered for a moment, and Kazareen felt sure he could hear his voice. "I wanted to say..." His voice cracked.

"I just wanted to say..." Kazareen sobbed. How could he get through this?

"I just wanted to say thank you. Thank you...for reminding me of my most important lesson. Without you, how would the deed have been done?" he whispered. He closed his eyes and placed his head on Geraldi's chest. It rose and fell only slightly. He felt the thin wisps of the king's breath on the back of his neck, and in them he found a tiny measure of solace.

How he wished he still had the Graystone. He knew its healing power could save his uncle. But to what end? The end of a noose? Perhaps it was better this way. Kazareen sniffled and opened his eyes. It was then he noticed a familiar shape leaning in the doorway.

"Leyrea!" Kazareen said, sitting up.

Leyrea's fingers were white from squeezing the jamb, and her eyes were intent on Geraldi. She held her longbow of yew at her side, though her quiver was not at her back. She took a hobbling step forward. A dull thump came from the floor and Kazareen looked down to see a thick stump of wood protruding from the pant leg where her mangled foot had once been. He winced. She looked from the king to Kazareen and back again, her lips pursed in silent fury. Kazareen saw something both fierce and pitiful shining in her eyes.

Her gaze lingered long on the gray face of the king. Then, without a single word, Leyrea turned to leave. But she stopped at the door, and with a guttural scream, thrust the arc of her bow upon the jamb, snapping it in two. She let it drop and slowly bowed her head. She sighed softly and disappeared down the hall.

Kazareen listened as the sound of her limping hobble, shuffling footsteps alternating with the dull thump of wood striking stone, faded as she withdrew. And he thought he heard a great burden in those steps, the weight of that which she had delivered in equal measures onto both herself and Geraldi: the weight of terrible justice, inconsolable sorrow and perhaps even regret.

Kazareen felt some of that weight himself and he scratched at his breast. He considered the wreck of Leyrea's bow lying in a heap by the door. How little satisfaction came from vengeance, even when it was fulfilled.

"It seems there's always more to be paid for. I suppose 'tis better this way." He touched Geraldi's hand once more. "May you rest Uncle, and find peace in the bosom of the Dragon," but it seemed to him now that all his tears were used up, and he stood.

Geraldi, lying crownless in his plain and simple dress, did not stir. They had long since stripped him of his scepter, and it struck Kazareen as unfitting that Geraldi meet what would surely be a pauper's grave without any sign whatsoever that a true king lay there. Even if he were a poor king for many years, in Kazareen's eyes he had, in the end, proven himself worthy.

So Kazareen lifted Rosari's necklace from round his head and curled Geraldi's limp fingers firmly round it. And there the necklace remained until both hand and token were turned to dust.

"I do forgive you," he said. And as the sound of his words passed into silence, the weight of all his troubles seemed to be whisked away with them, as gently as a leaf falls from the grip of a dying breeze.

Kazareen was never sure, but for a fleeting moment he thought he saw the faintest hint of a smile cross Geraldi's lips. But if it were ever there, it faded quickly.

He turned to leave.

Pausing at the doorway, he looked back at Geraldi one last time with the dim hope that he might suddenly wake. Instead, he heard the very last breath the king still had the strength to draw upon this earth. And when utter silence filled the cell, Kazareen turned and left.

Kazareen opened the door of the constabulary and the bright sunlight greeted him warmly. As he lingered on the threshold, he closed his eyes and turned his face to the sun; it seemed to fill the depths of his soul with a natural healing. Had he finally found the peace of mind he'd long searched for? There was nothing left to do, no one to run from, and perhaps—just perhaps—nothing beyond his ability to endure. But there

The Heart of the Graystone

was something else. He thought he finally understood the full depth of what it meant to be a man. And its terrible cost.

He'd faced death on countless occasions. Hardship. Loss. Just as Murro had. And Florin. Raízo. Even Leyrea. And still here he was. Trees still blossomed. The sun still had warmth. The stars would shine on tonight, as they always had, and always would. Of this he was certain.

He took a deep breath and felt almost whole. Almost.

Kazareen opened his eyes and spied a large eagle; its feathers tinged a golden hue, perched proudly on a thin bough high in a lemon tree across the street. He half expected to hear a familiar voice in his head, but there was only silence. The eagle returned Kazareen's stare for a moment, cocked its head almost knowingly, then ruffling its wings, it leapt to the air and lumbered off slowly into the pale blue sky. Kazareen found himself overcome with the desire to follow.

After Geraldi's passing, Kazareen couldn't think of a reason to linger long in Khürasé. All the words he had for Raízo had been said more than once. Besides, the Patri was busied with issues of great import to the kingdom. He doubted if he could ever close the rift that had opened between them.

Florin had said his goodbyes even before the king's passing because, he said, time was passing quickly, he was growing old, and he longed to be at Solia's side again. They were returning to Bethë Khür to live in his home in the forest once more. They thanked one another for all, and bid each other fond farewells. Florin was so moved he even gave Kazareen a warm hug. A first.

Leyrea was always welcoming to Kazareen when he visited her in those days, but there was something distant and joyless in her eyes now, and he knew that it sprung from more than just a lost limb. The spark he'd always seen in her had seemingly been doused.

Three days after Florin left, she told Kazareen that she and Cathio were going upriver to reclaim her family homestead, but when Kazareen went to visit them there, he found it empty and silent and undisturbed. He supposed that upon seeing it, the memories there were too painful for her to dwell among, and that they had rode back to Locnomina to collect their daughter.

That was the last straw. He didn't even bother to return to Khürasé to gather what little he had left to his name in his bare room there. He simply turned and walked off through the fields, without any particular destination in mind.

Around sunset, he happened upon a small glade in the hills, just west of the road that led north toward Crosston, then Dienaté, and eventually onto the Great Prairie. There he lay down for the night. After his long march in the southern sun, sleep came quickly under the diamond stars.

In the morning, he awoke to a vision he thought never to see again. At first he thought he was perhaps dreaming and he pinched himself. It hurt properly enough and so he became convinced he was well awake. Wingfoot stood grazing just a few yards away.

"Well, well!" Kazareen laughed.

The gray stallion raised its head, looked at Kazareen inquisitively, and seeing him awake and alert at last, neighed and stomped out its greeting in the dirt.

"I didn't think we'd ever meet again! How are you my good fellow?" They drew close and Kazareen embraced the great girth of his neck. "You look to be in need of a serious brushing!" he said, swatting at a patch of caked mud in his coat. Then noticing his bare feet, "Not to mention a good shoeing. Let us make for the nearest smithy."

Wingfoot stared back at him disapprovingly.

"I suppose you're right. I have led long enough. Very well. Where you lead I shall surely follow."

Wingfoot swooshed his tail and blew through his fleshy lips.

And so with his old friend to bear him away, the miles and miles of rolling hills and scattered farms passed more quickly. It wasn't long before Kazareen realized to where Wingfoot was bearing him.

Two days later he rode into town, and it seemed to Kazareen that Feria had changed not at all, except that there were no guards on the road now, and no tax collector to levy the toll. But he felt that once the kingdom was reordered, they too would reappear. Several people eyed him carefully as he rode by, and even if they thought his face familiar somehow, the color of his hair made them think twice. That was fine by him. He just wanted to go home and be left in peace.

He rounded the corner and dismounted before the quiet smithy he and Murro had long since abandoned. A pile of horseshoes, now a rusty brown, lay quietly where last he'd seen them. A thick layer of dust covered the anvil and the hammer atop it. It appeared as though no one had moved or stolen a thing since the day he was arrested.

Strange.

Kazareen picked up the hammer and struck the anvil, just to hear its familiar tone. It rang hollow somehow.

Murro's apron hung limply from a nail in the wall beside him. He fingered it absently.

The Heart of the Graystone

"Oi, there!" came a booming voice from behind. "Get out of here or I'll have your hide!"

Kazareen spun around to see his old neighbor Dargon's familiar, if not somewhat wider, face. He no longer wore the royal livery. Kazareen smiled at Dargon, but being more annoyed than curious, Dargon only scowled in return. "Go on! Scram you!"

"Dargon, it's me. Kazareen."

Dargon's eyes searched his face for a moment. "Kazareen! How can this be? Lords! What...what happened to your hair?"

"I'm afraid it's rather a long story."

"It seems then we shall have much to talk about. Come to the house, and you shall tell me your long story over dinner." He stopped suddenly. "Is Murro with you?"

"No. He fell when he freed me."

"Mmm. I suspected as much, though I never heard for certain. I'm very sorry."

Kazareen nodded. He'd long since laid his grief to rest. "Thanks. I think I'd like to get the house in order again first. Though to tell you the truth, I am rather famished."

"The house? Haven't you seen?"

"What?"

Dargon led him around the back of the smithy and pointed. Kazareen looked and where once his home had stood, now only a pile of splintered wood and black cinders littered the lot.

"Taken, on The Day of Fire. A direct hit, I'm afraid. The only house lost in Feria, though there were a few grass fires outside of town that had us worried there for a while. We could do little for your house, but we managed to save the stables and the smithy."

Kazareen surveyed the ruins of his home quietly and found it really didn't bother him that much. He had risked so much for so long that this seemed but a trifle to him, except that he had no place to sleep tonight. Even this he had become accustomed to.

"Can't be helped, I guess," Kazareen said. He clapped his hands. "You looked after the smithy all this time?"

"In a manner," Dargon shrugged. "Just kept the vandals away is all."

"Thank you."

Dargon nodded.

"Well. I guess I'll take you up on your offer then. What's for dinner?"

"Frog's legs and turtle soup, if that be to your taste."

"It is."

"Then I shall hear all your long story." Dargon smiled and led Kazareen next door.

Within a few short days he had the smithy cleaned up and ready to run, but he found that business was almost non-existent. It seemed it would take a long while to put to rights all the hurts in the kingdom. One afternoon, when there was little or nothing for him to do, he took a stroll through town. For a while, he tried to fool himself that he didn't really want to walk down Talisa's street. But he knew this was the only reason he'd gone for the walk in the first place. He knocked at the door of number seven. There was no answer. He went to the window and looked inside, but all was dark and empty. What did he expect? That Talisa's family should be spared the fate met by so many others?

Kazareen was relieved somewhat by the news, told him by a passing neighbor, that the Du Fe's had fled Feria just days after Kazareen's arrest. How Du Fe knew what doom was approaching, some in Feria still debated. But Gueren's fury over Kazareen's escape was taken out on others less responsible. Some said Du Fe got word of the approaching General from a strange old man who'd come calling in the night. Whatever the case, they had departed in great haste. Some said they went east, some said north, but it didn't really matter to Kazareen. Talisa was long gone.

He strolled back to the idle smithy, empty and disappointed.

A month passed, and summer was approaching fast. Kazareen watched as the first trade wagon of the day came rattling down the street. It was only half loaded. He struck the anvil with has hammer to get the driver's attention.

"In need of shoeing?" he shouted.

The driver's eye's widened as he saw Kazareen's pale locks. He spat on the ground as he passed by. Some things never changed.

Kazareen sighed and sat back down on a low stool. It was the only implement in the smithy that saw much use these days.

"I believe our mounts could do with a shoeing, yes," said a voice emerging from the door to the stables.

Kazareen turned and saw Raízo's familiar shape filling the doorway. His hands were behind his back. His youngest son Romath and his nephew Dregis peered over his shoulders.

"Twelve shoes, and stabling for one night at least."

Kazareen stood. "Raízo? What are—"

"We need to talk. Is there someplace a little more private?"

The Heart of the Graystone

"This is as private as it gets, I'm afraid. I'm staying with a neighbor. Our house was lost to the fires."

"Ah yes, we saw. Then I guess this will have to do," Raízo said, stepping forward. "I missed your departure. You left without a farewell."

Kazareen was quiet as he fingered the cold anvil.

"I have been greatly busied of late, and I didn't realize you'd gone until about a week ago. But the Council of New Pendoria's work is now over, for a while anyway, so here I am."

"What do you want?"

Raízo looked to his kin, "Excuse us." Romath and Dregis disappeared back into the stables. "Two reasons. First, I thought you should know that the council's first vote was to present you with the throne. You deserve it. I told them you had already refused it once, but I think they wished to make a point. We all did."

Kazareen blinked and held back a thin desire to smile. "Who won the second vote?"

"That still lies ahead of us."

Kazareen nodded, realizing such a decision was not going to be taken lightly again, not after what happened with Geraldi. "And the other reason?"

"To bid you fare well," said Raízo, looking at the dying fire in the forge. "But it would seem that saying it and granting are two different things."

"Business is still pretty slow."

"Aye," Raízo said, rocking on his heels in his familiar fashion. Then after clearing his throat, "then perhaps you would consider returning to Locnomina with us. It will be another three months before the counsel is recalled, and I'm sure we can keep you busy there."

Kazareen didn't hesitate. "This is my home. It always was. And it always will be."

Raízo nodded slowly and bit his lip. "Yet you have no dwelling, no business to speak of and no one to hold you here."

Kazareen's eyes narrowed.

"Sorry," Raízo said quickly. He turned his back to Kazareen. "I thought perhaps you might want to return. And I hoped that...after a while...you and I might...make amends. After all, we are blood." He took a deep breath. "I was wrong, Kazareen. I see it now. But my responsibilities are great. And I knew the people of Pendoria would demand his neck. But I didn't have the courage to stand up for him— even when you did. And for that, I am ashamed. Forgive a proud old man and his cowardice."

Kazareen's emotions suddenly came running to the surface, but he held them at bay. "You are the bravest man I know," he said softly.

Raízo slowly turned and faced Kazareen, and he saw a single tear running down his face before it disappeared into his bushy beard. The desire to embrace the Patri was strong. Instead, Kazareen just held out his hand.

Raízo shook it firmly, and the rift between them was closed.

At Raízo's invitation, Kazareen came and broke bread with the Knights of Pendi at a local inn that evening, speaking long into the night over more than one too many ales. The townsfolk who gathered in the common room were surprised to see Kazareen the orphan, the one they had long considered of so little consequence, garnering such honor and attention from the Hero of Pendoria and Lord of Locnomina, for here was the man most folks assumed would soon ascend to the throne. From that night forward, none in Feria dared to utter a harsh word to—or about—Kazareen, despite his odd appearance.

The next morning, a raucous crowd gathered at the stables to get a last glimpse of the Knights of Pendi as they departed for Locnomina. Kazareen stood in the middle of the throng, his head pounding only a little from the night before, and waved goodbye as the Knights of Pendi, his friends, his only family, rode away.

The rest of the summer passed slowly and when Kazareen began to feel he was wearing out his welcome with Dargon, not to mention his new wife and child, he started searching for a place to call his own. It wasn't long before he had a grand idea.

Standing beneath the twin poplars on the hill north of town, he looked out on where it had all started. Bethë Dien. Spying the once mysterious forest, he sensed it was not quite the same as before. The forest spirit had once again fallen into slumber, just as Arpento said he would, and to Kazareen's eyes it had become just another collection of trees. But he didn't mind. For these days, with his new-found notoriety, he found he longed for more peace than town life could now afford him, so he set himself about the business of building a cabin there.

He searched for a while until he found the clearing, and even the very stump where the Graystone had long lain hidden, and there by the knoll, he began to build. It was a humble house, more like the buildings of the forest town of Delasur than any found in Feria, but by the time the leaves began to fall, it was sound enough for him to move in. With Dargon's help, and the hands of a few others, who seemed eager to get in his good graces, it was completed, well before the first snows fell.

The Heart of the Graystone

Raízo was made king as most expected, and Kazareen's smithy thrived as his reputation as one favored by King Raízo spread. By now, his short trek from his home in the forest to the edge of town as he made his way to work each day had carved a narrow but well-defined path through the wood that anyone could find and follow. So it came to little surprise to Kazareen when someone did just that.

He was sitting by the hearth, for winter had now arrived, sipping a hot brew of his own recipe, not unlike tomporian—in taste at least, if not in effect—when a gentle knock came at his door.

No, he was not surprised someone had come, for the forest seemed to be losing its queer reputation, now that the king's favorite smithy had found the courage to build there.

He drew the latch and opened the door to see Talisa's sweet face beaming up at him. Her thick red curls shone like fire in the dusky shadows. And her eyes—those emerald eyes—filled with a glowing expectation, burned into him, and brought a leaping song of joy to his heart, one he'd not felt in years.

"Hello, Kazareen!" she said brightly. Her breath spread like a rolling fog in the frigid air.

He couldn't move. He didn't want to. He wanted this moment to last forever.

"May I come in? It's cold!"

He was about to offer her his hand when something moving at the edge of the clearing caught his eye. Framed by the gray skies of December, the wings of a great eagle, golden as the sun, spread out against the endless maze of leafless branches. And with a lonely screech and a few lumbering beats of its mighty wings it took to the air.

Kazareen took Talisa's hand. And as her fingers curled sweetly, gently round his own, he knew. He knew that at long last, he'd found his heart's desire—and a home he could truly call his own.

He helped her up, for he'd not yet fashioned a stoop, and she squeezed past him slowly, leaving the fragrance of dried wildflowers in her wake. Resisting the urge to turn to her, Kazareen lingered in the doorway and watched until he finally lost sight of the majestic eagle.

"Kazareen, what is it?"

"Oh...nothing."

"Are you going to close the door?" she asked, stomping the snow from her boots.

Finally he turned to her, "I am."

LaVergne, TN USA
23 June 2010
187133LV00004B/1/P